After
THE RAINS

Also by Deborah Raney
in Large Print:

In the Still of Night
A Vow to Cherish
Beneath a Southern Sky

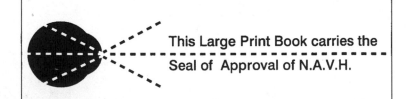
This Large Print Book carries the
Seal of Approval of N.A.V.H.

After
THE RAINS

Deborah Raney

Thorndike Press • Waterville, Maine

3 1257 01485 2437

Copyright © 2002 by Deborah Raney
Sequel to *Beneath a Southern Sky*

Scripture taken from the *Holy Bible, New International Version*®.
NIV®. Copyright © 1973, 1978, 1984 by International Bible
Society. Used by permission of Zondervan Publishing House.
All rights reserved.

Published in 2003 by arrangement with WATERBROOK PRESS,
a division of Random House, Inc.

Thorndike Press® Large Print Christian Romance Series.

The tree indicium is a trademark of Thorndike Press.

The text of this Large Print edition is unabridged.
Other aspects of the book may vary from the original edition.

Set in 16 pt. Plantin by Elena Picard.

Printed in the United States on permanent paper.

Library of Congress Cataloging-in-Publication Data

Raney, Deborah.
    After the rains / Deborah Raney.
      p. cm.
    ISBN 0-7862-4945-5 (lg. print : hc : alk. paper)
    1. Young women — Fiction. 2. Guilt — Fiction.
    3. Large type books. I. Title.
    PS3568.A562A688 2003
    813'.54—dc21   2002043005

*In loving memory
of my grandparents:*

Francis and Helen Reed,
married fifty-nine years
till parted by death

J. W. (Bill) and Dorothy Teeter,
married sixty-eight years
till parted by death

And with love to:

my husband's grandparents,
Bud and Lottie Turner,
married seventy-three years . . .
and counting

Prologue

The road rose and fell beneath the wheels of her car as though she were navigating a boat on a choppy lake. Why wouldn't the steering wheel obey her commands? Head throbbing, Natalie Camfield hunched over the steering wheel and narrowed her eyes, trying to see through the windshield. The highway continued to undulate before her, swells of black asphalt broken by erratic white lines.

The moon broke through a smoke-colored column of clouds and illumined the highway for a brief moment before disappearing. Gripping the wheel tighter, she glanced over at Sara Dever. Her best friend clutched the handle of the passenger door with her right hand and the dashboard with her left. Her eyes were wide, and Natalie wondered what they saw that her own eyes had not.

Natalie shook her head. The moon reappeared, only this time its beam shone through Sara's window and was as brilliant as a floodlight. Natalie put up a hand to shield her eyes. Sara screamed.

What was happening? Time had no meaning. She struggled to remember why she was in the car. Where was she? The road she was on seemed familiar, yet something about it was eerily foreign. Had she fallen asleep at the wheel? Or was she dreaming?

The light that poured into the car completely obscured her view of the road now, yet it lit the interior of the car as though it were daylight. A strange moon on a strange night.

Beside her, Sara's face was transformed into a mask of terror as she clawed at the dashboard, her cheeks bled of color. Sara opened her mouth, and Natalie watched her perfectly bowed lips form syllables. Everything was happening in slow motion now, and her friend's words came at her through an endless tunnel.

"Natalie! Look out!"

Another scream. She couldn't tell if it was Sara or if the high wail came from her own throat. Pain sliced through her ears, as the deafening sound of an explosion pierced the night. The screams were replaced by dead silence. Natalie felt herself being lifted high into the air. She was flying now, exhilarated, feeling no fear. She had to be dreaming. But just as suddenly, she was hurled to the earth again. Falling, falling, she grappled frantically for something to hang on to.

Something was wrong. Something was terribly wrong. Where was Sara? This wasn't a dream. It was too real.

"Sara? Sara!" Natalie's own voice echoed back at her.

For one split second in time everything became clear and sharp in her mind. She knew where she was — and why she was here. *Please, God, let me be dreaming. Please, God! Oh, dear Jesus, what have I done?*

And then everything went black.

Relámpago:
Lightning

One

Bristol, Kansas, one year earlier

The halls of Bristol High School were almost empty. Natalie Camfield was frantically trying to remember the combination to her locker when she heard Sara Dever's voice behind her.

"Having a little trouble here?" There was mischief in Sara's tone.

"Oh, Sara," Natalie wailed, "I'm going to be late for English. I can't get my stupid locker open, and if I don't have my book, I'll get detention!" She was near tears.

Sara put a consoling hand on her arm. "Hey, it'll be okay. How come it's locked anyway? You never lock this thing."

"I didn't. Somebody must've been messing with it."

"Here," Sara moved Natalie aside and picked up the clunky lock. "Okay, what's the combination?"

"I can't remember!"

"Didn't you write it down somewhere?"

"Sure." Natalie dipped her head and hid a wry smile. "It's on my notebook — in my locker."

Shaking her head and chirping like a solicitous mother, Sara pulled her backpack off her shoulder and unzipped it. She pulled out the needed English textbook and thrust it into Natalie's hands. "Here, you can use mine. Just be sure I get it back tonight. Hart gave us homework."

Natalie groaned. The first bell sounded, and she and Sara exchanged gasps and took off in different directions down the hall. "You're an angel, Sara," Natalie called over her shoulder. "I mean it. I owe you big time."

Still running, Sara formed her hands into a circle and held the resulting "halo" over her head. Natalie couldn't help but think that, with her strawberry-blond cascade of curls bouncing behind her, her friend did, indeed, look like an angel. Natalie was still smiling when she slipped into an empty seat in the back of the classroom.

"Nice of you to join us, Ms. Camfield," Dr. Hart said without looking up, inserting his chiding words smoothly into his lecture on proper use of the thesaurus.

The whole class snickered, and Natalie felt her face grow warm. She would have taken it in good humor in any of her other classes, but in this advanced English composition class, she was one of only three juniors among a throng of seniors. Worse yet, this was the one class she had with Jon Dever, who, she noticed, was laughing loudest of all.

She busied herself with getting a pen and notebook from her bag, but she felt very much like the dumb little twit Jon always accused her of being.

She swallowed back a sigh. For as long as she'd known him, Sara Dever's older brother had made her heart beat in a strange and wonderful rhythm.

Class ended and Jon walked past her with two of his senior friends. She watched him from the corner of her eye as she pretended to be busy with a stubborn zipper on her backpack. But to her surprise, he waited till his buddies were out in the hall, then plopped down in the desk beside her. "Hey, Natalie. What's up?"

Though she felt like her cheeks were on fire, she tried for an air of indifference. "Hey, Jon. Not much. What are you up to?"

"Oh, the usual . . . no good."

The ornery glint that had made her crazy when they were kids still did so, but it was a whole new brand of "crazy" now.

Natalie gave him her most charming smile and slid out of her desk. Students for the next class were just coming into the room. She glanced pointedly at the clock on the back wall. "You're going to miss the bell."

"You'll be late too."

"I aide for Kroger next hour," she explained. "She doesn't care if we show up or not."

"Must be nice."

She watched his Adam's apple slide up and down in his throat, and it struck her that Jon Dever actually seemed nervous. *What can he possibly be nervous about?*

The bell blared in the hallway. "Oh, man! I gotta run," he said. "But hey" — he put his head down and rubbed his thumb hard along the spine of his English book — "um, are you going to the homecoming dance with anybody?"

Natalie shook her head. "No, why?" *Camfield, you idiot. He's asking you out!*

"Just . . . wondered. I . . . I might call you tonight." He looked at his watch. "Oh, shoot! I am so dead!" Without another word, he raced down the hall.

She stared after him.

There was a God in heaven! Jon Dever was actually going to call her — tonight!

The rest of the afternoon dragged like a dull movie played in slow motion. Natalie was quiet at supper that night, her stomach in knots. At the other end of the big oak table in the kitchen, her sisters were singing and laughing at their own pitiful rendition of a new TV commercial. While she kept one ear tuned to the telephone, her parents were trying, over the clamor, to discuss the schedule at her father's veterinary clinic.

Finally Cole Hunter had apparently had enough. "Girls! Nicole, Noelle, please! That is just plain rude," he chided. "We can't even think with all the racket you're making, let alone hear one another speak."

"Sorry, Daddy," Nicole said.

He smiled his acceptance of her apology. "You guys can sing all you want while you do the dishes, but your mom and I are trying to carry on an intelligent conversation over here, and you're cramping our style."

Nicole and Noelle groaned at the reminder that it was their turn to do the dishes.

"Hey, speaking of intelligent conversations," Nicole announced, "I'm expecting an important phone call tonight, so everybody stay off the phone."

"No way," Natalie broke in. "I'm expecting a call too."

"Well, okay, but be sure and answer call waiting if it goes off."

Natalie affected a courtly bow. "Yes, Your Majesty. Who's calling you that's so important anyway?"

"My date for homecoming."

"Oh?" Mom jumped into the conversation now. "I didn't know you'd been invited? Who is it?"

"Well, I haven't actually been invited yet. But he's supposed to call tonight."

"And who is this mysterious 'he' anyway?" Daddy asked.

"Jon," she replied.

Natalie jerked her head up, and her heart started pounding.

"Jon Dever? Really? How nice," Mom said, clasping her hands in front of her. "I'm surprised Maribeth didn't say something about it." Maribeth Dever, Jon's mother, was Daria Hunter's best friend.

"It's not like it's that big of a deal, Mom. It's just a school dance," Nicole said.

"It's homecoming, Nikki," Mom said.

"That's a pretty big deal. And I think it's great that you're going with Jon. He's such a nice guy. Who are you doubling with?"

Nicole looked at Natalie. "Um . . ."

Daddy cleared his throat. "You know the rule, Nikki. Only group dates until you're sixteen."

"Daddy! C'mon! It's only Jon. You guys have known him forever. He's a saint."

"Sorry." He was unmoved.

Nicole rolled her eyes and grumbled under her breath, but it was obvious she knew better than to argue. "Just don't worry about it," she finally told them. "We're working something out."

Natalie pushed her chair back from the table. She couldn't believe what she was hearing. Maybe Nicole was mistaken.

The shrill ring of the telephone added to her confusion.

Nicole pounced on the phone as if it were the last cookie in the jar. She checked the caller ID display, then, smiling, picked up the cordless phone from the desk in the kitchen.

"Hello," she purred, taking the phone into the living room. Natalie excused herself from the table and went to the desk. She picked up the newspaper and pretended to be engrossed in "Dear Abby," while she strained to hear Nicole's end of the conversation.

Relief washed over Natalie when her sister came back into the kitchen holding the telephone out to her. She took it. "Hello," Natalie said, suddenly a bundle of nerves. She carried the phone into the living room, and when Nicole followed her she waved her away and went into the bathroom, locking the door behind her.

"Hi, Nattie," Jon said. "Did Nikki tell you why I called?"

"No-o-o-o." It suddenly hit her that maybe Jon had actually been afraid to ask her out. Maybe he had tried to find out from Nicole what his chances were. Her hopes soared.

"She didn't tell you?" Jon asked again. Then without waiting for a reply he said, "Well, here's the deal. I asked Nikki to go to the homecoming dance with me, but she said your dad has some stupid rule that it has to be a double date. So what we were wondering is if you'd go with Evan Greenway and we could double. Evan really wants to go with you . . ." His voice had lost its steam.

Natalie felt as though someone had just punched her in the stomach.

"Evan —" She couldn't get another

word to form over the lump in her throat.

"He's in our English class. You know, the kid that sits —"

"I know who Evan Greenway is. What? He couldn't call me himself?" She prayed Jon wouldn't hear the tremor in her voice.

"It's not that. C'mon, Natalie. He'll call you. He just — well, he wanted me to feel you out first. He was afraid you'd turn him down —"

"I'll have to think about it, Jon." She pushed the button to end the call and sank down to the floor with her back against the bathtub. She put her head on her knees, and the tears that had been threatening spilled over now.

There was a soft knock at the door. "Natalie, are you off the phone yet?" Nicole's voice was all sweetness.

Natalie swallowed hard. "Hang on," she shouted through the bathroom door, struggling to keep her tone from betraying her emotions.

That traitor. How could she do this to me? She knows that I have a crush on Jon. Natalie had let it slip once last summer during a rare heart-to-heart. She and Nicole had never really been close. It was always Nikki and Noelle. Noelle and Nikki. Her sisters were only a year apart in age, and until recently everywhere they went they'd been mistaken for twins. But over the last year Nicole had blossomed into a striking beauty, while Noelle, an eighth grader, was still in that awkward, gangly stage of adolescence. Now that Natalie and Nicole were in high school together, it could have been a time when they grew closer. Instead, having Nicole in the same school had created a whole new set of problems. Suddenly it seemed she was in furious competition with her sister — both at home and at school — over everything from clothes, to the use of the car, to grades.

But Nicole had hit a new low this time.

Natalie pulled herself up from the bathroom floor and looked at her face in the mirror. Her eyes and nose were red and ugly, her usually clear skin was puffy and mottled. Rubbing the tears from her cheeks, she turned on the faucet and splashed cold water on her face. She pulled a rumpled towel from the bar and scrubbed her face dry. Taking a deep breath, she opened the door.

Nicole was standing in the hallway, waiting for her with a desperately hopeful grin plastered on her face. She looked at Natalie and did a double take. "What's wrong with you?"

"Good grief! Can't a person have a minute of privacy in this house?" Natalie lashed out. "What do you want?"

Nicole took a step back, searching her face. Then she said in a syrupy voice, "Will you do it, Nattie? Please. Evan really likes you."

Natalie stared at her. "I can't believe you're asking this."

Nicole stared back "What? What are you talking about?"

"Oh, please. You know exactly what I'm talking about." She turned her back on her sister and started for her room.

Nicole grabbed her arm. "What? I don't know what you mean."

"You knew I liked Jon."

Nicole had the audacity to look shocked. "Nattie, you still like him? But that was . . . so long ago. Honest, I had no idea you still had a crush on him."

"Yeah, right."

"I didn't. I promise you. That was way back last summer, and you've never said another word —"

"Whatever."

"Nattie, please! I didn't know. Honest." She suddenly became pre-occupied with a loose button on her blouse. "But . . . well, the truth is, I like him too. And he likes me back." Nicole looked up at her, pleading now. "C'mon, Nattie, I'm begging you. You know Dad won't let me go if you don't go with us."

"It doesn't have to be me. Can't you get one of your little freshman friends to go with you?"

"Natalie. Come on. I promise, I'll do anything. You can wear my K-State sweatshirt anytime you want. You don't even have to wash it. I'll take your turn at dishes for a week — two weeks. Please. You've got to do this. I've been wanting Jon to ask me out half my life. You can't blow this for me."

The thoughts that assaulted Natalie's mind were definitely not ones she would be sharing in Sunday school class next Sunday morning. It was news to her that Nicole had wanted Jon to ask her out for "half her life." If that was true, why hadn't she said anything when Natalie made her confession last summer?

Turning her back on her sister, she mumbled, "I'll have to think about it." She went upstairs to her room and slammed the door behind her.

Two

The sun reflected off the asphalt in the church parking lot. Twelve-year-old Natalie listened as Daddy invited the new family to have lunch with them.

Sara, the new girl, eyed Natalie cautiously, while her brother leaned against the family's car with an air of indifference. Jon Dever was cute, no doubt about it, but Natalie had no intention of letting him know she thought so.

Feeling self-conscious, she turned her attention to the grownups' conversation. She thought her mother looked especially pretty this morning. Her hair fell in golden waves over her shoulders, and her blue eyes sparkled with life as she spoke. Natalie glanced at her own reflection in the window of the Devers' car. She had her mother's heart-shaped face. Her hair, too — well, the pale, straw color anyway. Mom's hair was coarse and wavy, not fine and silky like Natalie's.

She heard laughter, and her attention was

drawn to the sidewalk in front of the church where Nikki and Noelle were playing a bois-terous clapping game.

Mom called across the parking lot, "Girls . . . quiet down a little, please. We're trying to visit."

Maribeth Dever smiled in the girls' direc-tion. "I can't imagine trying to keep up with twins."

Mom laughed. "Well, they are a handful, but the girls aren't twins. They're a year apart. A lot of people make that mistake though."

"Oh, my!" Mrs. Dever exclaimed. "I would have sworn they were identical! They certainly are the spitting image of their father."

Natalie watched the smile that spread across her father's face, watched his chest puff out with pride. How she longed for him to feel proud of her the way he did of his own daugh-ters.

And that was exactly the problem. For though she called him Daddy, just as Nikki and Noelle did, she did not truly belong to Cole Hunter. Didn't her very name remind her of that fact every single day she lived? It was hard being a Camfield in a house full of Hunters — always having to explain why she had a different name than the rest of them.

"Natalie," her father called, "come on. Time

to go." The family climbed into their van. Sara was invited to ride with them, while the Devers followed in their car. Nicole and Noelle chattered together in the middle seat of the van, while in the back, Natalie and Sara gave each other sidelong glances and said not a word the entire way home.

Dinner was an apparent success. Natalie's mother made roast beef sandwiches, and the adults laughed and talked as though they'd known each other forever.

The kids were relegated to the kitchen table. Though Natalie was feeling rather timid in the presence of their visitors, Jon Dever kept them all laughing. He entertained them by telling stupid jokes and doing disgusting things with his Jell-O salad. And though she would never have admitted it to anyone, by the time dessert was served, Natalie had developed a serious crush on the boy.

After they ate ice cream, Mom called over the clatter of dirty dishes and silverware, "Natalie, it's a beautiful day. Why don't you girls take Jon and Sara outside and show them the barn?"

"Just don't let Rufus jump up on your good clothes," Cole Hunter interjected. "You watch him, okay, Nattie?" Daddy turned to Jon and Sara's parents. "Sometime you'll have to ask Natalie about the time she and Rufus took a *little impromptu swim in the creek."*

"Daddy!"

He winked and cautioned her again. "Just make him behave. I don't feel like playing lifeguard today."

"I will," she promised, as she led their guests out the back door.

They headed toward the barn. "Do you have animals?" Jon asked.

"Well, we have a dog — Rufus — that's who Daddy was talking about. And some cats. But not cows or horses or anything, if that's what you mean. My dad's a vet, so he gets enough of animals at work." She was repeating what she'd heard her mother tell people countless times, but talking to Jon, her heart felt all fluttery and funny in her chest.

The big golden Labrador came loping up the lane as fast as his old bones would allow. Jon Dever ran ahead to meet the dog. Nicole and Noelle dashed after him.

"You girls be careful," Natalie called after them. "Remember what Daddy said."

Nicole turned in the middle of the lane and put her hands on her hips. "You are not our mother, Natalie Camfield. Quit being so bossy." She whispered something in Noelle's ear, and the two giggled wickedly and ran on to the barn.

Natalie rolled her eyes to cover her embar-

rassment. "Sisters can be such a pain."

"Just like big brothers." Sara smiled knowingly, her pale carrot-colored hair glinting in the sunlight. Then, as though the discrepancy had just occurred to her, she asked, "How come your sister called you Natalie Camfield?"

Natalie rubbed a finger across the frayed edge of her coat sleeve. "Because that's my name."

"Oh. That's a funny middle name."

"No. It's my last name."

Sara wrinkled her freckled nose. "I thought it was Hunter."

"My last name is Camfield. Daddy isn't —" she pointed a thumb over her shoulder, back toward the house. "Well, see, he isn't my real father. It's a long story," she explained.

Sara inclined her head toward Nicole and Noelle, who were leading Jon through the gate to the barnyard. "Is their name Camfield too?"

She sighed. "No. Just me. Nikki and Noelle are Daddy's real kids."

"Oh." Sara brightened. "Kind of like me and Jon."

Natalie wrinkled her brow. "Huh?"

"I'm adopted, but Mom had Jon," Sara explained.

Something about those words made Natalie

29

feel energized, but she shook her head. "Oh, I'm not adopted. Daddy is my stepdad. My mom was married before."

"Really? Where's your real dad?"

Natalie usually hated telling her story, but something in Sara's eyes told her that this girl would understand. After all, Sara apparently knew what it was like to be the oddball of the family. She took a deep breath. "My real dad lives in South America — in Colombia. He's a missionary doctor."

Sara gasped. "A missionary? And he got divorced?" She said it as though it were the sin of the century, and Natalie felt her defenses rising.

"No," Natalie went on, "It was . . . well, see, there was a really bad fire in this village, and my mom thought my dad got killed — in the fire — so she came back over here, and that's when I was born. Then she got married again, but after that they found out my real dad wasn't dead after all. He was just, like, trapped there or something. It's kind of complicated. But anyway, when he found out my mom had gotten married again and I already had a really good dad and everything, he decided to go back to South America."

She waited for the disbelieving reaction she usually got when she recounted these events, but Sara only said, "Wow. That's amazing.

30

Have you ever met him?"

"Sure. I don't see him very often 'cause Colombia's, like, hundreds of miles away. But he comes back sometimes, and then I go visit him at my grandparents' house. They live in Kansas City. He's really nice — my dad, I mean."

"That's cool."

"Well, not always. It kind of stinks sometimes. I always have to explain it to everybody. And then they go crazy, like" — she laid a hand on her chest and put on her church-lady voice — " 'Oh, you poor girl, how awful, how tragic, how terrible it must be for you.' "

Sara broke into contagious laughter that warmed Natalie's heart and made her laugh too. When they finally quit giggling, Sara said, "Well, my story isn't quite as good as yours, but I know what you mean. I hate having to explain about Jon."

"Well, why is it you're adopted and he's not?" She hesitated. "Oh . . . sorry. Here I go making you explain it."

Sara put a hand on Natalie's arm. "No. I don't care if you ask. My mom had to have surgery after Jon was born. It made it so she couldn't have any more babies, but she and Dad wanted a whole bunch of kids, so they decided to adopt. That's where I came in. They might even adopt some more kids someday."

31

"That would be cool," Natalie told her. A thought struck her, and before she had time to think about it she blurted out, "Hey! If you guys adopted more kids, then Jon would be the oddball."

Sara screwed her face up and pronounced in a cartoon-character voice, "Oh, believe me, honey, he's already an oddball!"

They dissolved into laughter again, and Natalie decided then and there that Sara Dever would be her best friend forever.

The parking lot of the Sonic Drive-In was almost empty in the lull between the supper crowd and the late-night Coke-and-burger runs. Natalie sat behind the wheel of her mom's car, the cherry limeade in her cup holder barely touched.

Beside her, Sara sipped a slush and shivered. "So, are you going to tell me what's bothering you or not?" Sara asked.

Natalie had been stewing in silence, forcing Sara to carry the conversation, ever since the carhop had brought out their drinks. "Did you know Jon was asking Nikki to the dance?" she blurted.

Now it was Sara's turn to be silent.

"You did, didn't you?" Natalie accused. "Why didn't you say something, Sara?"

"And why would I think you'd care,

Nattie?" The knowing look on Sara's face made Natalie nervous. Sara looked at her lap. "Because I knew it would hurt your feelings."

It took Natalie a minute to process the implication of Sara's comment. "Why would you think that?" she hedged.

"Look, Natalie, you aren't even making sense. It's your business if you don't want to talk to me about your crush on Jon, but if I'm not supposed to know about it, then don't go getting mad when I don't report his every move to you."

Natalie looked hard at Sara. "You knew?"

"I guessed."

"How? Did Nicole say something to you?"

Sara shifted in her seat and turned toward Natalie. "I hate to break this to you, Nattie, but I'm your best friend. I can read you like a book. I've seen how you are when we're over at my house and Jon's around. And the way you're always asking about his plans. Why would you give a rip what my brother does if you *didn't* have a thing for him?"

Natalie's palms grew clammy, and she hoped the pinkish glow from the neon lights on the restaurant's signs hid the warmth she felt rise to her cheeks. "Is it that obvious?"

Sara nodded. "Did Nicole know you like Jon?"

Natalie's anger at her sister returned with a vengeance. "Yes, she knew. I told her last summer. I thought I could trust her."

"So, she's known all along that you like Jon?"

Natalie nodded.

"I'm sorry, but that just doesn't sound like Nikki. She's such a sweetheart," Sara said.

"Yeah, well, looks can be deceiving." Feeling strangely disloyal to the sister who had stabbed her in the back, Natalie picked up her drink and took a long slurp. "Does Jon like Nikki, Sara? Has he said anything?"

"Natalie, you are really putting me on the spot, you know?"

The last meager ounce of hope she felt dissolved. "So I take that as a yes?"

Sara nodded. "Yeah. I'm sorry. He likes her a lot. I . . . I didn't want to say anything because I thought this all might pass — either Jon's crush on Nikki or your crush on him. But I don't think it's going to, Natalie. Sorry to be so honest, but he likes Nikki a lot." She paused. "So . . . you really have it bad for him?"

Unexpectedly tears came to her eyes. "Oh, Sara. I think I love him. Sometimes I wonder if I've always loved him. Ever since we were kids he's been . . . I don't know. Just special, you know?"

Sara gave a smirk and held up a warning hand. "Hey, you forget the boy is my brother. I have a hard time seeing him as anything but the annoying pest he is."

Natalie smiled through her tears and stared, unseeing, out the windshield.

A pickup roared through the Sonic drive-through, rap music blaring, jarring Natalie to the present. She picked up her cherry limeade and rattled the ice in her cup. "Sara, I'm sorry I didn't tell you before. I just . . . well, I didn't figure I had a chance with Jon, and I didn't want you to feel like you had to play matchmaker or something."

Sara shrugged. "It's okay, Nattie. So . . . are you going to go with Evan?"

"I don't know," she sighed. "I guess it beats sitting home on homecoming night."

"I think you should go, Nattie. Evan Greenway is pretty cute, if you ask me."

Natalie gave her friend a close look. "Don't tell me *you* have a crush on him?"

"No way! You *know* who I like."

"Oh, yeah . . . Brad-ley." She singsonged the name like a playground taunt.

Sara blushed. "All right, all right. Back to the subject at hand. Are you going with Evan?"

"I guess I might as well," she sighed. "I've wasted years trying to get Jon to notice me, and look where that's gotten me. I've got nothing better to do."

"And nothing to lose," Sara pronounced with a bob of her chin. She looked at her watch and gasped. "But if you don't get me home in five minutes flat *I'm* going to have plenty to lose — like any curfew past nine o'clock for the rest of my natural life."

Three

The stadium was overflowing with a homecoming-night crowd when Cole and Daria Hunter arrived. They picked their way through the bleachers to their seats.

The evening was chilly with a brisk breeze that hinted of a bitter winter to come. Daria buttoned her jacket and tucked her arm into the crook of Cole's elbow. He gave her arm a quick squeeze, but he was already caught up in the excitement of the game.

A roar came from the track that encircled the football field, and Daria's attention was drawn to the high-school crowd. Despite the special section of bleachers reserved for them, the students chose to congregate on the track. It had been this way forever — at least since Daria had been a student at Bristol High herself. The teens were competing in a rowdy cheer with the fans from the opposing team, jumping up and down and yelling at the top of their lungs.

From her vantage point, Daria Hunter searched her daughters out, one by one. She felt like a queen counting the precious gems in her treasury.

Such beautiful girls. And each so different from the others. When had her little girls turned into young women? It seemed impossible that she and Cole had three teenagers. Why, she still felt like a teenager herself!

She spotted Nicole near the thirty-yard line, laughing with a group of her freshmen friends, her brown eyes flashing, the life of the party.

Noelle was there with her friends too, but the junior-high kids hovered at the fringes, not quite welcome in the fraternity yet. Noelle still had the coltish air of preadolescence, but the promise of impending beauty shimmered just beneath the surface.

Farther down the track, Daria spotted Natalie huddled head to head beside Sara Dever. Nattie's white-blond hair caught glimmers from the bright lights that illuminated the field. Daria smiled to herself, thinking what a godsend that flaxen hair had been when Nattie was a mischievous child. Cole and Daria had always been able to locate her quickly in any crowd, thanks to those blond tresses.

Daria watched Natalie and Sara and noticed that despite the noisy crowd and an imminent touchdown, the two of them remained deep in conversation. Daria recognized an all-too-familiar expression on Natalie's face. She was upset about something. Again. Poor Sara. How she continually put up with Natalie's moods, Daria wasn't sure. Daria felt a knot form in the pit of her stomach as she thought of the changes they'd seen in Natalie recently. Though she knew that some sibling rivalry was to be expected, it seemed that lately Natalie and Nicole fought almost constantly, and when they weren't fighting, they weren't speaking to each other. It broke Daria's heart to have her children at such enmity with each other. Daria sighed and turned back to the action on the football field. But it was a struggle to shake the melancholy that her fears had provoked.

The game was well under way when Daria spotted Don and Maribeth Dever, Sara's parents, stepping over boots and thermoses, making their way down the row behind her, where their own reserved seats were located. Daria waved and turned in her seat to move her stadium blanket out of the way while their friends got settled.

"Hey, guys. How's it going?" Daria asked.

"Good. How 'bout yourself?" Don asked.

Cole waved a brief greeting, then, when a time-out was called a minute later, he turned to shake hands with Don. "Hey, buddy, you just missed a whale of a play."

"Who? Jensen?"

Cole nodded. "First play of the game — Jensen to Laughlin. Great pass! Picture perfect. I mean, you talk about putting the ball right smack —"

"Cole, please . . ." Laughing, Daria took her husband by the shoulders and moved him in Don's direction. "Here, why don't you switch places with Mari and spare us the play-by-play."

"But I had that seat all warmed up," Cole griped good-naturedly as he stepped over the back of the bleachers and traded seats with Maribeth.

When the two women were settled side by side, they chatted while the men behind them cheered the game.

"Do you think Nattie's still upset?" Maribeth asked after a while.

"About what?"

"You didn't know that Nattie wanted to go to the dance with Jon?" she asked, her words halting.

"Natalie? With your Jon? Oh, my . . . Mari, no. I didn't know. Well . . . that explains a lot." She sighed in mock disgust. "Could you please tell me why mothers are always the last to know these things?"

Maribeth put a consoling hand on her sleeve. "Hey, you probably know Sara better than I do. That just seems to be the way it is. I've probably said way too much already, Daria."

Daria held up a hand. "No . . . I'm glad you told me. I should have seen it."

"You couldn't know, Dar. Kids are good at hiding this kind of stuff from their parents. And . . . I don't want to put you in a tight spot, but please don't tell Nattie I said anything. I don't want Sara to know I tattled. Ugh, that sounds so deceitful."

"Hey," Daria commiserated, "we are mothers of teenagers. It is our sworn duty to be conniving and devious." That made them giggle like teenagers themselves.

"Oh, that girl," she said to Maribeth now. "I don't know why she has to be so difficult. I'm sorry Sara always seems to get the brunt of it."

★ ★ ★

After the game, Cole and Daria were alone in the car since Noelle was spending the night with a friend and the older girls had gone to the dance. As they crept along in the long line of cars leaving the stadium parking lot, Daria snuggled beside him, trying to get warm.

"So, what were you and Maribeth in such deep conversation about?" he asked, kissing the top of her head.

"You were so involved in that game I'm surprised you even noticed," she teased.

"It was a great game. I can't believe you and Maribeth could yak through the whole thing." They reached the end of the drive, and he pulled into the street.

She sighed. "Oh . . . just Natalie . . . Mari told me something that kind of sheds a new light on things."

"What do you mean?"

"Did you know Nattie was upset that Jon asked Nikki to the dance?"

"Upset? Why?"

"Apparently Nattie has a crush on Jon."

"You're kidding."

Daria shook her head. "I've been thinking about Natalie, Cole. She's always felt like the odd man out. And lately the way she's been acting with her sisters." She cleared her throat, not quite sure how to broach the subject. "I . . . I wonder if some of her problem is the baggage of — well, of *our* history. I can't help but think that maybe some of what is weighing on her is the whole thing with Nate. I wonder if it would help if Nattie could talk to Nate. Maybe she's struggling with that whole identity thing. I mean, I know it's not practical for her to actually visit him right now, but maybe we could encourage her to write him more and even e-mail. Vera and Betsy hear from Nate quite regularly now that he has the computer . . ." She let her voice trail off, concerned with how Cole would receive her suggestion.

He was silent for several minutes. She watched his face in the light from the passing street lamps and wished she could read his mind.

Finally he turned to her. "My heart aches for Nattie. It really does, Dar. If she has feelings for Jon, it has to hurt to have him and Nikki going out now. But you can't *make* someone love you. There's really nothing we can do about this except just be there for Natalie."

Daria opened her mouth to speak, but Cole answered her counterpoint before she could even voice it. "And every one of us

43

has some kind of baggage from the past," he said firmly. "If anything, dredging up the whole thing with Nate will just make things worse. Don't get me wrong, I have no problem with Natalie corresponding more with Nate. I think that would probably be good. But I don't want to turn this into an excuse for her. She has no reason to act the way she's been acting. I don't know what her deal is, but somewhere along the way she got a chip on her shoulder the size of a barn, and I, for one, am just a little tired of it."

Daria knew he had a point, and yet she couldn't help but feel that he was letting his own attitudes about the past color the way he perceived things.

As they neared the city limits, the streetlamps grew fewer and farther between. Cole turned the car sharply onto Chaffee Street and headed east.

"What's wrong?" Daria asked.

"I need to stop by the clinic for a minute," he told her, looking straight ahead, his jaw set.

She recognized it as the excuse it was — Cole's way of telling her that he was finished discussing the subject tonight. Fourteen years of experience had told her that he would mull things over for a few days, and eventually he would come back to her, ready to talk openly and reasonably, ready to pray together about it, and maybe even to approach Natalie and try to offer her some comfort. But for now she knew better than to push it.

The Bristol High gymnasium shimmered under the eerie glow of black lights, and the blue-jeans-and-sweatshirt-clad teens swaying on the dance floor were an odd complement to the gold and silver balloons and streamers that glittered overhead.

Natalie spotted Sara sitting on the fringes of the room and waved. "Stay right there," she mouthed over the booming music. "Hey, Evan." She touched her dance partner's arm lightly. "I'll be right back, okay? I need to talk to Sara about something."

He didn't look too happy about being abandoned in the middle of a song, but he shrugged and let her go. Natalie wove her way through the crowd and squeezed beside Sara on the crowded bench.

"Hey, girl," her friend greeted her.

"Where's Brad?" Natalie asked.

"He's getting us some punch. Are you having fun?"

She rocked a flat hand, meaning "so-so."

"It's all right, I guess. How about you?" She was shouting to be heard over the din.

"The same. We've only danced twice all night."

"Lucky you. That's all Evan wants to do."

"Do you think he'll ask you out again?"

"Who cares? *He* didn't ask me out the first time."

"Nattie! You're so rude!"

"Oh, it's nothing against Evan. He's just not my type."

She turned to face the dance floor and sensed Sara do the same beside her. She didn't have to tell her friend that "her type" was on the dance floor not ten feet in front of them. But he was holding her own sister in his arms, flashing that darling boyish grin of his, whispering in Nicole's ear. Natalie watched him — watched *them* — with an ache in her throat, remembering back to the day when she'd first decided that she loved Jon Dever. She and Sara were in eighth grade, and Jon had just started high school, so instead of seeing him daily, she'd had to be content with the glimpses she caught of him when she was at Sara's house and at church.

"Natalie, would you like another slice of

pizza?" Maribeth Dever hovered over the table in the Devers' tiny kitchen. "How about some more salad?"

"Thanks, but I'm stuffed," Natalie declared. "Everything was delicious."

"Well, it's just pizza, but I'm glad you liked it. Sara, did you get enough to eat?"

Her mouth full, Sara waved her mother away.

"My mom never makes homemade pizza," Natalie told Sara's mother. "You'll have to give her your recipe."

"She's welcome to it. It's not that difficult."

The back door slammed, and Jon Dever filled the doorway between the kitchen and the mudroom. He was still in his gear from football practice, his dark hair plastered to his forehead.

Natalie's heart began to pound out its now familiar but strange rhythm, and she felt the blood rise to her face. She prayed no one would notice the effect Sara's brother always seemed to have on her.

"Hey, Jonny," Maribeth greeted her son. "How was practice?"

"It was okay. What's for dinner?"

"Pizza. You want to shower first?"

"Yeah, but save some for me. I'm starving."

Without giving her or Sara so much as a glance, he mumbled something unintelligible and headed to the basement where his room was. Ten minutes later he was back, wearing shorts and a T-shirt, his hair wet and tousled, his face freshly scrubbed.

He sat down at the end of the table, close enough that his arm brushed Natalie's when he reached for a slice of pizza. Natalie froze, suddenly finding herself speechless.

Maribeth started clearing the dishes off the table, and Natalie quickly stood to help her.

"Thank you, Nattie. I wish your manners" — Mrs. Dever cleared her throat meaningfully — "would rub off on certain people in this house."

"All right, Mom," Sara whined. "I get the hint." She unfolded her lanky height from under the table, went to the sink for the dishrag, and made a halfhearted swipe over the tabletop where her plate had been.

Jon brushed the hair off his forehead and looked up at Natalie, giving her a lopsided grin that made her knees weak. "Gee, thanks, Nattie," he said through a mouthful of pizza.

"Sorry," she said sheepishly.

He waved her off. "Aw, it's okay. We'll just have you over for supper every night so you can do the dishes."

That would be fine with me, she thought, heart thumping. But of course she didn't say that.

Over all those years, she never had told him how she felt, but something about that exchange had made her go home certain she was in love. What she felt for Jon had only grown over the years. In all her daydreams of the future, it was always Jon she saw beside her walking down the aisle of a church, holding her hand as she gave birth to their children, growing old with her. She'd always thought that someday, somehow they would be together.

Now, watching Jon hold Nicole in his arms, Natalie felt all those dreams begin to die. And it hurt too much.

She jumped up and put a hand on Sara's shoulder. "I'm going to go find Evan. Call me when you get home," she mouthed over the blaring music.

Sara nodded and waved her off.

Evan was just coming back in from the hallway where the snack tables were set up. He smiled when he saw her approaching, and she recognized a warmth in his eyes that she hadn't noticed before. *Oh, brother. What have I started?*

"Hey, Nattie," he said, running a hand through his hair. "Want to dance some more?"

"Um . . . not really."

"Well, you want something to eat?"

"Okay, sure."

"They've got sandwiches and chips. I think there was still some pizza out there."

"I'll just go with you."

She followed him back out to the hallway and filled a plate with food she had no appetite for. They took their plates outside, but a chill breeze soon chased them back indoors. Natalie pitched her plate into the trash can that sat by the door and waited while Evan refilled his plate.

When they went back into the gym, the lights were low and the DJ was playing a slow song. Without asking, Evan took her hand and led her onto the dance floor. She had to admit that it felt good to be held in strong arms, to feel cherished and desired. Evan was really a pretty nice guy. He was good looking, in a rugged sort of way, and he treated her with respect. But she knew he hung with a rough crowd sometimes and, well, he just wasn't . . .

He just wasn't *Jon*. That was it, plain and simple.

Four

"So, come on . . . give me details, girl," Aunt Betsy coaxed, her green eyes sparking with mischief. Betsy Camfield Franklin, Nathan Camfield's sister, blew a wisp of short, brunette hair off her forehead and eyed Natalie suspiciously.

The two of them stood side by side at the kitchen island in the Franklins' tastefully decorated home not far from the bustling, upscale Plaza in Kansas City. Aunt Betsy had inherited her cooking skills from Vera Camfield, and, like Grandma, Nathan's sister was always luring Natalie into one of her baking marathons. Today they were making cinnamon rolls.

"There's nothing to tell, Betsy," Natalie said, kneading the smooth, elastic dough with the heels of her hands. "Honestly. It was one date."

"You're not holding out on me now, are you?" Betsy was wearing a chartreuse silk tunic over faded jeans, and the silver bracelets and earrings that dripped from her wrists and ears jangled pleasantly as she worked. "What'd you say his name was?"

Natalie laughed nervously. "Evan."

"Ooh, that's a nice name."

Natalie elbowed her aunt good-naturedly. "Would you quit? I probably wouldn't even go out with the guy again — if he asked."

"So who *would* you go out with — if he asked?

"There really isn't anybody."

Natalie had always been able to talk to Aunt Betsy — her birth father's sister — but she wasn't sure she wanted to go into the whole thing about Jon. It was too complicated, especially now that things seemed to be heating up between Jon and Nicole. Ever since the homecoming dance six weeks earlier, Jon Dever had spent an inordinate amount of time at the Hunter house. Natalie had become resigned to the fact that her sister and Jon were "an item." Still, it hurt deeply to acknowledge that her dreams of being with Jon had been crushed.

"How's school going?" Betsy asked.

"It's good. I'm ready for summer though."

"Are you going to work this summer?"

"Yeah, I'll probably work for Daddy at the vet clinic again. Oh, and there's this summer class that the junior college over in Clayton is offering that I'm hoping to take. It's in advanced Spanish, and they have field trips and stuff like that. It would be a college credit."

"You've had a couple of years of foreign languages already, haven't you? You must really have a knack for that."

"Well, I don't know about languages in general. I only know Spanish."

A glint came to Betsy's eyes. *"¿Qué pasa?"*

"Hola. No hablo mucho español. ¿Podría hablar más despacio, por favor?"

Betsy laughed and held up a flour-dusted hand in protest. "Okay, okay . . . you lost me back on *hola*. I'm impressed."

Natalie gave her aunt a sheepish grin. "I'm not even sure what I just said. Something like 'Speak slowly, please, because I'm an idiot and I can't understand a word you're saying.' "

Betsy laughed. "Well, obviously it doesn't take much to impress me."

"It's just something we had to memorize off the tapes in Spanish II. But I do like studying Spanish. That and English are the only classes I ever ace."

"Well, I happen to know that anybody would be proud of the report cards you bring home. Grandma always cuts out the honor rolls from the Bristol paper," she explained.

"Oh yes, for her famous scrapbooks."

"Yes, but before they go in the scrapbook, she makes copies for your dad and me."

Natalie rolled her eyes. "Oh, brother."

"Yes, the honor rolls and the school lunch menus. Your grandma likes us to know what the Bristol High cafeteria is serving up on any given day."

"Are you serious? I guess I won't tell Grandma that I usually bring my lunch from home."

The two of them giggled like schoolgirls.

Natalie closed her eyes and breathed in the rich cinnamon aroma that hung in the air. Throughout her eighteen years, time spent with Aunt Betsy had always been a bright spot in her frequent weekend visits with her birth father's side of the family.

Now they worked together in companionable silence, flattening the supple lumps of yeast dough with a wooden rolling pin, then spreading each with butter and sprinkling a fragrant mixture of cinnamon and sugar on top.

Wiping a smudge of flour off her nose with the back of her hand, Betsy told Natalie, "Every time I make these I think of your dad. He used to polish off an entire batch of these things single-handedly."

"I can see why," Natalie said, putting a pinch of the rich dough into her mouth. She busied herself with buttering the baking dishes. "I think of him too — every time we make these." The truth was, she thought about her birth father often lately. She always felt closer to Nathan Camfield when she was with Grandma and Grandpa Camfield, Aunt Betsy, and Uncle Jim.

Her aunt was silent as she cut the roll of dough into slices and handed the swirled rounds to Natalie to arrange in the bottom of the pan. After all these years, they had their routine down pat.

Something about the warmth of the kitchen, the golden glow of afternoon sunlight that filtered through the stained-glass panel in the back door, and the quiet music that wafted from the stereo in Uncle Jim's den made Natalie feel at ease. She could remember a time when she'd been so little she'd had to stand on a wooden stool to see over the countertop. She thought back to a long-ago day in this very kitchen. She must have been about eight years old.

"I sure wish they'd invent a way that you didn't have to wait for the rolls to rise, Aunt Betsy."

Her aunt laughed. "Nattie, Nattie, that would be cheating! Half the fun is in the waiting."

"Then, I guess I don't know how to have fun. I hate waiting . . . for anything. Mommy says I'm too impatient for my own good."

"You get that from your dad," Aunt Betsy said. "But he learned . . . he learned how to be patient." A sad look came to her eyes, and for a minute Natalie thought Aunt Betsy had forgotten that she wasn't alone in the room.

"You mean because of — well, being lost in the jungle all that time."

Betsy looked up, seemingly startled. "Yes," she whispered. "I . . . I guess I didn't know you knew about all that."

"Mom told me some stuff. And Grandma. I don't know all of it, but — I guess the important stuff."

"Oh?"

Natalie licked a cinnamon-sugared finger and looked up at her aunt. "I know my dad went back to South America after he found out Mom got married again."

Aunt Betsy was silent, wiping flour off the countertop.

"I . . . I wonder how that made my dad feel . . . You know — finding out that Mommy had married somebody else."

Her aunt cleared her throat. "Well, Natalie, it was very hard for Nate — for your dad — to give up your mom. He loved her very much. But I sometimes think it was even harder for him to give you up. Here he had an adorable little baby that he hadn't even known about, and —"

Natalie held her breath, her heart skipping a beat. "What do you mean?"

"Mean?"

"What do you mean he didn't even know about me?"

A stricken expression replaced her aunt's smile. "Oh, honey. Maybe — maybe you should talk to your mom about all this."

"No! You have to tell me. My dad didn't know about me? I don't understand what you mean."

Betsy took a deep breath. "When your dad disappeared, your mom didn't even realize she was going to have a baby. So when he came back from Colombia, you were . . . a surprise to him — a wonderful surprise, of course. You . . . didn't know about that?"

Natalie shook her head.

"Oh, Nattie, I'm sorry. It wasn't my place to tell you. I hope your mom won't be angry with me."

*Natalie shook her head. "She won't mind."
But her thoughts were reeling — and Mommy
probably would mind. As Natalie had grown
older, she'd come to realize how unusual her
parents' story was. What else had her mother
failed to tell her? She wanted to know everything, and yet she wanted to forget what she
already knew.*

*"I bet it wasn't such a good surprise to him
about my mom, huh?" she risked now.*

"About her being remarried, you mean?"

"Yeah."

*"No," Aunt Betsy said slowly. "That was
pretty tough. On both of them. Your mom and
dad were very, very much in love."*

"You mean my Daddy-Nate?"

*Aunt Betsy nodded, and a soft smile curved
the corners of her mouth. "It gets kind of confusing, doesn't it?"*

*Natalie swallowed hard. "Then . . . why did
she get married again?"*

*"Well, honey . . . because she thought your
dad — Nate — she thought he was dead. You
did know that, didn't you, Nattie? Your mom
would never have married someone else if
she'd thought there was any chance that your
dad was alive."*

*"Yeah, but still, if she really loved him, how
could she ever marry somebody else?"*

"Honey, I know this probably seems all

mixed up to you, but you have to understand that your mom did what she thought was best. She had you to think about. You were just a tiny baby, and she wanted you to have a father."

"Grandma thinks she should have waited," Natalie challenged.

Betsy's nostrils flared. "Grandma sometimes has a mind of her own. And you've got to remember, honey, Nate is her son. She wanted him to be happy, and she sure didn't want him to go back to Colombia. Not after everything he'd been through."

Natalie thought about the ropelike scars that marred Nathan Camfield's hands and forearms, and for the first time she began to comprehend some of the suffering her father had endured during the time he'd been held captive in Colombia.

"So why did he go back?" she asked.

"Mostly, I think he just really felt like God was calling him to go back and help the people in Colombia. They kind of became like his family, you know?" She scrubbed at a countertop that was already spotless.

"Mommy loves Daddy now, though." It came out more like a question.

"Cole, you mean?"

She nodded.

"Oh, of course she does. Cole has been a

wonderful father to all of you girls. And I'm sure he loves you very much — and your mother."

"And she loves him," Natalie repeated defensively.

"Of course she does. Nobody doubts that, Nattie."

The timer on the stove buzzed, and Natalie jumped. She shook herself back to the present and held up a pan of rolls. "First batch, ready for the oven," she told Betsy, hoping her aunt didn't detect the quaver in her voice.

"It's hard to think about him, isn't it?"

Aunt Betsy's question startled her. It *was* hard to think about her father. She had a longing for him that she couldn't explain. And yet that longing made her feel like a traitor to the man she called "Daddy."

Natalie nodded now, aware that Betsy wasn't going to let her question go unanswered. "I . . . I wish I knew him better. I mean, sometimes when I read through all the letters he's written me, when I look at Grandma's picture albums, I feel pretty close to him. But then you say something as simple as 'your dad loved cinnamon rolls,' and I realize how much I *don't* know about him."

Her aunt listened with her head tipped to one side, a dangly earring brushing one shoulder, and Natalie let her thoughts pour out, unguarded.

"When I was little, I sometimes wondered what it would be like to be a *real* Hunter . . . Cole Hunter's natural daughter. I guess sometimes I still wonder. My name — being a Camfield — has always singled me out." She held up a hand and shook her head, aware that Betsy might misinterpret her words. "Not that I'm not proud of my name. I am. But sometimes it — well, it makes me feel like I don't quite belong in my own family." She cocked her head to match the tilt of Betsy's. "Does that make any sense at all?"

"Oh, honey, it makes perfect sense. Anyone in your shoes would feel the same way."

"I don't want to sound ungrateful. I mean, I think about Sara . . . you remember Sara?"

"Sure. The pretty redhead who was here with you last summer, right?"

Natalie nodded. "I wouldn't trade places with her for anything. She has great adoptive parents, but she didn't know either one of her birth parents. When she did find her birth mother, the woman didn't want anything to do with her. And Sara never did find her father. Even though I don't get to see my real dad very much, I've always been glad that I at least knew him. And I never had to wonder what he was like, or if he loved me. I've never doubted that. I know that what Sara has to deal with would be much harder than . . . than what I have, but . . ."

"But it still makes you feel like you're torn between two families," Betsy finished for her.

"Yeah. Sometimes it does. And in a way it's like I don't quite belong to either one of them. When I was little it used to make me so mad that Mom and Daddy would just drop me off here and then leave. I understood that, technically, Grandma and Grandpa weren't Nikki and Noelle's grandparents, but I always wished so bad that the whole family could stay. And — maybe it was just my imagination — but it seemed like every single time I came up here, something wonderful happened back home. I'm not kidding. I think half the kittens on our farm purposely waited to be born until I was gone!"

Betsy smiled sympathetically, and Natalie's words picked up steam.

"I can't tell you how many times we'll be

sitting around the dinner table and we'll start talking, and pretty soon someone will say, 'Oh, remember that Sunday afternoon when we stopped off at that little airport and watched those skydivers?' Or whatever the memory was. I just want to shake them and tell them, 'No! I *don't* remember! Because I wasn't there. You did that without me, remember?' "

Betsy put a warm hand to her shoulder.

"I'm sorry to be such a whiner," Natalie told Betsy now. "I . . . I know I have a lot to be thankful for, and I —"

"Hey, we do allow occasional whining in this kitchen," Betsy cut her off.

Natalie smiled and gave her aunt a hug. She loved Betsy so much. It felt good to voice some of her thoughts. But sometimes talking about her feelings seemed to stir up more questions than it answered.

Five

Summer was almost over. Clayton County had gone six weeks without rain. A black cloud of dirt billowed behind Natalie's car as it bumped along the country road. In spite of the hundred-degree heat and her car's faulty air conditioning system, Natalie rolled up her windows against the gritty dust. Her Grandpa Camfield had bought her the Camry at the beginning of the summer. It was far from new, but the car was Natalie's pride and joy.

As she neared the driveway to their farm, Jon Dever's car was just pulling onto the road, headed back into Bristol. She gave a halfhearted wave as he passed. Jon was leaving for college soon, and she would heave a sigh of relief when he was gone. Though she'd resigned herself to the fact that she would never have a chance with Jon, it stabbed at her every time she saw him and Nikki still together after almost a year.

She parked the car in the garage and went in through the kitchen. The house was quiet, but the savory fragrance of a roast and potatoes filled the air.

"I'm home," she shouted, leafing absently through the stack of mail on the kitchen table. "Hey, where is everybody?"

Mom's voice floated down the stairway. "Hi, Nattie. We're upstairs."

Natalie raided the refrigerator, taking an apple and a hunk of cheese up to her room. She plopped on her bed with the snack, popped in a cassette from her summer Spanish class, and put on her headphones. A soothing feminine voice was pronouncing Spanish phrases in her ears when Mom appeared in the doorway. Natalie clicked off the recorder and slid the headphones from her ears, letting them hang loosely around her neck.

"Hola, Madre."

"Hi, Nattie. How was your class?"

"Muy bien." She knew her constant use of Spanish since she'd started the class at the junior college over in Clayton was driving her family nuts. But the instructor had told them to use the language every opportunity they got, and Natalie took him seriously. Besides, in a perverse sort of

way, Natalie rather enjoyed getting under their skin.

Mom knew a little Spanish from her days in South America and sometimes she played along, putting Natalie's knowledge to the test. But now Mom ignored the challenge. She sat down on the edge of the bed and put a hand on Natalie's knee. "Hey, do me a favor and be nice to Nikki tonight, okay?" Her tone was serious.

"Why? What happened?"

"Oh, nothing happened really. But Jon's leaving for K-State tomorrow, and she's taking it kind of hard. He came by a little bit ago to say goodbye."

"Yeah, I saw him. He was just leaving when I drove in. Aren't they going out tonight?"

"I guess not. I'm not sure what's up, but Nikki's in her room crying her eyes out right now."

"Do you think they broke up or something?"

"No," Mom said, "I don't think so. She's just upset that he's leaving. Things will be different between them now. And maybe her feelings are a little hurt because he didn't want to go out tonight. Maribeth said they have to leave before six in the morning to take him up there, so I'm sure he has a lot to do tonight." Mom stood to leave. "Just go easy on her, okay? This is a tough time for her, and she doesn't need anybody giving her any grief right now."

Natalie hunched her shoulders in an exaggerated shrug and glared at her mother. "I didn't do anything."

"I know." Mom reached down to pat her knee again. "Hey, take it easy. I wasn't accusing you of anything. I'm just trying to head it off before —"

Natalie didn't wait to hear the rest. She pulled the headphones back over her ears, cranked up the volume on the Spanish tape, and turned toward the wall.

She felt the shudder of her door closing and looked over her shoulder to be sure her mother had left the room. Seething with resentment, she stuffed her fist into her pillow and flopped back against the headboard. She didn't recall her parents tiptoeing around *her* when she was so upset about Jon asking Nicole out. In fact, their attitude back then had been more like, "Get over it, sweetheart; we all have disappointments in life." It hardly seemed fair that Nikki was getting the "you poor thing" treatment now that *she* was the one mourning losing Jon.

Natalie thought about calling Sara to

complain, but things got too complicated with her when it came to the subject of Jon. Besides, Natalie was over Jon. She'd given up the right to cry over him months ago.

She turned the volume up another notch and rattled off the phrases with the voice on the recording.

¿Puede ayudarme? No comprendo. Me he perdido.

"Would you like more spaghetti, Nattie?" Maribeth Dever asked, a large spoon poised over the serving dish.

"Oh, no thanks. It was great though." She turned to Sara. "Hey, Dever, if we're going to get that book report done, we'd better book it." Natalie wiggled Groucho Marx eyebrows at Sara.

Maribeth laughed at Natalie's corny pun, and Sara rolled her eyes. "Very clever, Camfield. Why can't you ever come up with this stuff when we need it?"

Natalie grabbed her backpack from the floor by the front door, and Sara led the way to her room. They settled themselves cross-legged on Sara's quilt and spread their books and notebooks between them. Classes now that they were seniors required more homework than they'd bargained for.

"So, did you get invited to Lacey Franks' party Friday?" Natalie asked, uncapping her pen.

"Uh-huh. Did you?"

"Yeah."

"Are you going?"

"What do you think?" Natalie smirked. "You know Daddy. He thinks he has to do a background check on a girl's entire family before I'm allowed to associate with her. Don't tell me you're thinking about going."

Sara shook her head. "My dad *did* do a background check on her entire family, and they failed the test — miserably."

"Really?" This sounded juicy.

"Apparently her father has a bit of a problem with" — she etched quotation marks in the air — " 'the bottle,' as Dad so nicely put it."

"You're serious? He really checked up on them?" And she thought Daddy was bad.

"Well, not really. Dad works with Lacey's uncle. He heard all this from him. Did you know Lacey has two older brothers?"

"You're kidding."

"Yeah, one in rehab, another one dropped out of school. It turns out her mother manages the liquor store in Clayton."

"Oh, that's convenient," Natalie said wryly. "Well, that cinches it. There's no way I'll be going to *that* party."

Sara giggled. "I wish my parents didn't always have to make such a big deal about stuff like that, but to tell you the truth, it's kind of nice to have an excuse. I mean Lacey's okay and all, but . . ." Sara cocked her head to one side and wrinkled her freckle-strewn nose. "I don't know . . . I mean, it's not like I have any desire to get in with that crowd."

Natalie thought for a minute. "You know, if Daddy gave me permission, I probably wouldn't even want to go. But the fact that he thinks he has to make the big decision *for* me makes me want to go in the worst way."

"You rebel!" Sara teased, tossing a daisy-shaped pillow at her. "I feel sorry for your poor parents."

"Well," Natalie said defensively, "I am eighteen years old. I don't think I need my mommy and daddy to pick my friends for me."

"Well, I'm sure glad they picked me," Sara said, a glint of mischief in her eye.

"What are you talking about?"

"Don't you remember the first time we met? It was *your* dad who invited us over for lunch that day."

"Oh, man!" Natalie groaned, suppressing a smile. "That does it. I'm outta here. We are history, sister."

Sara hurled another pillow her way. Natalie lobbed it back, commencing full-scale war. Their hysterical laughter and squeals finally brought Maribeth Dever to the room to see why the house was shaking. Two hours later when Natalie got in her Camry to go home, their book reports were still unwritten.

Natalie growled under her breath. Her day was off to a lovely start. Daddy had informed her at breakfast that he needed her to fill in for the receptionist at the vet clinic as soon as school was out. Her plans to go jogging with Sara went out the window.

"It's okay," Sara said, when Natalie told her over lunch in the school cafeteria. "Maybe we can go when you get done at the clinic. What time do you get off?"

Natalie ignored Sara's question and let out a snarl of frustration. "I don't see how I can stand to be under their thumb for another whole year. They are driving me crazy! Especially Daddy. I can't make one plan that he doesn't mess up."

71

"Hey, just think about the money."

Sara had a point there. Daddy paid her well for helping out at the vet clinic. But that wasn't the issue here. Natalie was tired of always having her life dictated by the schedule at Daddy's precious clinic or by whatever he and Mom decided the family was going to do. She was practically an adult. She wanted the freedom to come and go as she pleased, to make her own hours.

All day long she fumed about her father changing her plans, but when school was out, she grudgingly went to the clinic to put in her hours.

At the supper table, her father thanked her for helping out. "I know you had other things you wanted to do, Natalie. But with Beth out of the office, I was really in a bind. I appreciate your filling in."

Natalie tried to keep her voice steady. "Yeah, well, I was wanting to talk to you about that, Daddy. Couldn't Nikki or Noelle fill in once in a while?"

"Huh-uh!" Nicole said over a mouthful of mashed potatoes. "I already give up every Saturday to work."

"Well, at least you know your schedule. I'm *always* having to change my plans when Beth calls in at the last minute," Natalie shot back.

"Well, at least you have your weekends free. It's not my fault that you didn't want to be put on the schedule," Nikki said.

"Well, now I do."

"Fine, you can have my Saturdays."

"Cut it out, you two," Daddy interrupted sternly. He turned to Natalie. "I know it's been a pain, Natalie, but Nikki's right. You're the one who didn't want to be put on the schedule. I seem to remember offering you a slot and you turning it down."

"But I didn't know 'on call' meant I'd have to change my plans practically every day," she whined.

"Well, what did you think 'on call' meant, Nattie?" Daddy said in the infuriatingly calm voice he used whenever they argued.

"I don't know, but I sure didn't think it meant this." She pushed her plate back and folded her arms. He was going to take Nicole's side. Of course. His precious baby.

"Why can't Noelle fill in for Beth sometimes?" she asked, testing.

Daddy shook his head. "No. She's not quite old enough. You and Nikki didn't have jobs until you were sixteen. Besides, Natalie, I've already invested the time and

73

money to train you for the position."

She sat unmoving while Nicole gloated from across the table. No use arguing now. It was obvious he'd made up his mind.

"I'll tell you what," Daddy said. "I'll try to get Beth to give me a little more notice before she takes a day off. There's not much more I can do than that."

"Fine," Natalie huffed, refusing to look at him.

Graduation could not come fast enough. She could not get out of this house soon enough. Freedom was going to be so incredibly sweet.

Six

Autumn deepened, and along with it the restlessness in Natalie's soul.

"I wish I had your faith," she told Sara one night as the two of them sat cross-legged on the floor of the Devers' family room finishing off a cold pizza by the flickering light of the television. They had the house to themselves, and the tearjerker movie they'd just watched had left Natalie feeling pensive and unguarded.

Sara wiped pizza sauce from the corner of her mouth with the back of her hand. "What are you talking about? You have the same faith I do."

Natalie shook her head. "No. I don't. I mean, I believe in the same God. I go to the same church you do every Sunday. I've done all the things I'm supposed to do. I asked Jesus into my heart. I even pray and read my Bible" — she shrugged — "well, maybe not as much as I should. But . . . I don't know . . . it's *not* the same for me."

"I still don't know what you mean."

"You just seem so sure about everything. I — I've tried to pray for God to show me what he wants me to do with my life — like you told me — but I don't ever seem to hear anything back. And I constantly want to do things I'm not supposed to."

"Like what?"

"Oh, I don't know . . . like go to the parties or smoke a cigarette — or even just haul off and use a swear word once in a while."

Sara stopped chewing and wrinkled up her nose. "You're tempted to do that stuff?"

"I guess . . . sometimes." Seeing the shocked look on Sara's face, she wasn't sure she wanted to continue what she'd started. "Those things don't even tempt you, do they?"

Sara shook her head. "But Nattie, that doesn't mean I don't ever sin. I guess it's just that I'm tempted by different things."

"Yeah, like what?"

Sara rubbed her jaw, and Natalie knew she was struggling to come up with something that Natalie would deem terrible enough to qualify. "I'm tempted to gossip sometimes. Or, like when Lacey wears one of her bimbo outfits, I'm tempted to be really judgmental and even make nasty comments."

Natalie flung a pizza crust at her. "You are a sick woman, you know that?"

Sara threw it back. "Quit. What's so sick about that?"

"If that is the only thing you can point to as an example of your sinful ways and your weak faith, then let's just nominate you for sainthood right now." She leaned across to the end table and picked up the cordless phone. "Where's the phone book? I need to call the Vatican."

Sara giggled, and the seriousness of the moment was lost. Natalie was relieved. She didn't like where that was heading. The truth was, she *was* tempted by those things. She'd never acted on her desires, but sometimes she just wanted to see what it would be like. Not for the rest of her life or anything, but just for a while — maybe even just once. Maybe that would get it out of her system.

As she drove home that night, a full moon illumined the country road. On a whim, she flipped off the headlights and drove by moonlight. Leaning over the steering wheel, she stared up through the windshield at the night sky. The myriad stars seemed to shout how insignificant she was in the universe.

She felt so utterly alone. *Something* eluded her, and she didn't know what it was. She knew the answer had something to do with God, but she didn't know how to reach him. It was as though she had this beautiful jewelry box, and she knew that whatever was inside would solve all her problems and finally make her happy. But she couldn't find the key. Couldn't even find the lock the key was supposed to fit.

"I'll be right back, Sara. Wait here."

Natalie left the car idling and ran into the house. "Mom? Daddy? Anybody home?"

"In here," her mother called from the laundry room. Daria emerged, peering over a pile of neatly folded towels. "Hi, honey. What are you up to?"

"Sara and I are going out. I just came home to change clothes."

Her mother hesitated. "Did you ask Dad?"

"I'm telling you."

"Well, I think you'd better check with your dad. You've been gone almost every night this week, and he wasn't too crazy about your coming home so late last night.

I think he might have some —"

Natalie let out a sigh of frustration. "Good grief, I am a senior in high school. Am I going to have to be asking you guys' permission for every little thing I do the rest of my life?"

"No," her mother said evenly. "Just the rest of this year."

At that moment her father came in through the back porch. "Hey, Nattie," he said, smiling. "You're home early."

"I'm just here for a minute," she said smoothly, purposely sidestepping her mother's admonition. "Sara and I are going to eat at Sonic, and then we're going to a show in Wichita. I'll probably spend the night at her house, so don't wait up for me."

He looked to Daria, then, without waiting for a response, cleared his throat. "No," he said slowly. "I don't think so, Nattie."

"What do you mean?" Natalie avoided her mother's gaze.

"You've been out late every night this week, and you've been way past your curfew more than once. I think you need to stay home for once."

She stared at him in silence, frustration and anger simmering inside her. He looked at her carefully, and his face softened. "I guess I don't care if you and Sara eat in town, but I want you to come home early."

"You're kidding, right?" She knew he was completely serious, and she saw from the hard set of his jaw that she'd used the wrong tone.

"No," he told her firmly, obviously reining in his anger. "I'm not kidding. You don't need to be putting any more miles on your car, and I'm sure you have homework."

"No, I don't. I finished it all in the library. Besides, it's my car, and I'm the one paying for the gas, so what do you care?"

"Natalie."

His stern tone should have been caution enough, but she plowed on, knowing even as she did so that this approach always backfired with him. "Well? What does it matter to you how late I'm out? I don't see what the big deal is. We're just going to a movie. Is that a crime?"

"That's not the point, Natalie," he said steadily.

"What *is* the point?"

His face became flushed. "The point is that you suddenly seem to think you don't answer to anyone but Natalie Camfield. You were gone every night last week; now you've been gone every night this week — and it was past eleven at least two of those nights." He didn't wait for her to answer. "Did you clean your bathroom like Mom asked? You know the rules of this house, Natalie. You suddenly seem to think they don't apply to you."

"I'm almost nineteen years old," she said through clenched teeth. "I think I can handle my own schedule, thank you very much."

"Well, apparently you *can't* handle it, thank you very much." His sarcastic tone matched hers, and his color deepened the way it did when he was about to lose his temper. He opened his mouth to say something, then apparently thought better of it. Instead he said simply. "I'd like you to be home early tonight."

He turned to go back through the porch door, and Natalie pulled out a weapon she'd been toying with for weeks, but had not yet had the courage to use. Now she fired it willfully. "I don't have to do what you say," she sneered at him. "You are not my father!"

Her mother stepped between them, her eyes flashing, utter disbelief in her voice. "Natalie Joan! Don't you *ever* speak that way to your dad."

Her father let loose of the doorknob and turned back to face her. His eyes narrowed, his nostrils flared, and his mouth hung open, but before he could say one word Natalie lashed out again, this time at her mother, "Well, he's *not* my father."

Natalie was a bit frightened by her own words, but she'd unleashed them, and she wasn't about to recant now. She was sure they could see her heart thumping against her sweater. She had never dared to speak to Daddy that way before, but it actually felt kind of good. The adrenaline surged through her veins, and she risked looking him in the eye. She expected to see his usual paternal arrogance that would justify her outburst and fuel her resolve, but what she saw there instead took her by surprise.

His face was etched with deep disappointment — and his eyes were filled with unmistakable sadness. Her breath caught in her throat, and an unfamiliar pang stung her heart. For a fleeting moment, she wanted desperately to run to him, to crawl up on her daddy's lap and feel his big strong arms around her, to feel safe and cherished. But she wasn't a little girl anymore. She saw things differently now. Saw the people in her life differently. Everything had changed. *She* had changed, and something inside her wouldn't allow her to take back her cruel words.

She pushed the door open and ran out through the garage. Sara was waiting for her with a questioning look on her face. Natalie slid behind the steering wheel and slammed the car door.

"What took you so long?" Sara wanted to know. She looked pointedly at Natalie's sweater. "Hey, I thought you were going to change clothes."

Natalie revved the engine and peeled out of the drive, scattering gravel in her wake.

"Whoa, girl. There's steam coming out of your ears. What's going on?"

"Oh, my stupid father is on one of his power trips," she growled. Mimicking her father's tone, she told Sara, "I have been forbidden from going out tonight."

Sara was silent for a moment, but Natalie could feel her friend's eyes burning into her like a laser. "So . . . if you can't go out, where are we going now?"

"Wherever we feel like," she declared, narrowing her eyes, and deciding even as the words left her lips that for once she wasn't going to cave in to her parents' asinine rules.

"Nat . . . I don't want to get you in trouble. Maybe you'd better just take me home," Sara said. "I don't mind, really. I have homework anyway. And Mom fixed lasagna. I can just eat with them."

She didn't bother telling Sara that her dad had at least given his blessing on them going out to eat together. Instead she said, "No. I am sick and tired of him treating me like a baby. I am eighteen years old, and there is no reason in the world why I should have to report every move I make to him. I don't know why he cares anyway. It's no skin off his nose. He just doesn't like it because Grandma and Grandpa *Camfield* bought me a car. Now he can't keep track of me every second of the day." She pushed her foot down hard on the accelerator, not caring that Sara had to grab for the dashboard.

"This time next year I'll be on my own at college," she ranted. "Do they think they're going to know where I am every second then?" She rolled her eyes and puffed out her cheeks in disgust. "Knowing them, they'll probably call me in the dorm every night to check up on me."

Sara laughed, but then she sobered. "Nat, you know parents, they only act like that because they love us."

"No, they act like that because they don't trust me. At least *he* doesn't. He

84

wouldn't be like this if it were his precious Nicole or Noelle."

"Natalie. Stop. You know that's not true. You're not being fair."

"You just don't know, Sara."

"What do you mean?"

"All my life I've had to compete with his *real* daughters. Nicole and Noelle have always gotten just about anything they want. He won't let *me* do anything."

Even as the accusations left her lips, Natalie knew they weren't true. The truth was, neither of her sisters pushed their father the way she did. The rational part of her brain knew that was the reason he treated them differently. She brought most of her punishment on herself. So why was she trying to convince Sara otherwise? Yet she felt powerless to take back the half-truths that poured so easily from her mouth.

Sara got quiet. After a minute — and against her better judgment — Natalie egged her friend on. "Okay, what are you thinking? You might as well say it. I know you're dying to give me one of your lectures."

Sara smiled tentatively. "I just think you're being a little paranoid, Nattie. You are so blessed to have parents who love you like crazy. And . . . well, it just seems like kind of a slap in God's face that you don't appreciate that."

Natalie shook her head forcefully. "Things aren't that simple."

"They could be . . . if you'd just trust God with all these feelings you're having." Sara dipped her head, as though she knew Natalie was ready to fire off a defense.

Sometimes Natalie hated the way Sara Dever always had to bring God into everything. Not that she didn't believe in God herself. She did. She'd asked Jesus into her heart when she was a little girl. She still remembered the warm feeling it had given her. But Sara had this just-put-God-first-and-everything-will-be-fine mentality that had no basis in reality.

"I'm not buying that, Sara," she leveled now. "Look at my dad. My *real* dad. He was a missionary. He devoted his whole life to God, and look where it got him. Permanent exile thousands of miles from his family."

"I know," Sara conceded. "I don't pretend to understand why God allowed that to happen. But still, your father loves you. And he's managed to be part of your life — as much as he could. I'm sure you've given him a lot of joy."

"Yeah, and if he was the one here, I can guarantee he wouldn't make all these stupid, strict rules. He would treat me like an intelligent adult. Sometimes I wish I lived with *him*."

"Natalie! You don't mean that!"

"Well, it would serve Daddy right."

"Nattie, your dad just wants what's best for you," Sara said gently. "It's not like he has those rules just to make you miserable."

Natalie shot her a look that said "Ha!"

"He loves you, Nattie. You know he does."

"Oh, Sara. I know it's not right, but sometimes I just want to run away and never come back."

A slow smile spread across Sara's face. "You know, if you can just hang in there for a few more months, you *can* 'run away' from home. College life beckons," she reminded.

Natalie smiled back, but Sara's words were drowned out by Daddy's harsh words echoing in her mind. *You suddenly seem to think you don't answer to anyone but Natalie Camfield.*

And what was so wrong with that?

Seven

"So what do you want to do?" Natalie asked Sara as they reached the dead end at Pine Street and made the traditional dragging-Main-U-turn for the fifth time. It had been raining off and on all day. Natalie and Sara were riding around after their supper, looking for something to do, bored out of their minds.

"I don't care," Sara shrugged. "Anything but dragging Main, wasting gas."

"Well, what? Do you have a better idea?"

"We could go back to my house. Mom and Dad won't be home till late."

Natalie started down the street again. "Man! Where *is* everybody tonight? This town is so dead."

Sara rolled her eyes. "It's Saturday night. Where do you think they are? They're all out at Hansens' getting wasted." She puffed out her cheeks in exasperation.

"Now there's an appropriate word if I ever heard one. Talk about a waste. I'm sorry, but I do *not* see the attraction."

Natalie ignored her. Sara was beginning to get on her nerves with her constant sermonizing, and after her father's sermon she was in no mood. Their argument twisted through her head. She wasn't about to go home. Maybe she should go out to that party. There sure wasn't anything else to do in this Podunk town. She didn't necessarily plan to *do* anything out there. She just wanted to see what it was like. Who cared what Daddy thought?

As they came to the dead end, instead of making another U-turn, Natalie headed south on Pine. She turned to Sara, testing the waters. "Hey," she said, as though the idea had just occurred to her, "Let's drive out there." She watched from the corner of her eye to see what her friend's reaction would be.

Sara looked at her as though she'd suggested they go rob a bank. "To Hansens'? You're not serious? I know you're still mad about what happened with your dad, but Nat —"

"Just for a little while. Not to stay or anything. I just want to see who all's there."

"Natalie, you know who all's there —
everybody."

"Which is why we're bored out of our
gourds! Come on."

"Your dad would kill you. Shoot, what
am I talking about? *My* dad would kill us
both if he found out we were out there."

"He won't find out. Besides it's not like
we're going to *do* anything. There's nothing wrong with just driving out there."

"I don't know, Nat . . ."

She kept driving, and Sara was silent in
the seat beside her.

Natalie could smell the bonfire before
they rounded the curve in the lane and
saw the sea of cars parked in the field. Her
palms were damp, and butterflies suddenly flitted in her stomach. She drove
slowly across the bumpy pasture and
pulled up to park beside Brian Wagner's
pickup.

Sara broke her silence, putting a hand on
Natalie's arm. "Let's leave, Nattie. Please.
I don't feel good about this at all. We are
both going to be grounded for the rest of
our lives."

"Nobody will even know we were here."

"Oh, you're not planning to get out of
the car?" Sara said, her voice dripping sar-
casm.

"You know what I mean . . . nobody that matters."

"Natalie, you know better than that. It'll be all over town by the time church starts tomorrow morning."

Natalie laughed, but she knew Sara wasn't exaggerating by much. "You can take my car and leave if you want to, Sara. I'll find a ride home. I don't care if you go. I won't be mad, I promise; but I'm staying."

She held the keys out, testing. Sara ignored them, so Natalie tucked them in her pocket and got out of the car.

"Hang on," Sara groused. "Let me find my umbrella."

Natalie turned her back on Sara and started walking, but she heard the passenger door slam, and she could sense Sara behind her as she picked her way across the field in the dark. The ground was rutted and muddy in spots from the recent rains.

The acreage they were on belonged to Joey Hansen's dad. Rumor had it that Mac Hansen was of the mind that kids were going to drink anyway, so he might as well provide a safe place for them to do it. Rumor also had it that he didn't mind supplying the kegs — or showing up now and then to have a drink or two himself. Some of the kids thought he was pretty cool, but most of them were glad he was Joey Hansen's dad and not theirs.

Behind her Sara whispered and scolded under her breath while they trudged toward the bonfire near the riverbank. As they got closer, Natalie started to recognize a few faces. She was surprised at how many kids were here. At least half the senior class, and she guessed twenty or thirty underclassmen, including a lot of freshmen. Everybody seemed to have a bottle or can in their hand, though the promised kegs apparently hadn't arrived yet. The smell of cigarette smoke — and something sweeter — mingled with the pungent scent of woodsmoke in the air.

A couple of kids had pulled their cars close to the party and their sound systems boomed — an odd battle between country and rap music. Between the fire and the river, Mandy Krispin was dancing suggestively at the edge of a loose knot of girls, but apparently Mandy heard a beat in her own head because her gyrations were not in time to any music Natalie could hear.

Natalie saw two figures angling toward them, headed for the make-shift parking lot. As they got closer, she recognized Rick

Boxman and Lacey Franks. Lacey was hanging on Rick and having more trouble walking than even the furrowed field warranted.

The girl caught sight of Natalie and Sara, and turned to Rick, laughing. "Well, I'll be —" She reeled off a string of slurred curse words.

"Shut up, Lacey," Rick laughed back. He waved at them and winked. "Hello, ladies."

"Hi," Natalie mumbled.

She figured they were too far gone to notice her greeting, but Lacey started pulling on Rick's coat sleeve.

"Come on," she purred. "Let's go back. This I gotta see . . . the saints go marching in . . ." She threw her head back and laughed until she almost fell over. Rick held her up, but kept dragging her toward the cars.

"Sheesh!" Sara rolled her eyes and tried to sound disgusted, but Natalie could tell she was nervous. Maybe even scared. Natalie was feeling a little nervous herself. Was everybody going to give them such a hard time for being here?

Evan Greenway spotted them and nudged his friends. "Hey! Look who's here! Come on, Nattie. Hey there, Sara. Here, over here." He motioned to them.

"What brings you two out here?"

Natalie put her hands in her back pockets, hoping she looked relaxed. "There's not much to do in town with everyone out here."

Evan smiled. "You ladies need something to drink." He dug around in the cooler at his feet and came up with two icy bottles of beer. He wiped them off on his shirttail and held out the offering.

Sara declined politely, but Natalie took one. She was thirsty, and she was curious to know what it tasted like. She'd smelled beer before — mostly on people's breath — but she'd never tasted it. It wouldn't hurt to have a sip. And if she carried a bottle around with her, then maybe they wouldn't bug her to drink anything stronger.

Evan reached into his pocket and pulled out a cigarette. He flicked his lighter and sheltered the flame from the breeze. He took a drag, then pulled another cigarette from the pack and offered it to Natalie.

Her laugh came out high and squeaky when she told him, "No, thanks. That's one vice I haven't taken up yet."

They all laughed as if she'd just told the funniest joke in the world, and Evan moved closer to her and put an arm around her shoulder. She shrank away a little bit. She'd had enough trouble getting him off her back after they'd gone to the homecoming dance together last year. She really didn't want word getting around that she and Evan Greenway had a thing going. She took a sip of her beer. It tasted nasty. But she'd always heard it was an acquired taste, so she took a swig, and then another, while the boys cheered her on.

She felt strangely elated. It was kind of nice to feel so welcome here. She'd almost forgotten about Sara when she felt an elbow in her side.

"Natalie, are you really drinking that?" Sara whispered.

"I just tasted it."

"It looked like more than a taste to me."

"Don't worry, I'm not going to do anything stupid."

"Well, let's go before you do." There was mild disgust in her friend's voice.

"Sara, I mean it. If you want to leave I'll give you my keys. It won't bother me one bit." She took another sip of the beer. Already it didn't taste so bitter. It was like eating a pickle. The first bite made you pucker up, but once your mouth got used to it, it really wasn't too bad.

"I'm not leaving you here by yourself,"

Sara told her. "Especially not if you're drinking."

"I'm not *drinking*," Natalie defended.

"What do you call that?" Sara pointed at the bottle of beer as though it were a vile insect.

"Well, I'm not getting drunk."

"Yet."

"Sara, it takes more than three swallows of beer to get drunk. Sheesh. I might as well have brought my daddy with me! I just want to see what it's like."

"Look around." Sara swung her head toward a group of senior guys gathered around the fire, laughing and teasing each other, a cloud of curse words rising in the air. "You can see what it's like," she said wryly.

Natalie wasn't sure how to answer that argument, so she ignored Sara and turned to Evan and his friends. Immediately Evan offered her another beer.

"I haven't even finished this one," she told him. But she put the bottle to her mouth and took several more swallows, as if that would prove her intentions to him.

She purposely closed her eyes and took stock of how she felt. Kids always said that if you weren't used to it you could get drunk pretty fast. But she felt fine. The smoke from the fire stung her eyes, but she didn't feel the least bit dizzy or light-headed, or whatever it was she was supposed to feel under the influence. She finished off the bottle and took the fresh, cold one Evan supplied.

By now, Sara was antsy and clutching her precious umbrella until her knuckles were white. "Come on, Nattie. Please, let's go."

Natalie laughed and reached out to put a hand on her arm. "Sara, quit worrying. I'm fine. It's really no big deal. I don't feel one bit different."

Sara met her gaze, but she said nothing. Natalie could see that there were tears in her eyes. "Hey," she said, softly. "Come here." She led Sara to the edge of the copse of trees, out of hearing of the other kids. "Sara, I'm not going to get drunk. I swear, I feel totally fine. I'll be careful."

"It's not that, Nat. It's just — I don't like us being here. What about our parents? What about your sisters? It just doesn't feel right."

"Why didn't I just bring my father with me?" She tried to make it a joke, but her words came out sounding more gruff than she intended. Sara started toward the car.

"Oh, good grief, Sara. Come back here." No response. "Sara!"

Her friend turned to face her. "I don't understand why you're doing this, Nattie. What are you trying to prove?"

"I'm not trying to prove anything. I'm just sick and tired of being treated like a baby, and I'm tired of everybody else having all the fun."

"You call this fun? I'm sorry. I don't get it. I don't get it at all." She wheeled and went on toward the car.

Natalie started to follow after her, but something made her turn back. Sara could sit in the car and mope for a while. If she wanted to leave she could come and get the keys. But Natalie wasn't going to let Miss Moral Police ruin her night. As she picked her way over the rutted field back toward the river, she took another drink from the bottle. She was suddenly feeling very thirsty. She finished the bottle and — without being quite sure how it got there — took a swallow from the fresh icy cold can of Budweiser that had appeared in her hand.

Evan and his friends pulled her back into their circle. In spite of the chill, they were all without jackets, the sleeves of their T-shirts rolled up to flaunt fake barbed-wire tattoos that encircled each of their arms.

Natalie eyed Matt Kimmell's impressive biceps. "So who's the artist?" she joked, feeling bold in the darkness.

"What do you mean, man? These are real!" Evan pouted playfully and struck a muscleman pose. His friends followed suit, hamming it up.

Natalie laughed. "Yeah, right. It looks more like somebody turned Matt's little sister loose on you with a Magic Marker." She'd never felt so witty and uninhibited. She ran a finger playfully over Matt's tattoo, then turned to see Jessica Gorman and several other younger girls sauntering over to join them.

"Hey, Amber. Hi, Jessi, how's it going?" she said.

Jessica beamed at her and shouted over the music. "It's a great party, huh?"

Natalie nodded. She thought she saw admiration in Jessica's eyes. So much for Sara's worries about setting an example. Wasn't she doing just that? She could prove that you didn't have to be drunk to have fun.

She stayed in the circle for a while, then, feeling braver, decided to see who else was here. Pulling another can from the cooler, she started walking, following the banks of the creek.

Judd Wright and his buddies did a double take when they spotted her. "Whoa! Natalie? Is that you?" But it didn't seem to take them long to warm to the idea of her being here. "Decided to get in on the action, huh?"

"Yeah, I guess so." She didn't like the suggestive tone of his voice.

Holding her watch at an angle to catch the light from the fire, she squinted and tried to make out the numbers. She was surprised to see that it was almost 11:30. With a stab of guilt, she realized that it had been almost an hour since Sara had gone back to the car. She threw the can of beer, still half-full, into the fire and started for the car to check on her friend. She decided that if Sara was still mad, she would just go home. Maybe she would anyway. She was feeling a little sleepy.

Halfway to the car, she saw Evan and Brian Wagner crossing the field ahead of her. Brian wasn't walking too straight. She remembered that his truck was parked right beside her car. She said a silent prayer that he wouldn't crash into her car when he backed out. Natalie breathed a sigh of relief as the pickup cleared her Camry and roared down the lane to the highway. As she reached the car, she saw

Brian's taillights headed west, away from Bristol. She wondered briefly where they were going, but forgot about it when she opened the car door and saw Sara sitting there, head bowed, tears streaking her cheeks.

She climbed in and turned on the motor, pretending not to notice Sara's tears. "I'm ready to go, okay?"

Sara nodded. "Are you okay — to drive?"

"Sara, I'm fine. I had a few sips of beer two hours ago, and you act like I'm the biggest alcoholic on the face of the earth."

"Well, I didn't know. I've been here awhile. How was I supposed to know what you were doing? Excuse me for wanting to be safe."

"Hey, I'm sorry I left you," she said, meaning it. "That wasn't very nice of me."

Sara waved off her apology. "It was my choice. Just forget it. Are you sure you don't want me to drive?"

Natalie ignored her question and revved the engine. "Are you cold? You could have had the keys and run the heater, you know." She knew she sounded defensive.

"I'm fine. Let's just go home," Sara said again, the question lingering in her voice.

Natalie put the car in reverse and maneuvered through the cluster of vehicles that were still parked haphazardly in the field.

She bumped along the road that led to the highway, squinting through the windshield. She flipped her dimmers back and forth, but it was hard to make out the edge of the lane in the dark. Her head hurt, and she needed to go to the bathroom in the worst way.

She breathed a sigh of relief when they finally reached the end of the lane and pulled onto the highway that led into town.

Eight

Cole snored softly beside her, and Daria looked at the clock before reaching up to turn off the lamp on her nightstand. It was seventeen minutes past midnight. Nicole and Noelle were sleeping, but Natalie still wasn't home. Daria lay there listening for her daughter's car on the drive, praying she wouldn't fall asleep until Natalie was safely home.

The phone rang. She was tempted to answer it before Cole could, but because Cole was a veterinarian and got so many late-night calls, the phone was on his side of the bed.

Beside her, he propped himself on one elbow, switched on the light, and picked up the phone. "Hello? Yes, this is Cole Hunter . . ."

Something in her husband's voice made her sit up in bed and switch her own lamp back on.

She heard the serious tone he used when there was an emergency at the vet clinic. She glanced at the clock. Twenty minutes past midnight. Daria prayed this call was for the clinic, but when she looked at Cole's face, her heart began to pound.

"Yes, that's our car," he was saying. "Yes . . . yes, that's the license number. What's happened?"

Daria gripped his arm and put a hand to her mouth. "Oh, please, Lord," she whispered. "Please . . ."

"Oh no," Cole said into the phone now, his shoulders sagging. He swung his legs over and sat on the side of the bed, elbows on knees. "When did it happen?" Daria had heard that tremor of horror in his voice only one other time in all their years together.

She climbed out of bed and began to pace and cry. From Cole's end of the conversation, it was obvious something terrible had happened. *Oh, please, Lord . . . not Nattie. Please, God. Please . . .* She thought immediately of Nathan Camfield. How would Nate ever bear it if something had happened to their daughter?

"We'll be right there," Cole told the caller. He dropped the receiver into its cradle, stood up, and looked at her with a stunned expression. "Natalie's been in an accident."

"No, no!" Daria moaned, shaking her head from side to side in disbelief. "Is she . . . ?" She couldn't bring herself to finish the sentence.

"She's alive. She's in the emergency room at Community, but . . ." He dropped back to the bed and put his face in his hands.

"What, Cole? What is it?" Panic rose in her. There was something he wasn't telling her. Something worse.

"They said . . ." He stopped and took a tremulous breath before going on, "There was a passenger in the car with Nattie. Her passenger was killed, Daria."

"Oh, dear God, no! Was it Sara?" Her thoughts spun out of control. "What happened, Cole? How did it happen?"

Already he was in the closet pulling on his jeans. Daria knew she needed to get dressed too. They had to go to Nattie. She would be devastated. Maybe she was critically injured herself. But Daria couldn't dwell on that possibility now. Her mind simply could not take in all the facets of this horrific news.

"Cole, how did it happen? Do you think it was Sara? Who else would've been with them?" she asked again.

"I don't know," he said, pulling a sweat-shirt over his head. "The sheriff's deputy said it was a two-car accident out on the highway. Apparently, some kids were leaving a party out at Hansens' —"

"Oh, Cole," she breathed. "You don't think Natalie was out there, do you?"

"I don't know, Daria. Hurry, get dressed. We need to go to the hospital."

She felt as though she were moving in slow motion.

"I'll leave a note for the girls," Cole told her, already halfway down the stairs.

She threw on a pair of jeans and a sweater and fumbled with shoes and socks. When she got to the kitchen, she could hear Cole starting the car in the garage. She'd just gotten her car door shut when he backed out of the garage and raced down the driveway. He pulled onto the road and drove far too fast on dirt roads that were still soft from the recent rains.

"Oh, Cole," Daria cried, as the reality of what had happened hit her full force. "What if it's Sara?"

He didn't answer but kept his eyes straight ahead as they sped through town, then found a place to park near the hospital's emergency-room entrance.

Inside, the halls were littered with people. Daria recognized a few faces, worried-looking teenagers mostly, though her muddled state of mind wouldn't allow her to put a single name with a face.

A nurse met them at the admissions desk. "Are you the Camfields?" she asked.

"I'm Cole Hunter," he said, correcting her. "We're Natalie Camfield's parents."

"This way," the woman said, leading them through a heavy door to the right of the admissions desk.

"Do you know anything about the accident?" Cole asked her as they dashed through the emergency ward.

"Right this way," she replied, ignoring his question.

The way she said it, it struck Daria that the woman must have known something she wasn't allowed to reveal. Daria's hands began to shake, and she wondered where Maribeth and Don were. *Oh, Father, don't let it be Sara.*

Then a numbing thought hit Daria like a punch in the stomach. *What if the wreck was Natalie's fault?*

The nurse stopped at an examining room and pushed the curtain aside. Natalie lay on her back on a cotton sheet.

Her face was pale, almost gray, and dirt smudged her cheeks, but Daria could see that her daughter was in one piece and that she was breathing. Relief coursed through her veins, leaving her drained and on the verge of tears.

But she felt another surge of relief when she realized that the doctor working over Natalie's still form was Marlin Davidson. Marlin was an elder in their church.

He looked up when they walked into the room. "Hi, Cole, Daria. She's unconscious, but she's alive. She has some cuts that will need sutures, and" — he brushed the hair off Natalie's forehead — "she has a pretty nasty bump here. We've already done a FAST exam, but we'll need to do a CT scan to make sure we're not missing anything. We're going to have you wait outside for a few minutes. You can sign the necessary papers. I'll let you know the minute you can come back in."

The nurse ushered them to a private waiting area. Daria stared at the forms they brought her, struggling to remember the simplest information, and clutching the pen with trembling hands.

Cole didn't sit but paced the short length of the room. Daria watched his lips move silently, and she knew that as she was, he was praying the most fervent prayer of his life.

After what seemed an eternity, Dr. Davidson appeared in the doorway. Daria jumped up, Cole at her side. She was horrified to notice, for the first time, the blood that stained the doctor's white coat. His face was unreadable as he nodded.

"Cole, Daria . . . please, sit down." He waited, then told them, "She has a pretty good bump on her head that we'll be keeping a close eye on. The cuts and abrasions are relatively minor. We have her stabilized right now, but the CT scan showed that her spleen is ruptured, so we need to move her into surgery. Dr. Grant is on his way in now."

Dr. Davidson assured them that Natalie was getting the best care possible, but he may as well have been speaking a foreign language for all Daria comprehended. She understood only that her daughter was seriously hurt — and they must face the unthinkable possibility that Nattie's dearest childhood friend was dead.

When Marlin left, Cole led Daria back to the chairs in the tiny private waiting room. They sat side by side, praying silently, interrupting each other every few minutes to ask aloud questions to which neither of them had answers.

"I wonder who found her."

"Do you think she knew what was happening?"

"Was Marlin going to be there — during the surgery? Oh, Cole, I hope she's not alone . . . oh, Natalie . . . Nattie." Daria finally broke down and wept.

The wait was interminable. Cole walked back and forth while Daria sat on the edge of a chair, her head in her hands. From time to time Cole went to the nurses' station, trying to get some clue as to how much longer they had to wait. But the nurses were frazzled trying to deal with the crowd that had gathered in the halls and could only tell him that they would let them know the minute they could see her.

Daria called her parents and asked them to go to the house to be with Nicole and Noelle. She couldn't bear to have the girls home alone now. She knew they would agonize over their sister — and over Sara, if what they feared was true.

Bill Simmons, the assistant pastor of their church, came and prayed with them, then sat with them while they waited. It went through Daria's mind that Pastor Vickers was probably with Don and Maribeth.

Finally, a haggard looking Dr. Davidson emerged from the ward and met the Hunters at the doorway of the waiting room.

"Let's go sit down, shall we?" He motioned toward a secluded corner of the room and closed the door behind him. "She's in ICU now. The surgery went well. I feel she's out of immediate danger, but we want to monitor her closely for the next few hours." He looked at the floor and cleared his throat, then turned to each of them in turn. "I don't know what you've been told about the accident . . ."

"Marlin, do you — Do you know what happened?" Cole asked. "The deputy who called us said Nattie's passenger was killed." His voice broke. "He said — it was a two-car accident. Do you know who was in the other car? Do they know — whose fault it was?"

"I don't know much, Cole. There were two fatalities, and —"

Daria gasped, "Two?"

Cole groaned, but Dr. Davidson ignored his reaction and went on in a soft, steady voice. "Witnesses have said that the kids left a party — a beer party — you know, out at Hansens' on the highway?"

Daria and Cole nodded in unison.

"Apparently the other vehicle ran a stop sign and hit Natalie's car broadside. The driver died at the scene, and his passenger was LifeWatched to Wichita. Natalie was thrown from the car. And her passenger was killed."

Cole interrupted now. "Can you give us any names, Marlin? Was it Sara Dever? Nattie's passenger? Do you know?"

Dr. Davidson nodded slowly and looked at the floor. "Yes. It was Sara."

Daria began to moan.

"From what EMS said, she was dead at the scene — probably instantly."

"But the wreck wasn't Natalie's fault, was it?" Daria wept, pleading for the answer she needed so desperately to hear.

"It doesn't sound like it, Daria," Dr. Davidson sighed. "But of course they won't determine that for a while. The sheriff has ordered blood samples on everyone. Witnesses said that both vehicles came from the party, and you know there was plenty of beer flowing out there."

"Both vehicles? They think Natalie and Sara were out there too?" Cole asked.

Daria could tell that he was near tears.

"I really couldn't say for sure. You'd have to talk to the sheriff about that." Dr. Davidson pushed his glasses up on his nose. "It's a miracle, really, that anyone survived at all. Be grateful that you have your daughter in one piece. You'll cross the other bridges when you come to them."

Cole rose from his seat, his voice choked with emotion. "Thank you, Marlin. Thank you so much for everything. We're grateful." He extended his hand to the doctor who stood to shake it.

"Can we see her now?" Daria rose too.

"Sure. I'll walk you to the wing. It's hard to say how long it might be before she comes to, but you can sit with her for a while."

He showed them through the halls and pointed toward the corridor that led to the ICU.

Daria clung to Cole's arm as they went down the hall. Natalie was lying in a hospital bed, her strong young body connected to the bed and the IV equipment by numerous tubes and straps. Daria rushed to her daughter's bedside and took a quick inventory. She couldn't help thinking of the moments immediately after Natalie's birth when she had inspected her baby, counting precious fingers and toes. Now she saw that there was a nasty bruise on Nattie's left forearm and that both her arms were bandaged. Her pale hair had been brushed away from her forehead, revealing a large goose egg of a bump. Her face had been scrubbed clean, and except for the bump on her forehead and the pallor of her complexion, her face showed no other sign of the trauma.

Daria gingerly stroked her daughter's cheek as tears coursed down her own face. Cole came and stood beside his wife, put his arm around her, and pulled her head to his chest, cradling it there.

She wept bitterly. It seemed unbelievable that they were here. She and Cole stood together that way for several minutes, quietly giving thanks to God that the life of their eldest daughter had been miraculously spared . . . and praying for the strength they would need to tell her that her dearest friend in the world was gone.

They stayed by Natalie's bed for hours, listening to the drone of the blood pressure machine and watching for any sign that she was waking up. Finally, Daria decided to go home long enough to break the news to Nicole and Noelle and to get some of Natalie's things to bring back to the hospital.

As she drove the few miles home in the gray light of morning, her mind reeled at all they still didn't know about the accident. Her heart went out to the Devers. She knew they would have to face Don and Maribeth, and she dreaded it, especially knowing that Natalie had been driving.

Please, God, she begged silently, *don't let it be Nattie's fault. Oh, Father, it will be hard enough for her to accept that Sara is gone. It will be unbearable if Natalie was responsible.*

She felt guilty even as she begged God for the fault to lie with someone else. She knew it was pointless to pray about something that was past, but somehow she hoped her words were true.

Daria pulled into the garage and went into the house. The farmhouse was quiet on this Sunday morning, and a sob escaped Daria's throat as she thought about waking the girls and telling them. Nicole, especially, would be devastated by Sara's death. Daria wondered if Jon might already have called her.

Daria walked through the kitchen into the dining room, where her parents were sitting somberly over coffee.

Margo Haydon jumped up and crossed the room when she saw Daria. "How is Nattie?"

"Hi, Mom." Daria walked into her mother's embrace. "She still hadn't come to when I left, but they think she's going to be all right. At least physically." Her shoulders slumped. "But I don't know how she's ever going to get over Sara's death."

Her father set his mug on the table. "So Natalie doesn't know yet?"

Daria shook her head. "The girls are still sleeping?"

Her parents nodded in unison.

"I'd better go tell them."

She went up to the room her younger daughters still shared. Turning on Nicole's bedside lamp, she shook the slight shoulders. "Nikki, wake up, honey."

Nicole stretched and rubbed her eyes. "What time is it?" she murmured.

"It's early. About five-thirty. But wake up, honey. I need to tell you something. There's been an accident."

The words brought Nicole upright in bed. "What happened? Is it Daddy?"

"No. Daddy's fine."

In the other bed, Noelle rolled over and sat up in bed. "What's going on?"

Daria looked over at her youngest daughter and braced herself to tell the news. "Natalie was in an accident last night. A terrible accident."

Both girls began to cry, and Noelle came and sat on her sister's bed, huddling up against her. "Is Nattie dead?" Noelle wailed.

Daria joined her daughters, weeping unashamedly. "No, I think Nattie will be all right, but — Sara was with her . . . And she — Sara didn't make it."

"Oh, Mom! No! Not Sara! What happened?" Nikki wailed. "Does Jon know?"

"I'm sure he does, honey. It just happened a few hours ago. We haven't talked to Don and Maribeth yet.

"There was another fatality too," she told them.

"Who?" the girls asked in unison, hands to their faces in disbelief.

She shook her head. "We don't know. No one at the hospital could tell us anything."

"Was — Was Sara at the hospital?" Nikki asked, her voice trembling.

For a minute Daria wondered if Nicole was in denial, not accepting that Sara was really dead. But then she realized that Nikki meant Sara's body. The thought took her breath away, made it all too real. "I don't know, honey," she finally said. "Dr. Davidson said Sara was . . . dead at the scene, so they probably didn't take her to the hospital."

"Then . . . where would they take her?"

"I don't know, Nikki. Probably the funeral home. But I don't know for sure."

Such hard questions. Their tears and weeping filled the room, and as Daria gathered her daughters into her arms, the three of them sat on the bed, lost in their separate thoughts.

How strange that a few short hours could change their world so suddenly. Yesterday they had been carefree and happy. Today Sara and someone else's son or daughter, brother or sister, were gone. And another young person was fighting for life in a Wichita hospital. Names they didn't know yet. Names that in all likelihood they would recognize and mourn.

And Natalie lay a few miles away, not even aware yet that her life had been devastated.

Nine

Natalie opened her eyes and strained to keep them open against the bright lights above her. Everything felt so heavy. Her eyelids, her arms, her head . . . especially her head. She couldn't move without extreme effort, yet it was a rather pleasant sensation — like the weight of heavy quilts on a wintry night. She gave in to its pull and closed her eyes for a minute.

A muffled sound reached her ears. She blinked and tried to open her eyes again, squinting against the harsh light overhead. The dull ache in her head had subsided somewhat, and with minimal effort she turned in the direction of the voice. Why were there rails on her bed? And what were all these machines whirring and beeping beside her? She must be in a hospital. *But why?* She tried to remember why she would be here.

Her eyes adjusted slowly to the light, and

without moving her head she took in her surroundings. Things began to come into sharper focus. There was a window opposite her bed, and though the heavy draperies were pulled, light leaked in between the two panels and around the edges of the window. It was daylight.

She racked her brain for a recent memory. Bits and pieces started coming to her. She remembered driving around town with Sara, bored, then ending up out at Hansens'. Something must have happened there. She formed a picture of Sara going off to sit in the car. Yes, she remembered that. And she had gone after her. Sara was angry with her for being at the party. But that was all she could recall.

She tried to sit up in bed and immediately fell back on the pillows as pain seared through her head from front to back. She moaned, and instantly two worried faces hovered above her.

"Natalie? Can you hear me, honey?"

It was her mother. Daddy was right beside Mom. She felt warm hands on her arms and a gentle palm against her cheek.

She heard her dad's voice as though from a long distance. "Hey, sleepyhead. How are you?"

She allowed the heavy feeling to take her

under again. She drifted off feeling happy that her parents were there, too sleepy to wonder anymore about where she was or why she was in this strange place.

There were voices calling her name. Over and over. *Natalie, Natalie, Natalie . . .*

She willed her eyelids open and saw her parents standing over her bed. She remembered waking up before. Sunlight was still coming in the window, but she had no sense of how much time might have passed.

"What — What happened?" she croaked.

"You had an accident, Nattie," her father said, so quietly she could barely hear him.

Beside him Mom turned away, but Natalie could see her shoulders heave as though she were crying.

"An accident? My car? What — ?"

"Shh." Her dad patted her arm. "We'll talk later . . . when you're feeling better."

"Why is Mom crying?" Something was terribly wrong.

She struggled to pull herself up in the bed, and instead of trying to stop her, her father helped her lean forward and plumped the stiff pillow at her back.

A nurse appeared on the other side of the bed and helped with the pillow, then began working over her, unclamping, then replacing what looked like a plastic clothespin on Natalie's index finger, and fussing with the tubes that led from various parts of her body.

She felt dizzy for a moment, then everything righted itself and she became oriented to her surroundings. She looked down at her arms and saw that there were needles and tubes running from the veins on the back of her hand to a metal pole beside the bed. Above her, hanging from the pole, a bulging bag dripped a clear substance into the tube. Her upper arm sported a blood-pressure cuff.

"What happened?" she asked again, seeking her father's face.

"Shh," he warned, indicating with his eyes that she should wait for the nurse to finish.

She submitted to the nurse's careful examination. Then, when the woman left her bedside, Natalie asked the question a third time.

"You were in a car accident, Nattie," her father told her. "Do you remember?"

She shook her head. "Where was it?" Even as she spoke the words, it struck her that if the wreck had happened after the party, Mom and Daddy probably knew that she had been there. They didn't seem angry with her, though.

"It was out on the highway, west of town . . . near Hansens'."

She bit her lip. "I'm sorry, Daddy. I . . . I went to a party out there. I shouldn't have gone. Sara tried to tell me —" Suddenly she remembered Sara with her in the car. "Where is Sara? Is she here too? Is she okay?"

Mom started crying again. Daddy sat down in a chair beside the bed so that his face was right next to hers. For the first time she saw that his eyes were red-rimmed and swollen. He reached out and put a hand on her arm. "We have something very hard to tell you, Natalie. Are you — do you feel well enough to hear it?"

"What?" She could feel her heart thumping beneath the thin hospital gown. "What is it, Daddy?"

He shook his head slowly. "Sara — Sara was in the accident too."

Like a bolt of lightning, a memory came to her. She and Sara were driving down the lane at Hansens', leaving the party. What had happened after that? She couldn't conjure any recollection beyond that moment.

"Is she hurt bad?" she asked now, looking into her father's eyes, knowing she would see the truth there.

Cole Hunter looked at the floor before he lifted his eyes to meet hers again. "Sara didn't make it, Nattie."

She heard her father's words, could picture the very letters in each word of his sentence. *Sara didn't make it.* But she could not get them to make sense. *Sara didn't make it? What is he talking about? What does he mean?*

Her mother knelt beside Daddy's chair now, and he put his arm around Mom, still keeping his other hand on Natalie's arm.

"Sara died, honey," her father said.

Natalie felt a fog descend on her.

Now her mother spoke. Her voice sounded tight and strained. "They said she was killed instantly, honey. She didn't feel any pain. Sara's in heaven now." Mom started to smile, but then her lips contorted into a ghoulish grimace, and her face crumpled.

Sara is gone? But how? None of this made one bit of sense.

"Do you understand, Nattie?" her father asked gently.

She felt tears run down her cheeks, and she wondered where they'd come from.

"I'm so sorry, honey," her father repeated.

"She's dead?" As if her own words had finally broken through to her consciousness, she started to weep. *Sara is dead.* Her vivacious, carefree, cheerful friend who had never done anything but good in her life, was gone.

"I — I was driving! No! I was driving, Daddy!" A sob escaped her throat. "Oh, God, it was my fault. I killed her."

Immediately her mother chided her. "No, Natalie. It was an accident. It wasn't your fault."

But Mom didn't know. Mom and Daddy didn't know the terrible truth. For though she still could not remember one thing about the accident, memories of the party were swirling in her brain, playing over and over in her mind. Vivid memories of bonfires and bottles and coolers and cans. And in one terrible moment, she knew the damning truth.

She had killed Sara Dever as surely as if she had put a gun to her friend's head and pulled the trigger.

Though the page never changed on the Fogelman's Pharmacy calendar that hung on the wall across from her bed, it seemed to Natalie that she woke up a hundred different mornings in the hospital. And each time she awakened, it was with a prayer on her lips — that this was all a bad dream, that she would open her eyes and Sara would be standing over her, strawberry hair glowing in the light from the window, mouth wide in that trademark angelic smile. And each time she had to stumble through the process all over again, taking the nightmare and making it become the reality that it was.

She'd had visitors, though with her skewed sense of time she couldn't have told anyone when or even, sometimes, who they had been. She vaguely remembered Grandpa and Grandma Camfield being there. And Pastor Vickers. But some of the faces that had huddled over her bed were a blur in her memory.

At some point during her stay in the hospital, Daddy came and sat by her bed. He picked up her hand and gently ran his fingers over the bruises on her arm. "How are you feeling today, punkin?"

"Fine." She couldn't tell anyone the truth. That she wanted to die. That she felt as though she were already dead. Except there couldn't be this much pain in death. Even if she went to hell.

"There's been some news about the accident I want to tell you, okay?" He waited, and when there was no response, he asked, "Do you feel well enough to hear it, Nattie, or do you want to wait awhile?"

"Tell me," she said in a monotone. What could be any worse than what she already knew? Sara was dead. How could it get any worse than that?

Daddy spoke as if he were reading the account from a newspaper, "Your car was hit broadside by Brian Wagner's pickup. Evan Greenway was with him, and apparently they took that shortcut through McLaughlin's pasture. They were both drunk. Brian ran the stop sign." Now bitterness had crept into her father's voice, and Natalie wondered what he would think if he knew the truth about her.

"Do you remember any of that, Nattie?"

She shook her head, and Cole tightened his grip on her hand.

"Brian was killed in the accident too, honey. And Evan was critically injured. They took him to Wichita right away . . . by LifeWatch helicopter. I think he's been upgraded to serious condition now, but he's got a long haul ahead of him."

It was all too much to take in. Brian ran the stop sign. And yet if she hadn't been drinking herself, perhaps they would've been able to stop in time. Perhaps Sara would be alive today. It was a question she would never have answered.

Sara's funeral was on the Wednesday after the accident — the day Natalie was to be released from the hospital. *Sara's funeral.* She couldn't even make those two words fit together in the same sentence. Secretly she was glad that she had an excuse for not being there. And yet, she felt even more guilty that she had missed the last event to mark her best friend's life. She wondered how her friends — Sara's friends — must feel toward her now. Ever since Daddy had told her that the highway patrol had determined that Brian had run a stop sign and slammed broadside into her car, she had tried to believe that the accident wasn't really her fault. And yet, in that deepest place inside herself, she knew that no matter what the details were, she *was* ultimately responsible for Sara Dever's death. After all, Sara had tried to talk her out of going to the party. Natalie had all but kidnapped her and taken her out to the river.

Afterward, Natalie was the one who'd insisted on driving. She still could not remember beyond pulling onto the highway as they left the party. But she did have a

vivid memory — a memory that played itself over and over and over again — of Sara
asking her, "Are you sure you're okay to
drive? Are you sure, Nattie? Maybe I
should drive." One split second could have
made all the difference in the world. If
only she had given the keys to Sara. Or if
she had simply stayed away in the first
place. She had known better. *Oh, dear
Jesus, I knew better.*

But she had let a stupid temptation draw
her in. Her stubborn will had taken over,
and now the consequences were more horrible than she had ever bargained for.
More terrible than she could have ever
imagined.

Ten

When Mom and Daddy came to take her home from the hospital that afternoon, they were still wearing their dress clothes from the funeral.

"It was a beautiful service, Natalie," her mother told her. She laid the program from the memorial service on the bed beside Natalie. Sara's face smiled up at her in living color. Natalie felt a twist in her gut.

"Don and Maribeth said to give you a hug," her dad said.

Natalie didn't know how to respond, so she said nothing.

"Well, I'm going to bring the car around," Daddy said finally. Mom nodded and began to help Natalie get dressed. She still had a nasty bump on her forehead. The incision from her surgery was tender, and every muscle in her body felt stiff and sore.

But the sharpest pain — the one that

was constant and unabating — was in a place deep inside her. A place she didn't think would ever heal.

A few minutes later, a nurse was pushing her in a wheelchair out to the waiting car.

When her father pulled into the garage fifteen minutes later, it felt as though she had been gone from home for months.

Daddy came around and opened the car door and helped her into the house. Nikki and Noelle were waiting. Natalie felt as if she were on exhibition in a freak show with all of them standing around, watching her shuffle across the room.

And then she saw Jon, standing behind Nikki, looking grief-stricken and ill at ease.

"Hey," he said, lifting a hand in a half-hearted wave.

Mom had told her that Jon and Nicole had come to visit her that first day in the hospital, but she had no memory of it. Now, seeing the pain in his eyes, seeing how uncomfortable he was in her presence, she wanted to shrivel up and disappear. She couldn't get one word to come from her mouth.

Her mother seemed to sense the awkwardness of the moment, and she put an arm around Natalie. "We'd better get you up to bed, honey . . . Noelle, could you bring Nattie's bags up, please?"

Noelle followed them upstairs with her bags, and Mom helped Natalie into bed.

"Do you need anything out of here?" Noelle asked, holding up a plastic bag of promotional items the hospital had sent home with her.

It made her heart ache to see her sister's attentiveness. She didn't deserve all the comfort and attention she'd been offered. She wanted to tell them, "Just leave me alone. It should have been me who died." But instead she whispered, "I just want to sleep, okay? Could you guys just close the door when you leave?"

Mom tucked the covers around her while Noelle hung in the background, a worried look in her eyes.

"I'm okay, Noelle. Really." Natalie forced a smile. "Maybe you can bring me some hot chocolate later, okay? When I wake up."

That seemed to make her little sister feel better. Mom gave her one last pat on the shoulder, and they left her alone.

She tried to sleep, but no matter how tightly she squeezed her eyelids shut, a parade of faces marched in front of her — people she could never face again — people who must hate her now for what she'd done to their daughter, their sister, their friend.

Jon. Sara's only sibling. Natalie felt sick to her stomach thinking what a big deal she'd made over her silly crush on Jon. Now it looked so trite in comparison. *Maribeth and Don.* They would never plan a daughter's wedding, hold her beautiful red-haired babies. She thought of her own grandparents, Grammy and Grandpa Haydon, who were in poor health and certainly didn't need something like this happening in their lives. And Grandma and Grandpa Camfield and Uncle Jim and Aunt Betsy who had always been so good to her. She had crushed every reason they might have to be proud of her.

And her father. Nathan Camfield, whose name she bore. The father who had never had a chance to really know her, would now have this badge of shame to carry because of her. All her silly daydreams of making him proud, of being one of the joyful things in his life of sorrow, had been shattered in one moment of horror, one idiotic choice.

If anyone found out the truth, they would never forgive her. Her agony, her overwhelming guilt almost paralyzed her. And as she fell asleep that night, she prayed in all sincerity that she would not wake up the following morning.

But she did wake up. The next morning. And the next, and the next. And only the pills they'd prescribed for the pain offered any relief — because the pills brought once again the sweet release of sleep.

On the third morning after Natalie came home from the hospital, Daria went into her room and sat on the side of the bed. She put a hand on Natalie's forehead. "How are you feeling today, honey?"

Natalie shrugged and closed her eyes.

Daria knew her daughter was suffering more than she could even express. But she feared that if Nattie didn't open up about how she was coping, depression would overcome her.

"Don't you think you should try to get up for a little while?" Daria asked now. "Come downstairs. Maybe you can sit out on the porch and get a little sunshine. It's really warming up out there today."

"Maybe later, Mom. I really don't feel up to it right now."

"Nattie, it's not good for you just to lie here and . . . and think."

"Mom. Please."

She didn't want to push too hard, but

134

Daria knew her daughter well. She knew Natalie had a tendency to be too analytical, to exaggerate things to the point that she didn't see the reality. *Oh, why did you let this happen, Lord? Nattie struggles enough as it is.*

"Would you just tell me what you're thinking about while you're lying up here?"

"What do you think I'm thinking, Mom? What else could I be thinking?" Suddenly her face crumpled, and she threw herself into Daria's arms as though she were five years old again. "Oh, Mom. It's my fault. Sara's gone, and it's all my fault."

Daria fought back her own tears and stroked her daughter's back. "Shh, shh," she whispered. "Natalie, it was not your fault. We've told you already, Brian ran the stop sign. The sheriff's deputy said that the highway patrol did tests that tell them exactly what happened."

She didn't want to upset Natalie, but she knew they needed to talk about what had happened that night. Gently, she pushed Natalie away from her and took both of her hands. "Honey, have you remembered anything else from that night?" In her heart, Daria knew the accident report told the truth: Natalie's car had been pulling out of the driveway that led to the river on

Hansens' property when it was struck. But she desperately wanted to believe that her daughter had had a good reason to be there on that night. "You . . . you and Sara were at the party before the accident happened?"

Natalie's eyes narrowed, her nostrils flared almost imperceptibly, and she nodded slowly. "Yeah, Mom. We were there."

Daria's pulse quickened. "Why?"

Natalie glared at her, then dropped her head. "We just drove out to see who was there."

Daria struggled to keep her voice steady. "How long were you there?"

"I don't know, Mom. Not very long."

"You two weren't —"

"Mom! Please," Natalie's head snapped up. "I really don't want to talk about this. It doesn't matter anyway. It doesn't change . . . anything." She started to cry again.

"Natalie, nobody is blaming you. You were in the wrong place at the wrong time, and something terrible happened, but it doesn't do anyone any good for you to sit here and beat yourself up over it."

Daria took her daughter into her arms again. She felt Natalie stiffen. She had stopped crying. After a few minutes, Daria gently pushed her away and smoothed a pale strand of hair off her forehead. "Honey, I know this is the hardest thing you've ever had to face. It's been hard for all of us. We loved Sara too. But now it's you we're worried about. You have to go on. You have to go on and live your life. You know Sara would have wanted you to."

"Sara would have wanted to live."

The hard edge in Natalie's tone frightened Daria. "Of course she would have. But God must have had something else in mind."

"Don't blame it on God, Mom. It was my fault."

"Natalie, stop it." She tried to make her voice firm. "I won't hear any more of this kind of talk. I'm very sorry that Sara died. You lost a wonderful friend . . . We all did. It was a terrible, terrible tragedy. But you can't go on blaming yourself for what happened."

Natalie swung her legs over the side of the bed and put her head in her hands.

"Mom." Natalie's voice broke, and something in her tone made Daria's heart beat faster. Natalie lifted her chin. Their gazes met, and Natalie opened her mouth as if she meant to say something.

"What's wrong, honey? Just let it out.

137

Cry if you need to; scream if you need to."

But then her daughter turned away again and sat motionless and mute on the edge of the mattress, her eyes fixed on some monster that Daria could neither see nor slay.

Eleven

Timoné, Colombia, South America

The clouds rolled in and the afternoon rains threatened as Nathan Camfield crossed the village commons and began loping toward the hut across the stream. He jumped the brook and almost made it to safety before the skies broke open to wash the jungle canopy. But the rainwater quickly pierced layers of palm branches and lush jungle foliage and ran in tiny rivulets on Nate's skin, trickling down to larger streams on the forest floor. Drenched and out of breath, he scaled the stairs two at a time and burst into the relative dryness of the hut that served as the mission office.

David Chambers looked up from the makeshift desk where he'd been engrossed in some document on his laptop computer screen. He laughed as he watched Nate try to dry himself with a thin rag not much bigger than a washcloth. "You'll never learn, will you, man?"

Nate gave his coworker a good-natured grin as he rubbed his close-cropped hair with the rag. "I always think I can get just one more thing done before it pours, you know?" He turned his head to one side and jabbed a corner of the towel into his ear, then turned his head and dried his other ear.

He hung up the towel and went to a small shelf in the corner. Picking up a grimy thermos, he shook it gently. "Is there any coffee left?"

"If you can call it that," Chambers muttered, already deep into his translation work again.

Nate poured a stream of the vile brown liquid into his stain-spattered mug and took a sip. "Man!" he complained, giving his head a shake. "How do we drink this stuff day after day?"

David Chambers looked up and smiled, stroking his neatly trimmed beard and taking a sip from his own cup. "I've been telling you, home-grown Colombian coffee ought to taste better than this. We're doing something wrong."

"At least it's hot. So how's it going today?" Nate asked him, indicating the laptop.

"Pretty good. I found some great info on that database I downloaded in San José. I'm just starting to sort through it all, but I think it's something I can really make use of. I want to try to get Tados in here for a few days this week and nail some of the intonations."

"Good luck," Nate said wryly. "You think he'll agree to that with a fishing expedition on the calendar?"

David shook his head glumly. "Good point. Oh, hey, don't forget you've got some e-mail."

"That's right! Did you print them out?"

"No, they're on the hard drive. Lucretia was griping about their paper supply as it was, and I'd already printed all these word lists." He patted a stack of wrinkled paper covered in what looked like an alien language. Looking sheepish, David said, "Sorry. I hope that's okay —"

Nate stopped him with an upheld hand. "It's not a problem. Just let me know when I can get on the computer." He crossed the room and sat down at his desk.

"I can wrap this up in a couple of minutes," Chambers told him.

"Thanks, Dave. No hurry."

If anyone had told him even ten years ago that he would be reading e-mail and watching his coworker use a computer here in Timoné, he would have told them they were crazy. But he had to admit that it did make their work easier. Of course, they weren't online in the village yet, but with the new airstrip at Conzalez just half a day away on the river, David could fly into San José del Guaviare every few weeks. There he had access to up-to-date computers and could download linguistic information and software for his translation work, along with an impressive array of medical data for Nate. In addition, it allowed them to order medical supplies and their own personal provisions with ease. Best of all, it made it possible for them to keep in closer touch with their families back home and with other missionaries, both in Colombia and around the world.

Nate sometimes regretted that he had been so obstinate with Daria when they'd first come to Timoné. He had been determined to win the hearts and minds of the Timoné people by becoming a part of their culture. He'd come to realize that with judicious use of technology, he had much more to offer the village. Though he still thought there was merit to his concept of living as one with the culture, he realized that he'd probably carried it too far those first years he and Daria were here. And she had suffered for it. Not that she'd ever complained, but he knew that as a woman and a homemaker, Daria had made far more sacrifices than he had for his precious philosophy.

He shook off the thoughts of Daria — it was a dangerous place for his mind to wander. Though nothing could ever make him stop loving her, Daria belonged to someone else now. He was grateful when, across the room, David Chambers shuffled some papers on the desk, closed the laptop, and stood.

"It's all yours," David said. He stooped to look out the window, then yawned and stretched his six-foot-five frame as much as the low ceiling of the hut would allow. "I think the rain's let up enough. I'm going to go home and do some reading, and if I should just happen to fall asleep in the process, well, so be it."

"I hear you," Nate laughed. "I might rest my eyes for a minute myself after I read my mail."

"Do you want me to check on Monni's baby on my way back?" he asked, referring to an infant Nate had delivered yesterday morning.

143

The little boy had been born with the umbilical cord wrapped around his neck. They had almost lost him. Nate had enlisted David's help with the difficult delivery, and now he smiled to himself as he realized that his colleague felt a special bond with the child he'd helped bring into the world.

"If you want to, that'd be great, but don't feel obligated, Dave. I was planning to check in on them on my way home tonight. They were both doing just fine when I stopped in this morning."

David nodded and smiled at the news. "That's good to hear." He gathered a few books off his cluttered desk and waved before ducking beneath the door frame.

Nate went to the shelf and drained the last of the thermos of muddy coffee into his mug. He got the laptop and settled in at his desk again. Through the window, he watched David dodge puddles as he made his way next door to the small hut that served as his living quarters.

Nate thought again, what a blessing the young man had been to him. David Chambers had been here just over a year now, sent by Gospel Outreach to begin the task of putting the New Testament in the Timoné dialect. It was a daunting assignment, given that Timoné had no written language and that the dialect had its roots, not in the Castilian Spanish spoken by most of Colombia, but in a peculiar mix of Portuguese and Spanish with a bit of Swahili thrown in for good measure.

David was in his late twenties. He had taught French and Spanish at an American university for several years before answering the call of the mission field. He had picked up the Timoné tongue quickly and was making amazing progress on an assignment that promised to take years to complete.

Nate crossed an ankle over his knee and propped the laptop in the resulting triangle. He began clicking on icons, rearranging the computer desktop, which David had left in disarray, as usual. Then, opening the e-mail program, he leaned back in his chair and scanned the short list of posts David had received in San José yesterday.

He was surprised to see Daria's name in his in box. She occasionally sent him news of Natalie, but more often that came via his parents or Betsy. He hoped everything was all right.

He opened the file and began to read.

Dear Nate,

I need to let you know what's going on with Natalie. I don't want to alarm you, and I don't think it's necessary that you come home, but she needs your prayers (and so do we). Last Saturday night Nattie was in a car accident. Physically she has recovered very well, but two other teenagers, including Natalie's best friend, Sara Dever, were killed in the wreck. The boy who was killed had been drinking. He ran a stop sign, and his pickup broadsided Natalie's car. Another boy riding in the pickup was critically injured.

Natalie's Camry was totaled, which seems a petty thing in light of the tragic deaths, but since your father bought it for her with your blessing, I thought you should know that.

We haven't been able to get her to talk about it much, but even though the accident wasn't her fault, I know Natalie is struggling with the fact that she was driving when it happened.

Nate tensed and scrolled to the top of the screen to check the date the e-mail had been sent. The accident had happened more than two weeks ago now. He read

146

Daria's description of the events, and tears filled his eyes.

His heart broke as he thought of Natalie's pain and despondency over the tragedy. He vaguely remembered Sara Dever. The girl had come with Natalie to his parents' house once while he'd been home on furlough. They had been at that silly, giggly stage of adolescence at the time, but he remembered thinking that she seemed to be a sweet girl, and it had been obvious that Natalie adored her. He sent up a prayer that the Lord would comfort his daughter and help her to heal emotionally as well as physically. He wondered if he'd done the right thing. Wondered if he would've been able to comfort the daughter he loved, had she not been a world away.

He forced himself to pause and pray more intently. But an arsenal of troubling thoughts assaulted him. These were the times when it still hurt — even after all these years — not to be a part of his daughter's life. He wished with everything in him that he could hop on a plane and go to Natalie, go to Daria. But another man had taken the place of protector and defender in their lives. Yet, in spite of the pain that was still raw at times, he never doubted that he had made the right decision in abdicating his role as Natalie's father, in coming back to Timoné and leaving Daria to continue the new life she had begun without him. From what he could tell from his conversations with Daria and his limited correspondence with Natalie, he believed that Cole Hunter was doing right by his family. Nevertheless, he sent up a silent prayer that the Lord would give the man an extra measure of wisdom now. That God would help Cole be the father that Nate could not be to Natalie.

He read the e-mail once more, lingering over Daria's final words:

Please don't worry too much, Nate. I hated to even have to tell you the news, since there's little you can do from there. But it didn't seem fair not to tell you. With God's help, I know Nattie will get through this. We all will.

Please pray for us, as I know you do. We'll keep you posted, and as always, we are praying for you.

Love and prayers,
Daria

His mind racing, Nate skimmed the other e-mails, and seeing that there was nothing urgent, he closed the laptop and bowed his head over the desk. The tears flowed freely as he placed his precious daughter — along with all the families involved in the tragedy — before the throne of the heavenly Father.

When Nate finally lifted his head, the village was just beginning to come alive with the smells and banter of the supper fires. With the heavy heart of a father far from his hurting child, Nate closed up the mission office and headed across the grounds to his hut.

He knew that tonight the silence would fill the empty space like thunder.

Twelve

"You sure you don't want me to come in with you, Nattie?" Cole Hunter asked as he pulled the car up to the drop-off zone at Bristol High.

"No, Daddy. I'm fine."

Natalie eased out of the car, her muscles still aching and stiff from the accident. She hoisted her backpack onto her shoulder and gave her father a halfhearted wave. His forehead was furrowed with worry lines, but he blew her a kiss — which she ignored — and drove out of the parking lot.

Monday morning. She had missed a whole week of school, and now, coming back for the first time since the accident, she was terrified. She couldn't remember when she had ever felt so alone. Every day of her life since the middle of sixth grade, she had arrived at school with Sara Dever by her side. Now, not only was Sara gone, but she had to face the entire school with the guilt of Sara's death on her head. It was all she could do to keep walking toward the wide front doors of the building, to not turn and run in the opposite direction.

It struck her what a cruel irony it was that she didn't even have a car in which to run away. Her Camry had been crushed almost beyond recognition. She hadn't seen it herself — hadn't wanted to. But the *Wichita Eagle* had run a photo of the scene of the accident, and Daddy had brought the paper into her room one night, saying something about what a miracle it was that she had survived.

Well, she didn't feel like a miracle survivor. She felt like an outcast — and one very deserving of the position.

She heard a commotion behind her and turned to see a gaggle of sophomore girls walking up from the parking lot. She turned away quickly, but she could tell by the way their voices dropped that they had spotted her and were making a wide berth around her. When they'd passed, she didn't miss the furtive glances over shoulders and the uneasy whispers. She knew what they must be saying.

She took a deep breath, went through the door, and started toward the office, head down, pretending to rummage for something in her bag.

In the office, Mrs. Oswell, the secretary, greeted her with the same pity in her voice that Natalie had heard a hundred times over the last ten days. "Oh, Natalie . . . Welcome back, honey. How are you getting along?"

Natalie shrugged and fought back the tears that sprang unexpectedly to her eyes. "I'm okay," she said evenly. She handed in the permission slip from the doctor and waited while the secretary read it.

Mrs. Oswell looked up from the paper. "Thank you, honey," she said, as though Natalie had given her a diamond tiara. "This is just what we need. Now do you have money on your lunch card and every-thing else you need?"

Natalie forced a smile. "I'm fine," she said, patting the pocket of her jeans where she kept the card.

"Okay, honey. Well, you just let us know if you need anything . . . anything at all."

"Thank you," Natalie muttered.

She had to get out of here. She turned away from the counter and hurried to her locker. Rebecca Jimison was working the combination on the locker beside hers.

"Natalie!" she shrieked when she saw her.

Rebecca pounced on her and gathered her up in a warm hug, but the pressure on her incision caused her to wince and take in a sharp breath.

Rebecca pulled away quickly, a hand to her mouth. "Ooh, I'm so sorry! Are you okay?"

Natalie laughed uneasily. "I'm fine. Just a little stiff and sore still." She hugged the girl back to give proof to her words, and relief flooded through her at her friend's response. Rebecca was in her first-hour class. At least she'd have someone to walk into the room with.

"Oh, man, Natalie. I'm so glad you're back," Rebecca said as they started toward the biology lab. "We were getting worried about you. You know Evan is still in the hospital."

"Yeah, I heard. I guess he's hurt pretty bad, huh?"

Rebecca nodded solemnly. "A couple of the guys went and saw him this weekend. I guess he might get to come home Friday, but he'll have to have a bunch of therapy and more surgery to get a pin out of his ankle or something. They're not even sure he'll be able to graduate with us. I still can't believe it happened," she said, shaking her head.

"I know . . . Me neither."

"It's been terrible here, Nattie. Everybody's been crying all the time. The wreck is all we can talk about. The teachers have been pretty cool about it, though. Masters even canceled a test 'cause he said our scores wouldn't be accurate, with everybody so emotional and everything."

As they made their way down the hall, other students and teachers started to notice her, and friendly shouts of "Hey, Nattie!" and "Welcome back, Nattie" greeted her. Maybe this day wouldn't be so bad after all.

She looked around the halls. "It feels weird to be back," she said, almost to herself.

"It won't ever be the same without Brian and Sara, will it?" Rebecca said, her face darkening.

A lump lodged in Natalie's throat, and she turned away.

"Oh, Nattie, I'm sorry. I shouldn't have said —"

The bell interrupted her, and Natalie willed a smile to her face. Grabbing Rebecca's arm, she said, "Come on. The last thing I want to do is be late for class."

Natalie sat on her bed that night, her

American history textbook spread open in front of her. Although her eyes were trained on the book, her mind was reliving the day at school. The hard knot that had bound her stomach since the accident loosened a bit. The kids had all been really nice to her, and by the end of the day things had actually seemed almost back to normal.

She remembered something funny Dr. Hart had said in fifth-hour English, and she picked up the telephone. She was halfway through dialing Sara's number when she realized what she was doing. The force of the truth took her breath away. She dropped the receiver back in its cradle and sat, numb, staring at the wall.

A knock on her bedroom door shook her out of her trance. "Who is it?" she asked in a monotone.

"It's me," Nicole's muffled reply came from the other side of the door.

"What?"

"Can I come in, Nattie?" Her sister's voice had the same gentle, sympathetic tone that everyone seemed to use with her since the accident.

"Sure . . . come in."

The door opened slowly, and Nikki's head appeared around the corner. "You busy?"

Natalie pointed to the textbook open on her bed. "Just doing homework."

Nicole stepped into the room and closed the door behind her. "How did it go today?"

Natalie shrugged. "I don't know. It was okay, I guess. You were there," she said sarcastically. She felt mean, and yet she felt incapable of responding any other way. It was the tone she had used with her sister for as long as she could remember.

"Everybody was really glad to have you back," Nicole offered now, sitting on the edge of the bed.

Natalie eyed her sister. Her head was tilted to one side, and her eyes seemed full of concern. Natalie softened a bit. "Yeah, they were pretty cool about it."

"We've all been worried about you."

She didn't know what to say to that, so she simply said, "Thanks."

"Jon's coming home this weekend, and we —"

"Again?" she interrupted. "He was just home last weekend."

"Well, he . . . he wants to be with his parents as much as he can . . ." Her voice trailed off, and she seemed suddenly intrigued with a loose thread on Natalie's quilt, running it through her fingers over and over.

Natalie nodded, guilt stabbing her afresh. She dreaded facing the Devers, but knew she couldn't avoid them forever. In fact, she had started a letter to them, asking their forgiveness. She didn't expect them to grant it. In fact, she wouldn't blame them one bit if they hated her now. But, for her own sake — so she could sleep at night — she needed to ask for it nonetheless.

As though she'd read her thoughts, Nicole said, "They don't blame you, you know" — she looked up to meet Natalie's gaze — "for Sara. Nobody blames you, Nattie."

Natalie felt hot tears well behind her eyelids. "Not even Jon?" she risked.

"He . . . He's taking Sara's death pretty hard. They had gotten really close before he left for college. But he . . ." She looked away. "Everybody knows it wasn't your fault, Nattie," Nicole finished weakly.

An all-too-familiar sick feeling planted itself in the pit of her stomach. "Don't just tell me that if it's not true, Nikki. I wouldn't blame them — him — if he did think it was my fault."

Nicole took her hand now. Her sister's hand felt small and warm, and Natalie realized that she couldn't remember the last time they had touched each other affectionately. The knot in her stomach loosened another notch.

"Nattie, I promise you, we just want to help you get through this." Nicole hesitated, as though she'd been about to say something and decided against it. Instead she told Natalie, "Jon said his mom really misses you. One of the things she misses most is not having Sara's friends hanging out at their house. It's awfully quiet there now with Jon at school and Sara . . ."

They let Sara's name hang in the air between them.

Finally, Natalie sighed. "I guess I should go see her."

"I wish you would, Nattie. I know Maribeth would love that."

Natalie smiled at her sister, and an unfamiliar surge of love for Nicole rushed through her veins. "When did you grow up so much?" she asked, feeling awkward, almost shy.

Nicole reached to embrace her, and Natalie swallowed back the tears as she returned the hug. Daddy always said that God could make something good out of the worst tragedy. Maybe there was one good thing coming out of Sara's death already.

★ ★ ★

The atlas was spread open on the passenger seat beside her, and on top lay a notepad from the vet clinic with detailed instructions for how to get to her Grandma and Grandpa Camfield's house. Daddy had written them out for her almost two years ago when Natalie made her first solo trip to Kansas City. She held the wheel with one hand and picked up the notepad, trying to figure out if she'd missed her turn.

It hadn't been easy to convince Mom and Daddy to let her come by herself. This was the first time she'd made the trip since the accident, and her parents were understandably nervous. But in the end they'd relented, and now Natalie was eager to prove that their decision had been the right one — especially since they'd let her drive Mom's new car.

She'd been nervous starting out, but after half an hour, the car began to feel a part of her, and she began to enjoy the solitude. She settled back in the seat and loosened her grip on the steering wheel. The countryside looked different now that winter had stripped the trees of their leaves and opened up the prairie vistas. The landscape stretched for miles, with little farmsteads dotting the patchwork of fields and pastureland at random intervals. Gradually factories and malls replaced the rural terrain. Natalie passed a familiar shopping center on the left and knew she was getting close to her grandparents' neighborhood.

When she pulled into their driveway a few minutes later, she was glad to see Aunt Betsy's car parked there. Betsy's presence would be a buffer against Grandma's well-meaning sympathy. She didn't remember her grandparents' visit to the hospital, but Vera Camfield had called a dozen times since Natalie had been dismissed. And while she appreciated her grandmother's concern, she had run out of ways to reassure the woman that she had survived.

Natalie unpacked her things from the trunk of the car and lugged everything to the front door, wondering why no one had met her in the driveway as they usually did when they were expecting her.

She barely had her hand to the bell, when Grandma and Aunt Betsy burst out the door.

"Nattie!" They squealed in unison, smiles as wide as the Missouri River flooding their faces.

"You're early," Grandma Camfield said.

"Am I? Sorry." She dropped her bags in

the middle of the foyer and returned their bear hugs.

"Don't be silly. Here, let me look at you," her grandmother said, holding Natalie at arm's length. "Oh, honey, you sure gave us a scare."

"I'm fine, Grandma. Hey, where's Grandpa?" she said, deliberately changing the subject.

"He's in there," Betsy said, motioning toward the den, where Natalie recognized the sounds of a football game on the television. "Sorry, babe, but you'll have to compete with your grandpa's precious Chiefs."

Natalie laughed.

"When he figures out you're here, he'll come out of hiding," Betsy said.

Natalie headed for the den. Jack Camfield was reclining in his La-Z-Boy with his back to her, but when he heard her cheery "Hey, Grandpa!" he maneuvered the chair into its upright position and stood to gather her into his warm embrace.

"Hey, squirt! When did you get here?"

"A couple of hours ago," she teased.

"I know better than that," he said wryly. "Here, sit down." He patted the sofa that sat perpendicular to his recliner. "Did you have a good Thanksgiving?"

She plopped down on the cushions. "Yeah, it was okay."

"That's good . . . that's good," he said, nodding slowly.

Natalie sensed that her grandfather wasn't sure what to say next, so she pointed to the TV screen where a beer commercial now blared. "How are they doing?"

"The Chiefs?"

She nodded.

He blew a raspberry. "They're not playing worth diddly," he said, but he warmed to the topic. "They'll come back . . . they'll come back. I'm not giving up on them yet." He turned and looked her in the eye with the same sympathetic cluck Grandma had made. "The question is, how is Miss Natalie doing?"

"I'm okay. Really I am."

"I'm glad, honey. You liked to scared us all to death. Sara's folks doing okay?"

"Yeah. It's been hard, but they seem to be doing really good."

"Well, I know you must miss her. She was a sweet girl."

"She really was, Grandpa." Natalie swallowed hard, tearing up.

There was an awkward lull while she tried to compose herself. Then the game came back on, and he slapped her on the knee as though she were one of his cronies. "Here we go . . . here we go."

"I'm going to go see if Grandma and Aunt Betsy need my help." Natalie rose to go. "You *will* come out and have dinner with us, won't you?" she said with feigned exasperation, trying to lighten the mood.

"I'll come out, but if these guys don't get on the ball I might come out a little grumpy," he said without looking up. "Come on, you bozo, get the ball!" he yelled at the television screen.

Natalie left the room laughing. The Grandpa Camfield she remembered from her childhood was reserved and rather solemn, but since he'd retired from his law practice a few years ago, something had clicked between him and Natalie. Though it made her feel mildly guilty, she sometimes pretended that her relationship with Nathan Camfield would have been as warm and fun-loving, had she had a chance to grow up with him for a father.

She found Grandma and Betsy in the breakfast room off the kitchen fixing tea. When she came into the room, Grandma bustled over to the cupboard to get Natalie a cup.

"So, no school tomorrow, huh?" Aunt

163

Betsy asked, as she settled herself at the table.

"Nope. It's a teachers' workday or something."

"Lucky you. How's school going? You suffering from senioritis yet?"

"A little." Natalie shrugged. "Maybe it'd be worse if I knew where I was going next year, but right now I kind of don't want the year to go too fast because I have no clue what I'm going to do."

Betsy patted her hand. "Don't sweat it. You'll know in plenty of time."

"I sure hope so. It's making me a little nervous." She took the steaming cup Grandma offered her. "Thanks," she said, testing a tiny sip.

"You know, Natalie," her grandmother said, clearing her throat, "there are some wonderful schools here in Kansas City. You could live with Grandpa and me and save a bundle on room and board."

"Oh, Mother," Betsy scoffed playfully. "Who wants to live with their *grandma* their first year away from home?"

Natalie smiled. "Thanks, Grandma, but I'm kind of looking forward to dorm life."

"Well," her grandmother said, flustered, but taking their rebuke in stride, "I'm just trying to help."

"And I appreciate it," Natalie told her, putting her hand over Grandma's wrinkled hand and winking at Betsy.

As she sipped the warm brew and listened to the lighthearted banter between the two older women, Natalie remembered a hundred other cups of tea at this table over the years. *How strange,* she thought, *that when I was little I hated having to come here because it made me feel so different from everybody at my house.* Now, she realized that she'd come to appreciate it for the very same reason. When she was surrounded by these people who shared her name and treated her like a princess, she could almost feel — for a few brief moments — that there was a place in this world where she belonged. A place she could escape the guilt and sorrow that haunted her.

Thirteen

Natalie pulled into the Devers' driveway and put the car in park. She knew Maribeth was home because the garage door was open and her little yellow Volkswagen Beetle was parked there. Sara had never had a car of her own, but her mother had occasionally allowed her to use the Beetle. Natalie had a collection of memories starring that tiny car.

Anticipation and fear mingled in her blood as she took the keys out of the ignition and opened the door. She'd dreaded this day, had put it off week after week. Now she just wanted to get it behind her. Mom and Nicole had assured her that Maribeth would greet her with open arms, and now that she was standing in front of the house that had been like a second home to her, she was suddenly anxious to see Sara's mother again.

It felt strange to go to the front door. When Sara was alive she'd always used the back door by the garage like one of the family. She heard footsteps inside. Butterflies warred in her stomach.

The door opened, and Maribeth stared at her for a minute as though she didn't recognize her. Then a tearful smile spread over her whole face. "Natalie!" She reached out and drew her into a warm embrace.

She ushered Natalie into the kitchen, and almost without knowing how she got there, she was sitting at "her" place in the Devers' cozy kitchen, Maribeth hovering over her with a cup of hot cocoa and a plate of homemade cookies.

"Oh, honey," Sara's mother said now, "you have no idea how good it is to see you. I've missed you so much!"

"I've missed you too," Natalie mumbled, a bit embarrassed. "Maribeth, I'm so sorry about Sara," she blurted out. "I'm sorry I took her to that stupid party." The words came out in a torrent, and as quickly as she spoke them, Maribeth was at her side, stooping to envelop her in tender arms.

"Honey, I forgive you. I forgave you a long time ago. You didn't mean for it to happen. I understand that . . . We all do."

Natalie didn't know how to respond, so she said nothing.

Maribeth's voice broke into her thoughts.

"Thank you for the letter you sent, Nattie. That meant a lot to us."

Natalie shrugged off the thanks, then suddenly burst into tears. "I miss Sara so much," she gulped.

Maribeth stroked her back. "I know . . . I know. We all do."

After a while, Maribeth pulled away and sat down beside Natalie. "You know, Nattie, I think —" She stopped short, and Natalie could see that she was struggling to regain her composure. "I think Sara would be so happy that you came today. I think it would make her glad to know that you still stopped by to give her ol' mom a hard time once in a while."

They grinned together at the thought.

Maribeth reached for a large album that was sitting on the other end of the table. She slid it in front of Natalie. "I've been putting Sara's things into a scrapbook. She had a baby book, but all her school things . . . Well, it's something I always intended to do and just never got around to." She rubbed her hand across the cover of the book. "It . . . it's been good therapy."

Natalie touched the album gingerly. "Can I look?"

Maribeth nodded, and Natalie could see that she was close to tears again.

She was almost afraid to see what was inside. She opened to the first page. There were a couple of blurry baby pictures and a smudged footprint on a note card. Across the page was what looked like a kindergarten photo. Natalie turned page after page and watched Sara Dever's life pass by on the pages of a dime-store scrapbook. It made Natalie ache to see her friend smiling up at her. Sara's smile hadn't changed from the time she was a little girl until death had wiped it from her face forever.

Natalie turned to the page that represented Sara's eighth-grade year. Her own face stared up at her. She and Sara stood arm in arm, toasting each other with ice-cream cones aloft. Their lives had been intertwined for almost as long as she could remember.

She looked up at Maribeth, expecting to see tears. But Sara's mom was smiling at the images in the photo. "You two had such good times together. Thank you, Natalie, for being such a good friend to Sara. I — I hope you know how much she loved you."

A stab of guilt pierced her. *You don't know everything.* She forced the thought from her mind.

For the next hour, she and Maribeth pored over the album and celebrated Sara's life. When Natalie got ready to leave, Maribeth hugged her again. "Oh, Nattie, you don't know how much good this day did me. Thanks so much for coming."

"It did me good too," she said, returning the hug, a lump in her throat.

As they walked to the door, Maribeth seemed reluctant to let her go. Finally, she blurted out, "Natalie, can I ask you something?"

A warning bell went off somewhere in her consciousness. "Sure . . ."

"I know . . . I think Sara was always, you know . . . *good*. But I want to be sure. She wasn't . . . drinking . . . at the party that night, was she?" Her words came out in a rush. "It's been eating at me because, well, I was kind of surprised Sara was even out there at all, and . . . sometimes parents are the last to find out, you know?" She looked embarrassed, as though she'd tainted Sara's memory by even asking. "They told us they took blood-alcohol tests on everyone," she explained. "But it's been almost six weeks now, and Don just found out that those tests can sometimes take three months to come back! I . . . I just thought you would know . . ."

Though blood was rushing through her veins, pounding in her ears, making every sound seem as though it came through a tunnel, Natalie heard her own voice, surprisingly calm, comforting her friend's mother. "No, Maribeth," she said. "Sara never drank — or anything like that. She *was* good. She didn't do anything wrong that night. Or ever. I can promise you that."

Maribeth Dever sagged in relief. "Oh, thank you, Nattie. You don't know what a gift you've given me."

Suddenly unable to speak, Natalie offered yet another hug before she put up a hand in a halfhearted wave and ran to her car. She hadn't lied. Everything she had said to Sara's mother was true. But like a mangy stray dog that wouldn't go away, one nagging thought scratched at the door of her mind. *They don't know everything. They don't know everything.*

Maribeth, Natalie's parents — everyone could forgive her because they had Brian Wagner to blame. After all, he was the one who ran the stop sign; he was the one who had crashed into them. And for the hundredth time, she pushed the telltale, badgering accusations into a hidden corner of her soul — the same corner where she now hid Maribeth's revelation that the blood alcohol tests had not yet come back.

It was a place in her spirit that she could never again visit if she hoped to keep her sanity.

Daria hummed the refrain of a Christmas carol softly as she folded the last of the warm clothes from the dryer. For the first time since the accident, she was beginning to feel as though they might make it after all, and the words of the song expressed her gratitude better than any prayer she could summon. *O come, let us adore him, Christ the Lord.*

She knew that Natalie still had some rough days, but they were fewer and further between, and now that they'd made it through Christmas and the new year was nearly upon them, the excitement of planning for college was taking center stage.

Still humming, she scooped a stack of neatly folded jeans and T-shirts and headed for Natalie's room.

The door was closed, and she shifted the stack of laundry to one hip and knocked softly.

"Come in."

"Special delivery," she said brightly. "There's one more load in the dryer, but I —"

Immediately she sensed that something was wrong. Natalie was sitting cross-legged on her bed, staring into space. Her face was a pallid shade of gray, and her eyes lacked the spark that usually animated them.

Daria's heart leapt to her throat. "Honey? What's wrong?"

Without a word, Natalie got up and walked stiffly to her dresser. She opened the top drawer, reached under a stack of socks and panties, and pulled out a white business envelope.

She held it out, and Daria saw that her hands were trembling. Natalie sat back down on the edge of her bed.

The envelope bore the return address of the local county attorney's office. Daria looked from the letter to her daughter and back again. "What's this?"

Putting her face in her hands, Natalie spoke in a voice that was flat and lifeless, "It — It came in the mail . . . Oh, Mom, I . . . I think I'm in big trouble." She nodded toward the envelope that now hung limply from Daria's hand.

Daria looked at the return address once more, then slowly opened the envelope and sat in stunned silence as the realization washed over her. The papers inside were a summons for Natalie to appear in the county courthouse on charges of driving under the influence.

"Nattie? What is this?" She forced the question over a knifelike lump in her throat.

"Mom . . ." Natalie's voice wavered. "I was — I must have been drinking too . . . that night."

Daria gasped. "No . . . oh, no, Natalie." There had to be some mistake. She thought of the argument Natalie had had with her father that night. They had known that Nattie had been flirting with rebellion. She'd been pushing the limits of her curfew and mouthing off, but they hadn't thought it had gone this far. Natalie had admitted that she'd been at the party that night, but in spite of the fact that her memories of the hours surrounding the accident were blurry, she had never given them reason to believe that she had been drinking.

Natalie's shrill moan broke into Daria's thoughts. "Sara never wanted to go to the party, Mom. It was *me*. I'm the one who wanted to drive out there. I — I wasn't going to *do* anything. But then they just kind of put a beer in my hands, and I took a sip and . . ." She dissolved in tears.

Daria felt numb. "You were *drinking,* Natalie? How — How much did you have to drink?" she asked in a monotone. She let the stack of folded clothes slide to the bed and sat down beside her daughter, her mind reeling. This was serious. How serious, she couldn't even guess. If Natalie was guilty — if she *had* been driving under the influence — the consequences could be grave. A rope of fear wrapped itself about her and constricted. What would happen to her daughter? Her mind churned with a thousand thoughts, each worse than the one before. Then another thought twisted that rope until Daria wasn't sure she could breathe.

Maribeth. *Oh, dear Lord. How will I ever face her now? After all the mercy she and Don have shown us, now it seems that Nattie was responsible for Sara's death after all. Oh, Lord Jesus, we need you, we need you desperately.*

Daria felt torn between the anguish she knew her daughter was feeling and fury that Natalie had deceived them all this time. She thought about all the people she'd had conversations with after the accident, and a sick feeling came to the pit of her stomach. How many times, and to how many people, had she confidently, even *smugly,* said, "Oh, we're just so glad that

175

Natalie wasn't drinking"?

She'd thought she'd been telling the truth. But how many of those people would now believe that she had lied to them? Even as the thoughts formed, she felt disgusted with herself for caring so much what other people thought. She cared more about that, if she was honest, than about the way her daughter was suffering, or the way the Devers were suffering. *Forgive me, Lord,* she prayed silently. Still, the thoughts bombarded her.

"Natalie," she said evenly, turning to force her daughter to meet her gaze. "I need to know the truth. How much did you have to drink that night? Were you drunk?" Disbelief and panic caused her voice to rise and crack, but she couldn't seem to bring it under control.

"No, Mom. I . . . I know I wasn't drunk. I felt perfectly fine. I don't know how much I had. I honestly don't know. I remember . . . a bottle and maybe a can, but I felt fine. I didn't feel a thing. And I didn't even drink it all. I poured some of it out . . . in the fire." Her eyes had a faraway look as though she were reliving the night in her mind.

Daria picked up the summons again and read it more carefully. And as she did, all hope that there might be some mistake dissolved. The damning words on the page shouted the truth. According to the document in her hand, tests had shown Natalie's blood alcohol content to be above .08, the legal limit. Of course, since Natalie was a minor, *any* percent was illegal. But .08 was legally drunk by anyone's standards.

Then she remembered. That night in the emergency room, Dr. Davidson had told them that the sheriff had ordered blood tests on the victims of the accident. This summons had obviously been delivered as a result of those tests. Could Natalie be charged with Sara's death? After all this time? Surely not. The evidence had pointed clearly to Brian Wagner running the stop sign. But Natalie had been driving under the influence of alcohol. *Drunk.* Their daughter had been drunk behind the wheel of a car! It was more than Daria could grasp.

"Natalie," she said, struggling to rein in her emotions. "Do you understand what this says? They took tests in the hospital that show that you were legally drunk. You — you must have had more to drink than you remember. Think, Natalie. This is important."

She watched her daughter and could see the memories continue to play themselves out behind haunted eyes.

"I shouldn't have been there," Natalie said almost to herself. "I should have listened to Sara." She put a fist into her pillow and cried out, "Oh, God, why didn't I listen to Sara?" She hit the pillow again, harder this time.

Daria stood up, but her legs had turned to liquid. She sank back to the bed, paralyzed. She needed to call Cole. They had to do something — but what, she couldn't even think.

Other thoughts assailed her, one a final twist in the taut rope that held her in its coils: *Nate*. If Natalie was in trouble with the law, Nathan Camfield would have to be notified.

Nate would never forgive her if they didn't let him know what had happened.

Daria's heart sank. Nate had given up so much. The one, small consolation for the enormous sacrifice he had made all those years ago had been his pride in their daughter. What would he think now? Would he blame Daria for Natalie's rebellion? Time reeled backward, and Daria relived the agony of the decision she had faced when Nate had returned from the dead, as it were.

If she had learned nothing else through that terrible time, she had learned whom to rely on at times like this. Putting an arm around her distraught daughter, Daria held Natalie close and silently offered up their crisis to the throne of heaven.

Natalie sat on her bed after her mother had left the room. She felt as though she were in a nightmare from which she couldn't awaken. Over and over she tried to replay that night, tried to remember how much she'd had to drink, how she'd felt. But again and again her concentration was disrupted by Sara's words. *Come on, Nattie. Please, let's go. I don't understand why you're doing this. What are you trying to prove? Come on, Nattie. Please, let's go.* The words assailed her, piercing her heart until she wanted to run, screaming, from her room, to escape their accusation. She covered her ears, as though that might stop the assault.

She remembered Evan handing a bottle of beer to her when they first got there. She had drunk most of it, and another one, too, she thought. And sometime during the night she remembered holding a can of beer. But she'd poured most of that in the fire, hadn't she? Had there been more? Maybe two or three beers was all it took. She didn't know. She'd never had so much as a taste of alcohol before, so she had nothing by which to gauge the effect it might have on her. But she had felt fine. It hadn't felt the way she thought it would. She hadn't felt out of control or giddy.

But blood tests didn't lie. What would happen to her? Could they actually put her in jail? She remembered a phrase from a newspaper article she'd read somewhere: *vehicular manslaughter.* If she was remembering right, it was almost like murder. She began to shake. For the first time since she was a little girl, she got on her knees. Sliding off the bed, she bent over the mattress, face in her hands, and wept. She poured her heart out to God, begging, pleading with him to save her. Only now, the word *save* had taken on a whole new significance.

She was vaguely aware of hearing a car crunching the gravel on the long drive that led to the house, and then the sound of muted voices in the kitchen below her room. Mom must have called Daddy to come home. What would he do? A nagging voice in her head told her that he had every right to be angry. The thought of facing him now terrified her. But if she was honest, her greatest fear was that he might be kind to her, that he might forgive her. She didn't deserve forgiveness.

A quiet knock at the door caused her to take in a sharp breath. "Yeah," she answered harshly, scrambling onto the bed, strangely embarrassed to be caught praying. She took a deep breath, steeling herself for what was to come.

Her father walked into her room, the accusing letter in his hands. The disappointment and hurt she saw in his eyes gouged a throbbing hole in her heart.

He sat down beside her on the bed and spoke softly without preamble. "I have a friend I'm going to call," he said, rubbing his hands together the way he did when he was upset. "He's a lawyer. He helped us when Nate — when your father came back. I think he can help us now." He leaned away to look her full in the face. "But you'll have to be honest with him, Natalie. He can't help you unless you tell him everything. The truth. All of it."

She nodded solemnly. "Will I . . . Will I have to go to jail?"

A shadow clouded his face, and he shook his head slowly. "I don't know. I don't know what will happen." He sat deep in thought for a moment, and when he spoke next, his voice was that of the disciplinarian that the rebel in her despised. "I don't want you driving, Natalie," he said.

"What?"

"Under the circumstances, I don't think it's wise for you to be driving — until we find out what this means." He indicated the letter on the bed beside him.

"You're not serious?"

"I am dead serious, Natalie. I'm sorry. But until we know what the consequences of this will be, I think it just makes sense. But Nattie . . ." His voice broke and he swallowed hard before speaking again. "I want you to know that we'll be with you no matter what happens. We'll get through this. With God's help, we'll all get through it." He reached out and put a hand on her shoulder.

But she turned away and shrugged him off, hating herself even as she did it. She desperately wanted the comfort of her father's touch, and yet she couldn't accept it. Not now. There was too much to be forgiven — on both their parts. A confusing pool of emotions whirled within her. She scooted to the foot of the bed, out of his reach.

He persisted, laying a hand on the bed

near her, palm up as though he wanted her to put her hand in his. "We love you, Natalie. You know that, don't you? Nothing you could ever do will change that."

She sat, unmoving and silent, her arms wrapped tightly around her, her head bowed.

After a few minutes, he stood and walked out of the room. She looked up in time to see that his shoulders were hunched and his head down. Something inside her whispered, *Go to him. Go to him now. Tell him that you love him.*

But she didn't deserve his love.

She sat paralyzed on the edge of the bed, unable to obey her own heart.

Fourteen

The snow was falling heavily. Daria had to run the wipers every few seconds just to see the road. She tapped the brakes as she approached the Bristol city limits sign and slowed again as she neared Harrison Street, wishing she could just keep driving. She felt like a prisoner going to the gallows. Even if she herself wasn't headed for death, she knew that her friendship with Maribeth Dever probably was. Her dear friend had extended more grace and mercy to Natalie — to their entire family — than anyone could expect. But no one would require Maribeth to forgive what Daria had to tell her today.

She pulled into the driveway, and a lump formed in her throat as she realized that this might be the last time she would ever be welcome at her friend's door. Trying in vain to compose herself, she got out of the car and trudged through the snow that had accumulated on the walk. She stood on the porch, letting the biting wind cut through her wool coat, then finally she lifted a gloved hand and touched the doorbell.

Maribeth, wearing her usual cheery smile, opened the door wide. "Daria! What are you doing out in this weather?" She took Daria's arm. "Get in here. Let me fix you a hot cup of tea." Then, taking one look at Daria's tear-stained cheeks, "What's wrong?"

"Oh, Mari. I have to talk to you."

Maribeth's face went pale. "What's happened?"

When Daria could only shake her head, Maribeth hurriedly pulled her into the warmth of the house and closed the door behind them. She steered Daria to the sofa in the living room and waited quietly. The warmth of Maribeth's hand on her arm was almost more than Daria could bear.

"I don't even know how to begin, Mari. You . . . you've been through so much. I don't know how you can take any more, how you can forgive any more."

"What are you talking about, Daria? What has happened?" she repeated, but her voice had taken on the dull timbre of dread.

"Mari —" Daria took a deep breath and plunged ahead. "Natalie was drinking the

185

night of the accident. The tests came back, and they . . . they showed that . . . she was legally drunk."

Maribeth put a hand to her mouth.

Daria watched the news slowly register on her friend's face. "I didn't know it before. I promise you, I didn't know. She — She got a summons in the mail yesterday charging her with DUI. Oh, Mari, I am so sorry!"

She waited for a response, but if she had expected anger and tears, if she had expected accusations and reproof, she was wrong.

Maribeth began to cry, but it soon became apparent that her tears were not for herself. She took Daria's hands in her own. "What can I do to help, Daria? How is Natalie taking it?" Maribeth asked.

"Not well. Not well at all. We were so encouraged right after the accident — and even more after she'd talked to you. It really seemed like her attitude had changed and she'd turned over a new leaf. She was opening up to Cole, and we could really see her making an effort with Nikki. But since the letter, she's turned cold again. She's hardly speaking to Cole . . . In fact, she's hardly been out of her room for two days. I'm worried about her, Mari. I don't know what's going to happen."

She looked at her friend, and though Maribeth's face bore only compassion, it struck Daria how unfair it had been for her to expect Maribeth to even listen to this. "Oh, Mari, I'm so sorry for dumping this on you. Forgive me. I will completely understand if you want nothing to do with us after today."

"Daria, stop it. I hope you know me better than that. I . . . I hate it. I hate every word of what you just told me, but I never stopped loving Natalie. I know she didn't mean for the accident to happen." She squeezed Daria's hands. "What are you going to do?"

Daria explained that they'd talked to Cole's lawyer friend, Dennis Chastain. "Dennis doesn't think the charge will go beyond DUI. It'll mean a fine and . . . probation. She'll probably have to do some community service and spend some time in —" Daria's voice caught, and she willed herself not to break down. She took a deep breath, reminding herself that, horrible as this was, she still had *her* daughter, living and well. "She'll probably have to spend forty-eight hours in jail."

Maribeth put a hand to her mouth. "Oh, Daria, no."

Daria nodded. "Dennis doesn't think the county attorney will go for manslaughter or anything like that — since they know that Brian Wagner ran the stop sign. It could be so much worse, Mari. I know you'd trade places with me . . . ."

Maribeth seemed overcome with emotion, but finally she asked softly, "Do you want me to talk to Natalie?"

"Oh no, Mari. No. That's not why I came. I didn't mean —" She stopped, fighting back tears. "I'm just so sorry," she choked. "I'm so sorry that Natalie . . . was involved at all. I . . . don't know what else to say."

"There's nothing to say, Daria. We all forgave Natalie long ago. This doesn't change that. But maybe she needs to hear it again. Now that we know —"

Daria cut her off. "I can't ask that of you, Mari. And to be honest, I'm not sure what Natalie's response would be. She's turned hard. She's — I don't know . . . she's not herself. I don't know what's going through her mind. But it's not good."

They sat talking quietly together, consoling each other. Finally they prayed together. As long as she lived, Daria would never forget the beautiful words of compassion and grace that her friend spoke.

"Father, comfort Cole and Daria," Maribeth prayed. "Let them know that you have everything under control. And be with Natalie. Help her to accept your love and forgiveness. Soften her heart, Lord. Don't let this keep her from you. Just let her feel your unconditional love, Lord. And somehow, Father, let even this be used for your glory."

Later, as she drove home through the snow, Daria prayed silently, *Oh, Father, bless Mari's willingness to forgive so quickly. Comfort her and Don and Jon. Be with all of them. Father, I'm so unworthy of Maribeth's love, but by your power, please make me worthy. Amen.*

The afternoon light was fading. Nathan Camfield moved out of his own shadow to the other side of the crude examination table where his patient lay. He peered into the bloodshot eye, trying to determine the cause of the irritation.

The elderly man was hard of hearing, so Nate had to shout the question three times before the man understood. "Andres, *pir aurdo?* Where does it hurt?"

But before Andres could do more than nod, a shrill cry pierced the air outside the hut.

The old man bolted upright and slid off the table, and he and Nathan went to gaze out the window of the medical clinic. A boy of about ten raced into the clearing, screaming Dr. Nate's name. In front of him, as though it were a snake, he carried a bag fashioned of coarse cloth and tied with a length of jute. It was clear from his bulging eyes that he was terrified of whatever was inside.

Nate signaled for his patient to stay put, and he ran outside to meet the boy. "What's wrong?" he asked in Timoné. "What's in the bag?"

The boy untied the bag and opened it to reveal the lifeless body of a small bat. From the child's breathless explanation, Nate gathered that the creature had bitten the boy's sister while they were playing in the trees. The boy had managed to capture the animal when it became entangled in his sister's hair. But now apparently there was swelling at the site of the bite, and his sister was having some sort of seizure and struggling to catch her breath.

Nate grabbed his medical bag from just inside the door and descended the steps two at a time. With the young boy in his shadow, he ran the short distance to the mission office, hollering for David Chambers as he crossed the stream.

Chambers appeared on the stoop of the hut. "What happened?"

"His sister was bitten," Nate shouted, indicating the boy. "I've got a patient waiting at the clinic. Can you explain and tell him to come back after supper? You'll have to speak up. He's very hard of hearing."

"Go," David told him, already sprinting toward the clinic.

Nate told the Timoné boy to take him to where his sister was and tore off across the village, easily keeping up with the lad. He led Nate to the family's hut where the mother sat in the doorway cradling a little girl who looked to be about four years old. The mother wailed and moaned while the child convulsed in her arms. A small crowd of neighbors were gathered around watching the drama unfold.

Nate climbed the ladder, knelt to examine the girl. The boy pointed to the soft flesh on his sister's shoulder where the bat had sunk its teeth. The tiny slits in her skin were barely visible now because the area surrounding the bite had swollen to the size of a small apple. Apparently she'd had a severe allergic reaction to the bite. "What is her name?" Nate asked, lifting the child from her mother's arms.

"Zari," the woman breathed, wringing her hands.

Nate carried her into the fresh air. He laid her out on the stoop and began to work over her, but within seconds she stopped breathing. Frantically, Nate performed CPR and mouth-to-mouth resuscitation, while the mother prayed loudly to *Jesu* on her daughter's behalf.

The toddler resumed breathing on her own once, only to begin convulsing again. But finally, Nate was able to get an antihistamine into her and stabilize her. Within minutes, little Zari had calmed down and was breathing normally.

When he placed the little girl back in her mother's arms, the woman smiled through her tears and looked heavenward. "*Égracita, Jesu!*" she cried.

"Yes," Nate agreed. "Thank you, Jesus." He knelt beside the woman, placed his hand on the child's head and prayed in Timoné. "Father in heaven, thank you that you love little Zari. Thank you for making her well. Thank you for giving her brother swift feet. Please bring Zari quickly back to perfect health. In Jesus' name. Amen."

Zari's mother smiled her thanks, and when Nate felt certain the child was out of danger, he trudged through the village back to the clinic to make sure Andres had gone home. The sun was sinking quickly, and David Chambers had closed everything up for the night. Nate walked back to his hut, bone-tired.

As he walked, he gave thanks. To his knowledge, the child's mother was not a Christian convert, yet she had prayed in *Jesu*'s name, and God had answered. Nate knew that by this time tomorrow night, the woman's testimony of *Jesu*'s provision would have spread throughout the village.

He climbed the stairs of his stilted hut and plopped down on the stoop, swinging his legs absently over the side. Grateful, but exhausted, he wasn't sure he could even summon the energy to fix himself something to eat tonight.

Suddenly remembering the e-mail David Chambers had brought back from San José del Guaviare this morning, he reached into his shirt pocket and pulled out the creased, water-stained paper. He had not had one extra minute today to read the post. He unfolded it and smoothed out the rumpled sheet with burn-scarred fingers. It was from Daria, dated just one week ago. He read it through once. Then he read it again, trying to make the meaning of the words register.

Dear Nate,

I'm so sorry to have to send you bad news again, but there's been a new development in the whole situation with Natalie since her car accident. Unfortunately, we didn't have all the facts at the time I wrote. Apparently, Natalie has been keeping the truth from us, and it only came out a few days ago when she received a summons from the county attorney. Even though Nattie's driving didn't actually cause the accident, tests they took at the hospital that night show that she had been drinking before it happened, and now she has been charged with DUI.

She will appear before the judge in county court next Tuesday to be arraigned. They are telling us that the system is so clogged that it can sometimes take months to get a court date. We just pray that it will all be resolved before she's supposed to be at college.

It's been difficult enough for Natalie to accept that Sara is gone, but the guilt she's feeling because she was driving after she'd been drinking that night is eating her alive.

I feel sorry for her, and yet, to be honest, Nate, I'm so angry with her for lying to us and for getting into this mess in the first place, that it's hard to know how to handle this.

We've hired Dennis Chastain to represent Natalie. As you can imagine, he has been very helpful.

Nate's pulse quickened at this distressing news, and his thoughts took him back to another courtroom — a long-ago day that had sealed his separation from Daria and from Natalie forever. It had, in the end, been a seal of his own choosing, and Dennis Chastain had been instrumental in turning their crucible into something they could all live with — even something that God had used for good. He located his place on the page and continued reading.

Dennis tells us that Natalie will probably get probation, but he's warned us that she will almost certainly have to serve some jail time — probably no more than forty-eight hours. He says the most likely scenario is that she'll be put on probation for a year, and, of course, she'll have to pay the fine and attend some kind of drug-and-alcohol counseling, and maybe do some community service. Oh, Nate, this all looks so cold and clinical on my computer screen. Our hearts are broken over this, and I know yours will be too. I don't know what else to say.

Since she confessed the truth to us, Nattie has become so withdrawn and depressed that I'm truly worried about her. The Devers (Sara's parents) have been wonderful and have completely forgiven her — even after finding out about her drinking that night — but Nattie can't seem to forgive herself.

I'm so sorry, Nate, to have to put this all on you. I know the last thing you need when you're so far away is to be burdened with something like this, but I knew you would want to know.

I will let you know the minute we find out her court date. Thank you for your continued prayers.

Love,
Daria

Nate looked up from the page, fixing his gaze on some unseen object in the distance. Tears filled his eyes, as he thought of his little girl standing before a judge and being sentenced for such a serious charge. Why hadn't Natalie told them the truth in the first place? He couldn't help but wonder if the angst his daughter suffered was — at least in part — a result of his absence from her life. If he'd been able to be a true father to her, maybe this wouldn't have happened.

He shook off the festering emotions before they erupted. He'd been over the regrets, the what-ifs, too many times to count. There was no use in rehashing them. What had happened with Daria all those years ago was done. It was inevitable that there would be some repercussions. He had done what was best under the circumstances, he reminded himself. What was important now was to help Natalie.

He folded the paper and tucked it reverently into the pocket of his cotton shirt. Resting his elbows on his knees, his forehead on the palms of his hands, he sought God's direction. After many long minutes, he lifted his head and rubbed his face with a heavy sigh.

Jumping down from the stoop, he started across the village toward the mission office. God willing, he would be able to radio Bogotá yet this evening and arrange for Gospel Outreach headquarters to get him a flight back to the States. He only hoped the airstrip in San José would be clear when he got there, given the rumors of sporadic guerrilla raids in the area.

Nate's heart beat with a sense of urgency. Yet strangely he sensed more purpose in this mission than he'd felt in any task for a long while.

Daria had the windows open. A brisk night breeze rustled the newspaper and a stack of bills and letters that were spread out on the kitchen table. Cole was attending a veterinarians' meeting in Kansas City, and Natalie and Noelle were already in bed for the night, but Daria was killing time while she waited for Cole and Nikki to get home. Ever since Natalie's accident, she hadn't been able to rest easy until her family was safely in bed for the night.

Jon Dever was home from college on winter break, and Nikki had begged to spend every possible minute with him during this last week that he would be in town. They'd been lenient, even letting her stay out late on school nights, knowing it would be two months before Jon might be home again.

Once more Daria whispered a prayer of gratitude that the whole mess with Natalie hadn't come between Nikki and Jon. In spite of their reservations about Nicole getting so serious about a boy at such a young age, she and Cole already loved Jon like a son. Daria thought it was a testimony to the two teenagers' maturity that they had weathered this crisis so well; if anything, they'd become even closer. She had little doubt now that Nicole and Jon would end up getting married.

It would have all been perfect if not for the tragedy of Sara's death and the part Natalie had played in it.

Daria's thoughts were interrupted by the sound of a car on the gravel drive. She glanced at the clock. It was not quite eleven. Sighing, she pushed back her chair and stood to look out the window. Cole's car slowed and stopped in front of the garage while he waited for the door to glide up.

A minute later he came through the kitchen door, looking surprised to see her. "Hey, babe. You still up?" He leaned to kiss her.

"Nikki's not home yet," she told him.

Cole looked at his watch, worry creasing his brow.

"Remember, you gave her till 11:30 tonight," Daria reminded him, sitting back down at the table.

He sighed and shook his head as though he regretted his decision now. But apparently resigned, he shrugged out of his coat and hung it on the back of a chair.

"Man, it's freezing in here," he exclaimed, looking around the room. "Why do you have all the windows open?"

"I don't know. It seemed stuffy. I'll close them." She started to get up, but Cole interrupted her.

"I've got it." He shut each window and straightened the curtains, then came to sit across the table from her.

"Do you want some tea?" she asked. "The kettle's still on."

"Sure. I can make it. You want some more?"

She nodded and held out the ceramic mug she'd used earlier.

"Nattie and Noelle are home?"

"Safe and sound."

He brought two steaming cups over to the table and sat down. "How's Nattie doing?"

"I don't know. The same, I guess."

He put his head down, ostensibly blowing to cool his tea, but she could see that he was troubled. She reached across the table and put a hand on his arm. "She'll get through it, Cole. We all will." She wished she believed her own words.

He shook his head. "I just don't know

what to say to her. She shuts me out."

"It's not just you, babe. She shuts everybody out."

"I miss the little girl who calls me 'Daddy,'" he said, his voice breaking.

He looked up, and the pain Daria saw in his eyes broke her heart. She pushed back her chair and went to him, standing behind his chair, wrapping her arms around him, leaning down to put her cheek against his. He took her hands in his and squeezed. They were still that way a minute later when the back door flew open and Nikki and Jon burst in.

"Hey, you two, break it up," Nikki teased, throwing her purse on the counter.

"Oh, you're home." Daria disentangled herself from Cole's embrace and tried to hide the emotions that were so close to the surface. "How was your evening?"

"Good," Jon said. "We've just been hanging out at my house. We were going to go to Wichita, but Mom kind of wanted us to eat with them, and then it got late."

"So, you're heading back tomorrow?" Cole asked.

"Yeah, back to the grind."

"Well, don't study too hard," Cole said wryly.

Jon shrugged and started toward the

door. "Well, I'd better get going." He dipped his head politely and waved. "See you guys in a couple of months."

Nikki followed him out the door, and when she came back a few minutes later there were tears in her eyes.

"Ah, parting is such sweet sorrow," Cole teased, with a thespian hand to his chest.

"Quit it, Daddy," Nicole pouted, but she punched him playfully.

Cole grabbed her arm and wrestled her into a bear hug. "Guess you'll just have to spend more time with your boring ol' dad now."

Their affectionate exchange touched Daria's heart, but at the same time it hurt. She would have given anything for Cole to have the same close relationship with Natalie. And he would have if Natalie hadn't pushed him away.

Nicole kissed them both good night and went up to bed. While Daria put their dishes in the sink, Cole turned off the lights and locked the doors. They walked through the mundane comfort of routine that had underpinned their marriage for almost two decades now. But as they fell asleep in each other's arms, Daria couldn't help but feel that the tranquil life they cherished was about to come further unraveled.

Fifteen

The sun rose high in the sky on a clear January morning one month before Natalie Camfield's nineteenth birthday. She crawled out of bed and went through the motions of getting ready for school, but the unseasonably balmy air was no antidote for the heaviness in her heart.

Eight weeks from now she would appear before a judge in the same courtroom she'd once visited on a seventh-grade field trip. How naive she'd been on that long ago day, pretending with Sara to be high-powered lawyers, and then taking turns playing the judge, never imagining that one day she would stand on the criminal side of the bench, accused of an act that had ultimately ended in Sara's death. The thought of it made her sick to her stomach.

She went down to the kitchen. She shook cornflakes into a bowl and sliced a banana over the top. Absently opening the local morning paper, her heart lurched when her eyes came to rest on the *Court Report*. The two-column article shouted the news in twelve-point type. The charge against her — DUI — and the date for her sentencing had been published for the whole world to see. Her shame and humiliation were complete now.

She shoved the newspaper into the recycling bin in the mudroom and went back up to her room and lay down on top of the quilt on her bed. Of course, the news of her DUI charge had gotten around school weeks ago, but once that first day of whispers and stares was over, everyone had seemed as sympathetic and forgiving as they had right after the accident happened. She was grateful for their kindness, yet it hadn't seemed right. She *deserved* the shame.

But now it was in the paper for Grandma and Grandpa Haydon and all of Mom and Daddy's friends to see. She hadn't just shamed herself, but her entire family would be publicly disgraced because of what she'd done. Natalie knew Mom had called Grandma and Grandpa Camfield to tell them. She hadn't had to face her grandparents since then, but she couldn't put it off forever. They'd felt sorry for her when they'd thought she was the victim of a terrible, fatal accident. What must they think now?

Natalie was still lying on the bed, dressed for school, when Noelle stuck her head into the room. "Natalie, hurry up! Nikki says she's leaving without us."

Nicole was driving since Daddy had decreed that Natalie could not drive until she'd completed whatever sentence the court imposed. Though she understood why he'd done it, it was an added indignity in this whole mess.

"I'm not going today," she told Noelle now.

Noelle stepped into the room. "What's wrong, Nattie?" she asked. Noelle's sweet concern tugged at something inside Natalie.

"Come here, Noey," Natalie said, sitting up on the side of the bed. "It was in the paper this morning. My — My DUI."

"Oh," Noelle said, her face falling.

Natalie's heart twisted, realizing that her sisters, too, would have to face all over again the humiliation that the morning newspaper announced.

"I can't go to school," she told her sister. "I just can't. And I really do feel kind of sick."

Noelle nodded, her unblemished face pale and ever innocent. "You want me to tell Mom?"

Natalie shook her head. "I'll tell her. Just go on . . . before Nikki really does leave you."

Noelle turned to go.

"Wait, Noelle . . . uh, would you stop by the office and tell them I'm sick?"

Her sister nodded. In the driveway below, Nicole laid on the horn. Noelle raced out of the room, leaving Natalie with a new load of guilt. Now she'd asked her little sister to lie for her.

Daddy always left the house by seven, but she heard Mom down in the kitchen, loading dishes into the dishwasher. Usually her parents read the paper together at breakfast. She wondered if they'd discovered the paper she'd shoved into the recycling bin yet.

Because her mother hadn't come up to check on her, she was pretty sure Mom didn't realize that she had stayed home sick. She was about to go down and tell her when the phone rang. Natalie froze. It was probably one of her mother's friends calling because they'd seen the paper.

She stood at the top of the stairs, listening. She heard Mom cross the kitchen and pick up the phone. Natalie started to steal back to her room, but something in the tone of her mother's voice as it drifted up the stairs made her halt.

"Oh, my goodness. You're here — in the States?" Then, very quietly, her voice quavering, "You didn't have to do that."

Natalie's pulse quickened. *In the States?* She sat down at the top of the steps and eavesdropped.

"Oh, Nate. I don't know what to tell you. She's . . . she's a stranger. She's shut us all out. I don't even know how she's feeling."

Natalie's face flushed, and her mind raced. He'd come back because of her. What must her birth father think?

"I'm not sure that's a good idea," Mom was saying. "I just think it would be awkward, Nate. For all of us. Cole is — Well, I just don't think that would be wise." There was a long pause, then her mother said, "No. Cole isn't letting her drive now that — Well, you know . . . but, we — I can bring her to your parents'. I'd be glad to. Maybe it will do her good to get away from here for a few days. I know it will do her good to see you."

Natalie's heart was pounding. Nathan Camfield wanted to see her. How could she ever face him now?

Below her, the tone of her mother's voice changed, and Natalie scooted down a couple steps, straining to hear.

"Nate, I'm — I'm so glad you came back." There was a long pause, then, "No, I don't think Cole would mind. He . . . he's handling it the best way he knows how. And I don't know what he could do differently. Things have been pretty strained between them lately. Oh, Nate, I'm so sorry this had to happen . . . No, of course not. It's not your fault. There's nothing you could have done."

Natalie listened to her mother's anguished explanations, imagined her father's response on the other end. As if they hadn't already been torn apart by everything that had happened to them when she was a baby, now her actions were causing them to suffer all over again. The despair that had been flirting with her since the accident wrapped itself around her heart and squeezed.

She tiptoed back to her room and lay down on the bed. The next sound she heard was her mother's gasp.

"Natalie! You scared me half to death. What are you doing home?" Natalie lifted a sleep-weary face.

"I don't . . . feel well."

Her mother sat on the side of the bed, her forehead creased with worry lines. She put a cool hand on Natalie's cheek. "You don't feel like you have a fever. What's wrong, honey?"

Natalie rolled over on her side, turning away from her mother's scrutiny. "I'll be fine. I just need to sleep."

She felt a tender hand on her shoulder. "Nattie, I want to talk to you about something. Nate — your father — called this morning. He's in Kansas City, and he wants to see you. I thought maybe I could take you to Grandma and Grandpa's this weekend, and you could spend some time with him. It — Well, it might be good if you could talk to him . . . about everything that's happened."

Natalie turned and sat up in bed. "Mom! No! I . . . I can't face him."

"Nattie, please. He's your father. He loves you, and he wants to help."

"It's not like he can do anything that will make any difference, Mom."

Her mother was silent for a few minutes. Finally she looked Natalie in the eye. "Natalie, no one can make a difference unless you *let* them."

"So, are you telling me I have no choice? I have to go to Kansas City?"

"Nate came all the way from Colombia, Nattie. It wouldn't be fair to refuse to see him."

"I didn't ask him to come home!"

Her mother's voice was maddeningly steady when she said, "Well, Natalie, we're all dealing with a lot of things we didn't ask for. I'd like you to go see your father this weekend."

Natalie knew it was not a request. She threw herself on the bed and turned toward the wall. She heard the door close, and she flopped over onto her back to stare at the ceiling. But instead of feeling angry or manipulated, she felt a small spark of hope ignite inside her. Maybe her father could help her. Maybe he could tell her how to shed this unbearably heavy burden that threatened to drag her under.

Nathan Camfield stood shivering on the driveway of his parents' house. Jack and Vera had gone back inside, leaving him with Daria and Natalie. His daughter had barely spoken two words since their arrival twenty minutes ago.

"I should go," Daria said for the third time. "You're freezing."

"This weather is hard to take after the jungle," he admitted, burying his chin in the collar of his jacket. But even as he said it, he knew that he was trembling from more than the chill air. "Why don't you come in for a few minutes?" he said. "Have something hot to drink before you start back."

She shook her head again. "Thanks, Nate, but I really need to get on the road."

It was a game they'd played for a decade and a half. And he still hadn't figured out the rules. He wanted to talk to Daria, discuss Natalie's situation with her. And yet, the current that still flowed between Daria and him was disconcerting. He suspected that she still felt it too — that she was protecting herself, as well as him, by refusing to come in.

Because Natalie had driven to Kansas City by herself the last time he'd been back in the States, it had been almost five years since Nate had seen Daria. He was struck by how little she had changed over the years. She wore her hair shorter now, and the sun had etched fine lines around her eyes and mouth. But she still had the athletic posture and the becoming smile he remembered. Natalie looked so much like her mother that it made him ache to look at her.

He turned to his daughter now. "Well,

Nattie, shall we go see what your grandma has cooked up for dinner?"

The girl nodded and put up a gloved hand. "Bye, Mom. Be careful."

Daria came around the car and gave her a quick hug, but in spite of the show of affection, Nate saw that tension was stretched taut between them.

"See you Sunday night, honey," Daria told Natalie.

"Okay."

Now Daria approached Nate with her arms out. She hugged him briefly. It was a polite gesture, and an awkward one, especially with Natalie there watching them. After all these years it still hurt to hold Daria in his arms, however briefly, knowing that it could never mean what it once had. He'd forgotten how difficult it always was to see her — how hard it was to convince himself that he had made the right decision all those years ago, that no matter what his heart told him, there was no way things could ever be any different — no way he could ever regain what he'd lost.

He shook off the dark thoughts. "Thank you for bringing her," he told her quietly, putting a hand briefly on her arm.

She nodded and got in the car. But Nate

didn't miss the tears that welled in her eyes.

Natalie went into the house, but he stood in the drive and watched Daria's car back away and disappear around the curve in the street. After several minutes, he rubbed his face with his hands, trying to compose himself, and trudged up the drive to the house.

"Nathan," Vera Camfield said, "don't you want some more steak? You haven't eaten enough to keep a bird alive."

Natalie watched as her father pushed away from the table and patted his belly. "Mom, I couldn't eat another bite if my life depended on it," he said. "Everything was delicious, though. Maybe I'll raid the refrigerator later tonight."

Grandma Camfield looked pleased at that.

Natalie looked around the table. Across from her, Uncle Jim and Aunt Betsy sat side by side. They'd put Natalie beside her father, and Grandpa Camfield was at the head of the table. Grandma sat at his left, near the kitchen — although "sat" hardly described it. Throughout the meal Grandma had jumped up and down, waiting on all of them, bringing out dish after dish —

more food than the six of them could possibly consume in one sitting.

Natalie was grateful that the adults had kept the conversation going all evening. She'd been able to listen, without feeling that their eyes were all on her. Not one word had been spoken about her "situation," and while she was thankful for that, a part of her wanted to get it out in the open and get it over with. She knew from the telephone conversation she'd overheard that her reason for being here was so her father could talk to her. Whatever that meant. She felt jittery just thinking about it. She wondered what he wanted to say. Would he scold her and tell her how ashamed he was? In some ways that would be easier to take than Daddy's quiet acceptance had been. Maybe if someone just chewed her out good, she'd feel as if she'd gotten what she deserved.

"Right, Natalie?" Her thoughts were interrupted by Aunt Betsy's voice.

"I'm sorry," Natalie said, embarrassed to have been caught daydreaming. "What did you say?"

"I was just telling your dad that you're about to surpass even Grandma in the cinnamon roll–baking department."

She smiled nervously. "Oh, I wouldn't

go that far. Grandma still makes the best rolls in the world."

Her grandmother beamed. "Well, yours are a close second, honey."

"Hey," Betsy protested. "What am I? Chopped liver?"

Uncle Jim put an arm around his wife and kissed her cheek. "You're still *Numero Uno* on my list, sweetheart." Then he put a hand next to his lips, leaned across the table, and said in a stage whisper, "Sorry, Nattie. But I've got to protect my own best interests here if I ever want to see another cinnamon roll on my breakfast plate."

Natalie grinned and nodded conspiratorially, whispering back, "I understand."

After dinner Natalie helped Grandma and Aunt Betsy with the dishes while the men watched television in the den. She was drying the last of the silverware when Nate came into the kitchen.

Natalie sensed that this was the moment. Butterflies flitted in her stomach, and she busied herself putting forks and spoons in their compartments in the drawer. She didn't even know what to call him. Lately, when she thought of him, she'd simply thought of him as *Nate.* But that didn't seem appropriate. He was her father, after all. When she was little, everyone had referred to him as her "Daddy-Nate." But that seemed unnatural and a little silly now.

Nate was giving Betsy a hard time about the wildly flowered peasant blouse she was wearing. "I would have thought you'd have grown out of this hippie phase by now, Bets," he teased.

"Hippie is back in style, if you haven't noticed." She snapped a corner of the dishtowel at him, but he caught it and wrested it from her. Betsy squealed and backed into the corner cabinets.

Natalie smiled at their antics. It was good to see them enjoying being together. It reminded her of the way her mom and her Uncle Jason were with each other. Mom and Daddy clowned around like that sometimes too. Yet, she couldn't help but think that if her birth parents had stayed together, Mom might be in on this cheerful scene now.

"Hey, Natalie," Nate said, suddenly serious. "I got some pictures back — from Timoné. Would you like to see them?"

She shrugged. "Uh, sure, let me finish putting this stuff away," she told him. She put the last of the forks in the drawer and closed it slowly. *Help me, Lord. I'm scared.*

When she turned around, she saw that

everyone had left the kitchen. She went out to the living room and found Uncle Jim and Aunt Betsy getting their coats on.

They said their goodbyes, and when they closed the front door, Grandpa stretched and yawned. "Well, I don't know about you guys, but I'm heading for bed. If it's not snowing tomorrow, I've got an early golf game."

"Big surprise," Grandma said wryly. But she told him, "I'm going to turn out the lights, and I'll be up in a minute."

Natalie could hear her grandmother walking through the downstairs rooms, flipping light switches. Natalie followed her father into the dining room, where he had several envelopes from a local photo developer spread out on the table. She stood there, rubbing circles in the glossy finish of the cherry wood table, not knowing what to say.

Vera Camfield finished her rounds and popped her head around the corner. "Well, good night, you two," she said. "Nate, will you be sure and turn out this light before you turn in?"

"Sure, Mom. Good night. See you in the morning."

Natalie pulled a chair out from the table and sat down. "Did you just get these developed?" she asked, feeling awkward to be alone with him.

"Yes. Mom — Grandma — sent a bunch of film back with me last time, and thankfully I remembered to bring it with me."

"There's no place to develop pictures there?"

"Well, there is in Bogotá, of course — and I think there's even a place in San José — but it's expensive, and I'm never there long enough to wait on them. It was just as easy to bring it back here."

"Oh," she said. "Can I?" she indicated the photos with a nod of her head.

"Yes, sure." He picked up one of the packets and riffled through the stack of photos. "Here, these are the earliest ones. They were taken about a year ago."

Natalie began to flip through the pictures. In several of the shots, he posed arm in arm with various native men, and he was surrounded by smiling children in another shot. Many of the pictures depicted the surrounding countryside or huts in the village. A few were apparently taken at a small airport. Natalie was so intrigued by the images that she soon forgot about her nervousness. It was amazing to see her father in the environment in which he lived and worked. She couldn't help but notice how relaxed and happy he appeared in these photos. "That's the airstrip at the mission in Conzalez," he told her, peering across the table. "It's just a few minutes' flight into San José from there. That's where we get our e-mail."

Natalie was surprised how much it meant to her to now have mental images of the places her father had spoken about in his letters and e-mails. For the first time his life in Colombia seemed more than some fairy tale she'd heard all her life. Here were real people who knew and spoke with her father every day.

She leafed through another packet of pictures. Holding up a photo of a bearded man who appeared to be an American, she asked, "Is this that guy you told me about — the one who's translating?"

"Yes. That's David Chambers. Great guy . . . I don't know what I ever did without him. David is making tremendous progress in preparing to get the language into written form. He started altogether from scratch since the Timoné don't have a written language. It's been a real challenge. He's already doing the work of three people, and with our limited computer equipment and having to make a two-day trip just to get to a decent printer, or to get on the Internet, it's a wonder he hasn't given up."

"He's going to translate the Bible into Timoné?"

"Well, that's the ultimate goal, but when you're beginning without so much as an alphabet, there's a long way to go before that will be a reality. David is just now beginning to speak Timoné well, and since none of the Timoné people are fluent in English, that was an important first step. Now that he has a handle on the mother tongue, he can begin to actually work with some of the native people, getting the tones and inflections just right, and creating an alphabet. That will be a major victory."

"I never thought about how much was involved in translating something into another language," Natalie told him.

"I didn't either, Natalie. I've learned a lot from David. I bet he was a great teacher."

"He was a teacher?"

"Yes. He taught languages at a small college somewhere back East. I forget the name of it now. His background has served him well. The Timoné people accepted him very quickly. I've never seen them so eager to learn how to read. Somehow — even before he spoke the language well —

he was able to convey his excitement about getting God's Word into print in Timoné. Pretty amazing when you realize that 'in print' has no real meaning for them."

As her father spoke of his life in South America, Natalie felt drawn into her father's world in a way she'd never been before. After a few minutes, she realized with a start that she had almost forgotten his reason for being back in the States.

She looked up from a photograph to find him watching her intently.

"Is something wrong?" she asked.

Nathan Camfield reached across the tabletop and put a hand on her arm. "I'm sorry. I just can't get over how much you've changed since I was home last." He dipped his head slightly. "And how much you look like your mother."

She smiled, embarrassed by the tinge of longing in his voice, and went back to thumbing through photos. When she'd lingered over the final envelope for a while, she stacked the photos and slid them back into the packet. "Thanks," she told him. "Those are really good."

"They did turn out nice," he agreed. "I guess I should take more pictures. We took so many — your mom and I — when we first got there . . ." His voice trailed off.

Then he simply spoke her name, "Natalie?"

She looked up and met his gaze, and it struck her that he was as nervous as she was.

"Let's talk about what's going on with you, okay?" he finally said.

"Okay," she whispered.

Sixteen

Natalie swallowed hard. "What do you want to know?"

"Well, your mom told me most of the details, I think," he said. "What I want to know is how you're feeling about things. Are you doing okay?"

"I'm okay," she muttered, staring down at the table.

"Define *okay.*"

She could tell that he was trying hard to put her at ease, but she couldn't seem to find the words. She looked up at him and suddenly — though he still seemed more like a kind counselor than a father to her — what she saw in his eyes opened a door. There was a kindness there, an acceptance without judgment. There was love. Strangely, she found herself wanting to pour out everything. And maybe it wasn't so strange. Nathan Camfield would leave in a few days, go back to Colombia halfway across the world. Maybe she could tell him things that she could never tell someone she'd have to face day after day. Maybe somehow he could take her shame and guilt with him when he left.

She took a deep breath. "If you want to know the truth, I honestly don't know how I'm doing. I — I broke the law . . . did something totally stupid . . . and my best friend is dead because of it. I'm not sure how I can ever live with something like that. I feel like it's — like it's totally unfair that I'm sitting here in one piece, breathing and living."

He shook his head slowly. "I guess I can understand how you might feel that way," he said quietly. "But you don't have much choice *but* to live with it. Right?"

"I guess. I mean, I'm not going to kill myself or anything."

"Good," he said. He cleared his throat. "From what your mom said, it sounds like you've done everything you can to make this right —"

"Nothing will ever make this right!" she cried.

He held up a hand. "I know . . . I know." His tone became apologetic. "What I mean is that you've asked for forgiveness from everyone involved. And your mom said that they've all forgiven you."

"What choice did they have?"

"Oh, they had a choice, Natalie. Nobody *had* to forgive you."

"They *didn't* have a choice — they're all Christians — all of Sara's family. They *have* to forgive me." Jon Dever's face came to her mind, and she wondered, *had* he forgiven her yet?

"Oh, Nattie . . ." Her father laughed softly, not unkindly. "It would be nice if forgiveness were that cut-and-dried — even for Christians. But it's not that easy."

She didn't know what to say, so she waited, her gaze trained on the shiny table.

"Do you consider yourself a Christian, Natalie?"

She jerked her head up, taken aback by his question. "Sure. I guess . . . I mean, I believe in God and everything."

He waited for more.

"I asked Jesus into my heart, if that's what you mean," she told him, "when I was four years old."

"And is he still there?" He thumped his chest. "In your heart?"

"I guess so."

"You need to *know*, Nattie. You *can* know for sure, you know."

"Well, I — I never kicked him out or

anything," she smiled wryly. "And I know the Bible is true and all that stuff. I — I've never doubted that."

Her father smiled back at her. "Then he's there — in your heart. For sure. God promises he will *never* leave us or forsake us."

She sighed involuntarily. "Sometimes it seems like it might be easier just not to believe in God at all. Maybe then this stuff wouldn't bother me so much."

"Oh, Nattie. Even if you didn't believe, you'd still have a conscience. It'd be so much worse to have the guilt and not know what to do with it."

She sat thinking about what he'd said. What *had* she done with her guilt? She'd said she was sorry. But that didn't bring Sara back. *Sorry* seemed a pretty pathetic penance for the horrible, irreversible thing she'd done.

"I just wish God would have kept this from happening in the first place," she said now.

"I do too, Nattie. I wish it worked that way. But belonging to God doesn't mean we won't ever have troubles. We're human . . . We're all going to make mistakes. And other people are human . . . They're going to make mistakes that affect us. But belonging to God means that when we do come up against trouble, he'll be right there with us, helping us get through. But you have to *let* him help you."

He was quiet for a minute, and then he said, "You know, my friend David Chambers — the guy you saw in the pictures — had something a little bit like this happen to him when he was younger. He didn't set out to hurt anyone, but things got out of hand and everything played out differently than he thought it would and — well, it's a long story, and not really mine to tell — but when it was all said and done, David felt like he had ruined someone's life. But his testimony now is that the thing that seemed so terrible at the time, ended up being the very thing that brought him to faith in God, brought him ultimately to Timoné. And he's doing incredible work there now. Making such a difference in our little world."

He looked down thoughtfully, and when he looked back up at her there was determination in his eyes — and something else. Sadness?

"I want to tell you something, honey."

The way he called her *honey* made her feel warm inside.

"The hardest thing —" He stopped

227

short, swallowed hard, and pressed his lips together for a moment before starting in again. "The hardest thing I've ever done was to give up your mother — and you. I . . . I didn't think I could do it. It seemed impossible. And yet, God was more real to me during that time than he's ever been. It was like —"

"Yeah, but you hadn't done anything wrong," she protested. "None of what happened was your fault. You —"

He stopped her with an upraised palm. "Hear me out, okay?"

She nodded, intent on his words.

"When I went back to Colombia, I had to forgive a lot of people for what had happened. And I *did* have a choice. I did. And for a while — not very long, praise God — but for a while I made the wrong choice. I was hurt and angry and bitter, and I wanted someone to blame for the way my life had turned out. But I came to realize that even if I could blame someone — say I'd decided to lay all the blame on your mom — it wouldn't change my circumstances. And in fact, all it would do was eat me up inside. When I made the decision to forgive — everyone, even God, for letting things happen the way they did — *I* was the one who was set free. And the most wonderful thing happened then."

Natalie watched his face, and she could see by the faraway light in his eyes that he was remembering something from the past.

"I started to love all those people in a new way, a way I'd never imagined I could. I realize now that it was God loving them through me." He shook his head, as though rousing himself back to the present. "Do you understand what this has to do with you?"

She shook her head, confused. "I — I don't think so . . ."

"Natalie, you have been given the most precious gift. Not only has God forgiven you, but the people who were hurt because of the accident have chosen to forgive you for the part you played. That's a rare gift. I've been in the position of someone who had to forgive when it was really hard to forgive. And because of that, I know that those people love you more today than they did even before this all happened. When you forgive someone, you kind of make an investment in them." He looked at her, eyebrows knit as though he wanted to understand *for* her. "Does that make sense?"

She nodded, and tears came to her eyes

as she realized how true his words were. She had been forgiven so much.

When he saw that she was crying, his voice softened and he reached out and put a rough hand over hers on the table. "I know that what happened was — Well, you didn't do it on purpose. You didn't mean for it to happen. But it's probably a safe bet to say that you weren't asking for God's direction when you went to that party and when you got in that car after you'd been drinking."

He waited for her acknowledgment, and she nodded, her mind reeling with all he'd given her to think about.

"The result of your actions was something more terrible than you could have ever guessed would happen. It was the same with your mom back when —"

He hesitated for a second, and Natalie could see in his eyes that he was struggling with how much to say.

"She didn't know I was still alive. She couldn't have been expected to know that, but —" Again he paused. "I don't know how much your mother has told you about what happened with us, Natalie — and maybe it's not my place to tell you this — but Daria told me that she wasn't asking for God's direction when she married

Cole. And the consequences for that were huge. Not just for her, but for all of us. But what made the difference, Nattie, is that she acknowledged her mistake and started asking what God wanted her to do to make it right. Like you, she apologized. But she went a step further: When people gave her the gift of their forgiveness, she accepted it. She was grateful. And I know — for me at least — it made me glad I'd offered her my forgiveness. It made it easier to complete the process of forgiving — made it easier to resist the temptation to pick up my unforgiveness and carry it around with me again."

Natalie looked down at the burn-scarred hand that covered hers. There was an odd comfort in knowing that they had all managed to survive in spite of what had happened. She thought of Mom and Daddy and the deep love they shared. She thought of the man sitting across the table from her, and the joy and fulfillment she had seen on his face in the photographs they'd looked at just minutes ago. And for the first time, she could envision a future ahead of her — a future that might even include some moments of happiness and fulfillment. A tiny seed of hope cracked open, and a fragile sprout emerged.

Nate patted her hand, then in one smooth motion pushed his chair back from the table and stood. "Well, that's probably enough of the lecture circuit for me tonight. I hope I didn't overstep my bounds —"

"No. You . . . you didn't," she said, rising and moving toward his side of the table. "I — I needed to hear that. Thank you, Nate — Dad —" She shrugged, embarrassed. "I don't ever know what I should call you."

"I liked that last one," he said.

His hopeful smile made her heart soar. "Okay . . . Dad."

Her father pulled her into his arms, and she let the tears flow freely.

With Dennis Chastain leading the way, Daria and Cole passed between the towering columns of the county courthouse and ascended the wide cement steps. Natalie walked between them, her head bowed, shoulders stooped. Daria fought back tears.

Their attorney opened the door and held it for them, but Cole held up a hand. "Hang on, Dennis. Could we have a moment?"

"Sure," he said with a nod. "I'll wait inside for you."

Cole put an arm around Daria, and taking Natalie's hand, he guided them to the side of the portico. "We'll say our goodbyes now, honey, okay?"

Dennis had warned them that Natalie would be required to serve forty-eight hours of mandatory jail time immediately following the sentencing.

Natalie nodded, her chin quivering, but she didn't break down. Cole bowed his head, and Daria wept silently.

"Father God," Cole prayed, "we know you will go with us into that courtroom today — and after. We trust that what happens will be your will. Father, give Natalie — give us all — the strength we need to make it through."

Daria heard the emotion in his voice and knew that Cole was struggling to continue. Finally he whispered, "Amen." They embraced Natalie, and though she willingly accepted their hugs, she seemed stiff, wooden.

As they walked through the doors, Daria couldn't help but remember another day long ago when they'd entered a different courthouse with equally anguished feelings about the verdict that would be handed down. Daria vividly recalled the warring emotions that had filled her heart as the judge had declared her marriage to Cole intact. She was glad and yet unspeakably sad that Nathan — her first love — had had to sacrificially and lovingly relinquish his rights to her as his wife and to custody of their daughter.

Today Daria, too, had — in her heart — given up her rights to Natalie, turning her daughter over to the heavenly Father, trusting that whatever he allowed, he would also give them the strength to bear.

Weeks that seemed an eternity ago, Natalie had stood before a judge and pled guilty to the charge of driving under the influence. Today she would be sentenced.

Dennis Chastain met them inside the door and led them down the long corridor and into the courtroom. They all followed him blindly, their footsteps echoing on the polished floor. Daria had never been so grateful for their lawyer's reassuring authority. There were half a dozen people scattered throughout the large room, and Daria wondered vaguely what had brought each of them here.

Dennis stopped and pointed to the first row of seats in the gallery. Cole stood aside, and Daria started to slide into the narrow space between the rows, but Natalie turned to them suddenly, a look of desperation on her face. Daria thought her heart would break. At that moment, she would gladly have taken Natalie's place beside Dennis, would have willingly faced the judge on her daughter's behalf. But this was something no one could do for Natalie.

Daria reached out and ran a hand down Natalie's arm. "It'll be okay, honey," she whispered.

Cole patted Natalie's shoulder and turned away. Daria knew by the hard set of his jaw that he, too, was struggling to contain his emotions. Cole put a steady hand on Daria's back and guided her to a seat in the gallery.

Dennis pulled out a chair for Natalie at a large desk in front of the judge's bench. Alicia Barstow, the prosecuting attorney came into the courtroom. She and Dennis shook hands and exchanged sober greetings.

A few minutes later, Judge Sanders appeared through a door behind the bench. Everyone stood as he took his seat above them.

"You may be seated," the judge said, looking out over the nearly empty room. He acknowledged each attorney with a slight nod of his head, then slid a pair of reading glasses over the bridge of his nose.

For what seemed an eternity, he shuffled through a sheaf of papers that he'd taken from a folder.

Daria shifted in her seat, and Cole reached for her hand. Finally the judge looked up to address the county attorney. "Ms. Barstow?"

Though Dennis had informed them of how the proceedings would go, still Daria's ears rang with humiliation as the charges against their daughter were read aloud. The prosecutor made her request for sentencing. As Dennis had predicted, her recommendations were mild.

The prosecutor took her seat, and Judge Sanders gave the floor to Dennis Chastain.

Dennis rose from his chair and stepped from behind the desk. "Your Honor, the prosecutor's recommendations seem reasonable and prudent to us. We have no argument against them."

Judge Sanders focused his eyes on Natalie. "Is there anything you wish to say, Miss Camfield? Or any evidence to present in mitigation of sentence before I pronounce the sentence?"

Daria couldn't see her daughter's face, but she could tell by the judge's demeanor that Natalie was meeting his gaze. Natalie's shoulders rose and fell, and Daria heard the deep intake of air before she spoke.

"Y-Your honor." Daria could hear the torment in her voice. "I just want to say that I am very, very sorry for what I've done. I would give anything —" Natalie's voice broke, and she shook her head, unable to go on. She turned to Dennis, and Daria saw that her face was contorted with pain, and tears were streaming down her cheeks.

Dennis nodded reassuringly.

"I'm sorry," Natalie croaked out, her voice rising an octave. "That's all . . . sir . . ."

Again, the judge studied the papers before him. Finally, he took off his glasses and raised his head to look directly at Natalie. "Miss Camfield, I'm going to follow the recommendations of the prosecuting attorney — and the recommendation of the DUI Work Restitution. I sentence you to a fine of $500 and forty-eight hours in the county jail. You will serve a probationary period of one year, during which you will report regularly to your probation officer. And as per Kansas law, you will also be required to attend an alcohol information school. Do you understand the conditions of your sentence, Miss Camfield?"

Natalie nodded, and her breath caught on a violent shudder.

The judge closed the folder and looked from Dennis Chastain to the prosecuting attorney. "Custody of the defendant is hereby remanded to the sheriff for execution of the sentence. Unless there is anything further, that concludes this proceeding. This court is adjourned."

Though Natalie's sentence was one of the mildest she could have been given, still it was painful for Daria to hear these words spoken and realize that they were meant for her firstborn. Her little girl would not go home with them today. It seemed unbelievable.

And yet Daria and Cole both heaved audible sighs of relief when the sentence was delivered. The mandatory jail sentence was an alarming prospect, and Daria knew that Natalie was frightened. It would not be a picnic, but Dennis had assured them that Natalie would be safe during her stay in the facility. And it would all be over in forty-eight hours — a pittance compared to the weeks of uncertainty that had imprisoned them all since the night of the accident. Daria was so grateful that this terrible time was finally nearing an end.

With tears in their eyes, and gratitude

mingled with sorrow, Daria and Cole went forward to thank Dennis. They went to Natalie then and each hugged her for a moment, weeping quietly.

She could not bear to watch as Natalie was led from the courtroom. She let Cole put his arm around her and lead her outside. They walked together through the parking lot, joined in their silence. Cole opened the car door, waited for her to slide across the seat, then closed it after her. He came around and got behind the wheel. For a long minute, they both sat, heads bowed, unspeaking.

What would they have thought if they could have seen this moment from those other courthouse steps so long ago, from that other day of decision in the past? Would they have made the same decisions? Chosen a different way to raise Natalie? Could they have done something that might have spared Sara's life? Daria shivered involuntarily at the thought.

No, it was good that God did not allow a view into the future. And yet now she couldn't help but long for a glimpse into Natalie's future. A year from now, two years, would they be able to look back on this day the way they now looked on that other verdict? Would the passage of time allow them to rejoice that something good had come of this crucible, too? Would time benevolently diminish the anguish they had all experienced over the past weeks and months? Or did the future hold something even more bleak?

Finally, Cole sighed heavily, buckled his seat belt, and reached quietly across the front seat for Daria's hand. Without looking her way, he squeezed her hand tightly in his own, and she knew that, in the tender language shared only by long-wed lovers, he was telling her, *We'll be all right. We cleared another hurdle, and we're still breathing, still living, still loving.* She squeezed his hand in return, and in her spirit, she whispered a prayer for her daughter.

Seventeen

The heavy door slammed shut. Its thunder reverberated down the corridor and back again, over and over, as though it would never end. Natalie put her face in her hands, but she could not weep.

She was grateful to find that the two beds in the room were empty. She could hear voices outside the door and knew that there were other prisoners in the pod, but for now, at least, she was alone in the small room. She looked down at the ill-fitting bright orange jumpsuit she'd been given to wear, and her face burned with humiliation.

Her lawyer had told her exactly what to expect from her time in jail. But her worst imaginings could not have prepared her for the degradation of being stripped of every personal belonging, searched, forced to shower and shampoo, and then being shown to this cell by the none-too-pleasant officer.

And yet she had received the treatment she deserved. She had no one to blame but herself. Sinking onto the bare mattress of the nearest bed, she sat with her elbows on her knees. Somewhere deep inside, a part of her desperately wanted the release of tears. She longed to cry and scream and wail. But it was all she could do to make herself continue breathing in and out.

She knew Mom and Daddy had tried to be strong for her sake, but she hadn't missed the looks of agony on their faces as they left the courtroom. She had humiliated everyone she ever cared about. If she lived to be a hundred, she didn't think she could ever make it up to them.

Time seemed to stand still, and her thoughts swirled in a swift current, like a whirlpool threatening to suck her into its vortex. Finally, her back and arms began to ache from sitting in one position for so long. She crawled onto the mattress, not bothering to put on the sheets that lay folded at the end of the bed. She curled into a fetal position and sought sleep, but instead, the accusing thoughts assailed her. Her breathing became shallow, and her skin felt clammy and cold. Panic rose in her throat, and she wondered if she was having some kind of attack.

"Oh, God. Help me. Forgive me. Please, God, forgive me!" she whimpered. "You have to forgive me!"

She waited, feeling nothing. But slowly the panic subsided, and she was able to stretch out on the mattress. Her racing heartbeat gradually slowed. Staring at the empty ceiling she prayed. Pleading for mercy, forgiveness. Begging God for a chance to redeem her life. But Sara was as dead as she'd been yesterday and the day before. How could that ever be made right?

Natalie grew drowsy and reached for the thick blanket that lay under the stack of unused sheets. She pulled the scratchy fabric around her shoulders and finally drifted off. When she opened her eyes next, harsh light from the central room of the pod shone in through the windowed door. Her room remained in shadow. She closed her eyes again and slept deeply.

When she woke again, she somehow knew it was morning. The smell of burnt toast hung in the air. She heard the clatter of some sort of cart being wheeled down the corridor. She sat up on the side of the bed and waited, not knowing what to expect. Her door opened, and a uniformed woman deposited a tray on her desk.

Natalie got up and went to sit in front of the congealed oatmeal and soggy toast but soon returned to her bunk. After an hour, the same guard came to pick it up.

"You ought to eat something," the woman said without emotion.

"I'm not hungry."

The guard lifted broad shoulders in a halfhearted shrug. "Suit yourself." She picked up the untouched tray and left the room. Natalie was alone again.

The next thirty hours crept by. Natalie was barely aware of her surroundings, scarcely moving from the utilitarian mattress on the stripped bed. When offered an opportunity to exercise in the facility's gym, she declined. She wasn't asked again. She'd been told that she would be allowed to call home, collect. What would she say to them, she wondered. It was better not to call at all. Besides, she couldn't make herself go out among the other inmates.

Inmate. A label that — like the orange jumpsuit — she'd never, in a lifetime of thoughts and dreams, imagined she would someday wear.

Natalie refused the lunch they brought her as well, but when the supper tray came, she went to the desk, pulled out the chair, and ate the tasteless food. Later, after they'd taken the tray away, she could not remember what it was she had eaten. A Gideon Bible lay on the desk. Natalie stared at it, feeling drawn to it. But she couldn't bring herself to open the cover and accept the comfort she knew it offered. These hours were part of her punishment. She didn't deserve comfort. She deserved the dull ache, the numbness she felt in this place — this hell of her own making.

She scarcely moved from the bed for the rest of her incarceration. When the door swung open and the same uniformed officer who'd admitted her informed her that her parents were waiting to take her home, it was as though she'd awakened from a macabre dream.

She shed the orange jumpsuit and put on her own clothes again, but she could not shed the guilt that she'd worn into this place. That burden remained as heavy as it had been when she'd walked in through the doors of the county jail.

Natalie fell asleep in her own bed that night, one more debt for her sins allegedly erased from the ledger. But she knew in her heart that forty-eight *years* in jail would not be enough to atone for what she had done.

The music of children's laughter floated across the playground, and an April sun turned the afternoon air balmy. Natalie walked across the winter-bare lawn, gathering abandoned toys as she went. Here and there the cracked, parched earth beneath her feet had given way to brave blades of yellow-green grass. She came upon a set of building blocks at the edge of the yard. Stooping to collect them, she looked across the lawn. From this angle, closer to the ground, she could see that a fine, green haze covered the yard. With one good, soaking rain and a few days of sunshine, the whole lawn would wear a mantle of green. What a difference they would see in the barren countryside when spring truly made its appearance. Her heart felt lighter at the mere idea, and she thought how much she had come to enjoy her work here at the childcare center. Somehow it didn't seem right. Wasn't the whole point of community service supposed to be punishment — or at least restitution?

She looked up and spotted a toddler on the glider near the swing set. The little girl's bright pink shoestring sailed back and forth with her as she swung. "Wait a minute, Jessi," Natalie called out.

She left the pile of toys lying where they'd accumulated and trotted across the playground. Jessica Benson slid off the glider and stood waiting for her, an inquisitive expression on her cherubic face.

Kneeling beside the little girl, Natalie smoothed away a sweat-damp curl that clung to her rounded cheek. Natalie smiled. "Let me tie your shoe before you trip on this shoestring, okay?"

The petite girl nodded and plopped down on the ground beside her. Offering her foot to Natalie, she gazed up at her with wide, blue eyes. With her strawberry-blond curls, pale eyelashes, and a button nose sprinkled liberally with freckles, she reminded Natalie of someone. A lump formed in her throat as she realized that it was Sara. Sara Dever had probably looked much like little Jessica when she was a toddler. And Sara's children could have looked like this child. Natalie wondered how often Maribeth Dever would be confronted with moments like this. She didn't like the direction her thoughts were taking, and yet it somehow seemed wrong for her *not* to ponder such things.

She swallowed hard and realized that the old ache was still there. Like this lawn she knelt upon, fresh green shoots of happiness had cropped up here and there in her life, but underneath, the ground was still hard and black and unyielding. When, she wondered, would the quenching, soaking rains fall to soften the hard soil of her heart? "Please, Lord," she whispered, "help me." It was all she knew to pray. But it was a beginning.

She finished tying the girl's shoe. "There you go, punkin. You be careful now, okay?"

"Okay, Miss Natalie," Jessi chirped as she ran off to play.

Natalie walked slowly to the other side of the playground to collect the pile of toys she'd left there.

It was strange, and rather frightening, that time was passing so quickly. Her physical scars from the accident had healed so that she scarcely thought of them anymore. Her time in jail was a vague memory that appeared only in an occasional nightmare. At Bristol High, the whole incident seemed to have been forgotten. The high-school yearbook was being dedicated to Sara and to Brian Wagner. It was as though, with that action, their classmates had paid their dues to the memory of two good friends. They could get on with their lives now. Natalie wondered when *she* would move on.

Evan Greenway had not been back to school since the tragedy, but rumor had it that he was staying with an aunt in Kansas City while undergoing physical therapy at a facility there. He was supposedly working on his GED at the same time, but no one seemed to know whether he would be back to graduate with their senior class.

The parties out at Hansens' had come to an abrupt halt after the accident, and then the harsh winter had set in, keeping everyone indoors and close to home. But just two weeks ago, Natalie had heard that they were having a big "bonfire" out on the property. She wondered if anybody thought it made a difference if they called it a bonfire instead of a beer party. She had no desire to go and was disgusted that nobody seemed to have grasped the connection between those parties and Bristol's greatest tragedy in years.

This last semester of her high-school career had been odd. She wasn't sure if it was because of the accident and Sara's death; or maybe it always felt weird to be ending a time in your life that you'd never been able to imagine being over.

Of course, how many high-school students spent time in jail or spent their evenings attending alcohol and drug rehabilitation sessions? And her hours here at the community childcare center — three or four hours after school every day for the past few weeks — had ruined any possibility of other extracurricular activities at school. When she got home each evening, most of her remaining hours were spent on homework and filling out college applications and admissions forms.

There were less than three weeks to go before her community service would be complete. A nagging thought itched at her subconscious mind: Two days in jail and a few short weeks of entertaining adorable toddlers were not going to do the trick, would not convince her that justice had been done. The court system, the law, could dish out what they saw as punishment for her crime, but it was going to take a far more powerful detergent to absolve a guilt as immense as hers.

Daria Hunter clenched a wad of tissues in the damp palm of her hand. She glanced up at Cole, who sat beside her in the gymnasium bleachers. Beneath the sun-roughened skin of his square, clean-shaven jaw, a muscle tensed. Daria knew he was struggling as much as she was to contain his emotions.

"Natalie Joan Camfield," the principal solemnly intoned the name, as the president of the school board held out the imitation leather folder containing Natalie's diploma. Wobbling a bit in a new pair of heels, their daughter crossed the gym floor and stepped onto the temporary dais.

Daria knew Natalie was feeling nervous and uncertain about this moment in the public eye, but she managed to look poised and happy as she accepted her diploma. While Cole stepped into the aisle and snapped pictures, Daria tried in vain to hold back a flood of tears.

Hannah Dickson was next to cross the stage. Daria wondered if anyone besides her and Don and Maribeth Dever realized that Sara would have been next in line behind Natalie to receive her diploma. Daria took one look at Natalie's face as she returned to her seat, and she knew that she, too, was remembering Sara. *Please, Lord, let this be the last hard thing. Let this be the last time Nattie has to mourn her friend so deeply — and so publicly. Let college be a new beginning for her.*

Daria looked down the row and spotted Don and Maribeth Dever. She immediately felt guilty for her prayer. Daria knew Sara's parents were here for Natalie's sake.

Maribeth had a serene smile on her face, but this had to be one of the most difficult days of her life since Sara's death. So many dreams had died with their daughter. Daria couldn't even imagine. Guilt stabbed her again when she whispered a prayer of thanksgiving for her own three beautiful, healthy daughters.

The posters were gone from her bedroom walls, the paraphernalia of her childhood cleared off the tops of the dressers and off the shelves. Her life had been reduced to a dozen cardboard boxes that were now stacked neatly in the back of Daddy's SUV. Even the wallpaper had been stripped in preparation for the anxious future occupant of the room.

Now, while Natalie packed the last of the clothes from her closet, Nicole whirled around the room, crowing, "I can't believe I'm finally getting a room of my own!" Eyeing the full-length mirror that hung on the back of the closet door, she ventured, "Hey, Nattie, are you gonna take that mirror with you?"

"Probably not, but don't get too attached to it yet," she told her sister. "Man, I can't get out of here fast enough to suit you, can I?"

Nicole looked at her closely, as if trying to determine whether she'd hurt her sister's feelings.

Natalie offered a reassuring smile. "Hey, I don't blame you. I'd be all over it too. But do me a favor, will you?" She affectionately elbowed her sister out of the way and brought another load of clothes from the closet. "Give me a few minutes alone to finish packing."

"Okay, okay . . . sorry," Nicole said with a sheepish grin.

Her sister slunk from the room, leaving the door open a crack behind her, and Natalie was left alone. She slipped a sweater off its hanger and folded it slowly. The air around her echoed with a strange emptiness, and for a moment she was overcome with sadness. There were happy memories here, yes. But there were a lot of difficult ones, too. More of the latter, it seemed — or maybe they were just too recent. She'd begun to feel that it was a gift that she'd be able to leave those behind. College seemed to promise a new beginning. Yes, she would think about that, force herself to dwell on the hope the future held for her.

Though she hadn't a clue what she wanted to study, it had always been assumed that she would go on to college. But the uncertainty of her situation had greatly limited her choices. In the end they'd decided it would be simpler to attend a college in the state. Her mother and father — Nate — had both graduated from the University of Kansas in Lawrence, and Natalie was strongly drawn to that school. Then she'd received a letter of acceptance from Kansas State University in Manhattan that essentially made the decision for her.

Nicole was ecstatic about Natalie's decision, since Jon Dever was at K-State too. "Now I can come up and visit both of you," she'd chirped when she heard the news.

Natalie didn't tell her that Jon's presence there was one of her biggest reservations about going to the school. But on such a large campus the chances of their running into each other with regularity were probably slim. Still, it gave her pause. She had seen the way he looked at her since the accident, the vague sense of disdain in his eyes. It broke her heart, but she didn't blame him. Still, she feared the old feelings were still there, buried not far enough beneath the surface.

Take away my wrong desires, Lord, she whispered within her spirit. She sighed as, almost immediately, a psalm she'd memorized in a long-ago Sunday school class came to her. *Delight yourself in the Lord and he will give you the desires of your heart.*

Yes, Lord . . . put your desires in my heart. It was new to her, these two-way conversations with her heavenly Father. There was not one moment she could point to when she'd suddenly decided to seek God wholeheartedly. But through the awful time of Sara's death and the aftermath of the tragedy — and especially since her talk with Nathan Camfield — she had slowly begun to take her questions, her problems to the Lord and then to listen for his quiet, gentle voice in reply. She was learning that she could trust him, and there was no denying that a new peace had begun to fill her heart. Yet neither could she deny that there was still an ache there . . . a longing for something she couldn't quite grasp.

She thought of her two fathers. Sometimes she felt she didn't belong to either one of them. When Nathan Camfield had come back to the States after the accident, they had shared a warm, close time, and yet that very closeness had caused her to feel like a traitor to Daddy.

It seemed she and Daddy were so often at odds. She wasn't sure why. Since the accident — no, even before then — he had distanced himself from her. Or maybe it was the other way around. She felt awkward in his presence, and he seemed to feel the same. And yet, her throat ached with the sweetness of treasured memories of him. In her little girl's mind, she could see the view from his broad shoulders as he carried her all the way to the end of the lane to get the mail and pick a bouquet of wildflowers for Mom.

She walked to her bedroom window and peered out over the backyard vista that was as familiar to her as her own face. Outside, the cottonwoods whispered their ancient song, and she could almost hear Daddy's deep laughter the way it had sounded the night they'd captured dozens of fireflies and put them in a Mason jar. They had sat on a blanket in the grass on that hot summer night, their firefly lantern and a billion twinkling stars the only light for as far as she could see.

She'd never been afraid with her daddy by her side.

When had it all ended? When had they become strangers — or worse, enemies? She winced as the echoes of her own voice rang in her ears. *"You can't tell me what to do. You're not my father."*

Oh, Lord. I don't want to leave with things like this between us. Help me make things right.

She went to her bed and dropped to her knees beside it. Bowing over the brightly flowered comforter, she poured her heart out to the one Father whose love she was discovering never felt divided or uncertain. "Lord, sometimes I think I'm a hopeless, mixed-up mess. Please be with me as I go off to college. I'm . . . I'm kind of scared, Lord. And Father, please help me work things out with Daddy before I go." Tears wet her cheeks as she prayed, "I can't stand thinking of leaving with things the way they are between us right now. But I don't know what to do."

As if in instantaneous answer to her prayer, there was a tentative knock and the door swung open. "Hey, what else needs to go in the car, Nat —" Her father stopped short, seeing her on her knees. "Oh, I'm sorry," he muttered, sounding almost embarrassed.

She brushed at her tears with the back of her hand, but before she had time to get to her feet, he dropped to his own knees on the floor beside her. He placed a strong arm around her shoulders, and the love in his voice when he spoke her name covered her like a warm quilt. "Natalie? What's wrong, honey? Is everything okay?"

She nodded her head against his chest. Now that he was here beside her, comforting her, she truly did feel as though things would be okay.

"Oh, man," he whispered, his voice thick with emotion. "I'm sure going to miss my girl."

She turned and buried her head on his shoulder. "Oh, Daddy . . ."

"It's been a rough year, hasn't it?"

She could only nod again and soak the front of his shirt with her tears.

Silently, he rocked her back and forth, the way he had when she was little, with a scraped knee or a stubbed toe. After a while, he pulled her up to sit on the edge of her bed beside him. Again, he put a comforting arm around her shoulders. "Nattie, I'm — I'm sorry if I haven't been —"

"Oh, Daddy, I'm sorry too."

"Let's" — he swallowed hard — "let's just forget all the bad stuff. We've got an awful lot of good stuff to remember, don't you think?"

She pulled away and looked up into his face, nodding solemnly. There was no denying the love she saw in his eyes. It filled her to the core.

"Remember that time Rufus knocked you into the creek?" he asked, a mischievous glint coming to his eye. It was a story that had been told fifty times through the years.

"Yeah," she said. "You laughed so hard I thought you were going to fall in too." She looked up at him and grinned through her tears. "It would have served you right if you had."

"Hey, watch it," he said, but his voice was so tender it made her ache.

They talked then, remembering the good times, the happier days before things had gone sour. There was contrition in the remembering — unspoken, yet as clear as though it had been given voice.

Finally he put a hand on her head. "Can I send you off with a prayer?" he asked.

Natalie nodded, tears springing to her eyes again.

Daddy took her hand and slid again to his knees, bowing over the bed. She followed, willingly, sinking to the floor beside him.

"Lord Jesus, thank you," he said. His voice wavered and cracked, and something twisted in Natalie's heart. "Thank you for putting this girl in my life. Thank you for the privilege of being her father all these years. I know — I know it's not one I deserved, or ever managed to earn, Father, but I thank you just the same. Help us to forgive each other. Help us to stay close even though we'll be far apart —" Natalie felt her big, strong daddy tremble beside her, and the silence seemed interminable. When Cole Hunter spoke again his voice was steady, his plea to heaven fervent and honest. "Keep us close, Lord. Put your angels around Natalie and bring her back for a visit with her ol' dad every once in a while."

Natalie could hear the smile in his words, and she couldn't help smiling too.

"And Father God," he continued, serious again, "I know you have a wonderful plan mapped out for Nattie's life. Reveal it to her in your perfect time, Lord. Amen."

Her throat was so full of sadness and joy it was painful. And yet it was the sweetest ache she'd ever known. Natalie opened her mouth, but she couldn't croak a word. In the depths of her heart, she echoed the pleas of the man who knelt beside her. And she clung, as though drowning, to the raft of his prayers.

Trueno:
Thunder

Eighteen

Natalie hoisted her knapsack onto one shoulder and studied the sign, then looked down at the directory in her hands. Her psychology class was supposed to meet in one of the ballrooms in the student union this morning to hear a guest lecturer. But the banquet rooms were empty, lights out, molded plastic chairs turned upside down atop dozens of long tables. She looked at the sign on the wall by the wide doors again and double-checked the paper the professor had handed out. She was definitely in the right place.

In the middle of a Tuesday morning, the union was crawling with students. They streamed by Natalie as though she were a rock in a raging river current. Most of the students seemed to saunter with the confident nonchalance of upperclassmen, but here and there Natalie could pick out other freshmen in the crowd. They were the ones dressed a little too nicely, carrying back-packs that were a little too new and neatly organized, and swinging their heads from side to side, desperately looking for their destinations.

Natalie sighed and stood in the flow of bodies, trying to decide what to do. Her class must have been cancelled. Maybe the speaker hadn't shown up. She hoped that was it, or this would make the second time she'd missed a lecture in this class. And the semester was barely three weeks old. Oh well, she thought, she may as well head back to the dorm. Heaven knew she had plenty of homework to do.

She whirled around, and her backpack sailed away from her shoulder, hitting a tall, athletically built student square in the chest.

Natalie gasped, then put her hands to her face when she saw that he was on crutches. "Oh no!" She reached out and put a hand on his arm. "I am so sorry! Are you all right?"

"Holy cow! Natalie Camfield? What in blazes are *you* doing here?"

She looked up into the twinkling eyes of Evan Greenway. "Evan! Oh, I'm so glad it was only you."

"Well, thanks a lot," he laughed wryly.

She hid her eyes beneath the visor of her hand. "That didn't come out right. I just meant, I'm glad it wasn't —"

"Glad it wasn't a complete stranger you almost steamrolled?" he teased.

"Oh, you know what I mean. I am so sorry," she moaned again. "Are you all right . . . really?"

"I'm fine . . . really." Smiling, he playfully mimicked her tone of voice.

She reached out and put a hand on one of his crutches. "Is this still from . . . the wreck?"

He nodded. "How are you?" he asked. "I haven't seen you in forever."

She dipped her head. "It has been a long time. I wasn't even sure if you'd — well, if you'd finished school."

Evan had not received his diploma with their class. In fact, as far as she knew, he had not been back to Bristol at all after the accident.

"Oh, yeah," he said now. "I graduated. I actually got better grades my last semester — in the hospital — than I ever got when I was healthy. I had plenty of time to study."

"I heard you had several surgeries."

"Five to be exact."

"Wow. Are you done now? Is this it?"

She indicated his crutches again.

"Probably." He lifted the cuff of his wide-leg jeans to reveal a short cast. "I'm supposed to get this off in a couple of weeks, and they'll see where I am then. But I think I'm good to go."

"I'm glad." Natalie suddenly felt awkward with Evan. Seeing him here brought the accident back as freshly as if it had happened yesterday. She felt as though they had unfinished business between them.

In spite of that, she couldn't help but notice that Evan looked wonderful. Aside from the crutches he leaned on, he looked healthy and muscular. His skin was tanned, and his brown hair flaunted highlights that looked as if they'd been put there by the sun. Most noticeable of all, his eyes seemed to hold a glint of something that Natalie hadn't seen there. Not the rebellious edge they'd possessed before. Something good.

"You look great, Evan. Really great."

"Thanks," he beamed. "So do you. It's good to see somebody from home." He looked at his watch. "Hey, are you busy? You want to get some lunch?"

She laughed nervously. "At ten-thirty?"

"Well, okay then . . . something to drink?"

She scrambled to think of an out, then realized she didn't want an excuse. "Sure, why not," she decided, tilting her head toward the empty ballroom. "I'm going to flunk out of this class anyway, since I can't ever seem to find where they meet."

He laughed and steered her toward the open stairway that led to the food court on the first floor. They melted into the flow of the crowd, talking over the din. "So what's your major?" he asked.

"I have no idea," she laughed. "Do you know what you want to do?"

He dipped his head. "I'm thinking about physical therapy. I got a lot of experience at it over the last few months," he said with a shy grin.

"That's wonderful, Evan. Really great." She turned serious. "It — it was hard, wasn't it? The whole accident . . ."

He just nodded, and his thoughts seemed far away. She understood. Her mind wanted to travel the same direction. But she shook it off.

"I heard your folks moved to Kansas City?"

"It was just easier, I guess. They were going up there all the time anyway — to see me in the hospital."

"Weren't you in a hospital in Wichita?"

"Yes, at first. To be honest I barely remember that part. They moved me to Kansas City for a couple of the later surgeries and the physical therapy."

"Oh," she said, not wanting this conversation to carry her where it seemed to be leading. "So are you in the dorms?" she asked.

"Yeah," he said, smiling at her. "I'm in Haymaker."

"You're kidding? I'm in Ford." The two dorms were adjacent to each other on the northeast end of the sprawling campus.

"Seriously?"

"Seriously."

"Great! Maybe we'll see each other around."

She followed him through the line at the coffee shop in the union. Evan ordered a Coke, while Natalie got coffee.

"How can you stand that stuff?" he asked her, wrinkling his nose at her cup.

She giggled. "To be honest, I can't. But isn't that one of the first things you're supposed to learn in college? I thought Coffee Drinking 101 was a freshman requirement. I mean, how else are we supposed to get through all the late-night-cramming-for-finals stuff?" She took a deliberate sip. "They say it's an acquired taste —"

Immediately the words brought back stark memories of another night that they'd discussed acquired tastes in beverages.

They sat in awkward silence for a while, watching the busy parade of students that filed through the wide corridors of the union. After a few minutes, Evan got up to refill his Coke at the fountain. When he came back he was smiling.

"What?" she asked, curious.

"I was just thinking how funny it is that I ran into you."

"Funny?"

"Well, strange funny."

"What do you mean?"

"Well, I" — he rubbed his hands together — "I guess all along I kind of thought I was getting away from Bristol, and — everything that happened there. By going to Kansas City and then coming here, you know? And here, the first thing I do is run into you . . . practically the first week of school. I just think it's kind of interesting."

She tilted her head and wrinkled her brow, entreating a further explanation. He looked at her for a long minute. She could almost see the wheels turning in his mind. He took a deep breath. "Nattie, I don't know how bad you were hurt in the accident — or how you've handled everything since then. I know you and Sara Dever were like this" — he clasped his hands tightly together, demonstrating — "so I'm guessing it was pretty tough on you. But even if you were hurt as seriously as I was — injured, I mean — I'm guessing that the physical part has been nothing compared to the . . . emotional junk."

She nodded slowly, thinking of what to say. "Evan . . . I don't know if you know that I . . . well, I got a DUI for the accident." She stirred her coffee, not meeting his gaze.

"I heard that. I'm sorry. To tell you the truth, I wish I would have gotten one."

"You don't know what you're saying."

"What I really wish is that it'd never happened, that I'd never been there. But since I was — well, I deserved a DUI too."

"But you weren't driving."

"I let Brian drive. 'Friends don't let friends drive drunk,'" he quoted the public service announcement.

Natalie smiled wryly. "And friends don't get behind the wheel — drunk — with their best friend in the passenger seat." She was surprised that she could say it without emotion. In all the months since the accident, she had never spoken the truth so forthrightly to another human being. It felt good to admit it. And it felt especially good to talk to someone who had been there, who truly knew what it had been like.

"So, how do you deal with it?" he asked, as if he'd read her thoughts.

She shrugged. "People have been really good about it. I — I've been offered a lot of . . . forgiveness. I've had a lot of support. But, I guess . . . you don't have much choice. You just . . . deal with it. How about you?"

"Mostly God," he said. "I mean, I've had a lot of support, too. But I've spent an awful lot of time alone. All those hours in the hospital . . . I've had a lot of time to think."

"And what did you think about?"

"Mostly about God." He looked at her as if to gauge her reaction, then blurted, "Do you believe in God, Natalie?"

"Yes. Definitely."

"You know, if you'd asked me that question a year ago, I would have answered the same way . . . and I wouldn't have had the slightest clue what I was saying."

"What do you mean?" Natalie asked.

"You're a churchgoing girl. I remember

271

that. You guys went to the same church Jon and Sara did, right?"

She nodded.

"I never had that. I mean, my folks were good people and all that. I think they even believed in God. But they — We didn't *know* God. But that's all changed now. You know, Nattie, I said I wished the accident had never happened. And I mean that — for Brian and Sara's sake, I truly mean that. But if it wasn't for the accident I might not *know* God, know Jesus personally, as my savior. I know that might sound corny to you, but —"

There was such excitement and discovery in his voice that Natalie couldn't help but feel a surge of joy in her own heart.

"No, Evan. I know exactly what you mean. The same thing's happened to me. I mean, I asked Jesus into my heart when I was a little girl. And I meant it — as much as I could understand things at that age. But I — I guess I kind of forgot about it when I got older. No, I didn't forget about it," she corrected herself. "I was running from it. I think that was the whole reason I was at the party that night."

Evan looked heavenward. "So things are okay between you and him now?"

"Yes. I . . . I still have some things I'm working on, but yes. We're definitely on speaking terms."

He smiled.

They sat in companionable silence, watching the comings and goings of the student union.

After a while, Evan said, "Hey, there's a Bible study group that meets Wednesday nights at this church down by Aggieville." He nodded his head in the general direction of the little community-in-a-community area that was a longstanding institution in this college town. "I've only gone a couple of times, but it was great. It's all college kids. Some really great discussions. You want to come? With me?"

She looked at him, and found it hard to realize that the good-looking, engaging man who sat across from her now was the same Evan Greenway she'd barely tolerated in high school. "I'd love to," she told him, almost without thinking.

"Okay. I'll pick you up in the lobby of Ford at 6:15," he said. "Oh . . . I don't have a car here. Hope you don't mind walking."

"That's a long way to walk on crutches," she said, eyeing the metal contraptions propped against the booth beside him.

"Hey, I wasn't named all-state running back for nothing." He all but swaggered from the waist up.

Now *that* was the Evan Greenway she remembered. "Fine," she laughed, "but I'm not carrying you if you wimp out."

"Not gonna happen," he said, flexing his biceps. Then he pulled the sleeve of his sweatshirt back and looked at his watch. "Oh, man. I better book it. I have to go back and get something in the dorm before my one o'clock."

"You'd better hurry Mr. All-State Running Back," she teased as he got up and left.

Her heart felt strangely lighter as she jogged across campus toward the dorm. She couldn't help but laugh at the irony of it. If anyone had told her, the night she went with Evan Greenway to homecoming at Bristol High, that there would come a day when she would anxiously anticipate seeing him again, she would have laughed them out of town.

Nineteen

Natalie dashed across the hall to the dormitory bathroom, makeup case in hand. She looked at her watch. Evan was probably waiting for her in the lobby right now. She'd stayed at the library far too long, but at least she had enough material to finish the English assignment that was due Friday.

She dusted blush across her cheekbones and applied a smudge of lip gloss. Her hair was in a messy ponytail atop her head, but she didn't have time to do anything different with it. She studied her reflection in the steamed-over mirror. She'd had better days, but this would have to do.

She stuffed everything back into her makeup case, ran back to her room to scrawl a note for her roommate, shrugged into a jacket, and raced down the hall, praying she wouldn't have to wait for the elevator.

When she stepped into the front lobby,

Evan was standing there, holding his wrist-watch to his ear. He wore a bulky lime-green sweatshirt that flattered his tan and made his eyes appear sapphire blue. Why did she not remember him being this good-looking in high school?

"Hi," she said, suddenly feeling nervous. "Have you been waiting long?"

"Just a couple of hours." He grinned. "I was starting to think either my watch was broken or you stood me up."

"I'm sorry. I lost track of time at the library."

"Oh, the studious type, huh? I suppose you're here on a full-ride academic scholarship or something."

"Please. Not hardly. But I do have to keep my grades up if I want my parents' help with tuition."

He eyed the light jacket she wore. "Are you sure you'll be warm enough? It'll be pretty cold when we're coming back tonight."

"I'll be okay."

"Well, I'm not loaning you mine if you wimp out," he said, echoing her rebuke from their last conversation.

Feeling instantly more at ease, she punched him in the arm.

Laughing, he led the way through the

doors of Ford Hall and out into a crisp September evening. They walked in silence, headed south on Manhattan Avenue along the edge of the university grounds. The campus was on the threshold of its usual autumn glory. The recent chill weather had turned the treetops into molten gold and crimson, and the ivy that scaled the distinctive limestone buildings shimmered in the fading evening sunlight. The few leaves that had already fallen crunched underfoot, and the pungent scent of woodsmoke drifted on the air.

Evan managed his crutches effortlessly, gliding gracefully beside Natalie.

"Sheesh, slow down, will you?" Natalie said after she'd struggled to keep up with him for several blocks. She put her hands on her hips and puffed as if she'd just run a mile. Evan beamed.

"Told you they didn't name me —"

"Yeah, yeah," she interrupted, singsonging, "Mr. All-State Running Man."

"Running *man?*" He almost doubled over laughing.

"What?" she said.

"It's running *back,*" he corrected, still laughing.

"Whatever."

"I take it you don't watch much football?"

"Is that the one where they try to get the little white ball through a hoop and score a home run?" she asked.

He howled and turned a pirouette around his crutches in the middle of the sidewalk. "Okay. That does it. Saturday afternoon begins the *real* education of Miss Natalie Camfield."

"Oh, no," she moaned, catching on.

"Oh, yes," he said. "You *will* be in the stands with me bright and early Saturday when the Wildcats kick off."

"How bright and early are we talking?"

"You goose," he joked. "The game starts at two. You can sleep till noon. Unless you want to eat pizza with me before the game." Now his tone was hopeful.

"Sleeping till noon I can handle. But pizza — even better."

"So it's a date?"

"Unless you do something that really annoys me before *this* date is over."

He paused to wrap an arm around one crutch. Balancing himself, he put a hand to his chest and affected a shocked expression. "*Moi?*"

"Yes, you."

"Hey, wait a minute . . ." Now he leaned

on one crutch and faced her. "You said before this *date* is over . . . So this is a date, huh?"

She felt the blood rise to her face. "Well . . . you know what I mean. 'Date' in the 'social engagement' sense of the word."

"Oh, so now we're *engaged?*"

"No! Evan! Good grief!" She folded her arms in front of her. "I'm not saying another word."

"Good idea . . . at the rate you're going, we'll be married, have three kids and a house in the suburbs by the time I get you back to the dorm."

She couldn't hold back the laughter now, and he joined in. His full lips parted to reveal white, even teeth, and his eyes crinkled at the corners when he laughed. *Get a grip, Camfield. It's only Evan, remember?*

They walked for ten minutes before they came to Aggieville. The often-raucous college section of town was relatively quiet early on a Wednesday evening. A couple of the bars and eateries were doing a pretty good business, but most of the shops were closed for the day. and the streets were almost empty.

They continued on a few more blocks until Evan stopped in front of a pale brick church building. A sign in the front declared the facility to be COMMUNITY CHRISTIAN CENTER.

"This way." Evan followed a jog in the sidewalk and led her around to a side entrance. They went through the door and down a narrow flight of stairs, then wove their way through a maze of hallways until the sound of laughter drew them into a room at the end of one hall. There were at least a dozen other college-age students there.

A husky, bearded man jumped up from his perch on a shabby sofa. "Hey, guys! Welcome! Come on in." He extended a hand to Evan. "I'm Rob Gray. You were here last week, right? Evan, isn't it?"

"Yeah." Evan nodded, then turned to Natalie and winked. "This is my date, Natalie Camfield."

"Good to have you here, Natalie. You guys help yourselves" — he indicated a long table laden with drinks and snacks — "and we'll get started in just a minute."

Natalie and Evan found seats together in the circle of castoff sofas and easy chairs that furnished the large room.

A couple of coeds accompanied them on guitar while they sang worship choruses, and then Rob led a short study of the New Testament book of Romans. Natalie didn't take part in the discussion, preferring just to listen, but she was surprised at how vocal — and how articulate — Evan was. Judging from the insights he shared, he had changed a great deal in the months since the accident.

When they walked out of the church around nine o'clock, the sky was dark and there was a nip in the air. Natalie pulled her jacket tighter around her torso and put her head down against the brisk breeze.

"So what did you think?" Evan asked.

"I liked it," she said, honestly. "Rob gets a tad too excited about some of that stuff, but it *was* interesting."

Evan laughed easily and tilted his head toward her. "Wait up," he said and paused. He took off his coat and handed it to her. "Your lips are turning blue," he explained. "Put it on."

Natalie blushed. "But you said —"

"I don't want you to freeze to death on the way home." He smiled, then said, "Wimp."

"Hey!"

They walked back along Manhattan Avenue, and before she knew it, they were standing in front of Ford Hall.

"Thanks for inviting me, Evan," Natalie told him, one hand on the door to the lobby. "It was a fun *date*."

He grinned. "Well, don't forget we have another one Saturday."

"I wouldn't miss it."

"I'll pick you up at noon sharp, okay?"

"I'll be waiting. Oh, don't forget your coat." She took if off and handed it to him, then went inside, and hurried to the stairwell. She ran up to the third floor and watched him from a lobby window until he disappeared into the night. She was still smiling when she flopped onto the bed in her dorm room.

Evan Greenway got off the elevator on the fifth floor of Haymaker, hobbled down the hallway to his room, and turned the key in the lock. Good. His roommate was still out for the night. He and Tom DeVane got along fine, but he wasn't in the mood to answer any questions. Not to mention that he was in terrible pain.

Evan leaned the crutches against the wall and grimaced. He turned his hands over and inspected them. Angry blisters had risen on his palms and on his right hand, a raw sore between his thumb and index finger oozed. Gingerly, he pulled his sweatshirt over his head, along with the long-sleeved T-shirt he wore underneath. The muscles in his arms throbbed. What had he been thinking, walking such a distance tonight? Well, he was going to pay for it, that was for sure. *Macho man, indeed.*

He smiled to himself. It didn't matter. It had been worth it. In spite of the nagging pain he'd managed to hide from her, he had loved every minute he'd spent with Natalie Camfield.

It was strange. After suffering from a desperate crush on the girl since at least the fifth grade, in the months since the accident he'd almost gotten over her. He knew God deserved some of the credit for that. The old Evan Greenway had had some pretty messed-up priorities in his life BTW — before the wreck. In the process of finally getting some things straight — of realizing that he made a lousy lord and master of his own life — he hadn't given Natalie much thought. But wasn't it just like God to allow Natalie back in his life now?

He showered, wincing as the hot water stung the chafed flesh on his hands, but sighing as the heat soothed his aching muscles. Later, as he lay in the dark, his hair damp on the pillow, he wrestled with a troubling thought — a dormant memory that he knew had been disturbed by Natalie's nearness these past few days. He didn't know what she remembered about the night of the accident. They hadn't talked about it since that very first meeting in the student union. His own memories of the events leading up to the tragedy were pretty fuzzy, but he did have one clear image in his mind from that night. It played in his mind like a silent movie now: Natalie in front of him, her face luminous in the flickering light from the bonfire. And him, reaching into a cooler, drawing out a bottle of beer and offering it to her. He couldn't be sure, but given his modus operandi of those days, chances were good that he'd given her more than one beer that night. Did she know that? Did she remember that he'd been the one to supply her "poison" that night?

As he drifted to sleep, he prayed that he would have the courage to talk to her about it. To — What *was* it he needed to do? Ask her forgiveness? Yes. He needed to do that.

The thought terrified him. He longed to bury the memory, pretend it had never been roused. He realized with chagrin that it was within him to do just that — to deny the holy nudging he'd felt only moments ago. Yet he knew that would be wrong. Temptation latched on to him like a snare, and he fell asleep in its hungry claws.

Twenty

The crowd streamed out of the stadium and across the network of parking lots and fields that led back to campus. Natalie had enjoyed the game and had actually learned a few things about football.

Beside her, Evan maneuvered through the mob, using his crutches to cut a wider swath for the two of them.

"I have to admit that was kind of fun, but I still don't see what the big attraction is," she said. "It's just a funny-shaped leather ball, and a bunch of guys in weird outfits are chasing it around."

He secured the crutch under his right arm long enough to slap the ball of his hand against his forehead in mock frustration. "Uniforms, Natalie. Uniforms."

"Huh?"

"Not 'outfits.' They're called *uniforms*."

"Whatever."

He laughed, and she rewarded his good

humor with a smile.

"You want to go somewhere for dinner?"

"Oh, let's just eat at Derby, Evan. You've already spent too much money on pizza at lunch."

"Okay. Do you need to go back to the dorm first?"

She shook her head. "You?"

"Nope. I'm good to go."

They laughed and joked all the way across campus, and it suddenly hit Natalie that she couldn't remember when she'd felt so happy. It had been a long time . . . a very long time.

She looked over at Evan and was troubled to see him wince. He caught her watching him and glanced away, quickly wiping the grimace off his face.

"Hey," she said, "are you okay?"

He nodded and otherwise ignored her question. "I wonder what's on the menu tonight," he said.

"Evan, are you all right? You look like you're in pain."

He stopped midstride, and arranged the crutches side by side in front of him. Then, leaning his elbows atop the crutch handles, he looked her square in the eye. "If you must know, I am in agonizing pain." The truth of his statement was evident in the squint of his eyes and the creases etched on his forehead.

"Evan! What's wrong?"

A strange, embarrassed smile came to his face as he confessed in minced syllables. "These crutches are rubbing my hands raw." He held out his palms for her inspection.

"Oh, ouch," she said. But suddenly, thinking about all his strutting and swaggering the other day, she wanted to laugh. Her efforts to hold in her laugher resulted in a very unladylike snort, and finally she quit trying to appear sympathetic. "So, ol' Mr. All-State Running Back got some bwisters on his widdle hands?" she snickered.

"Okay," he cut in wryly, looking like the proverbial cat who'd just swallowed the canary. "So I'm not quite as macho as you were first led to believe."

She snorted again, and he lifted a crutch and wielded it as a lance. "Stop, I say."

Skipping ahead of him, she parried his blows. With surprising speed, he hobbled after her on one crutch, thrusting the other in her direction. Natalie squealed when she glanced back and realized he was gaining on her. She left the sidewalk, but the path she took went uphill. She stumbled, and the grassy hillside came flying to meet her.

Fortunately, his "weapon" was within handy reach, and she grabbed it for support. Unfortunately, he was off balance when she did so, so when she went down, she dragged him with her.

She landed on her back in a pile of leaves, squeezing her eyes shut as she toppled. But when she heard leaves crunching in her ears, she opened her eyes and saw that Evan was precariously balanced over her, his hands planted on either side of her head, holding him up. She struggled to sit up, which undid the tentative chance Evan had of remaining upright.

They both went sprawling, and when she opened her eyes again, Evan was gazing at her with an expression on his handsome face that could only be interpreted as "I want to kiss you."

For one moment panic rose in her. He was going to ruin everything. She wasn't ready for their relationship to move so quickly. But before she could think of an escape, he struggled to his feet and turned away from her. He bent at the waist and began vigorously brushing crushed leaves from his hair.

"Are you okay?" he asked, breathless.

She could only nod.

As if he'd just realized she was still on the ground, he said, "Here, let me help you."

She took the hand he offered, and he pulled her up in one smooth motion, but when she let go he clenched his blistered palm in pain.

"Ooh, sorry about that," she said, taking his hand, turning it over, and inspecting the raw flesh. "That looks painful."

"I'm okay," he said between gritted teeth. He pressed his fingers to hers, matching fingertip to fingertip, and they stood that way for several seconds, not speaking.

She'd felt grateful that she had evaded his kiss, but now, with his warm fingers gently intertwined with hers, and his gaze upon her, she wondered if she was in any less peril. She willed her heart to begin beating again and wrested her hand from his grasp, ostensibly brushing grass and leaves from her own hair and clothing.

"I didn't hurt you, did I?" he asked. The genuine concern in his voice touched her.

"I'm fine." She forced a laugh, then turned serious. "Are you okay?"

"I'm fine." As if to prove it, he hopped over to collect the crutches, which had gone two different directions in the skirmish.

She giggled.

"What?" he asked, a hint of amusement in his own voice.

"I wish somebody had caught that on video." She giggled harder.

"No you don't," he assured her.

"Seriously. I don't think we could repeat that again if we choreographed it. Not like we'd want to," she added quickly.

He gave her a sidewise glance. "Oh, I don't know. It was actually kind of fun."

"Are you kidding? My heart is still beating a hundred beats a minute."

"Yeah, I have that effect on all the women."

You have no idea, buddy, she thought.

Man! You blew it, Greenway! he chided himself. *Why didn't you just kiss her and get it over with? You know you wanted to.*

He had just walked Natalie to Ford Hall and was headed back to Haymaker. He hadn't tried to kiss her good night there either. Two perfect opportunities blown. And he'd had the sneaking impression that she wanted him to kiss her as badly as he wanted to oblige. He must be losing his nerve. He'd never been hesitant with the

290

ladies before. He'd always been a smooth talker and a smoother performer.

But Natalie was different. She was special.

And he was different now too, he reminded himself. Maybe that was the deeper reason. If his priorities had truly changed since he'd started trying to live for a higher purpose, then what was his hurry?

The old fear rose in him, and he felt a strong urge to call Natalie. He needed to hear in her voice that she felt about him the way he did about her.

He took the elevator to his floor and let himself into the cluttered dorm room. Almost without thinking, he crossed to his desk and picked up the phone. *No. Wait.* He set the receiver back in its cradle.

He sighed. What was really going on? As he had awakened to the spiritual side of himself, he had learned that his motives were often different than even he realized. "Show me the truth, Lord," he whispered. "What's going on here? With me? Show me *your* truth."

He slumped into the desk chair and put his head in his hands, purposefully quieting his mind, listening for the still, quiet voice that had so recently become familiar to him.

After a while, a feeling of peace settled over him. And as though someone had drawn a diagram, he suddenly knew what was really eating at him. He smiled to himself, thinking that if his roommate were to walk in now and see him carrying on this conversation, he would never understand.

Now his smile faded as he faced the revelation of his motives. He had gone to sleep just three nights before feeling deeply convicted that he needed to confess to Natalie the role he had played in the accident — even in her being convicted of the DUI charge.

But now he saw a deceitful, scheming side of himself that had hoped to "capture" Natalie — or at least her affections — before he made his confession. He had sought to give her a deeper incentive to forgive him. How unfair that would have been to her. He resolved that moment that he would not go forward one more step with Natalie until he had asked for her forgiveness. And he would accept the "verdict," whatever it might be.

He sent up a hopeful prayer that he would be granted the gift of Natalie's forgiveness. He didn't dare to pray that he might also, eventually, be beneficiary to the gift of her love.

Natalie slid from behind the cramped desk, hiked her backpack onto one shoulder, and filed out of the classroom with the rest of the students. High-tech tennis shoes and Gore-Tex boots echoed on the tiled floors of the antiquated Anderson Hall.

When she reached the exit, Natalie was surprised to see that it was raining. *Rats!* She'd not thought to bring an umbrella. Sara would never have been caught umbrella-less. She smiled at the thought. Thanks to Maribeth's indoctrination, Sara Dever could always be counted on to have rain protection in her car, in her book bag, in her locker. The girl must have owned half a dozen umbrellas. It had been one of her delightful quirks.

Natalie stood in a portico by the door, waiting for the rain to let up, watching the chaos the downpour had created. Students raced across campus, books and backpacks tented over their heads. Several girls sought shelter in Anderson Hall, yelping and groaning as they wrung icy rainwater from their hair and clothing.

Natalie thought again of Sara, and waited for the familiar ache of sadness and regret to come over her. Perhaps they would have gone to different colleges, gone their separate ways by now, but she couldn't help but think for a minute what fun it would have been to have Sara here on campus. Maybe even sharing a dorm room. Natalie and her roommate, Amy Stinson, got along fine, but Amy was no Sara Dever. No, there would never be another Sara. Never.

"Nattie! Hey!"

A familiar voice broke into her reverie, and she looked up to see Jon Dever standing in front of her, water dripping in rivulets down his face, off his nose.

"Jon! Oh, you're soaked!"

"Tell me about it. And the sad thing is I've got the world's best umbrella right here." He grinned awkwardly, with that same twinge of sadness that Natalie had seen on his face before and patted the soggy knapsack slung over his shoulder. "I was halfway across campus and the sky just opened up. I was drenched before I could even *say* 'umbrella.' " He slid the knapsack off his shoulder, unzipped it, and knelt down to rummage inside.

Nikki and Jon were still dating and as serious as ever. Of course Natalie knew Jon was here at K-State, but in the month since school started, this was the first time she had run into him. She felt suddenly uneasy, wishing she knew what to say to him to make things right. Nikki and Maribeth had both tried to make excuses for him, assuring Natalie that Jon would "come around." But she wondered.

"Are you headed to class?" he asked, standing up with the umbrella in hand.

She nodded. "I've got a ten o'clock in Denison, but I refuse to arrive looking like" — she pointed at his wet attire — "like that."

He gave a short laugh. "Well, hey, I'm heading that way. Would you . . . want to share an umbrella?" He pushed a button, and the canopy mushroomed, filling half the entryway.

She hesitated a moment, feeling a tug at her heartstrings. Jon still had a beloved place in her affections — maybe he always would — but at this moment it was more that he reminded her of Sara. How strange that Jon should appear just when she had been thinking of her friend. And with an umbrella, no less.

Deciding suddenly, she pulled her jacket tight around herself and ducked under the canopy beside him. "Let's make a run for it."

Without another word, he pushed open

the heavy glass door, maneuvered the huge umbrella through the space, and took her arm. They ran, skipping over puddles on the sidewalk, heads together, trying to stay dry.

It was disconcerting being so close to him. Memories of her childhood crush fell with the rain. Natalie breathed in the citrus scent of his shampoo and felt a twinge of guilt at the thoughts that danced at the edge of her consciousness.

Jon delivered her to Denison Hall dry, save for her boots and the hem of her jeans. They stood under the awning that covered the walkway in front of the building that housed the English department.

"Well, thanks for the . . . rescue," she said, feeling awkward and uncertain.

"Anytime," he said. His smile seemed genuine.

Natalie surprised herself with her next words. "You know," she said, pointing to his umbrella, "I always think of Sara when I see an umbrella. She would have loved that one."

"It was hers, actually, Nattie."

Was she imagining the hard edge to his voice? "Oh . . . it was?" Tears sprang to her eyes.

"Yeah." He looked at the ground, and Natalie wasn't sure if he was fighting the emotion of missing Sara, or if he was fighting feeling angry with her.

"I'm sorry, Jon. I'm so sorry." She felt better just for having said the words.

Head still bent, he looked up at her through hooded eyes, holding out a hand as if to keep her at a distance. "I know. I know you are, Nattie."

For an awkward minute they stood, not speaking. "Well, thanks again for the umbrella," Natalie said finally. "I'll probably see you around."

"Yeah, sure."

Jon had just turned to leave when Natalie spotted Evan Greenway coming out of the building.

"Hey, Nattie!" Evan shouted when he noticed her.

Jon heard Evan and turned around. Natalie didn't miss his slight hesitation when he realized it was Evan Greenway who had called out her name. But Jon didn't turn away. He came to meet Evan, putting out a hand. "Hey, man. How's it going? I didn't know you were up here at school."

Watching them, Natalie could tell that Evan, too, was apprehensive about seeing

297

Jon for the first time since Sara's accident. But the two shook hands.

"It's been awhile," Jon said now. "I don't think I've seen you since I graduated."

"Yeah," Evan said. "I heard you were up here, but you know how that goes. It's a big campus. Natalie's the only one from Bristol I've even crossed paths with yet."

"I just ran into Nattie today for the first time too," Jon told him. He turned to her. "So, you knew Evan was here?"

She felt her face flush. "Yes," she told Jon. "We ran into each other, like, the third week of school."

" 'Ran into' being the operative words," Evan told Jon, with a wry grin. "She practically killed me."

Natalie laughed, but inside she cringed at Evan's use of the word *killed*. Every word seemed ripe with double meaning.

But their conversation was polite enough. Natalie stood and listened while they caught up on each other's lives.

After a while, Jon nodded toward Evan's crutches. "So, how are you getting along?"

"I'm all right," Evan told him. "I'm through with surgeries at least."

"That's good." Tension filled the air again, and finally Jon looked at his watch and gave a low whistle. "I've really got to run," he said. "But, hey, good seeing you guys."

"You too," Evan and Natalie said together.

When Jon had gone, Evan draped an arm casually around Natalie's shoulders. "He's a nice guy. I . . . I'm not sure I could have stood there and been so nice — to us."

"I know," she said.

"Speaking of which . . . I'd like to talk about that, Nattie . . ." He kicked at a leaf that the rain had plastered to the cement. "There's something I need to get off my chest. Could you meet me at Derby for dinner tonight?"

She looked at him carefully, knowing her curiosity was emblazoned on her face. "Okay. Sure. What time?"

"Maybe six?"

"So I'll just meet you there?"

"Six o'clock."

She nodded, and they hurried off to their separate classes.

She may as well have skipped her next class for all the attention she paid the lecture. She wondered what Evan wanted to talk to her about. She couldn't imagine, but he'd seemed awfully nervous and uncertain. Perhaps it had to do with Jon.

Running into Jon like that, and being re-minded of Sara and all that had happened, had certainly left her emotions in a knot. She wondered how many years would have to pass, how far from Bristol she'd have to go, before the reminders would stop catching her unawares. She wondered if anyone could ever truly forgive what she'd done.

Twenty-One

The cafeteria was crowded, and it took Natalie a few minutes to spot Evan. But there he was, leaning on his crutches, waving madly, flashing that charismatic smile — one she was quickly coming to adore. She snaked her way toward him through the crush of bodies.

"Hey, Nat," he said when she was within hearing.

Sara was the only one who had ever called her that, but she liked Evan's nickname for her and smiled when she heard it. He closed the short distance between them and gave her a quick hug. She was learning that Evan was a physical person. It had been disconcerting to her at first, always having him reach out for a hug or to throw an arm around her shoulder, but she had quickly become comfortable with it, realizing that it was simply his way of showing friendly affection.

"What're they serving tonight?"

"Can't you smell?"

She took a whiff. "Mmm, something Italian. Lasagna?"

"Spaghetti, I think," he said.

They went through the line and found a table. Natalie tried to make conversation, but Evan seemed preoccupied. Her curiosity about what he wanted to talk to her about edged up a notch.

When they'd cleared their table and had started back toward the dorms, Evan turned to her. "Did you remember that I want to talk to you about something?"

She gave him a sidewise glance and nodded.

"Where do you want to go?" he asked. "I think Tom's studying for a test tonight, so the dorm probably isn't a good idea."

"I'm not sure what Amy's doing," she said. "Do you want to go to the library?"

"Sure. That'd be good."

They crossed campus and entered Hale Library. The massive facility was built in the gothic architectural style to match the original wing. Inside, they found a quiet spot in the first floor study hall. They claimed two overstuffed chairs flanking a low end table, then took off their jackets and piled them on a nearby table. Natalie slipped her boots off and curled up, stocking-footed, in the chair. Evan sat slumped in his chair, his hands tented in front of his face, one foot nervously tapping the carpet.

"Okay," she said, trying to keep her tone light. "Out with it."

He looked at her out of the corner of one eye, barely turning his head. "I don't know where to begin."

"At the beginning?"

He cleared his throat. "Man, Nattie. I've been trying to get up the nerve to talk to you for a week now. I . . . I don't even know where the beginning is. Seeing Jon kind of brought everything crashing back."

She waited, suddenly afraid of what he was going to say.

Evan scooted up in the chair, turned slightly toward her, and took a deep breath. Eyeing a couple of coeds engrossed in conversation at a table at the opposite end of the large room, he dropped his voice to a low whisper. "Nattie. I . . . want to talk about the wreck. About that night. I don't know what you remember about . . . about the party . . ."

He waited, as though he hoped she would fill him in, but she wasn't going to make it that easy.

"There's something I need to get off my chest." His Adam's apple bobbed in his throat. "I know that I — I gave you something to drink that night. You might not remember . . . I mean, I hardly remembered it until recently. But Brian and I had bought a whole cooler full of stuff that night, and I was handing it out like candy at Halloween. I was so —" He stopped short, looked at the floor, and raked his fingers through his hair before he spoke again. "I was so glad to see you walk up that night. You don't know how many times I'd fantasized about that — about you coming to one of the parties out there, and us, well, you know . . . being together. I wanted to impress you so badly. Anyway, I gave you a beer . . . maybe more than one, I honestly don't remember —"

She reached out and put a hand gently on his arm. "Evan, I do remember that. But I've never blamed *you*. Not once. I mean, it's not like you were forcing it down my throat. I could have said no. Sara managed to refuse you."

He shook his head. "I guess I never thought about that. Man, I *hate* what I was back then, Nat. It's just so weird. I thought I was so stinkin' cool. I look back not even a year later now, and I wonder, what was I thinking? Where was my brain? You know?"

She nodded. Oh, how she knew. She'd asked herself those very questions again and again.

"I hope you know that I've changed since then, Nat." His eyes had the hopeful shine of a puppy at the pound.

"Oh, Evan, of course I know that. Hey, you're looking at someone who knows exactly what you're talking about. I thought I was pretty cool that night too." A lump lodged in her throat, and she bowed her head. "What I wouldn't give for a do-over of that night."

He nodded slowly. "I know. I've thought that myself . . . a thousand times. Still . . . I want to ask your forgiveness. For my own sake." He looked at her now and leaned across the low table between them to take her hand. He sandwiched it between both of his, and a tiny shiver went up her spine. "Will you forgive me, Natalie? I'm so sorry for my part in the whole thing. Please forgive me."

His voice was steady, and she had the impression that he had rehearsed his speech. Tears sprang to her eyes, and she swiped at them with the back of her free hand. His hands felt wonderfully warm, and his touch was excruciatingly tender.

"Of course I forgive you, Evan," she whispered. "I'm just sorry it's bothered you for so long. You should have said something long before this. There was no reason to . . . to . . . agonize over it all this time."

"Oh, but there was."

She met his gaze with knitted brows. "What do you mean?"

He sighed and brought her hand to his lips. "I probably don't have to tell you that I've been crazy about you half my life."

She smiled, but underneath, her mind was racing, scared to death that he was going to say something they'd both re-gret — like "marry me."

He returned her smile and said, "I don't want to rush you. Maybe we aren't even — I don't know — *meant* to be. But I couldn't go one more step with you until I was sure that you knew the truth about my role in the accident and until I knew that you would forgive me for it."

She shifted in the chair. He let go of her hand, but she sensed his reluctance to do so.

"You know," she said wryly. "It's actually kind of nice to be on the other end of this forgiveness thing for a change."

He smiled, and the sweetness in his expression emboldened her to try to explain to him how deep her guilt ran, how confused and alone she sometimes felt. It was after ten o'clock when they left the library. Evan walked her back to the dorm, and when he left her at the door, he gave her the usual hug. He didn't try to kiss her, but she guessed that they both sensed something had changed tonight; and that first kiss wouldn't be long coming now.

To her surprise, the thought made Natalie's heart feel lighter.

Thanksgiving Day dawned cold and clear. Daria Hunter awakened with a light heart. For the first time in almost three months, her family was all together under one roof, Natalie sleeping in Nicole's old bed in the room that Noelle now had to herself.

Though they'd talked on the phone often and exchanged e-mails several times a week since Natalie left for college, she had not been home until now. Cole and Daria were both elated by the changes they saw in their daughter.

"It's like we have the old Nattie back," Cole had whispered in Daria's ear last night as she lay in his arms before they drifted off to sleep.

It was true. The bitter, wounded child who had lived in this house before had seemingly been replaced by a more mature version of the carefree little girl they cherished so much.

In the few short hours Natalie had been home, they'd heard the name *Evan Greenway* no less than a dozen times. Daria couldn't help but wonder how much the boy had to do with Natalie's newfound happiness. She prayed that it wasn't merely a case of the wounded comforting the wounded. And yet, from the things Natalie said, it seemed that Evan Greenway had done some growing up himself in the months since the tragedy.

The anniversary of Sara's death had passed quietly a few weeks ago. Daria wondered too if traversing that milestone had been a relief to Natalie. It had certainly been so for her and Cole.

Daria had taken Maribeth to lunch, to a new little café that had opened in Clayton. They had marked the anniversary with shared tears. But the day had been mostly a joyful celebration of their friendship, of the fact that time had already begun to heal some of the pain. And that because of Jon and Nicole's growing romance, they, too, had a hopeful future of shared holidays and celebrations, and eventually, God willing, shared grandchildren.

Beside her, Cole stirred. "You getting up?" he asked, squinting at the digital alarm clock on his nightstand. "Don't you have to get the turkey in the oven?"

"In a few minutes," she said, rolling toward him and nestling into the warm shoulder he offered. She breathed in the familiar, sleepy scent of him and thought that today it would not be difficult to give thanks for the blessings in her life.

"Hey, sleepyhead," a voice very close to her ear said.

Natalie mumbled and pulled the quilt over her head. She was awake now, but the dream still perched on the edge of her consciousness like a vulture.

"Come on, Nattie, wake up." Noelle's voice was a pleasant distraction.

Natalie threw off the covers and sat up in bed, rubbing her eyes, trying to erase the last vestiges of the nightmare. Her younger sister scrambled to the end of the bed and sat there, smiling, rocking on her knees. Though Noelle had grown taller and her figure had begun to bud, she still had the look of a little girl. Natalie kicked her playfully from under the quilts and sent her sprawling.

"What's your big hurry, Noey?"

"Don't call me that!" Noelle shrieked.

But Natalie recognized an old game in her sister's protest, and she played along. "Okay, Noey. Whatever you say."

"Stop it! I'll tell Mom."

The two tussled on the bed until Natalie, decidedly on the losing end of the scuffle, finally gave in.

"We better go see if Mom needs help with dinner," she told Noelle. "Do you know what time Grandma and Grandpa are coming?"

"I think they said eleven. But you know Grandma. They'll probably get here at ten. Did you know you snore?"

"I do not!"

"Yes, you do. I tossed and turned half the night because you were over there sawing logs."

"I was not — Noey!"

And they were at it again. The door burst open, and Nicole joined the fracas.

"I sure do like your room, Nattie," Nicole said when all three finally lolled, out of breath, on the beds.

"Oh, so you admit it's my room?"

"Excuse me — your *former* room."

"Your old bed is pretty comfortable, actually. Although I did have trouble sleeping with all the snoring going on." Natalie looked meaningfully in Noelle's direction.

"That was *you!*" Noelle shot back playfully.

"Was not."

"Was too."

Ten minutes later, Natalie padded down the hall to the bathroom with a smile on her face. It was so good to be home.

In the shower though, flashes of the nightmare returned. It was torture to relive that last night of Sara's life over and over again, as her dreams compelled her to do, and yet she was strangely drawn to the mental images of her friend. Sara always seemed so real, so alive, in her dreams.

Natalie adjusted the faucet and let the sharp needles of scalding water pelt her, wishing she could wash away the heaviness that lingered in her spirit as easily as she washed the grime from her body.

Twenty-Two

It was hotter than blazes inside the hut. David Chambers sighed and pushed his stool away from the desk. He peeled the sweat-damp shirt away from his back, then kneaded his temples with tapered fingertips, trying to tame the monster of a headache that had stalked him all morning. "Need an aspirin?" Nathan Camfield asked, eyeing him from behind his own desk.

"Maybe. I can't seem to shake this thing."

Nate closed the laptop he'd been working on, opened a drawer, and tossed David a small brown bottle. The younger man nodded his thanks and downed two of the tablets with the cold dregs of his morning coffee.

"Will you have some e-mail ready to send when I go to San José next week?" David asked, inclining his head toward the computer.

His colleague nodded, opening the laptop again.

A few minutes later, Nate burst out laughing.

David looked up, startled, but Nate continued to gaze at the computer screen, chuckling. "I guess you had to be there," David said wryly.

"Oh, sorry," Nate said as though he'd just realized that he had laughed aloud. "I'm just reading an e-mail from Natalie."

"Ah," David said. "I take it things are going well with her?"

Nate looked up and smiled. "Things are going great, actually. She seems to be thriving in college."

"That's good," David replied. Then, with mock accusation, "Although I don't see how she could be doing *too* well in a place like that."

It was a running joke between the two University of Kansas graduates. David liked to give Nate a hard time for allowing his daughter to go over to "the dark side" of KU's Division I rival, Kansas State.

"Hey, I've had to swallow my pride, Chambers," he said. "I think you're just going to have to learn to do the same." His expression turned serious. "I can't tell you how relieved I am to know that she's getting along so well. It's been a rough road for that girl. It's hard to believe she's about to finish her second year of college already."

"Well, I'm glad things are going well for her. It's nice that she's been writing you so often."

Nate nodded his agreement and leaned back in his chair, balancing the laptop on one knee. "I don't mind telling you that it's been the biggest blessing of the past two years — getting to know Nattie a little better. You know, when I came back here, I never thought . . ." His voice trailed off and he looked away, as though embarrassed by his show of emotion. But he swallowed hard and continued, "I never thought I'd get a chance to have any kind of relationship with my daughter. Who would have thought an invention like e-mail would make it possible?"

David smiled. "Pretty amazing, isn't it?"

Being the only two Americans in Timoné, David Chambers and Dr. Camfield had spent hours discussing their families and friends back in the States and sharing the emotional struggles and heartaches each had brought to the jungle with them. And though the man wasn't quite old enough to be his father, David's relationship with Nate was the one he'd always longed to have with his own absent, uncaring father. The friendship that had grown between him and Nate was truly one of the foremost blessings of his thirty-two years. He sometimes suspected that God had called him to Timoné more for his own sake than for the benefit of the people for whom he hoped to translate the gospel.

"Ready for a lunch break?" Nate asked now, glancing at his watch.

David looked at his own watch. "I'd better not yet. I really want to finish with this first." He indicated the stack of papers scattered across his desk. "But thanks. I'll grab something later."

"Okay. I guess I'll run by and check on Carlos on my way home."

Still sharp of mind, Carlos Muentes was the patriarch of Timoné, and though there was no way to know for sure, village lore claimed that the man was one hundred and ten years old.

"I don't think the man is long for this earth," Nate said, shaking his head.

"That's what you said six months ago," David reminded him with a wry smile.

Nate gave him a glib wave that seemed to say "touché" and left the office whistling a tuneless air.

David capped his pen and rose from the hard stool that served as his desk chair. He stretched his weary muscles and sighed heavily. In spite of his prayers to the contrary, a fog of melancholy had settled over him. Sometimes he felt elated that he had accomplished so much in his short time working with the translation of the Timoné dialect. Other days he felt his was a nearly impossible task and that even if he lived to be as old as Carlos, he would still be a thousand years from realizing his goal. This day was definitely one of the latter.

He gathered the reams of word lists and computer printouts he'd been working on and shuffled them into two semi-tidy piles. If only he had some help. Of course, Nate assisted him with the translating whenever he could, and David had begun to work with some of the Timoné people. But Dr. Camfield's role here was as a physician, and he couldn't be expected to sacrifice the care of the people for David's work.

He eased his tall frame back onto the stool, scooted up to the desk, and arranged the pages of the word lists in front of him again. Stroking his beard, he did some quick calculations. He was already putting in fifty hours or more each week, but maybe if he added just one extra hour each day, he could begin to feel that he was making some headway.

Natalie put the heavy books on the checkout counter and waited for the librarian to scan them. She wasn't looking forward to lugging these all the way back to the dorm, but she needed them for a history paper that was due Friday.

She managed to zip the volumes into her backpack, hoisted it onto her shoulder, and pushed open the wide doors that led outside. She smiled to herself as the balmy air hit her face. Spring was in the wings, and her heart felt lighter just thinking about it. She was almost at the halfway mark of her college years. Where had the time gone? It seemed as though only yesterday she was packing up her room at home and moving into the dorm, an anxious, wounded, but beginning-to-heal teenager.

She had grown up a lot in the past two years. And yet even after all this time, she had so many regrets for the way her life had turned out. Sometimes her guilt over Sara's death hounded her until she wasn't sure she could bear up under the weight of it. Too often she awakened in the middle of the night feeling a pressure in her chest that she knew no medicine would relieve.

It helped to have Evan to talk to about these things, but even Evan Greenway couldn't completely take away the sting. Still, his presence in her life was a blessing. The profound history they shared had forged a steadfast bond between them. Together they had hashed and rehashed their thoughts and feelings about the tragedy that had so changed their lives. And together they had come to a tentative peace about what had happened to them. It was good to have someone with whom they could each openly acknowledge their guilt, but also rejoice in their redemption.

Natalie didn't know what the future held with Evan. It was hard to contemplate, when she was still struggling to know what she wanted to be when she grew up. Although they'd acknowledged the chemistry that existed between them, they'd also agreed to take it slowly. Still, neither of them had dated anyone else since that first impromptu meeting in the student union over two years ago now.

She slowed her pace, deep in thought. She did love Evan. And he had told her that he loved her too. But she sometimes wondered if their love for each other was based too much on mutual sympathy, even on a strange gratitude to each other because they could share the history of the tragic accident that had taken their friends' lives.

Her thoughts were interrupted by the muted jangling of her cell phone beneath the canvas of her backpack.

Without breaking stride, she slid the bag off her shoulder and rummaged through it, searching for the phone. It was probably Evan. He had invited her to go with him to a film in the student union tonight. She was tired, and she had a ton of homework, but she'd probably go. It had been a few days since they'd been able to spend any time together, and she missed him.

She pressed a button on the face of the trim phone. "Hello?"

"Hey, Nattie!" her sister's voice chirped. "I was beginning to think you weren't going to answer."

"Oh, hey, Nikki. What's up?"

It had been good to have her sister on the same campus this year, although the two sometimes went for days without running into each other.

"Where are you, Nattie? Right this minute."

There was a peculiar tone in her sister's voice.

"Why?" Natalie asked. "What's going on?"

Nicole giggled. "Just tell me where you are," she insisted.

Natalie stopped in the middle of the sidewalk. She turned three hundred and sixty degrees on the walkway, as though she might see Nicole lurking behind one of the huge oak trees on the lawn. "I just — left the library. I'm on my way back to the dorm. What is going on? Where are *you?*" she persisted.

"I'm just leaving Ford. Just keep heading this way. I'll meet you halfway."

"Nikki! What —"

The phone clicked and went dead.

Quickening her pace, Natalie headed north, her mind reeling with possibilities. Had something happened at home? But no, whatever it was must be good news. Nicole had definitely seemed happy and excited, not worried or upset.

A few minutes later, she spotted her sister walking — no, trotting — toward her on the walk. "Hey! What's up?" she yelled, lengthening her stride.

Nicole ran the last few steps, closing the distance between them, and almost bowled Natalie over with a bear hug.

Natalie struggled to get out of her clutch. "Nicole Hunter, if you don't tell me what is going on this very second, I'm going to strangle you!"

Nicole released her, laughing joyously. She backed away a bit and held out her left hand. "Oh, Nattie, look." Just as suddenly as she had laughed, tears sprang to her eyes.

A glint caught Natalie's eye, and she grabbed her sister's hand. An expensive-looking diamond solitaire glittered on her sister's ring finger. "Nikki!" she shrieked. "You got your ring!"

"Jon gave it to me for my birthday," she beamed.

Natalie pulled her sister into a hug again. "I can't believe it. You're engaged? Oh, Nikki — Hey, wait a minute," she protested good-naturedly, "your birthday's not until April."

"Jon couldn't wait." Nicole grinned. "He picked it up this morning and officially proposed over lunch at Applebee's."

Natalie gave her sister another squeeze, genuinely happy for her. "Oh, Nikki, I can hardly believe it. My little sister, soon to be a married woman. Have you set a date?"

"Over Christmas," Nicole said.

"Really? Have you told Mom and Dad yet?"

"No. I haven't told anybody. You're the first."

Natalie felt tears well unexpectedly behind her eyelids. "Oh, I am so happy for you."

They started back toward the dorm together, chattering like the squirrels that played on the telephone wires overhead.

"Can I tell Evan?" Natalie asked, before they parted ways in the lobby of the dorm.

"You can tell the whole world as far as I'm concerned. Well, wait . . . better tell him not to say anything until I call Mom and Daddy and Noelle." Nicole cocked her head and eyed Natalie. "I bet you'll be next, Nattie. I bet you and Evan will be following us down the aisle."

"Whoa, whoa!" Natalie held up a hand, palm out. "Slow down there, sister. I don't think so."

"Well, don't say I didn't tell you so," Nicole said, a lilt in her voice and a teasing gleam in her gold-flecked brown eyes.

"No, Nikki, I'm serious." She shook her head vigorously. She didn't want any rumors starting. "We haven't even discussed the subject."

The doors to the elevator glided closed, and if Nicole responded it was lost in the soft hum of the conveyance's motor.

Natalie took the stairs to her floor two at a time, her mind racing. So Nicole was getting married. Not that she was surprised by the news. Everyone had always known that Jon and Nicole would end up married. But this was sooner than she'd expected.

She wondered what it would be like for Jon to be officially a part of their family — present at every Thanksgiving table, every Christmas gathering. Would he find it easier to forgive her when she was his sister-in-law? Or would she be an even harsher reminder of the true sister he'd lost? *Oh, Father, will the pain ever stop? Will every good thing that happens always be ruined by memories of what I did?* She stopped short, realizing how self-centered she was being. *Help me be happy for Nicole.*

She thought about what Nicole had said about her being next. Did she dare to dream that she might someday know the same kind of happiness that Nicole had found with Jon? Could Nicole be right? Was Evan part of the future God had in mind for her?

Twenty-Three

The strains of Lohengrin's "Bridal Chorus" filled the sanctuary. From her place beside the other bridesmaids at the front of the church, Natalie watched her sister come down the aisle on Daddy's arm. Nicole Hunter's smile, the beatific glow on her face, said it all. This was the fulfillment of her dreams, the thing she had desired above all things since she and Jon Dever had fallen in love as young teenagers.

Natalie stole a furtive glance at Jon, who stood soldier-stiff at the helm of the contingent of groomsmen. He was as handsome as ever, and there was no mistaking the love in his eyes as he watched his bride walk slowly toward him.

For a brief instant, old feelings welled up inside Natalie — the ache of longing for what might have been, the niggling pangs of jealousy at seeing one of her sisters get all the attention. When she was thinking rationally, she could recognize the feelings for what they were: vestiges of her first innocent crush and remnants of the insecurities that had plagued her for too much of her childhood.

And regret. She would probably always feel a twinge of regret for what could never be changed. But relics though they were, the emotions still stung sometimes — especially on a day like today. *Sara.* Sara Dever should have been standing here beside her. Oh, how tender Sara's memory was on this day. Natalie could look out at the wedding guests and see it in the faces of Sara's parents — Maribeth's valiant effort at a joyful demeanor betrayed by the missing sparkle in her eyes. Don's furrowed forehead, and hair gone gray too early, gave him away. And everywhere she looked, friends of Sara. People who would never again be graced with the gift of Sara's sweet smile or the joy of her laughter. And all of them knowing full well Natalie's part in their loss. *I'm so sorry, Sara.*

She shook off the mounting accusations and sought out Evan's face in the congregation. She found him, gazing at her with the same fervor in his eyes that she saw in Jon's when he looked at Nicole. *Oh, Evan.*

I don't know if I can ever be worthy of that gaze, ever deserve such love.

She was halfway through college now — finally the adult she'd always longed to be. So why did she still so often feel like a confused little girl who didn't know what she wanted from life?

Nicole reached the foot of the altar, and Daddy placed her hand in Jon's. Natalie could read in the tension of her father's jaw that his emotions were close to the surface. She couldn't help but wonder what she would see on his face on *her* wedding day. *Probably relief,* she smiled to herself.

When the pastor asked, "Who gives this woman in holy matrimony?" Daddy answered in a quavering voice, "Her mother and I." Nicole and Jon presented red roses to each of their mothers and laid a pink rose on the altar in memory of Sara. Then Natalie turned with the rest of the wedding party to face the altar as Jon and Nicole ascended the platform. Nicole offered her a bright smile as she relinquished her bridal bouquet to Natalie for safekeeping while they exchanged their vows. Natalie returned the smile and forced herself to focus on the present, to celebrate this most consecrated day in her sister's life.

In voices that were strong and sure, Jon

Dever and Nicole Hunter promised to love, honor, and cherish each other until death parted them. And as the last notes of Mendelssohn's "Wedding March" floated away, and Natalie took the arm of the best man to follow her sister and new brother-in-law down the aisle and out of the church, she compelled her saddened heart into submission, surrendering up a prayer of gratitude.

She caught Evan's eye once more, and the smile that upturned the corners of her mouth was true, the light that twinkled in her eyes genuine.

Daria Hunter balanced on the top rung of the stepladder and paused to wipe beads of perspiration from her forehead. She blew a wayward strand of hair from her eyes and took another box down from the top shelf of the big walk-in closet in their bedroom. How in the world had they managed to accumulate so much junk in the few short years they'd lived here? She corrected herself. The years had been short, but not so few.

Holding a stack of dusty shoeboxes in the crook of one arm, she climbed down the ladder and took them out into the bedroom and stacked them on the end of the bed. Blowing a cloud of dust off the lid, she opened the first one. Peeling away a layer of brittle tissue paper, she smiled as she recognized the low-heeled pumps she'd worn at her wedding to Cole. The ivory satin was yellowed with age, and the shoes were hopelessly out of style. She rewrapped each shoe carefully and nestled them back in the box.

Two decades had passed since the day Cole had carried her over the threshold of this farmhouse on their wedding day. Oh, how time had stolen away those years. But they'd been given many happy memories in return.

A tear slid down her cheek, and she felt guilty for feeling gloomy when there was so much for which to be joyful. Nicole and Jon were married and due home from their honeymoon at the end of the week. Noelle was halfway through her senior year of high school. And Natalie — *oh, dearest Natalie* — finally seemed to be healing from the wounds of her youth. Her eldest daughter still had another week of Christmas break before beginning the second semester of her third year at the university. Their time with her had been a treasure.

Yes, it had been a wonderful winter.

Filled with emotion and impending good-byes, but wonderful all the same.

Daria put the wedding shoes in the pile designated for the church's rummage sale. One couldn't save *everything*. She opened the next box.

The sight of the cassette tapes and newspaper clippings caused her heart to leap. Keepsakes of Nate. The memories came crashing back, as clear as if they had happened yesterday. And yet, somehow the things that had happened to them — to her and Nate and Cole — seemed at the same time surreal.

Picking up one of the audiocassettes, she read the label. *Timoné — Language*. How well she remembered the day these tapes had come back to her in the mail. She had been in love with Cole, trying to get over Nate, believing him to be dead. Unable to bear listening to them, she had packed them all into this box, save one that she set aside for when Natalie grew up. She had shipped them off to the old missionary woman who had served in Timoné before them, to be forwarded to the mission headquarters, in hopes that they would be of help to the next missionaries Gospel Vision might send to Timoné. Someone had copied the tapes and returned the originals to her with a warm note of gratitude.

Only one time in the ensuing years had she gotten this box down from the closet. Only one time had she played one of the recordings. It had probably been a dozen years ago now. She sighed, replaying the memory in her mind.

Cole's partner, Travis Carruthers, had decided to strike out on his own, leaving Cole to work eighty-hour weeks. Daria had gone back to work at the clinic, but she deeply resented having to leave their three little girls in childcare. The stress of those months had precipitated a severe crisis in their marriage. One night she and Cole had had a huge argument. In the midst of it, he stormed out of the house, leaving her so angry she was shaking.

She had gone up to bed, but she couldn't sleep. She crawled out of bed and, in an effort to burn some of the anger that was still raging inside her, she'd started cleaning this very closet. As she pulled things from the shelves, she made a mental list of Cole's faults. She had crucified him in her mind that night, and to make matters worse, at her most vulnerable moment, she had come across Nate's tapes hidden away in the closet. As the recording played, she had deliberately allowed her love for Nathan Camfield to be resurrected. Listening to his strong, sure voice, she remembered only the sweetness of first love, recalled only Nate's admirable qualities. And in the space of an hour she had believed that life with Nate would have been perfect. She compared the two men to whom she had pledged her love, and in her mind Cole came up so pitifully short that she wondered if she could ever again find the love she'd once felt for him.

The clock in the hall downstairs chimed the hour, and Daria realized with a start that she'd been staring into the past, entranced by her memories, for several minutes.

She smiled now as she remembered the stern lecture Maribeth Dever had delivered when Daria had gone whining to her after that fight. Bless her dear heart, Maribeth had set her straight. Daria saw now, more clearly even than she had that day, how true her friend's words were. Every marriage had its valleys — and sometimes they seemed treacherously low, the walls insurmountable. Yet how many of their friends had tragically traded the valleys of one relationship for another whose gulf turned out to be far deeper?

She had gone home from her friend's

house that day and packed the tapes away. She hoped someday Natalie would treasure them, but she knew that they represented a part of her life that she could never revisit.

How grateful she was that she had stuck it out, that she had chosen to love Cole again. The love they now shared was precious beyond belief. Cole completed her, made her whole. It was more than she deserved, but she embraced it, accepted it fully as a gift from God, a reminder of his power to redeem even the most impossible dilemma.

She put the cassette gently back into the box and dropped the lid in place. Maybe it was time to pass the tapes on to Natalie. Her daughter had grown up so much over the last two years. And to Daria's great joy, Natalie and Nate had forged a solid friendship via e-mail.

She shifted the box on the bed, putting it with a small collection of things reserved for Natalie. And with a heart overflowing with gratitude, Daria Hunter continued to sort through the tangible reminders of a life that — in spite of her grim fallibility, in spite of her grave mistakes — God had chosen to bless richly.

Natalie drove slowly across the gravel

and parked at the back of the rambling old house. She turned off the ignition and went around to open the trunk of her car. She shaded her eyes and gazed up at the dormer windows that jutted out from the third-floor apartment. *Her apartment.* It still gave her a little thrill to turn the key in her own door. Last summer she had finally managed to convince her parents that living in an apartment instead of the dorms would round out her education in the proverbial "real world."

She and Amy Stinson, her roommate in the dorms, had seen the little *For Rent* sign planted in the yard one day last spring when they'd been out jogging. They'd quickly composed a jingle to help them remember the phone number and chanted it all the way back to Ford Hall, lest they lose the apartment to someone else. But not only was the apartment still available, but the landlord was also willing to hold it for them over the summer for a minuscule monthly fee.

Natalie had enjoyed every minute of apartment life. Well, almost every minute. She rarely felt like cooking, and it got expensive eating out all the time. But she did enjoy the peace and quiet and the freedom from the rules of the dorm. She was looking forward to having the place all to herself during the upcoming week. Amy's brother was graduating from college back home in Indiana, so Amy wouldn't be back for another week.

Natalie unpacked the last of her things from the car's trunk and climbed the open stairway that hugged the side of the house.

She smiled as she heard Daddy's fatherly caution echo in her ears: *This is an accident waiting to happen, Nattie! You girls be careful on these steps this winter.* Love for Cole Hunter welled up in her unexpectedly. Things had been so much better between them since she left home. *More regrets.* Why hadn't she been able to see what she had until it was almost too late? Why had she wasted so much time provoking quarrels with the people she loved most?

She brushed away the troublesome thoughts and unlocked the door to the apartment. The space had been closed up for two weeks, and the air inside smelled musty, but already it felt like home. She looked around the high-ceilinged room with its white painted woodwork and beaded-board paneling. The mismatched collection of furniture and the flea-market knickknacks she and Amy had collected only added to the cozy feel of the place. It took two more trips to carry everything in from the car. She dumped it all in a heap on the living room floor, then went to take a quick shower.

Refreshed and comfortable, with a thick terrycloth robe around her, she began unpacking the latest batch of goodies from her parents. Mom had been cleaning closets like a madwoman since Nicole's wedding, and the girls had reaped the rewards of her efforts. Nikki inherited the extra bedding and some decorative items for the house she and Jon hoped to buy. Natalie had gotten some dishes and glassware for the apartment out of the deal, along with some other odds and ends she'd rescued from Mom's rummage sale pile.

She unwrapped the glasses and plates and put them to soak in the kitchen sink, then went back to sort through the rest.

The old shoebox was at the bottom of a grocery bag, underneath some well-worn dishtowels and potholders. Natalie lifted it carefully from the bag and slid off the lid. A dozen or more cassette tapes were filed in a neat row in the box, and beside them, an assortment of yellowed newspaper clippings, old letters, and brochures from Gospel Vision.

When her mother had given her the box,

she had seemed nonchalant about it. "I don't even know if these old things will play anymore," she'd said, thrusting the box into Natalie's arms. "But, well, I thought you might enjoy listening to them."

Natalie felt she'd been offered a hallowed gift.

Picking up a small stack of airmail envelopes, she took the top one and pulled out a thin sheet of paper. It had been years since she had seen this letter, but she recognized it immediately. It was the very first letter her father — Daddy-Nate — had sent after his return to Colombia. Sometimes, on Nathan Camfield's birthday, before Natalie signed a card or colored a picture for him, Mom would let her read the letters he had written to his infant daughter. She couldn't remember when or why they had ended the tradition. But she read the words now as though they were freshly penned.

Dearest Natalie,
I am back with my Timoné people now, and I am happy to be here. I know I am where God wants me to be. Someday your mommy can tell you about these people and this village where your life began.

I hope you will always know how much I love you and how precious you are to me. I pray for you every day, as I know your mommy and daddy there in Kansas do too. God has blessed you with a wonderful home in which to grow up, Natalie. I hope you will never forget how greatly God has blessed you. You are a special girl with so many people who love you, and I know God has great things in store for you. I will write again soon, but for now, remember that I love you with all my heart.

> Keeping you in my prayers,
> Your Daddy-Nate

She leafed through the sheaf of letters, and her eyes misted with memories. She folded the letter and slid it carefully back into the envelope. Plopping down cross-legged on the floor in front of the stereo, she chose a cassette from the box and inserted it into the slot.

She waited for a few seconds, adjusting the volume knob, suddenly realizing how disappointed she would feel if her father's recordings had not survived the years. The tape droned softly, as though it were blank. She was just about to hit the *fast forward* button when a resonant voice filled the room. Natalie adjusted the volume again and sat back to listen. It was Nathan Camfield's voice she heard — there was no doubt about that — but the voice coming from the stereo speakers was deeper and missing the gravelly tone that Natalie knew.

She remembered Grandma Camfield telling her that Nate's voice had been damaged by the smoke he'd inhaled in the fire that nearly cost him his life. Still, it shocked her, hearing this tangible evidence of one of the many things he had lost in his ordeal. Tears sprang to her eyes, and a lump formed in her throat. Several minutes went by, and she realized that she had become so mesmerized by the timbre of her father's voice that she had been paying little attention to the content of his words.

She swiped at her damp cheeks and reached up to punch the *rewind* button. She hit *play* again, hanging on to every nuance of sound the stereo speakers emitted.

"I just returned from a hunting expedition with some of the men," the voice began again. "The rainy season is coming, and the village is busy laying up provisions."

In the background Natalie could hear

338

the intermittent squawks and twittering of tropical birds and what sounded like water trickling over stones. She could almost smell the damp floor of the rain forest, could almost see the dense foliage. Never had she been so enthralled by what might have, under ordinary circumstances, seemed boring. But this was her father! This was a glimpse into the life of the two people who had given her breath.

Her father went into some detail about his experiences on the hunting trip. Then he paused and cleared his throat. "We're making progress with the language," he continued. "Daria has struggled with the rather guttural tones of the dialect. For some reason, it seems to come more naturally to me. Daria claims it's because I snore. I didn't dare tell her that she does too." His laughter filled the room. It was a joyful sound — one that was naively oblivious to the sorrows that were perhaps mere days away.

Natalie stopped the tape and pressed *eject*. She popped out the cassette and inspected it for a date, some indication of when it might have been recorded. The tape was labeled *Timoné — Impressions*, followed by a number that seemed to denote the chronological sequence in which the recording had been made.

She started the tape playing again, stretching out on the carpet on her belly, chin resting on one fist.

"For instance," Nate went on, "the word for coffee is *cazho*." He pronounced the word with a rough inflection, as though he had something caught in his throat. "Daria is inclined to pronounce the word as *cash-o*, which is the Timoné word for *nose*. The natives find it quite hilarious when she offers to put sugar in my nose." Again his laughter filled the room, and Natalie found herself smiling too.

"It has been a little frustrating for her," he said now, his tenor suddenly more serious, "but she's hanging in there."

For nearly three hours, Natalie listened as her father's voice recounted with humor the everyday details of the life he had once shared with her mother.

She was mesmerized, astonished by the realization that at the time he had recorded these words, he could not have known that he would someday have a daughter named Natalie Joan, and that through no fault of his own, his little family would never know life together on this earth.

As his words soaked into the core of her being, something she could not name began to emerge in her spirit. And like a fledgling on the frayed cusp of the nest, she somehow knew that this nameless emotion would soon give her wings.

Twenty-Four

"Okay, Evan, listen to this." Natalie pushed the *play* button on the tape recorder and waited for the now familiar voice of her father. Evan had just arrived back in Manhattan after the Christmas break, and Natalie had waited impatiently all through supper to surprise him with the recordings. She adjusted the volume, plopped on the floor by the stereo, and watched Evan's face as Nathan Camfield's voice filled the room.

Evan sat on the edge of the big over-stuffed chair in Natalie's apartment and listened politely, but she could see that he wasn't catching the same excitement that she had felt in discovering the tapes. She'd intended to play an entire cassette for him, but after fifteen minutes, he leaned back in the chair and began to fidget. She waited for a lull in her father's narrative and ejected the tape.

"Well?" She looked at him expectantly.

"What do you think?"

"That's really neat, Nattie," Evan said. "I can see why you were so happy to get those tapes."

She had been holed up in the apartment listening to the recordings for three days, and her excitement had grown each day. She knew it was unfair to expect Evan to share her enthusiasm or to comprehend the profound effect that listening to this account of her parents' life in Colombia had had on her — especially since she barely understood it herself.

But an idea was germinating, one that seemed more real and more possible every day. She had thought she might share her thoughts with Evan tonight, but something caused her to keep silent.

Evan stretched and yawned as if he were getting ready to leave. She knew he still had unpacking to do, and she didn't blame him for wanting to get back to his dorm, but still it frustrated her that he hadn't reacted the way she'd hoped he would.

She fiddled with the cassettes, struggling to get over her annoyance at his lack of interest.

"Hey," he said, letting the word hang in the air until she finally turned to look at him. He beckoned her with a curve of his finger and a glint in his eyes. "Come here."

She went to him, and he pulled her down onto his lap. "I missed you," he said, brushing her hair off her forehead.

"I missed you too." He took her face in his hands and kissed her, and the irritation she'd felt toward him earlier dissolved. But his kiss didn't make her forget the dream that had been kindled by her father's recordings. As they sat, cuddling and talking quietly, she couldn't stop the plans from forming in her mind, taking on a life of their own. She knew that Evan sensed her preoccupation, but he didn't press her for an explanation.

It was barely nine o'clock when he gave an exaggerated yawn and picked up his coat from the back of the chair. "I've got a ton of stuff to get done before I can even go to bed tonight, Nattie. I'd better get going."

She didn't argue with him, but she walked him to the door and returned his good-night kiss.

"You want to have lunch tomorrow?" he asked from the landing of the stairway outside her door.

"Sure. Meet you in the union at noon? Usual place?"

"Okay. Good night." He leaned to place

one more gentle kiss on her lips.

Natalie wondered if he was sensing the same odd feelings that she was. She couldn't put a name to it, but something was changing between them.

Classes started for Natalie the following Wednesday, but she attended in body only. Every minute she could, she went back to the apartment and listened to the tapes. As she played tape after tape, for hours on end, she'd found herself in an almost trancelike state while she relived her parents' early life vicariously. She played the cassettes until she had some of them memorized. She rewound certain sections, delighting in Nathan Camfield's wry sense of humor and in the musical sound of his laughter. She realized that in the brief periods of time she had spent with her birth father over the years, she had seldom heard him laugh in the unfettered manner she heard on these tapes. Yet the recordings were marked by frequent expressions of this mirthful side of him. On some of the tapes, Nate had persuaded a reluctant Daria to say a few words. Natalie played those sections, too, over and over again. Her mother's voice sounded younger and more callow. But what startled Natalie more than anything was the love for Nathan Camfield that — even dimmed by the wear and tear of twenty-five years on the cassettes — came across strikingly. The subtle nuances of her mother's voice brought yet a deeper understanding of how profoundly the tragic events in her parents' lives had shaped them — and herself.

She went to the library and searched out everything she could find on Colombia. Though there was almost no information about the village of Timoné, she almost cheered to discover *National Geographic* stories about the Rio Guaviare, and *Newsweek* articles that mentioned San José del Guaviare, the town her father flew into from Bogotá. She made copies of everything she could find and, on a whim, even called her mother and asked her to send the books and tapes they'd used in the Spanish class she'd taken at the junior college a few years ago.

The following Sunday night Natalie sat down at her computer to compose an e-mail to her father. She hoped to convey the new sense of respect and admiration she had for him. She started and deleted half a dozen paragraphs. Nothing she wrote seemed to adequately express the deep emotional chord that had been struck within her.

Finally, she decided just to write honestly what she was feeling and to quit worrying about how he might interpret — or misinterpret — her words.

Dear Dad,
Mom gave me a bunch of cassette tapes you made when you guys were first in Colombia, and I've been listening to them ever since I got back to Manhattan. Don't worry — I'm not neglecting homework or anything.

Dad, I can't tell you how much I've enjoyed getting to know about your life there in Timoné — and especially the life you and Mom shared before I was born. I've even learned a few Timoné words (which I'd try to cleverly slip into this e-mail if I had the faintest idea how to spell them! How is that guy coming with the translation? Sorry but I forget his name now. David something-or-other, wasn't it?).

Anyway, I can't believe everything was so primitive when you lived there twenty years ago. Not even an airstrip nearby! It's kind of hard to picture Mom living like that. (Or Grammy Haydon letting her!) But at the same time, it explains a lot about the way

Mom is. I mean that in a good way, of course. Now I know why she was always after us for wasting stuff! You wouldn't believe how much trouble we'd get in for throwing out three kernels of corn or half an old brown banana! "That would have been perfectly good in a soup," she'd say. Or "I was going to make a banana bread with that." Ha! I guess I probably do take the luxuries we have here in America for granted.

Which brings me to something I want to ask you. I'm almost afraid to put this in writing because I don't know if it would even be possible, but listening to the tapes makes me realize that I want to come and visit you. I know Aunt Betsy has visited you in Bogotá before, but I want to come all the way to Timoné. Could you send me some information and let me know what it would take for that to happen? I've been studying about Colombia, and I've even brushed up on my Spanish. I know what I learned in high school probably won't get me far — and I know they don't actually speak Spanish in Timoné — but Señor Edmonds always said I had a knack for languages, so I think I could learn Timoné pretty quickly.

Natalie stared at the words she had just typed. Until she saw them on the page in front of her, she hadn't realized just how strong her longing was. But now, daring to give her yearning voice via the keyboard of her computer, she realized that this was exactly what these days of introspection had culminated in — a deep desire to go visit her father in his village. There was no way she would ever truly get to know him unless she visited him on his own turf. And her world was far too small, her perspective on everything limited by her myopic view.

Before she could chicken out, Natalie clicked the *send* icon in her e-mail program.

And thus began the wait. She knew that it was sometimes weeks before her father could get to San José del Guaviare, where they were able to receive e-mail and letters. But that didn't keep her from anxiously checking her e-mail the minute she got back to the apartment after classes each day.

And though there was a twinge of fear in the waiting — fear that he would deny her — the predominant emotion was still that shadowy anticipation that something, something big, was about to change in her life.

Nathan Camfield turned up the flame in the lamp that sat on the crude table in the mission office. It was late, and the rest of the village was asleep. He read Natalie's e-mail one more time, and a sinking feeling roosted in the pit of his stomach. What had he done? It had never been his intention to influence Natalie to come to Colombia. That had been the furthest thing from his mind in all the time he had been writing to her, telling her of his life here in Timoné. Yes, he was delighted to be corresponding with his daughter more frequently. It had been wonderful to finally feel he had a connection to this child he'd never been privileged to parent. But he had never meant to encourage her to want to come here.

He heard a sound on the stoop outside the door and called out, "Who's there?"

The door opened, and David Chambers stuck his head in. "I thought I saw a light. You're still here?"

Nate sighed. "Oh, I'm just reading my mail — and praying."

David looked at him, a question in his eyes. "Is everything all right?"

"It's nothing serious. Natalie seems to think she wants to come and visit me."

"Here?"

He nodded.

"I take it you don't think that's a good idea?"

"No. Of course not . . . not with the political situation the way it is. I think she has this image of some tropical paradise vacation spot. I don't think she has a clue about what things are really like here. It . . . it just wouldn't even make sense for her to come. This place isn't set up for a woman . . ." He knew he was rambling, but he also knew that David would listen patiently and perhaps help him sort through his emotions. "I don't know what her motive is for coming, but there are a million reasons why this isn't a good idea. And if something happened to her while she was here, or on the way, I would never forgive myself. She's not even twenty-two, Dave."

David cocked his head. "How old were you when you came to Timoné, Nate?"

Nate rubbed his brow sheepishly. "Okay . . . not a whole lot older than that."

"And your wife?"

"Okay, okay . . . I get your point. But it

seems like Natalie wants to come for all the wrong reasons."

"What are her reasons?"

He flung out a hand in frustration. "Oh, I don't even know exactly. Maybe I'm making more of this than I should. I think maybe she has this desire to connect with the father she's never gotten to know."

"Would that be so bad . . . if she got to know her father better?"

He looked hard at his friend and shook his head. "Don't tempt me, David. I haven't even dared to imagine that I might get a chance to . . . to know Natalie like that. I'm afraid her mother will think I've put her up to this . . . or persuaded her in some way. I think that's what's bothering me the most about this whole thing. I gave up my rights to my daughter a long time ago. I've trusted Daria and her husband to do right by her. And I don't mind telling you that it wasn't easy when this whole thing with the accident happened. But I didn't make waves then, and I sure don't intend to start now."

"So you're going to tell her no?"

"What else could I say, David? I don't know . . ." He ran a hand through his close-cropped hair. "Maybe if I just ignore it, this will all blow over." He blew out his cheeks in frustration. "I'm probably making too much of it. She hasn't even graduated from college yet. She surely didn't intend to come before that. I'm probably getting all worked up over nothing."

"Well, don't just dismiss the idea out of hand, Nate. I don't think it's all that impossible. For all you know it's just a little vacation." David reached out and gripped Nate's shoulder. "I'll be praying for you."

"Thanks, Dave. Go on to bed. I won't be much longer."

"Okay. Good night."

David latched the door behind him. Nate thought about the things he'd said. The truth was, his heart beat with excitement at the possibility of Natalie coming to Timoné, of getting to know her better, of finally being able to share his life with his daughter. He hadn't dared to even imagine that he might someday have a relationship with her, and now the opportunity was staring him in the face. All he had to do was say yes, offer a little encouragement.

He reminded himself that, as David pointed out, Natalie was not a child anymore. He could tell from the thoughtful letters she wrote that she had grown —

both spiritually and emotionally — in the years since the tragic accident that had taken her friend's life. But this couldn't be his decision. He didn't want the responsibility of having said yes, if anything should go wrong.

He rose from the table, feeling a heaviness in his spirit that he hadn't felt for many months. He closed the laptop and straightened his desk, then put the copy of Natalie's e-mail in a folder for safekeeping.

He locked up the office, and holding the lamp high, he walked through the village to his hut. He undressed and crawled onto his sleeping mat, arranging the mosquito netting over him. Reaching underneath the net, he turned the knob to extinguish the lamp. The flame inside the glass chimney sputtered and faded. But he lay awake for many minutes, staring into the blackness, composing replies to his daughter's request — none of which seemed right.

For — he realized with clarity as he finally drifted off to sleep — the answer he wanted to give with all his heart was, *Yes, daughter! Yes, please come.*

"Evan, it's *not* a crazy idea! Why can't you support me in this?" Natalie glanced around her and realized that she had raised her voice to a level that was attracting the attention of fellow diners in the food court at the student union. She pushed her fried rice around on her plate with a plastic fork and lowered her tone to a whisper. "Can't you understand why this is so important to me?"

Evan held his palms face out to her, and she recognized the long-suffering look that came to his face. He was going to pretend he understood even as he tried to talk her out of it. She was too tired to call him on it.

"Natalie, he's your father. Of course I understand why you'd want to go see him. See him 'in his element,' as you say. But, come on, admit it: Your timing makes no sense whatsoever. Why don't you at least wait until summer — or better yet, wait until the following summer. Then you'll have your degree under your belt and possibly even a job to come back to. You have less than three semesters to go. I don't see why —"

"Evan Greenway," she broke in, "you know as well as I do that there's no way I'll graduate in three semesters."

"Well, if you hadn't changed majors ten times . . ." His voice trailed off and he remained silent.

"Hey, can I help it if I still don't have a clue what I want to do with my life? But don't you see? That's just it. Maybe this will help me decide."

"What are you talking about, Natalie? Decide what? What is it you want?" The look on his face was that of a frightened boy, and she decided this would not be a good time to voice the thoughts that had refused to leave her alone for the last two weeks.

Instead she looked pointedly at her watch. "You're going to be late."

He looked at his own watch, and she could tell by the way his eyes darted between her and his book bag that he was seriously considering skipping class to finish their discussion. But she knew if he missed this economics class he would regret it later, and that would add a whole new dimension to their argument.

"We can talk about this later, okay?" she told him, sliding out of the booth and picking up her tray of half-eaten vegetables and rice from the tabletop.

He sighed and slid out behind her. They emptied their trash into a nearby receptacle, and he gave her a quick kiss before he melted in with the throng of students headed for afternoon classes. Natalie watched him walk away, and her heart twisted.

Though he was finished forever with casts and crutches, Evan still walked with a mild limp. Though many wouldn't even notice, she saw it clearly — more pronounced when he was tired or troubled, like now.

Watching him until she could no longer find him in the crowd, her heart ached.

She cared deeply for Evan. So why did she feel so melancholy watching him walk away? She wasn't sure. And yet she suspected that it all had to do with this unknown impending *something* in her own life.

As she walked back to her car, and later as she drove to the apartment, she prayed. *Lord, I'm not sure what's going on, but help me sort it all out. Help me find what I'm looking for, Father. Please.*

Twenty-Five

Natalie brought her fingers down hard on the keyboard of her computer and harrumphed under her breath. Nobody ever took her seriously. She deleted the errant alphabet that had skittered across the computer screen at her outburst of anger, and, sighing, she read her father's e-mail again.

Well, at least he hadn't completely ignored her question this time. The first time she'd written to him about her desire to visit him in Colombia, he had sent back a friendly e-mail that discussed the weather and not much more. She had e-mailed him back promptly, telling him that she was quite serious and that she was, in fact, thinking about coming soon.

This time he had started his reply with the usual news and thoughtful questions about her life, but at the end he'd placed a carefully worded response that seemed to purposely misunderstand the fact that she wanted to visit soon — and that seemed intent on discouraging her. It was almost as though he'd discussed it with Mom and Daddy, and with Evan.

Once again, she read his words.

Naturally I'm delighted that you want to visit me, Nattie. Of course, things are always very volatile in Colombia. One never knows from day to day whether the airports will be open, or whether it will be safe to navigate the Guaviare. We've had paramilitary at the airport in San José del Guaviare routinely throughout this year, although there haven't been any violent incidents recently. The mission's airstrip at Conzalez has not been affected so far, but that doesn't mean I'll be able to say the same next year.

I assume if you come it would be the summer after graduation. I'd hoped to surprise you and come for your graduation. Maybe we could arrange to fly back together. And perhaps I can help with your expenses as part of your graduation gift. At any rate, I am excited to think of showing off Timoné to you, and I do hope it will work out for you to visit. But we have plenty of time to work out the details.

I assume this is all acceptable to your mother and to Cole. I'm sure you can understand that I want to be certain they have given their go-ahead and their blessing to this before I get involved.

We'll talk about all this more when the time gets closer.

With much love,
Dad

She sighed again in frustration. Like everyone else, he seemed intent on putting her off. But he didn't know her well enough — she would not be discouraged so easily. In fact, the more she thought about it, the more she longed to make this trip.

Mom and Daddy had been cautiously in favor of her plan — until she told them that she wanted to go before the end of the school term. Until she told them that she wanted to stay indefinitely. Then they were adamantly against it.

"That would be foolish, Nattie," Daddy said. "You'd be throwing away a whole semester of college."

Mom agreed, adding, "Besides, I don't think you realize the danger involved, honey. You don't just hop on a plane and you're there. Even in the best of circumstances, it's a rough trip through dangerous territory."

Evan, too, though he claimed to support the idea of her going, did not approve of her timing. Even Grandma and Grandpa Camfield and Aunt Betsy — whom she'd thought would be 100 percent on her side — encouraged her to get her degree first, or at the very least finish the semester and wait to go in the summer. She understood the concerns they all had. She knew that it seemed foolish to waste a semester that was already paid for. But something stronger than a mere desire to see her father was pushing her toward this destiny. She had prayed about all the advice she was getting. She didn't want to do something foolish, and still she felt that there was some reason that she must go.

Unbidden, Natalie's thoughts turned to Sara, and a battle began in her mind. The happy memories of the friendship she and Sara had shared warred with the memories of the accident and its aftermath. As always, the good memories quickly turned bittersweet in the fray, and a painful twist in the pit of her stomach proved her guilt. Long forgiven, yes, but never forgotten. "Forgotten" was a joke. She might have played along at the game that everyone seemed so set on playing — pretending that the tragedy was over, that they had all healed from the damage she'd done. But she knew the truth. They might have forgiven her — truly forgiven. But no one would ever forget. *Ever.*

The doorbell relieved her of the troubling thoughts. She glanced at the clock on her computer and gasped. It was six o'clock! She had promised Evan she'd go to dinner with him, and here she sat still in her rumpled jogging pants, her hair a mess.

She raced to the bathroom, yanked a hairbrush through the tangled curtain of hair, ran back to the door, and opened it.

Evan took one look at her and made a face that said, *I knew you wouldn't be ready on time.*

She made a visor of her hand and hid her eyes behind it. "I'm sorry," she whimpered, trying to appease him. "I was on the computer, and I completely lost track of time." Her voice gained steam as she made her excuses. "But I got an e-mail from Dad, and I had to answer it."

He looked at her, and she could tell he was mildly amused but not buying her explanations.

"Give me five minutes, and I'll be out the door. I'm more ready than I look. Really."

He just stood in the doorway and shook his head, as though she were a hopeless case. She planted a penitent kiss on his cheek, took his arm, and escorted — or rather dragged — him to the sofa. He fell onto the cushions and took a pose that said he expected to be there awhile. She opened a magazine and placed it on his lap — never mind it was the new issue of *Today's Christian Woman* — and raced back to the bedroom to change clothes and freshen her makeup.

When Natalie had not appeared after ten minutes, Evan put the magazine down and wandered through the large combination living-dining-kitchen area. Natalie's computer sat on an old desk at one end of the dining area. He didn't really intend to pry, but the e-mail was right there on the screen and difficult to ignore. Only part of the letter was visible, but Evan read Nathan Camfield's words. It seemed Natalie was more determined than ever to make this crazy trip to South America. He and Natalie had argued about it for two weeks. In fact, it was all they'd talked about since she first got this crazy bug in her ear.

He went back into the living room and paced back and forth on the worn green carpeting, his growing impatience caused by more than Natalie's tardiness for their dinner date.

He sighed. He truly didn't have anything against her going to see her father, at least for a short visit. But she seemed intent on something longer. It seemed ridiculous to go now. What was her rush? Maybe, if things went as he hoped, she'd be ready to settle down then. If he was established in a good job, maybe they could get married. They could visit Colombia together then.

She had been right when she told him that there was no way she would graduate a year from May. But if she didn't blow it, she might make it by the following December.

His own career plans had been carefully thought out, and he was right on schedule to achieve them. He didn't appreciate her throwing this wrench in the plan. He knew what he wanted in life, and he'd worked hard for it. As much as he loved Natalie, she sometimes frustrated him to distraction.

But he was a soft touch where Natalie

Camfield was concerned, and he had to admit that none of what he wanted in life would be worth it without her at his side. He just didn't like her forcing his hand this way.

She punctuated his thoughts by appearing in the doorway, looking beautiful as ever. Her hair swung just above her shoulders like a glossy yellow silk curtain, and her skin glowed from a fresh scrubbing. She had changed into a pair of olive corduroys and his favorite sweater. He knew at that moment that he was a goner. He would never be able to deny this woman anything.

She had turned his life upside down for more than a decade now — ever since she'd walked into their fifth-grade classroom at Bristol Elementary and stolen the stubby No. 2 pencil off his desk. She'd stolen more than a pencil that day — she'd stolen his heart. And in the loving, they'd both healed from the wounds of their shared tragedy.

Yet Natalie seemed so restless lately. He couldn't seem to fill her longings the way he had at first. He didn't seem to be enough for her anymore.

"Are you going to be mad at me all night?" Natalie's affected pout jerked him to the present, and he realized she'd been standing there for a while.

"What? No . . . no, I can't ever be mad at you for very long."

"Just not speaking to me?" she asked, her head cocked coyly.

He shook his head like a dog trying to shake off a bath. "Sorry. I was . . . I was thinking."

"About?"

"Nothing you need to worry your pretty head about." He went to the door and held it open for her. "Ready?"

She gave him a strange look but went down the stairs ahead of him.

They were both quiet on the way to the restaurant. They ate at a corner table, making small talk, but when the waitress cleared away their dishes and brought coffee, Natalie said, "So, are you going to tell me what has you so pensive tonight, Mr. Greenway?"

"I've been thinking about us."

A flicker of worry crossed her face. "Judging by the look on your face, I'd say they weren't necessarily good thoughts."

Suddenly it seemed the right thing to do. He took a deep breath and plunged in. "I don't think I appreciate you enough, Natalie."

Her face was a mask of bewilderment. "Appreciate me?"

He reached across the table and took her hand. "I don't tell you often enough how much you mean to me, how much I love you."

She smiled. "Oh, Evan. That's so sweet. I love you too."

"Natalie, I've just assumed you'd always be there for me, assumed you'd always love me. But lately when you talk about going to be with your dad, going half a world away, to the most dangerous place on earth — well, it's made me think about some things."

His heart was beating a hundred miles an hour, and the restaurant suddenly felt like an oven. He pulled his chair closer to the table and leaned his head toward hers. Squeezing her hand, he looked into her eyes. "Natalie Camfield, I love you. And I want to marry you."

"Evan —" There was disbelief in her voice. He wasn't sure if that was good or bad.

He held up a warning hand. "I know we both have to finish school and there's a lot to consider financially. But if you're going to be running around with guerrillas and poisonous snakes and" — he shrugged —

"whatever else is out there, well, I just want you to know where you stand with me. I love you, and I want you in my future more than I've ever wanted anything in my life."

"Oh, Evan. I — I do love you. But I'm not sure . . ." She stared at her plate.

His heart seemed to quit beating while he waited for her to finish.

Finally she looked up and there were tears in her eyes. "Evan. I don't know what to say. There's something I haven't told you . . . something I'm not sure I even knew until now . . ."

"What are you saying?"

"I don't even know how to explain it."

"Try." He somehow knew that what came next was going to hurt him deeply.

She took a deep breath. "Evan, I don't think I'm ready to talk about this yet. I need some time. I'm so sorry, but there are some things going on in my head that I have to figure out before I can even think about marriage."

"What kind of things? What are you trying to say, Natalie?"

"I promise we'll talk this out, but I have to think about what I want out of life. I have to pray about it."

He spread his hands in a gesture of

368

dismay. "I tell you I love you and that I want to marry you. You're evading the question — It's obvious you don't feel the same about me as I do for you." He took out his wallet and dug out a twenty and slapped it on the table. *Never mind the change.* He pushed the chair back and grabbed his coat off the back of it.

Natalie scrambled for her coat and purse and followed him out of the restaurant, calling his name. "Evan, please. I'm sorry. Evan . . . wait."

He kept on walking.

Twenty-Six

They drove through the dark in complete silence. Though Natalie knew she had hurt Evan's feelings, she also knew that voicing her thoughts would only make things worse.

He pulled into the driveway at her apartment, but he made no move to turn off the ignition.

"I'm sorry, Evan. I . . . I know I just blurted things out that I shouldn't have. I wish I could make you underst—"

He put a hand on her arm. "Hey, we both said some things we shouldn't have. Maybe we both just need to go home and pretend this night never happened." He immediately looked remorseful. "I'm sorry. I didn't mean it that way. But I guess — Well, we need to think things through, pray about things. We'll talk later, okay?"

She nodded, but a deep sadness came over her. She knew that over the last few weeks, something had changed between them. Or maybe she was the one who had changed. Whatever it was, she wasn't sure they would ever be the same.

She let herself into the apartment and threw her purse on the desk. Amy was on the phone, but she waved a tacit greeting. Natalie pillowed her head on her hands, indicating that she was going to bed.

She showered, put on her warmest pajamas, and climbed under the quilts on her bed. But nothing could ward off the chill in her heart. Poor Evan. She'd been so unfair to him. He had proposed, and all she could do was give him a lame answer about some mysterious thing that she wasn't even sure of herself.

But Evan's declaration of love had frightened her. He had forced her to finally admit to herself what she'd known deep in her heart for some time now.

She was going to Colombia.

And not just for a visit. She wanted to live there with her father, to work among the Timoné people, to make a difference. She had spent too many years feeling that the only difference she'd made in people's lives was a horrific one — one that had taken away a daughter, a sister, a friend. Forever. Too much of these past few years had been lived in regret for one mistake that could never be undone. But she had the rest of her life to make up for what she'd caused. Nothing before had ever been *enough*. She'd done her time in jail. She'd done her community service, but that had been no sacrifice on her part. In fact, she'd enjoyed the work at the childcare center immensely. She'd done what she could to set things right with Sara's family. And that, too, had backfired and ended up being a blessing to her. Except Jon — he had seen through her, and deservedly so. Now she had a chance to truly make a sacrifice that meant something. To give her whole life over to a mission of eternal consequence.

She thought about how she would break the news to Evan. What would this mean for them?

Tears came to the surface as she thought of what a blessing Evan had been to her. His love, his complete empathy, had been an important part of her healing. But she felt torn now between him and this new direction that compelled her.

She thought about telling Mom and Daddy, but she knew they, too, would try to discourage her.

But she'd thought this through. Ever since she had listened to those cassette tapes, Timoné was all she *could* think about. Wasn't it possible that this was the way a call from the Lord came? In the form of a desire that became almost an obsession? Her classes at the university seemed more boring and useless than ever. The money she spent on her apartment, on her car, on her clothes, all seemed wasted and pointless. The only thing that held any excitement or meaning for her now was the idea of going to Colombia, working beside her father.

"Oh, Lord," she whispered into the darkness of her room, "is this your voice I'm hearing? Are you in this, Father? Is this my chance to finally make up for what happened? Please don't let me do anything foolish."

The temperature was in the low forties, and the sky was overcast, but Natalie and Evan had agreed to meet at the small park near her apartment where they could talk without risking a roommate's interruption or running into someone they knew on campus.

Evan sat stiffly on the backless bench beside Natalie, bouncing his knees up and down to keep warm. She turned the collar of her jacket up and burrowed into it.

Clasping her mittened hands together, refusing to look him in the eye, she said the words as simply as she knew how, "Evan, I'm going to Colombia."

"Okay . . ."

"I don't mean just to visit. I — I'm not sure, but I think God might be —" She started again. She wanted him to hear confidence in her voice. "I think God is calling me, to be a missionary there."

He shook his head. "You mean, like short-term missions? A couple of months or something?"

"I honestly don't know. Maybe longer. Maybe much longer, Evan. I — I don't think I'll really know until I get there."

He stared at her. "And where exactly does this leave me? Us?"

Tears sprang to her eyes. "I don't know." For a fleeting minute, she dared to hope. A sad smile curved her lips. "You . . . You wouldn't want to go with me, would you?"

"If you can wait a year or two, Natalie. Let me get my degree. Let me pray about it. Not be in such an all-fired rush." Anger tinged his voice. "Be reasonable. Look at what you're throwing away."

She assumed he meant her education. "You don't understand. A degree will just be a piece of paper in Colombia. What difference would it make in *your* decision if you had your degree, Evan?" She forced a smile, but her heart was breaking.

They sat in silence for a while. Finally he turned to her.

"You seem to have this all figured out. When are you leaving?"

"No, Evan, I *don't* have it all figured out. I'm confused about a lot of things." She reached out and put a hand on his arm, testing.

He didn't push her away, but neither did he touch her in return, as he would have before. "Have you prayed about this, Nattie? Do you know for sure this is God's calling and not just Natalie Camfield's desires?"

She felt her defenses rising, but made herself answer calmly — and honestly. "I've prayed more these last few weeks than I have since . . . since Sara died. And . . . I don't know how anyone ever knows for sure that it's God's voice they're hearing until they step out in faith. I'm as sure as I *can* be. I just know that if I don't go, I'll always wonder if I made the biggest mistake of my life. I — I can't afford any more mistakes in my life, Evan."

He did push her hand away now, gently, but meaningfully. He rose from the park bench and began to pace in front of her. "But you don't wonder if leaving me would be a bigger mistake?"

"Oh, Evan. Don't make this so hard!"

"Don't make this so hard?" he echoed, a sharp edge coming to his voice. "You think you've made this easy for me?"

"I didn't mean it like that . . ."

"Natalie, I love you. I thought we loved each other."

"Evan, I do love you. I do. But I . . . I just know . . . somehow I know that I have to do this. I believe this is God's desire . . . I'm sorry if I've hurt you. I truly am. But —"

"No," he stopped her, and though his words were measured, there was no longer anger in his voice. "I don't ever want you to feel like you're making a choice between me and God . . . or like I'm keeping you from doing what God has called you to do." He continued to pace back and forth in front of the bench.

She sat in silence. She truly didn't know what to say to him. Finally she rose from the bench and approached him. "Evan, I'm sorry."

He turned toward her, and she opened her arms, longing for the comfort of his nearness.

But he held up a warning hand and shook his head vigorously. "You're going to have to give me some time to . . . to get over this."

"Okay," she said softly, stinging from his rebuff, yet knowing it had been unfair to expect a different response.

She turned and walked away from him, head bowed against the cold and against the pain. She felt as though she'd been rent in two. Part of her longed for Evan to run after her, to beg her to stop this foolishness. And yet now that she'd told him her plans, the pull toward Colombia and her father was stronger than ever.

She kept walking, and when she was beyond the reach of his voice, she broke into a jog and ran the rest of the way home. Inside the empty apartment, her resolve dimmed. She missed Evan already. He'd been so much a part of her life for the last two years, it was almost as though she were losing a part of herself. She knew he was feeling the same way. And that seemed all the more reason to go to Colombia — now — as soon as she could possibly make arrangements. Before she could change her mind.

"Natalie, you can't be serious. This is

crazy!" Cole Hunter put his hands on either side of the big oak table in the kitchen and all but shook it. Natalie had the distinct sense that he wished it were her shoulders he was shaking.

How many times had she heard these very words over the last week? She sighed and prepared to defend herself one more time. "Daddy, I know it seems sudden, but I *have* thought it through. I really have. And I feel like this is what God wants me to do."

Daddy sighed and looked at Mom as though she might have the magic words to talk some sense into this daughter.

Natalie turned to her mother. "You understand, don't you?" she said, appealing to the former missionary in her mother.

Mom patted Daddy's leg as if to reassure him that, in spite of the words to come, she was on his side. "Honey, I guess I do understand your wanting to go, wanting to get to know your father better, even feeling that God has called you to this. But Daddy's right. It does seem a little rash. Why wouldn't you finish school first? Even your father had to finish medical school before he answered the call to go to Colombia. And do you realize how long it takes to raise support for something like this? Do you understand how dangerous it is there and how —"

"Mom, please . . ." Natalie breathed deeply, struggling to rein in her frustration. "I've been in school for over two years. Until a few weeks ago, I still didn't have the faintest idea what I wanted to be when I grew up. Now I finally know. Please . . . support me in this. Please don't make me do this against your will. Please."

Her parents looked at each other, and when Daddy spoke she thought there was resignation in his voice. "Natalie, let me ask you one question. What exactly is it that you hope to accomplish if you go to Colombia?"

She thought for a minute. For her sake as well as theirs, she wanted to give as honest a reply as she could. But she couldn't tell them that she wanted to make up for Sara's death. They would give her the same line they always had about God's forgiveness. But they'd never murdered their best friend. They didn't know how it felt. She took a deep breath. "Daddy, I know the right answer . . . is that I want to share the gospel of Christ with the people of Timoné. And that's true. But I also —" She paused, knowing that her next words could so easily hurt her father. She reached out and took his hand. "Daddy, you know I love you with all my heart. You are the best father I could ever ask for. It's taken me too long to realize that. But . . . well, I want to be honest."

She looked at the floor, then forced herself to look him in the eye. "One of the reasons I want to go to Timoné is to get to know my father — my other father. I don't know how to make you understand how important this feels to me. Daddy . . ." Her throat filled, and she gulped back the tears, desperately needing to finish her thought. "I wouldn't hurt your feelings for the world. And I'd feel terrible if you took this the wrong way . . ." Her words caught in her throat, and she swallowed a sob.

Daddy let go of her hand and drew her into his arms, then he reached for Mom and she came to them, completed the circle. They held each other and cried together.

After a few minutes he drew back, and his eyes seemed to bore through her. "Natalie, if you are absolutely sure this is God's call on your life, then I give you my blessing. I understand your desire to get to know Nate — your . . . father. And I will help you in any way I can to explore the possibilities."

"What does Evan think about all this?"

Tears filled Natalie's eyes again. "He's hurt. He thought we'd end up getting married. He even proposed."

"And you don't feel the same about him?" Her mother lifted her chin, and Natalie saw the hope in her eyes.

She shook her head. "I don't know, Mom. I . . . maybe I do love him. But I can't not go because of him. I . . . I dared to hope that Evan might want to come with me, and that's not happening. Our — Our lives seem to be going in different directions . . ."

Her mother swiped at a tear. "Give him time," she said. "Maybe he'll still come around."

Natalie nodded. "Maybe. I don't know what the future holds for us, but I can't ask Evan to wait for me when I don't know if —"

"If you'll ever come back?" Her mother finished the sentence for her. "Oh, Nattie. Now I know how my parents felt when I followed Nate to the ends of the earth. I know this isn't right, but to be honest, I think I'd feel better if you were following a big strong man to Timoné."

"Or at least dragging one kicking and screaming behind you," Cole said wryly.

Natalie and her mother both tried to laugh, but what came from their throats was more like a sob, which made them laugh, and then cry even harder.

The phone rang, and Daddy gave Natalie another hug before he went to answer it. "I love you, punkin," he whispered, using the childhood endearment she treasured.

The telephone summoned Cole back to the vet clinic for an emergency, but after he'd gone Natalie and her mother sat and talked for a long time.

"Mom?" Natalie ventured, "How did you know . . . for sure that it was God calling you to go to Timoné in the first place?"

Her mother thought for a minute. "You know, Natalie, in all the years since everything happened with your dad — with Nate — I've had to be honest with myself and admit that I'm not sure I really was called of God. I felt it was right for me to go — and I still believe that — because I loved your father and *he* was called. It was kind of the 'whither thou goest, I will go' mentality. I think I let that be enough. But I know now that if I'd really been seeking God, if I'd waited for my own calling, I might not have made the mistakes I made.

I might not have been so quick to leave when Nate . . . things might not have turned out the way they did."

Natalie saw a faraway light in her eyes, and she was amazed that her mother seemed so serene, speaking of that most terrible time in her life.

"It's hard for me to think about what might have been," Mom went on now, "because if I hadn't married Daddy, then I wouldn't have Nicole and Noelle and the happy life we've all had together. My life would have been so very different. But I can't change anything that happened now. Some mistakes can't be fixed." The expression that passed between them acknowledged that they both had suffered tragic events only God could redeem.

Mom patted her knee. "Honey, I'm glad that you are strong enough to hear God's call over your love for a man. I guess I still kind of hope Evan will come around, and maybe God will call him, too. Or maybe you'll only be away for a short time, and Evan will wait for you."

"I can't ask him to do that, Mom," Natalie said quietly.

"No. I don't suppose you can. But maybe he'll wait anyway."

It was a while before Natalie could speak

again. The reality of letting Evan go was sinking in, and it hurt more than she'd ever thought it could.

Feeling the sudden need to get away, to mourn the end of that sweet love in private, she turned to her mother. "Thanks, Mom. For understanding. For giving your blessing."

Her mother gave a sad smile. "I'm not saying I like it."

"I know. I'll be okay, though. You know that, don't you?"

"Yes, I know."

Haymaker Hall was unusually quiet on a January evening. The lobby of the dormitory was almost empty. Natalie stood by the windows that overlooked the parking lot, waiting for Evan to come down from his room.

She felt as nervous as she had on their first date. She just wanted this evening to be over. She'd only seen him once since that day in the park when she'd told him that she was leaving school and going to Colombia. She'd spent two weeks at home working on arrangements for her departure. Everything had happened so quickly since then. It all seemed surreal.

The door to the stairwell swung open,

and she watched Evan step into the lobby and search the room. When his eyes landed on her, there was no mistaking the sadness in them. But she saw something else there too. Resignation?

She started toward him and forced a smile. "Hi."

"Hi, Nattie." He put a hand on the small of her back and led her toward the door. "You want to get something to eat?"

She shook her head. "I'm not hungry, but if you want something, that's fine."

"I'm all right. You want to just go to the library then?"

"Sure."

"Let's walk, okay?"

She nodded and they started across campus. This politeness between them now was unbearable. She ached for the teasing, brother-sister-punch-in-the-arm way they'd always had with each other.

"So I don't suppose you've changed your mind?" he started, but she detected no hint of hope in his tone. He knew her too well.

She shook her head.

"And your parents are okay with this?"

"I wouldn't say they're thrilled, but I have their blessing."

"So how soon do you leave?"

She couldn't stop the smile that spread across her face. "Oh, Evan, everything is just falling into place. It makes me feel all the more like God has his hand in this. Grandma and Grandpa Camfield want to pay most of my expenses, and Mom and Daddy are going to pay my airfare. Since I'm not going under the auspices of Gospel Vision, but as Dad's guest, it actually simplified things. I sent for my passport, and Daddy's working on finding a good rate with the airline. Aunt Betsy is going to fly out with me, and then —"

"Whoa. You're going way too fast for me." Evan stopped in the middle of the sidewalk and looked at her. A grin played at the corners of his mouth, and it was the old Evan she saw behind the smile.

"I'm sorry. I'm just so excited. I can hardly wait to get there."

They had come to the entrance to the library. Evan held the door for her. They went to their favorite spot in the all-night study hall and settled into the overstuffed chairs — the same chairs they'd claimed on their first date together here. It seemed an eternity ago. That had been the night Evan had first declared that he thought they had a future together. Natalie wondered if he was remembering too.

"So," he said, breaking into her thoughts, "you're really going then?"

"I'm really going."

"I'm not going to sit around and pine for you, you know."

"I wouldn't want you to."

"Well, I might pine for a little while." He grinned.

"Oh, Evan . . ." The tears took her by surprise. "I'm going to miss you so much."

"Stop it," he said. "You're going to make me start crying."

She laughed through her tears.

A noisy trio of coeds came into the study hall and plopped down at a table a few feet from them. Evan stood abruptly. "Let's walk some more. It's really not that cold out."

Natalie nodded and followed him out the door.

The night campus was quiet and friendlier than it had ever seemed. She took his arm and looked up at him. "Why is it we never appreciate things until we're leaving them behind?"

"Hey, you tell me. I'm not the one who's going to the end of the earth."

"I know. Oh, Evan, I don't want to say goodbye. I just want to go and take the memories of everything we've had together with me."

"It doesn't work that way, Nattie. You have to say goodbye. You can't move on otherwise."

She took a deep breath and felt her throat constrict again. "I know you're right. But I've always hated goodbyes."

"Well, they don't have to be forever . . ."

"No, they don't. But I don't want to leave you with any false hopes. I don't know what the future holds for me, but I just have a feeling that I —"

"That you're not coming back."

"Maybe."

They walked in silence for a few minutes, then Evan stopped in the middle of the path and turned to her. "What happened to us, Natalie?"

She looked up, forced herself to meet his gaze. "What do you mean?"

"Were we in love? Because I'm confused. Did I take what we had for granted?"

"No, Evan. You didn't. And yes, I think we were in love. Maybe we still are . . . I don't know. But I think —" She paused. What *did* she think? She was quiet for a long minute before she spoke again. "Maybe God brought us together because he knew we each needed someone who understood what we were going through — with the accident. I'm not sure I could

388

have made it this far without you. And I'll never forget that . . . as long as I live. But maybe it's time to be strong now — on my own."

"There's nothing wrong with people needing each other, Natalie." There was hurt in his voice.

"Oh, this isn't coming out right at all. That's not what I meant."

"What you're trying to say is that I'm the best thing that ever happened to you, but you're willing to throw it all away to run off and live in some jungle with the snakes and spiders."

She gratefully recognized his effort to re-capture their bantering way, and she thanked him by slugging him playfully in the arm.

He rubbed his biceps. "Ouch."

They had circled back to the parking lot at Haymaker where Natalie had parked her car. He walked her to the driver's side and opened the door for her.

"Let's just get it over with, okay," he said as he pulled her into his arms. He held her as though he would never let go. "Natalie, I love you," he whispered. "And — not that I have a choice, but — I love you enough to let you go. With my blessing. I — I hope that doesn't sound presumptuous . . ."

She buried her face in his coat and held him tight. She felt the kiss he planted in her hair, and the tears came again. "Thank you, Evan," she choked. "I treasure your blessing. I really do."

He pushed her gently away from him and looked her in the eye. "You be careful, you hear?"

She could only nod.

"You'll write?" he asked.

"I promise."

"Okay." He wrapped her in a bear hug again, then abruptly let go. "Now get out of here," he said, his voice ragged.

Lluvia:
Rain

Twenty-Seven

"Are you sure you have everything?" Cole asked for the tenth time. His face was drawn, and the sadness in his eyes clutched at Natalie's heart.

"I have everything, Daddy," she assured him, her tone of exasperation covering for the tears that threatened to spill over.

"If she had one more thing, we'd have to charter a separate plane for her luggage," Aunt Betsy teased.

They stood in a tense knot on the concourse at Kansas City International Airport — Mom and Daddy, Grandma and Grandpa Camfield, and Uncle Jim all there to send her and Aunt Betsy off. Natalie's throat was full. She dreaded the goodbyes, wished she were already in the air, winging her way toward her future. Her nerves were raw with excitement and, if she was honest, a good measure of fear. Now that the day had finally arrived, she was more grateful than ever that Betsy had agreed to travel with her. Betsy would stay a week in Timoné before returning. More than once, her parents had reminded Natalie that she could always come home with Betsy if she changed her mind.

A velvet-smooth, dispassionate voice came over the public address system, announcing boarding for their flight — as though it were nothing to step onto an airplane that would carry her to a faraway place from which she might never return. She hadn't told her parents, but she had promised herself that no matter what happened, she would not come home with Aunt Betsy. She didn't want to give herself an out. There was too much riding on her staying.

The announcement came again over the PA system.

This is it.

Natalie forced a smile and gave one last hug around the circle, fighting back tears. "Bye, Mom, goodbye, Daddy. I love you."

"You be sure and e-mail the minute you get to San José," her mother said.

"I will. I promise."

Aunt Betsy disentangled herself from Uncle Jim's arms. "I'll see you in ten days, sweetheart," she said, giving her husband one last lingering kiss. She let him go, and she put an arm around Natalie's shoulder. "Are you ready for this?"

Natalie nodded resolutely and hoisted her carry-on bag over her shoulder. She popped up the handle on her overnight bag and tipped it onto its wheels. Her luggage suddenly felt as if it contained lead.

They fell into line with the other travelers, putting their bags on the conveyor belt and stepping through the metal detector. Once through security, she turned to wave one last time before gathering her bags again. She saw that Mom had slumped against Daddy, weeping, and for one wrenching moment, she felt pulled between two worlds. She forced herself to turn away and keep walking.

They made it to Eldorado International Airport in Bogotá without incident, and the following morning they flew into San José del Guaviare. Nate was waiting when they stepped off the plane into the sultry tropical air.

Natalie spotted her father first, as they waited with the other passengers for their baggage to be unloaded. "There he is!"

Betsy followed her gaze, and when she saw her brother, she shouted his name and started weaving her way through the crowd. Natalie followed.

When they reached him, they both fell into his arms. Natalie pulled away first and looked into her father's eyes. "Hi, Dad." She'd forgotten what a beautiful smile he had.

"You two are a sight for sore eyes," he said, still beaming.

"You, too," Betsy told him. She looked around the bustling airport. "Is this little airport always this busy?" she said.

He shook his head, and Natalie thought she saw worry etched in the lines on his face.

"Is it always guarded like this?" Natalie asked, watching the fully armed soldiers that milled around the airport. They had seen soldiers at the airport in Bogotá, too.

"Sometimes," her father said, obviously preoccupied. He inclined his head in the direction of a group of camouflage-clad men. "The thing is, it's hard to know if these guys are legit, or if they're guerrillas — rebels."

They waited for an hour, Nate going to check flight information every few minutes. Though her father couldn't get any clear answer, it seemed that the military in San José was on alert due to a rumor that a plane carrying a load of cocaine worth a small fortune was en route to San José.

Nate told Natalie and Betsy that he'd considered staying over in San José, but he had been afraid they might shut down the airport and leave them no choice but to make the trip to Conzalez by boat — a trip that could take as long as three days.

"Even if planes are flying out of San José, we can't always count on the airstrip in Conzalez being open so we can land," he explained.

Natalie almost hoped they'd be forced to travel the river all the way. She was anxious to see as much of the country as possible. It was almost noon when they boarded a flight, and by the time their plane finally took off from San José, she was so exhausted she wasn't sure she could have survived a long boat trip.

The flight to Conzalez took less than an hour. Hank and Meghan Middleton, the young missionary couple stationed in the small village, were waiting with a feast of roasted chicken and vegetables and corn on the cob.

"More corn, anyone? There's plenty," Meghan said, as they all sat around the table in the Middletons' large dining room. The young couple's living quarters were behind the medical clinic where Meghan, an R.N., saw patients from Conzalez and outlying villages. Natalie was surprised at how modern the house and clinic were. She knew from photographs that the mission office at Timoné and her father's living quarters there were little more than huts like those in which the villagers lived.

Nate patted his midsection and winked in Hank's direction. "The whole meal was wonderful, Meg, but I have it on good authority that a prudent man would save a little room in his belly."

"Hank! You spoiled my surprise!" Meg said. She smiled and went to the kitchen, returning with a frosted chocolate layer cake. She cut generous slices for each of them.

"I thought you guys would *never* get here," Hank teased, digging into his dessert.

Meg gave her husband a playful punch in the arm. "He actually tried to get me to cut a slice for him before lunch!"

Hank shrugged sheepishly.

"Mmm, I can see why," Nate said over a mouthful of the confection. "This is a real treat, Meg. Thank you."

Natalie enjoyed the time spent with the Middletons, but she was eager to see

Timoné. While they worked together clearing the dishes from the table, Nate glanced at his watch. "I hate to eat and run, but if we don't go pretty quick, we won't make it home before nightfall."

Natalie shivered involuntarily at the thought of being on the river after dark.

The Middletons walked with them to the dock, and Meghan helped Natalie and Betsy slather on insect repellant before they climbed into the boat.

Conzalez was barely out of view when Natalie began to see why Meghan had been so insistent about the foul-smelling repellant. She and Betsy swatted at mosquitoes almost as big as dragonflies, and other insects that she didn't recognize buzzed around them like flies on honey.

There was a primitive beauty to the river. The water of the Rio Guaviare was dark brown, like milky coffee, Natalie thought. At many places along the waterway, the trees hung low over the river, the branches on one bank laced together overhead with those on the opposite shore, forming a sort of tunnel through which they traveled. Inside the tunnel it was dark and cool, the air dead still. Natalie felt as though she were traveling back in time.

The river looped south and then back

east again where it widened. Though Natalie didn't think the native pilot spoke English, he seemed amused as she and Betsy bombarded Nate with questions about the things they saw along the way.

"Are there villages back in the trees?" Natalie asked, trying in vain to peer into the dense forests on either side of them.

"One or two that we know of, but they're far into the jungle, off of the smaller tributaries. On the shores of this main artery, there's nothing between here and Timoné. Then once you get twenty miles or so past Timoné, there are several villages right along the river." He cleared his throat. "That's where Chicoro is."

Natalie's pulse quickened. Chicoro was where her father had been held captive for more than two and a half years.

"Oh, Nate," Betsy whispered. "Do you . . . have you ever been back?"

He shook his head. "In all these years, there's never been reason to. But I would go . . . if I was called."

Natalie wasn't sure if he meant called by the villagers of Chicoro or called by God. She saw Nate swallow hard and stare into the distance.

After a few minutes he spoke. "I think God knows it's best that I stay away from there — at least for now."

"Why is that?" Betsy asked tentatively.

"The people there set me up as some kind of god — because I survived the fire and the sickness. I don't want to give them any reason to see me as some resurrected savior."

"What about the Timoné? When you came back after they thought you were dead, didn't they think you had been . . . resurrected too?" Natalie asked.

"I think there were some who did . . . at first. But the Christian converts in Timoné back then understood what had happened, and they quickly set the story straight. It became a real testimony of God's care for me." He was thoughtful for a minute. "I know it could someday be a testimony for the Chicoro people, too, and if God asks me to go back, I will. But I won't deny that I'm very grateful he *hasn't* asked me to go back yet." His sheepish smile made Natalie think of a little boy.

"Do you think they know that you're back in Timoné?"

"The Chicoro? Oh, probably." He smiled. "In spite of the fact that we don't have a telephone system, news manages to travel pretty fast from village to village."

Betsy eyed him. "You don't worry that

they might still want —"

"Some kind of revenge?" he finished for her. "No. I doubt that whole event is much more than a myth to the Chicoro by now, Betsy."

The current grew stronger, and the boat's pilot cranked up the motor, its roar making conversation difficult. They rode without speaking. Natalie's thoughts raged like the water around them. But as they journeyed deeper and deeper into the rain forest, her excitement grew. She was almost there. It was really happening.

Her first glimpse of Timoné was just that — a mere glimpse before the sun faded behind the dense forest, leaving the village in gray-green shadows. She stepped onto the dock while Dad steadied the boat. She would sleep in Timoné tonight.

Dad helped the pilot tie up the boat and hoist their bags onto the primitive dock. When they'd distributed the bags among them, he led Natalie and Betsy along a muddy pathway. He lit the way before them with a bright lantern, but more than once Natalie slipped and stumbled, catching herself, only to come up with a handful of mud.

"I thought this was supposed to be the dry season," she said after falling yet again.

Her father only smiled and trudged on.

In spite of the heavy-duty insect repellent she'd put on back in Conzalez, the mosquitoes buzzed around her face and hummed in her ears. She swatted at them with mud-caked hands and dreamed of the warm shower she had enjoyed in the luxurious hotel in Bogotá.

As the sun slipped farther below the horizon, Natalie squinted into the half-light, seeing wild creatures in every looming shadow. The jungle seemed alive with strange and haunting sounds. Natalie gripped Betsy's hand tightly as they tried to keep up with Nate. She took some comfort in the fact that her father seemed unconcerned by the ominous chorus. He plodded ahead, occasionally stopping to help them over an especially treacherous spot in the path but for the most part tramping silently ahead of them.

Without warning, a shrill squawk split the air, and Natalie and Betsy both let out a squeal.

"What was that?" Natalie asked, her eyes darting from side to side.

Her father laughed softly. "Probably a macaw," he said. He waited a beat. "Or it could be a jaguar."

The women gasped in unison.

"Just kidding," Nate laughed. "It's a bird — probably a scarlet macaw. After a few nights you won't even hear him."

"That's hard to believe," Betsy said wryly, as the bird's ear-piercing screech filled the night again.

Fifteen minutes later the path widened, and the mud puddles became fewer and farther between. Now, on either side of the trail, Natalie could make out the skeletal forms of huts raised on stilts.

They came to a large open-air pavilion covered with a thatched roof. Nate held the lantern high. "This is the village commons," he told them. "This is where your mother held Bible classes for the children, Nattie — after our hut got too small to hold all the kids. The village meetings are held here, and the *féstas*. Parties. Festivals," he explained.

"Like fiesta," Natalie said, proud of herself for making the connection.

"Right," he confirmed.

She had studied Spanish for three years in high school, along with the advanced class at the junior college. Dad had told her that a few Timoné words were similar to the Spanish. She'd picked up quite a few Timoné words from listening to the tapes her father had made when he'd first come

404

to Colombia. She was hopeful that the language barrier wouldn't be too difficult a hurdle.

"We're almost there," Dad said now, slowing his pace a bit. "Watch it here, you have to jump the stream. Our little footbridge washed out during the last rainy season, and we haven't had time to rebuild it yet."

The water glistened under the light from the lantern, and though the stream appeared to be only about four feet wide where it flowed across the path, judging by the rushing sound of the water, the current was quite swift.

Dad held the lantern until she and Betsy had safely hurdled the gully, then he turned and continued down the lane. He pointed to a larger hut that sat on a clearing to the south of two smaller ones. "Over there is the chapel. It was where Daria and I lived when we first came here. We enlarged it and held church there for a while, but happily we've outgrown it again. Now we have services in the commons down in the village and use the chapel for Bible classes and prayer meetings."

Through the dense thicket of trees Natalie saw a flicker of light in one of the smaller huts.

Her father apparently saw it too. "Oh, good. It looks like David is still in the office." He shouted into the darkness "*Hollio?* Hey, Dave!"

As he led the two women up the sturdy steps to the covered stoop, the door flew open and a grizzly bear of a man appeared, smiling. Natalie recognized him from Dad's pictures.

"Hey! You made it!" The man and Nathan Camfield shook hands and clapped each other on the back before ushering Natalie and Betsy into the hut.

The space inside was surprisingly large and quite bright with the light that Nate's lantern added to the one already burning, suspended from a hook in the middle of the ceiling.

David Chambers towered a good two inches over Dad's six-foot-three height, and behind his well-groomed beard he had an expression of amusement on his face and a twinkle in his eyes. "David, I'd like you to meet my sister, Betsy, and my dau—" Nate turned proudly toward them, then stopped midsentence and burst out laughing.

Now the restrained amusement on Chambers's face blossomed into a full-blown guffaw, and the two men laughed until they were red-faced and nearly breathless.

Natalie stared at them in wide-eyed astonishment, then turned to Betsy to see if she got the joke. Betsy turned to her at the same time, and when their eyes met, they both gasped.

Betsy was plastered with mud from her knees down, and her hair and face were speckled with the stuff, now dried and cracking. Only the circles around her eyes were free of mud giving her the appearance of a raccoon in reverse. Natalie put a hand to her own face and knew immediately that she must look at least as bad.

"You two look like you just lost a mud-wrestling contest," her father said when he finally caught his breath.

Natalie lifted her feet and inspected the bottom of her boots. Her shoes and the hem of her khakis were caked. "I thought my feet felt awfully heavy," she said sheepishly.

David Chambers was still looking at the two of them with amusement. Natalie felt suddenly self-conscious — this was certainly not the first impression she'd hoped to make on her father's colleague.

"Be grateful for the mud," Nate told them, "It's probably the only thing that kept the mosquitoes from eating you alive."

Betsy scratched at an arm through her mud-splattered blouse. "I think the mosquitoes must have gotten to me before the mud did," she groaned.

"Well, in that case, there's no better poultice than rich Colombian mud," Nate countered.

Betsy grinned at her brother. "You make it sound like coffee."

"Oh, wait till you taste his coffee." David winked. "You'll see just how apt the comparison is."

Nate laughed good-naturedly, then put a hand on his sister's arm. "Don't worry, Bets. The swelling won't last for long."

"Gee, thanks, Dr. Camfield. Must you always be so positive?" she teased. "Can't I just wallow in my misery for a while?"

"Wouldn't you rather wallow in a warm bath?"

"Oh, *is* there such a thing here?" Natalie piped up eagerly.

"Well, probably not in the sense you're thinking of," her dad said. "But we'll do the best we can. David, can you help me get some water on to heat?"

An hour later, Natalie and Betsy were

mud-free and dry, and stretched out on soft grass mats on the floor of the mission office. David had offered the bed in his hut next door to the office, but they'd declined politely.

Betsy's calm, even breathing soon filled the room. Natalie had expected that she, also, would fall asleep the moment her head hit the pillow, but here she was, wide awake, her thoughts careening like a hard-hit pinball.

She looked over at Betsy's still form under the mosquito nets they'd brought with them and whispered a prayer of thanks that her aunt was here to share the experience with her.

Natalie rolled over onto her back and reached into the darkness to make sure the netting over her own mat was in place. Outside, the sounds of the jungle roared. Yet none of it seemed real. Her dream of coming to Timoné, of living and working among the people with whom her birth father and mother had lived and worked — the very place where she had been conceived — was being ful-filled.

So why, now that she was finally here, was her brain swarming with thoughts of Mom and Daddy and her sisters back home? Of Sara? And most of all, of Evan Greenway?

"Please, God," she whispered into the cacophony of the Colombian night. "Don't let this have been a mistake. Let me make a difference here. Let me find what I'm looking for."

Twenty-Eight

Natalie woke with a start. The sun was laid in yellow patches across the floor of the hut. It filtered through the gauze of mosquito net that swayed above her with every movement. The light had an ethereal quality that made it seem even more unbelievable than it had last night that she was actually here in the village she'd daydreamed about for so long. She stretched and sat up, rubbing the sleep from her eyes.

Beside her, Betsy stirred, then resumed her slow, even breathing.

Natalie lifted the netting and looked around the room, taking in the details that had been hidden in the shadows last night. There were two wooden desks arranged in an L-shape in one corner of the room. One desk was scattered with open Bibles and concordances, stacks of papers, and a collection of stained coffee mugs. A long shelf for books hung over the window, but it appeared that most of the books intended for it had migrated to the desktop. Neat rows of science texts and classic novels were lined up along the back of the other desk, but — except for an open Bible concordance — the rest of the surface was clear. By the titles of the books, Natalie guessed that the tidier desk belonged to her father.

Along the wall opposite the desks, there was a primitive bench made of hollow cane poles lashed together with a thin, jutelike rope, and on the north wall was a small table that held the two-way radio flanked by two straight-backed chairs. A large bulletin board cluttered with maps and photographs and a calendar hung on the wall above the desks, but other than that the room was devoid of decoration.

Natalie rolled over onto her stomach, rested her chin on her hands, and listened to the sounds outside the window. The birds still sang in a discordant chorus, but the sound had a different quality than it had last night. Pushing aside the mosquito net she got to her feet, stepped over Betsy's prone form, and went to the window that overlooked the front stoop. She bent to peer through the taut mesh screen. The hut apparently faced east, for the arc of the sun was an orange sliver just climbing over the farthest emerald swell of trees.

This hut, which served as the mission office, sat in a clearing at the top of a rise. From her vantage point, Natalie could peer down into the village, which still seemed to sleep in darkness under the canopy of foliage. The peaked, thatched rooftops of dozens of stilted huts jutted through the greenery, and here and there thin curls of smoke rose from outdoor stone grills like the one just outside the window. Natalie's stomach growled as she caught a savory whiff of something cooking. The Middletons had sent food with them for the boat trip from Conzalez, and Dad had even cut down bananas for them to eat along the trail last night, but suddenly she was ravenous.

She was just about to rouse Betsy when she heard footfalls on the steps of the hut. A soft knock sounded at the door.

She grabbed a wrinkled chambray shirt from her duffel bag and threw it over the cotton nightshirt she'd slept in. Finger-combing her hair, she opened the door to find David Chambers towering over her.

"Good morning," she muttered.

"I hope I didn't wake you," he said quietly. Then looking past her to Betsy, who was stirring again, he said, "I apologize, but I forgot to get something I need for the laptop last night. I'm pretty much at a standstill without it."

"Oh, sure," she said, stepping aside to let him in.

He ducked beneath the doorframe and went to the desk on the south side of the room. Natalie watched as he slid a drawer open and rummaged quietly until he came up with a computer floppy disk.

"Oh, I'll need this, too," he whispered to no one in particular, closing a large dictionary and tucking it under one muscular arm. He was obviously making an effort not to wake Betsy. Natalie appreciated the gesture and felt guilty that they had taken over his office.

She tipped her head toward the gold watch he wore. "What time is it anyway?" she whispered. "Should we be getting up?"

He shook his head and matched her hushed tone. "Nate — your dad said to let you sleep as late as you like this morning."

"Is Dad awake?"

Behind the neatly trimmed beard, the corners of his mouth turned up. "Your dad is up long before dawn every morning. He's put in half a day's work already."

"Oh." She wasn't sure if his words were meant to be scolding because they'd slept so late, or if David Chambers was simply stating a fact. "Well, I'm awake," she told him. "I'll get dressed and be out in a minute."

He didn't respond, but held up the computer disk in tacit thanks before ducking outside and disappearing down the steps.

Natalie closed the door behind him and went to her duffel bag to find something presentable to wear. As she unfolded the creased and rumpled clothes, she saw movement from the corner of her eye. She turned in time to see a tiny brown lizard slither into an open compartment of her duffel. She screamed and kicked the bag into the corner of the room.

Natalie's screech brought Betsy bolt upright on her sleeping mat. "What? What is it, Nattie?"

The lizard chose that moment to come out of the bag and scurry toward Betsy.

Betsy spotted it and leapt to her feet, shrieking even louder than Natalie had. But when she tried to run, she got tangled in the mosquito netting and fell back to her knees. Her sudden movement sent the lizard running back in Natalie's direction.

Natalie jumped onto the sleeping mat beside Betsy — as if the two-inch-high pallet offered one iota of protection from a lizard. The two women clung to each other squealing, then laughing, then screaming again when the lizard zipped up the wall.

Suddenly the door flew open and David Chambers rushed in. "What happened?" he asked, his eyes darting around the room, his broad-shouldered form poised for combat.

Sheepishly, Natalie and her aunt pointed to the now empty wall.

"There was . . . a lizard," Natalie explained, breathless.

"A big one?" he asked.

"Well . . . he wasn't really big, but he was —"

"Fast —" Betsy filled in for her. "He was so fast."

"Did he look like that?" David asked, pointing toward the ceiling above their heads.

They looked up, and Natalie saw the lizard clinging to the thatch directly above their heads, beady eyes blinking at them, tongue flicking in and out like a snake's. She squealed and jumped off the mat, running to stand at the far end of the room. Betsy started to giggle like a little girl, and Natalie couldn't help but join in.

David Chambers reached up, knocked the lizard easily into the palm of his hand, carried it to the door, and tossed it over the stoop. "Better get used to those little fellows," he said when he ducked back through the door. "Would it help if I told you they eat mosquitoes?"

"A little, I guess," Natalie said in a small voice.

"You're both okay?" David asked as he turned to leave.

They nodded in silence. He left the room, closing the door behind him, but when they heard him burst into laughter at the bottom of the stairs Natalie and Betsy turned to stare at each other.

Natalie gingerly shook out a long cotton skirt and blouse and started to dress. She worried about the first impression she must have made on David Chambers. Dad had assured her that his colleague had given his blessing on Natalie joining them. So far the only thing he'd seen of her was a giggly, skittish adolescent. Of course, the same thing could be said of her forty-something Aunt Betsy. But then Betsy wasn't planning to stay.

As she pulled on her socks and boots, Natalie made up her mind that she would redeem the silly schoolgirl image she'd established. Somehow, she would prove that she had plenty to offer the mission at Timoné.

By the time Betsy and Natalie walked out the door, Nathan Camfield was crossing the stream to meet them. *"Hollio!"* he called cheerfully.

"Hollio," they replied.

"Ce mangura?" he asked.

She and Betsy exchanged blank looks.

"Are you hungry?" he translated.

"Oh, you have no idea," Natalie told him. "I could eat a horse."

"Sorry. No horse on the menu in Café Timoné, but I make a mean fruit salad. And there's corn bread. I have everything ready at my place," he said.

"Sounds great."

They followed him across the stream and into the heart of the village. Nate's hut was no more than a four-minute walk from the office. Along the way, brown-skinned natives stopped their work to stare at the two American women who followed behind Dr. Nate like ducklings after their mother. The children chattered and pointed, and Betsy and Natalie waved and called out shy greetings of *hollio.*

"Aren't they adorable?" Natalie whispered to Betsy, as a pair of dark-eyed brothers waved shyly from the stoop of a tidy hut. They looked to be about six or seven.

"Ah, don't let those two fool you," Dad told them. "They're twins. Double trouble — as ornery as the day is long. They're Tommi's boys, Nattie. Maybe you've heard your mother talk about him. He was one of her favorite students when he was little, and now he and his wife are some of our best workers in the church."

She didn't tell him that Mom rarely spoke of her days in Colombia.

"How many converts do you have now, Nate?" Betsy asked.

He rubbed his chin. "Oh, we usually have anywhere from thirty-five to fifty in the service on Sunday morning, but I wouldn't say they are all converts. There are usually some there out of curiosity — and some come just to make trouble. There are half a dozen young men who come every week without fail, but they refuse to step under the shelter. They stand outside, rain or shine, and watch everything that goes on. David has even caught them singing and clapping to the worship choruses on occasion, but they still won't join us."

"Are they spies or something?" Betsy asked.

"I'm really not sure," Nate said. "I can't get anything out of them. I'm just choosing to see them as elders in training."

He turned and flashed them a conspiratorial grin, and Natalie's heart warmed. It was so nice to be with her father. He seemed so relaxed, not tense like he was at Grandma Camfield's. Here he was . . . at home.

"Here we are," Dad said, as they approached a small hut at the edge of a grouping of the primitive homes.

The steps that led to his stoop were steeper, more ladderlike than those at the mission office. Her father led the way up and opened the door to reveal a table laid with three bowls overflowing with fruit, some of which Natalie couldn't even identify. Mismatched mugs held juice, and slices of corn bread sat on shiny leaves that served as plates. They viewed the appetizing spread through a layer of nylon netting, put there to keep the bugs at bay, she guessed.

"Nate, this is lovely," Betsy exclaimed. "You turned out to be quite the homemaker!"

He waved off her compliment, dipping his head and looking self-conscious. "You might want to hold your praise until you've tasted it."

He removed the sheet of netting and

pulled out stools for Natalie and Betsy. While they got settled, he poured coffee from a thermos, then sat and bowed his head. They followed suit.

"Father God," he prayed in the husky voice the long-ago fire had given him, "we come before you this morning with praise and thanksgiving for the many blessings you have given us. But especially, Father, we thank you for bringing Betsy and Natalie safely here."

He paused, and Natalie suspected that his emotions had choked him up. A lump lodged in her own throat.

"Bless this food to the nourishment of our bodies, and guide and bless the work of our hands today and every day," Dad finished.

Natalie looked up to find him smiling at her. She ate her first real meal in Timoné amid warm conversation and happy laughter. She had so much to be thankful for, so much to look forward to. Maybe here she could finally put the pain and guilt of her past behind her.

A silly cliché sang in her head: *Today is the first day of the rest of your life.* This morning it seemed neither silly nor cliché.

Twenty-Nine

"Where do you want me to put these, Dad?" Natalie asked, holding up a stack of what appeared to be foreign language medical brochures.

"Oh, I don't know," Nate said. "They came with the supplies some clinic in the States sent — or maybe it was a church. I've forgotten. But since they're in Portuguese, they don't do me much good." He scratched his head. "Maybe you should give them to David. He might be able to tell if there's anything in them that would be helpful."

"David speaks Portuguese, too?"

"Not fluently, but probably well enough to get the gist."

On their fifth day in Timoné she and Betsy were helping Dad clean out the mission clinic. Situated beside Nate's hut, the timber structure stood in rather stark contrast to the primitive architecture of the rest of the village.

Natalie laid the pamphlets by the door so she wouldn't forget them and turned back to sorting through the books and magazines on the shelf. As far as she could tell, the cabin that housed the clinic was the only concession to modern civilization her father had allowed in Timoné. Well, besides David's bed. The revelation that David Chambers slept on a real bed — box springs, mattress and all — had niggled at Natalie for two days now. She hadn't had much trouble adjusting to the heat and humidity of the tropics, and she was even learning to take the lizards in the hut in relative stride. But she did miss her bed. And since learning this piece of information, she'd become nearly obsessed wondering how David had gotten his bed here, and what it would take to get one for herself. She fully intended to mention it in her next e-mail home. Or better yet, in her next letter to Grandma and Grandpa Camfield.

"What do you want me to do with this?" Betsy held up a cardboard box with an illustration of a fancy macramé hammock on the front.

"Hmm? I forgot I even had that. I think Mom sent it in one of her care packages a couple of years ago. I just never got around to putting it up. I guess . . . just store it in one of those cupboards."

"Hey, I'll take it," Natalie said.

"Help yourself," he told her. Then, with a wink, "Just don't expect to have a lot of time to spend *using* it."

He picked up a large box of books and started for the door. He paused for a minute to watch Betsy, who had started scrubbing down the examination table. "Hey, Bets," he said, "doesn't this remind you of the good ol' days when I used to pay you to clean my room?"

"Yeah, and don't think you won't get a bill for this, too," she deadpanned.

He laughed and pushed the door open with one hip. "I'll be right back," he said.

"Sure you will," Betsy teased. "I know that old trick. You'll be back when the work's all done is what you mean."

Natalie smiled at their banter. She was going to miss Betsy something fierce. She enjoyed watching the camaraderie between her father and his sister. It did her heart good to see how happy Dad seemed to have them here; how happy he was here. She realized that ever since she'd learned her parents' story as a young girl, she'd pictured her father pining away, sad and lonely in a remote place, living among strangers.

But in the few short days she'd been here, she'd come to see that Nathan Camfield was quite content with his life in Colombia. She heard her father's voice outside the window. He was speaking with one of the native men. The man was gesturing broadly. Nate listened, then said something that caused a wide smile to stretch across the bronzed face of the Timoné man. Nate clapped him on his bare back, and they laughed together. Though Natalie couldn't understand a word of their conversation, it was obvious that they shared the amity of friends.

It still intrigued Natalie to watch her father with the natives, to see a strange language flow effortlessly from his lips. She tried, and failed, to visualize herself interacting this way with the villagers. She was doing well to spit out a *hollio* each morning as she walked through the village with her father. Without a written language, there was really no way she could study or practice. She longed to be able to speak with the children who had taken to following her around the village.

A few minutes later, Dad came back into the clinic and pulled several file folders from the four-drawer cabinet in the corner of the room. He sat down at his small desk and began to sort through the contents of the first folder.

"Hey, Dad, how do you say 'My name is'?" Natalie asked.

He looked up from the papers and smiled. "*Ne apronez* Natalie," he translated, putting a foreign inflection to her name so it sounded like Nat-ah-LEE.

She repeated the phrase.

"Very good," he said. "And don't forget, the minute we put Betsy on that boat, you'll not hear another word of English."

She groaned. David Chambers had suggested this torture at dinner the other night when Natalie and Betsy were complaining about how much difficulty they were having with the dialect. "It's for your own sake, Natalie," David had told her. "Studies have shown that people learn a new language much more quickly if it's all they hear or speak."

It had sounded to her like an excuse to make things more difficult.

"Betsy, are you sure you don't want to stay a couple more weeks?" she moaned now.

Her aunt laughed. "You don't think that would stop them, do you? They'd just impose the same punishment on me."

"Hey," Dad said, a note of seriousness in his voice. "It's not punishment. It's called education."

"It's just a lot harder than I thought it would be — the language."

"It'll come. Goodness, you haven't even been here a week yet. It's not worth losing any sleep over."

"Easy for you to say," she shot back. "You're not the one who's going to be suffering."

"I put in my dues."

"I know. I'm just griping."

Nate looked from her to Betsy, smiling. "What is it with you women anyway? Gripe, gripe, gripe. Is that all you do?"

"Hey, buster," Betsy countered, "I can take this dust rag and these work-blistered hands somewhere else if that's all the appreciation I'm going to get."

"Ouch," Dad said dryly. He smiled and held his hands palms out in submission. "Okay, okay. I guess I better quit while I'm ahead."

Natalie and Betsy laughed and set back to work.

That night the four Americans shared dinner together one last time. Tomorrow

David Chambers would take Betsy downriver to Conzalez where they would both be flown to San José del Guaviare. Betsy would fly back to the States the next day via Bogotá. David would remain in San José for a few days buying supplies, doing research on the Internet, and collecting the mail and e-mail that had come for the mission.

"Can I pour you another cup of *cazho?*" Nate asked, getting up from the table and reaching for the thermos of coffee on the stoop behind him. His hut was too small to accommodate all of them comfortably, so they had brought a table from the clinic and put it in front of Nate's hut. They were enjoying the relative coolness of the evening. Citronella candles and an abundance of repellent lotion kept the mosquitoes to a tolerable minimum, and the candles provided a pleasant remedy for the early darkness that came to the huts under the forest canopy.

Natalie pushed her plate away from the edge of the small table. The remains of her tamale-like entrée sat untouched. "That was wonderful," she said. "But I can't eat another bite. And here I thought I might lose a couple of pounds eating jungle food."

David Chambers laughed. "Jungle food?"

"Well, you know — I thought it would all be fruits and vegetables and rice and all that healthy stuff. Who knew that everything would be deep fried?"

"In lard, no less," Dad said, rubbing his stomach.

Natalie detected a glint in David's eye as he turned to Nate. "Should we tell her now or wait until the getaway boat has already gotten away?"

"Tell me what?" She shot them a suspicious look.

"Better tell her now," Dad said conspiratorially. "It's only fair."

"What?" she demanded.

Dad cleared his throat. "David and I had an executive meeting, and we've decided to appoint you to a very special position — a position of great honor and responsibility —"

"No-o-o . . . oh no . . ." she protested. "You're going to make me cook, aren't you?"

"You got it," Dad said, making his hand into a pistol and pulling the trigger.

"You male chauvinists." She turned to Betsy. "I've landed in the dark ages. Save me, Aunt Betsy."

"Hey, don't look at me. Did I twist your

arm to get you here?"

It was all in good-natured jest, but suddenly Natalie felt a bit panicked. "Dad, I'm a terrible cook. And that's with a microwave and refrigerator at my disposal! I don't know if I can *ever* learn to cook like this." She spread her hands over the remains of the sumptuous meal they'd just enjoyed.

David reached over and gave her arm a fatherly pat. "We'll help you out — for a few days. And we really don't always eat like this. Besides, we promise not to make fun of your cooking for one full month. Right, Nate?"

"Whatever you say, Dave."

"Betsy! Help!" she whined again.

When their laughter died down, David changed the subject. "Natalie, if you want me to transmit any e-mails for you when I'm in San José, you'll need to get them on the computer tonight. We need to get an early start in the morning."

"Okay," she said. "Will I have to start up the generator or anything?"

"You shouldn't. But I'll walk you back to the office later and get you set up on the laptop," David told her. "Betsy, do you have anything you want to send?"

"Nate already helped me put a post in the

outbox for my husband, but maybe I'll have Natalie send another quick message to Jim. Should we have her send something to the folks, too, Nate? Just to let them know we're all right and that I'm on schedule?"

"Good idea," he agreed. "You will write your mother, Nattie? I'm sure she's anxious to hear from you."

Natalie nodded.

The rest of the evening was spent in quiet conversation, and later when David delivered her and Betsy by lantern-light to their makeshift bedroom in the office, Natalie felt a pang of sadness and a moment of dread. Tomorrow Betsy would leave, and Natalie's last opportunity to change her mind about staying here would be gone.

She had left so much behind to come here. For some strange reason, David Chambers had made her think of Evan tonight. It seemed ridiculous. The man was nothing like Evan Greenway, not to mention that he was practically old enough to be her father. But something about the camaraderie they'd shared around the dinner table had made her miss Evan deeply. If she did not get on that boat with Betsy tomorrow, she knew it might be months before she'd have another opportunity to go home. If a year went by and she discovered she'd made a terrible mistake by coming here, would Evan still be there for her? They'd made no promises, but had she thrown something precious away by letting him go? *Oh, Lord, could you still change Evan's heart?* But even as she prayed the words, it seemed implausible.

She reminded herself of why she was here in the first place. She had felt a call from God. If she tried, she could still remember the feelings she'd had as she listened to her birth father's voice on the worn cassette recordings.

No. She couldn't go back. She *wanted* to stay. Needed to stay. She was here for a reason, she reminded herself. To make a difference. But oh, why did saying yes to one thing so often mean giving up something else? Something good. And Evan had definitely been something good in her life. Something very good.

While Betsy finished packing, Natalie cleared off a spot on David's desk, opened the laptop, and launched the e-mail program the way David had shown her. She was almost afraid of what she might say if she tried to write to Evan in her present state of mind. Instead she typed out a long letter home.

Dear Mom and Daddy,

Well, Betsy goes home tomorrow, and David Chambers, the translator who works with Dad, says that he'll send some e-mail for me if I write it tonight. Dad and David made a great dinner for all of us — fish and rice and some weird-looking vegetables that I couldn't pronounce — but they were good! Then Dad informed me that from now on the cooking duties are mine! You don't happen to remember any good Timoné recipes, do you, Mom? Help me out here. And pray for the men! You know what a terrible cook I am! :)

Things have gone very well since we arrived. Betsy and I have been sleeping in the mission office. (It's right near the hut where you and Dad lived, Mom. They use that hut as a chapel now for prayer meetings and stuff.) It was really the only place there was room for us, but it's been quite an inconvenience to the men, so tomorrow Dad is going to work on finding another place for me.

Natalie reread her last paragraph and deleted the parenthetical comment. It seemed like something that might hurt Daddy, and perhaps Mom already knew anyway. She began typing again.

Speaking of sleeping, David Chambers has a bed here! I'm so jealous. I haven't said anything to Dad yet, but that's what I'm asking for for Christmas. I don't know what it takes to get one here. (I don't think a bed would have fit on the boat we came on.) But I sure haven't slept very well on the floor!

She wrote about her experiences for another half-hour until her eyelids grew heavy. She still needed to compose a short note to send Grandma and Grandpa, and she did want to send something to Evan. It was hard telling how long it might be before she would be able to send e-mail again.

She opened a new file and carefully typed Evan's e-mail address in the appropriate field. Rubbing her eyes, she began to type.

Hollio, Evan!
Que ésta? That means, "How are you?" in Timoné. Beginning next week I'm not "allowed" to speak English, so I'm trying to get a head start on using

Timoné. David Chambers (you re-member the translator I told you about who works with Dad?) says that the best way to learn a language is to be forced to use it, so I guess I'm being forced. I don't think I've made a very good impression on David so far. Too many stories to tell you right now, but suffice it to say that he probably wasn't too impressed with the way I handled the creepy-crawly things here. Oh, Evan, you wouldn't believe how dif-ferent things are here. Beautiful beyond words, but sometimes in a very scary way! I'm living with lizards and walk-ing within inches of huge snakes and spiders the size of small rodents every day!

Oh, there's so much to tell you that I hardly know where to begin. It doesn't seem possible, but today I celebrated my one-week anniversary in Timoné. It's been wonderful getting to know Dad better. He's so happy here. You can imagine how much peace that has given me. He's more alive here than I've ever seen him. I guess that's what happens when you are right where God has called you to be.

Well, this is terribly short, but David

is taking Aunt Betsy to catch a flight home out of San José del Guaviare tomorrow, and he sends all the e-mail from there, so I need to finish.

Are your classes as hard as you thought they'd be this semester? Oh, Evan, your world seems a lifetime away from here. I miss you. There's so much of this world that I'd love to share with you.

Please write to me. We only get e-mail whenever someone goes in to San José, but I promise to answer every post.

Love and prayers,
Natalie

She closed the laptop. There was so much more she wanted to say to him. But it wasn't fair to him. She knew it would pull up those old longings in him, just as it did in her. She missed him desperately, wished he were here sharing these new experiences with her. And yet, even as she thought of him back in Kansas, she knew that in one week they had already grown away from each other. This past week had already changed Natalie Camfield in ways she couldn't yet define. But she knew she was not the same woman who had boarded the plane in Kansas City.

She looked over at Betsy who was sleeping soundly under the mosquito net. She wished Betsy could stay. She would miss the presence of another woman — well, one who spoke her language anyway.

But she had resolved to stay. No matter what Mom and Daddy said. No matter what she knew Evan wanted her to do. *No matter what.* She'd felt a call and she'd answered it. Everything depended on her making this work. *Everything.*

Thirty

Natalie waved from the rickety dock and tried desperately to hide the tears that welled behind her eyelids from her father. She stood watching and waving until the boat carrying Aunt Betsy and David Chambers disappeared around a bend in the murky waters of the Rio del Guaviare. In spite of Dad's presence beside her, Natalie had never felt quite so alone. All the things she had to learn just to survive here seemed overwhelming — the rigors of life in the tropics, communicating in the native language, learning to cook meat and vegetables she'd never heard of, in the most primitive circumstances imaginable.

Her introduction to the Timoné kitchen — if one could call it that — began that very evening. Nate showed her how to get a fire going in the open grill outside his hut. Though a few of the natives had cookstoves and a few more had built mud

438

ovens, the majority of the Timoné still cooked over an open fire in the *fogoriomo* in the way of their ancestors.

Natalie had learned quickly that Nathan Camfield believed strongly in fitting into the culture of the people to whom he ministered. He saw himself as a guest in their land. One who could offer the healing gift of medicine and, most important, the gift of a Savior. But a guest, nevertheless.

As they stirred up a batter for corn bread inside Nate's hut, Natalie asked him about his reluctance to bring modern equipment into Timoné.

"It just seems a few simple, inexpensive things would make your life so much easier," she said.

"You mean *your* life, don't you?" he winked. "Now that you're the chief cook and bottlewasher."

Her motive uncovered, she smiled. "Well, sure. But seriously, Dad, I'm curious about your thoughts on this."

He grew pensive for a moment before replying. "When your mom and I first came here, especially before we spoke the language, I was very conscious of being an outsider. I didn't want to set myself up as being superior. For us to bring in all this modern equipment — things that seem almost magical to such a primitive people — would have been like flaunting our wealth and position. So much of what we could bring in would have to be run by a generator — something very few of the people here will ever have access to."

"But you do have a generator," she pointed out.

"We do now. For years we didn't. It's mostly for the computer and the office equipment and the fridge in the clinic. Things necessary for our work here. I've tried to make that my criteria for bringing in anything new: Is it furthering the gospel or just making Dr. Nate or his lovely daughter" — he put his hands on her shoulders and gave her a playful shake — "more comfortable?"

She laughed but nodded in agreement.

"And you know," he continued, "now that David is working on the translation, I see even more the wisdom in not trying to modernize things."

"Why is that?"

"Since I've lived among the people, shared their way of life for over twenty years now, I understand the way they think."

He handed her a wooden spoon, and she stirred the corn bread batter while he talked. "For instance, when you try to relate a truth of the Bible to an American unbeliever, you might use an example of . . ." He thought for a moment. "Oh, say, a car: The Holy Spirit is like the engine that makes the car run . . . that sort of thing."

She nodded, beginning to see where he was going.

"Of course such an analogy would be meaningless here. But I can use the *fogoriomo*, for instance — the grill — saying how until the fire is lit the grill is powerless, just as we are powerless without God's Spirit in our lives. That means something to them."

"So if you were over here cooking with an electric stove in your cabin, they might not see that the faith you are trying to share with them is the same faith you live?"

"Well, that's true," he said. "But more important, if the *fogoriomo* wasn't part of my everyday life, I might not even think to use the analogy in the first place."

"Ohhh," she said. "I see what you mean."

Spooning the batter into the greased metal pan Dad had placed in front of her, Natalie grinned and asked, "So why does David get to sleep in a real bed?"

"David has problems with his back, and sleeping on the *mittah* — the grass mat —

seemed to aggravate it. He found a bed in San José and brought it here."

"Are you okay with that?"

"David and I are colleagues, Nattie. I'm not his boss. He defers to me sometimes because I've been here longer — or when it's a medical matter — but I don't try to impose my views on him. And when it's an issue concerning the translation, I certainly concede to him."

"Do you think he's okay with my being here?" she blurted out, seizing the unexpected opportunity to ask a question she'd been wondering about.

"David? Of course." Dad's forehead wrinkled, and his eyebrows met in the middle. "Why wouldn't he be?"

"I don't know. It's just that I know for a while I'm going to be more trouble than I am help."

"More trouble than you're worth?" he teased. But he must have understood her need to have her question answered, for he turned serious. "David understands that. The same could have been said for him when he first arrived, you know."

"Oh. I guess I never thought about it that way."

He patted her arm. "I'm glad you came, Nattie. You can't imagine how much it means to me to have you here."

She couldn't speak over the lump in her throat.

"But let's get that bread to baking," he said, picking up the pan of batter, "or I might starve to death before it comes off the grill."

She followed him outside, and they sat together visiting, taking turns basting the vegetables on the *fogoriomo* until the delicious aroma of hot corn bread, fresh trout, and exotic varieties of grilled squash, peppers, and other vegetables filled the air.

"Dad," Natalie said, as they washed the pottery together in a galvanized tub on the stoop, "you know that rule David has about only speaking Timoné?"

"Oh. I guess we've broken that already, haven't we?"

"Big time. But think what we would have missed. Can we . . . well, can you and I have maybe just one night a week when we get to talk like this? At least until I get the hang of Timoné?"

He put an arm around her shoulders and squeezed. "I'd like that, honey. David might not be crazy about the idea, but we'll just let it be our little secret, okay?"

"Hey, if that man can sleep in a real bed, I think I can have one night to speak my native tongue with my own dad."

Her father's laughter filled her with unspeakable joy.

To Natalie's delight, her father secured a
small hut for her less than a hundred yards
from his. Apparently real estate in Timoné
was not precious. Natalie was amazed to
learn that Nate had traded some good
lumber, a flashlight, and a coffee thermos
with one of his neighbors, Polo del
Juarique, for the hut.

When Natalie expressed her astonishment at how seemingly easy it had been to
acquire the hut, her father told her mod-
estly, "Well, there is the small matter of my
saving the life of Polo's eldest daughter
after she nearly drowned a few years ago.
That may have sweetened the deal." He
winked.

Natalie spent a happy morning moving
into her new residence. Though only one
room and less than half the size of the hut
that housed the mission offices, her new
quarters boasted a covered porch that was
large enough for a picnic-sized table and
rustic benches — which Dad had also bartered for — and the hammock Betsy had
found when they were cleaning out the
clinic.

Now, as the sun grew hot and the air became a sauna, she sought the shade in the sumptuous embrace of the hammock — and the obligatory mosquito netting — and laughed to herself. She had realized the American dream — a home of her own. The house itself might not be much, but her "garden" rivaled any she'd ever seen featured on the pages of *House & Garden*. Just outside her veranda grew foliage in every shade of green and generously dotted with lush orchids, pink and orange hibiscus blossoms the size of platters, and other tropical flora that she could not yet call by name. Tiny hummingbirds flitted among the flowers, sipping nectar, while brightly colored parrots punctuated the more melodious birdsong with their squawking.

Natalie allowed herself half an hour to savor her surroundings before she set off to the mission office. She wanted to get it cleaned before David returned from San José. Dad expected him back today, although Natalie was learning that Timoné operated on a much different time schedule than the world to which she was accustomed.

She filled a small bucket with water from the stream, and with cleaning tools in hand, she entered the office that had served as her bedroom for more than a week. She knew David would be relieved to have his work space back.

She swept the floor and walls and brushed the day's spider webs from overhead. She moved the furniture — which had been pushed against the wall to accommodate their sleeping mats — back into place and dusted it with a damp rag.

She tidied the few items on her father's desk. Then she looked at David Chambers's desk and sighed heavily. He might be nice, but the man was a slob. That was all there was to it. His desk was littered with books and papers, pencils minus their lead, and stained coffee cups. There was even a molding banana peel poked into one of the mugs.

She set the dirty dishes on the stoop ready to take back to her hut. She would wash them with the lunch things and bring them back this afternoon. Entering the office again, she gazed at the two men's desks. The contrast was stark. How could anyone work amid such chaos? she wondered. She closed the covers of two worn dictionaries and plugged them into empty spots on the bookshelf above the desk. Another stack of books lay on a stool beside the desk. A dozen brightly colored sticky notes protruded from each volume. Natalie left the markers in place, but lined the books up on the crowded bookshelf beside the dictionaries. There seemed to be no rhyme or reason to the way the books were arranged, and feeling suddenly inspired, she began to reorganize them, shelving them alphabetically by title. It took some time, but it was a small favor she could offer in exchange for David's sharing his office so generously with Betsy and her. She couldn't help thinking how pleased he would be to find his office so well organized and tidy. She wondered how long it would stay that way.

The papers and computer printouts spread across his desk looked important, and she didn't want to disturb them. She did gather them into one neat stack so she could dust the top of the desk. She sharpened his pencils and cleaned half an inch of lint and dirt from the jar that held pens and scissors and other office supplies. She resisted the temptation to open his desk drawers and organize them as well. She didn't want to violate his privacy, but perhaps when he saw what she'd done with the rest of the office, he'd give her permission to do just that.

Giving the desk one last swipe of the dust rag, she stepped back and viewed the room with satisfaction. She emptied the pail of water over the edge of the stoop, loaded it with the dirty dishes and the rest of her cleaning supplies, and started back to her own hut. It felt good to be able to contribute.

David Chambers pulled a dingy handkerchief from the back pocket of his jeans and wiped the sweat from his brow. He shaded his eyes with one hand and tried to gauge how long it would be before the boat docked. After making this trip on the water almost a dozen times, he was beginning to recognize the landmarks along the river.

He hadn't liked the feel of things in San José one bit. It wasn't just the paramilitary hanging around the airport. That wasn't all that unusual. But something was afoot. He could sense it. And he wasn't the only one. All his contacts in San José had seemed to be on edge.

Though the man hadn't said anything, there seemed to be caution in the way Pedro Alejandro, the spice vendor at the market, talked, his eyes shifting as if he were searching for something. And Lucretia at the library had been downright frightened. For some odd reason, she had been ready to deny him access to the computers until he reminded her kindly that she owed him a favor for translating an American Web site into Spanish for her the last time he'd been in San José.

David was anxious to talk to Nate about his impressions. And yet he hesitated to say anything. Of all the rotten times for things to turn shaky — with Nate's young daughter visiting. Or staying, it appeared. The girl was obviously not cut out for the rough life Timoné offered. And yet she was still here. He would have bet his beard that she'd have been on the first boat back to the States with Nate's sister. Now she was stuck here for who knew how long.

Still, even when the rest of the country was volatile, their village remained fairly safe. The Timoné had no interest in politics, and except for a few isolated incidents, they had not become involved in the drug trade that seemed to be at the heart of so much of the violence.

David shifted on the uncomfortable seat and checked to be sure his duffel was safely beneath the bench. He smiled to himself as he thought of the thick sheaf of e-mail letters bundled inside. Half of them were for the girl. He wondered if the letters would make her regret her decision to stay. A fair number of the posts were from someone named Evan. He hadn't actually read the notes, of course, but he'd been young and in love once himself, and as the pages rolled out of the printer, he couldn't help but notice a few phrases that seemed to go beyond friendly hellos. But maybe things were different nowadays. Heaven knew that whenever he went back to the States, he felt the English he heard on television and on the streets was a completely different language than he had spoken growing up in Ohio. Still, he doubted the language of love had changed all that much since he was a starry-eyed young man. If he tried, he could remember what it was like, and a part of him felt envious of what these pages of Natalie's e-mail represented.

After what had happened with Lily, he tried not to remember those emotions. He'd long ago put aside any notion of ever having those feelings again. It was too painful.

Wiping the sweat from his forehead again, he glanced at his watch. They'd been on the water for almost four hours. It wouldn't be long now till the dock at Timoné came into view. It would be a welcome sight.

Thirty-One

When the afternoon rains ended, Natalie and her father trekked down to the dock, thinking they might meet David's boat. Natalie heard the commotion at the landing before she saw the boat. Though this dock, which served a tributary of the Guaviare, was almost half an hour's walk from the village, it was a popular place for the adolescent boys of Timoné to play. They swam and fished and watched for the occasional motorboat that docked there.

Sure enough, the boat David was on was just mooring as they rounded the bend in the pathway. The boys hung off the pier and dog-paddled in the water, greeting David and the pilot of the boat with whoops and cheers.

When her eyes met David's, Natalie waved a greeting, but she hung back while her father exchanged welcoming handshakes and pats on the back with him.

451

They began to unload the supplies, and when Natalie saw that there were many boxes and crates to carry, she went to lend a hand.

When they were each loaded down with all they could carry and there were still supplies on the boat, David motioned to two of the younger boys who stood apart from the others watching them work. *"Ceju na,"* he said, reaching into his pocket. He pulled out a crumpled pack of chewing gum, saying something in Timoné that caused the boys' eyes to light up. They loaded the lads down with boxes, and the five of them hiked back to the village.

Darkness was encroaching under the forest canopy when Dad set his cartons on the stoop and unlatched the door to the mission office. Natalie went in first and put her load on the small table. Hot and sticky and out of breath, she wiped the sweat from her face with her shirttail and watched David, anxious to see his response to the pristine office.

He put down the boxes he was carrying, relieved the native boys of their burden, rewarded them with the gum, and dismissed them. He glanced around the room, then took the laptop in its padded case over to his desk. His eyes widened, and his Adam's apple bobbed in his throat, but he said nothing.

While they sorted through the supplies, repacking boxes that belonged in the medical clinic and those that went to each of their individual huts, Dad and David talked nonstop — though Natalie couldn't understand a word, since they spoke only in Timoné.

She tried to pay close attention to pick up the gist of what they were saying, but not one syllable sounded like anything she had ever heard. Their exchange seemed to be friendly banter, and Natalie guessed that David was asking how things had gone while he was away.

At one point she interrupted, holding up a box of supplies. "Whose pile do these go in?"

"*Ni,*" David said, shaking his head with a condescending smile. "*Timoné.*"

She groaned, then yielded. Smiling sweetly she raised her brows in a question mark, and pointed to the box. "*Que?*" she asked simply. There was more than one way to skin a cat, and sign language was the same in any dialect.

The two men laughed.

"*Mi utta,*" David answered, amusement in his eyes. But he did proffer the benefit of sign language back to her, pointing in the direction of his hut. Of course. *Mi utta.* My hut. She added the box to the stack near David's desk.

He and Nate went back to their conversation, leaving Natalie out of the loop. Soon their voices changed, and she thought she detected the tenor of anxiety in David Chambers's tone. She watched her father's face carefully. Once she caught his glance as though they might be talking about her, but when their eyes met his expression gave nothing away. She felt the blood pump a little faster through her impatient veins.

They finished their sorting, and Natalie picked up two boxes of supplies intended for the clinic. She'd been helping her father in the clinic long enough that she knew where things belonged. It would be a good excuse to get out of here. She cleared her throat to get their attention. Both men looked up at her, but they didn't break stride in their conversation.

She lifted her chin smugly, indicated the boxes, and turning on her heel said, "Dr. Nate's." Well, after all, that *was* his name in Timoné, too.

Still rattling off something to her father and all but ignoring her, David Chambers opened the door for her.

"Égracita," she said curtly. Then, pointedly, she told her father, *"Mi utta."*

She huffed down the path toward the clinic. The further she walked the more furious she became. She began to mutter to herself — in defiant English. "I'd like to know what makes him think he can decree what language I speak? By George, I'll speak English if I feel like speaking English. And not so much as a 'thank you' for cleaning off his pigsty of a desk."

The boxes were heavy, and by the time she reached the clinic she was sticky with perspiration and indignation. She worked the combination on the padlock that secured the door and went in to put away the supplies. Then she went to her own hut.

It was too early to retire for the night, and she was anxious to see if David had brought any e-mail for her, but she decided that she would go to bed anyway. She had no desire to see David Chambers again tonight — or anyone, for that matter. She was relieved that she had her own place to sleep and that it was a good distance from there to a certain hut on the other side of the stream.

Alone in her *utta* for the first night, sleep did not come easily. She tossed on the grass *mittah* under the gauzy netting and made a mental list of all the Timoné words she knew. It wasn't very impressive. And when she thought of how few of those words in her meager vocabulary could be strung together to make an intelligible sentence, she almost despaired. She certainly hadn't realized how much she liked to talk. Though she and Sara had had their share of all-night chats, she'd never seen herself as a typical gabby female. But now the thought of not being able to communicate on a level deeper than grunts and hand gestures — for who knew how long — overwhelmed her.

She threw back the mosquito netting from around her mat and rose to her feet, padding barefoot across the small room and back, then back again. She clenched and unclenched her fists. She wished Evan were here. He would know what to do. No, Evan wouldn't have let things go this far in the first place. He would have stood up to David's ridiculous rule.

Well, she would show him. She would study the Timoné language and learn more quickly than even the precious David Chambers.

David came into the mission office the

following morning low on sleep and even lower on patience. He looked again at the damage that had been done to his desk, and with a plea heavenward for self-control, he began to try to sort through the mess.

He had just located his misplaced dictionaries when Nate made his usual morning appearance at the office.

"Whoa!" Nate exclaimed lightheartedly after taking one look at David's desk. "Are my eyes deceiving me, or did you actually clean off your desk?"

"No, I did not," David answered. He tried to keep the resentment from his voice, but apparently without success.

"Ohhh, I see. You had some help?"

He shook his head and bent over his work, hoping Nathan would catch the hint that he wasn't in a mood to talk about it.

"Did Natalie do that?" Camfield asked.

"I assume so," David replied, busying himself sorting through the papers she'd desecrated.

"I'm sorry, Dave. I'll have a word with her."

"No!" It came out more stridently than he intended. He deliberately softened his tone before speaking again. "It's all right. I'm sure she meant well."

"Yes, I'm sure she did. But if I don't say something, she might make this a weekly habit. I'd better speak with her."

"Please . . . don't say anything. I'll talk to her myself."

He felt Nathan's eyes looking down on him. After a minute, he glanced up and met the older man's thoughtful gaze.

"Go easy on her, will you, Dave?" Nate said softly. "I'm sure she thought she was doing you a favor."

"Don't worry. I'll be nice." He went back to sorting through the mess on his desk. When he left for San José, there had been carefully indexed books laid out in precise order on his desktop, pages of word lists and definitions organized by category. Scraps of important notes had been strategically placed where he could easily find them. Natalie might as well have been a Kansas tornado. He could not find one thing he needed. The word lists were a jumbled mess. He was beginning to fear she'd thrown some pages away.

After a while Nate stood and headed for the door. "Well, I think I've done about all the damage I can do," Nate said. "I need to get over to the clinic. If you want to take a look at that radio later on and see if you can fix it, be my guest."

David grunted. *Wrong thing to say, buster,* he thought. He would be doing well if his desk was "fixed" by this time next week. He sure wouldn't have time to work on that piece-of-junk radio.

He sorted and reorganized for another hour, and the steam began to subside. All his papers did seem to be here after all, and once he figured out that the books had been filed in alphabetical order by title, he realized that it was actually kind of nice to have them off the desk and out of the way. Still, that was no excuse for her to take it upon herself to clean off his work area. He was lucky she hadn't tried to clean out his desk drawers. If she'd gone that far, he would have personally escorted her to the dock to wait for the next boat out.

"*Hollio,*" Natalie said, coming into the office. Then, with almost perfect inflection, she said in Timoné, "Dad said you wanted to see me?"

"Yes." He leaned over the desk and cleared off a chair for her. "Please, sit down."

She smiled and actually shook a finger at him. "*Ni. Timoné,*" she scolded, taking a seat.

Why that impudent little . . . . He couldn't help himself. He leapt from his chair and launched into a diatribe like he hadn't delivered since his best Spanish student had told him he was dropping out of college. "What makes you think you can come in here and rearrange my things?" he said, arms spread wide, fingers splayed. "Every single book on my desk was exactly where I needed it to be. I have passages marked for my reference in every one of those books." He strode back and forth, his words gathering steam. "Now I can't find one thing I'm looking for. You have set my work back weeks. I might as well be starting from scratch! What were you thinking, girl? Well, let me tell you. You *weren't* thinking."

He ranted and paced behind his desk, saying everything aloud that he'd muttered under his breath since he'd first realized the damage her little cleaning spree had inflicted. When he'd finally run out of words, he took a handkerchief from his pocket and wiped his forehead, realizing how foolish he must appear to her.

He looked at Natalie, who sat in front of him with her mouth hanging open in stunned silence. And he realized that it was only by God's grace that he had delivered his entire speech in the Timoné dialect.

Natalie looked at him for a long minute.

"Excusez, ni comprendé," she said with a shrug. Her words were a jumble — more Spanish than Timoné — but he got her drift. And then he realized that she had got him — and got him good. He started laughing. Which was apparently the wrong thing to do.

The girl burst into tears, pushed the chair back, and made for the door.

"Wait!" he shouted.

She struggled with the latch, still trying to escape.

"Natalie, please. Just a minute." He spoke clear English as he came from behind the desk and went to where she stood. Haltingly he put his hand on her arm. "Natalie, I'm sorry."

She turned toward him but kept her eyes on the floor.

He felt like a fool — the scholarly linguist, suddenly tongue-tied. He was disgusted with himself for letting a mere girl get to him like this. He put his fingers under her chin and gently raised her head, forcing her to look at him. "Natalie, please forgive me. I know when you — when you cleaned off my desk, you were only trying to help. I shouldn't have yelled at you — in any language."

He thought he saw a hint of a smile play

461

at the corners of her shapely mouth. He knew he should say something more. Explain to her why he'd been so upset. But looking at her lovely face, the thoughts that pelted his brain frightened him. Suddenly he realized that her chin still rested on his hand, the warmth of her skin searing his fingers. He dropped his hand as though burned and took a step backward.

What was he thinking? He'd been down this road before. He thought he had escaped temptation's clutches long ago, and now — completely without warning — it stood mere inches from him. With her pale, silky hair and her sun-kissed complexion, Natalie Camfield was as opposite from Lily's dark beauty as she could be. Yet something about her — the emotion that sparked in her eyes, the vulnerability in the tilt of her head — caused memories of Lily to swirl around him. Memories of the good times. Before —

He yanked his thoughts back to the present and turned away from Natalie, muttering a few more feeble words of apology.

"It's all right, David," she said quietly, swiping at a tear-stained cheek. "I was trying to help when I cleaned off your desk. But I see now that what I did wasn't helpful at all. I . . . I wasn't thinking. Please forgive me."

He stroked his beard, chastened. "No, I'm the one who needs to ask forgiveness. I know you meant well. I let my temper get completely out of control . . . I acted like a complete *brihacho*. There was no excuse for that."

"*Brihacho?*" Her inquisitive smile was a gift.

"I'm sorry. I sometimes lapse into Timoné without even realizing. It means 'idiot' or 'jerk.'"

"Oh," she said, her grin widening. "I'll remember that."

Thirty-Two

Rain pelted the ground, and thunder rumbled in the distance. The rainy season had begun in Timoné, and the work of each day was now determined by the weather. Natalie grabbed an umbrella and headed for the village commons. She could think of plenty of things she'd rather be doing today than helping her father vaccinate dozens of screaming babies and toddlers. But this particular vaccine had been hard to come by, and now that he had it, Dad was anxious to get it into the Timoné children. He had even asked David to set aside his translating work for the morning to help with the task.

When Natalie arrived at the commons, David and her father were dragging the decrepit examination table from the clinic into the center of the gazebo. They were both soaked to the skin.

"*Hollio*," she called out cheerily.

David lifted his hand in a greeting.

"Oh, good, you're here," Dad said, obviously preoccupied. "Could you go to the clinic, Nattie, and bring that box of supplies from the bottom of the cabinet in the exam room?" He described the box to her — in English. He apparently didn't have time or patience for language lessons this morning. "Be sure and wrap it in plastic so it doesn't get wet on the way over here. David, I think I'm going to need that small table from the clinic after all. Could you bring that over too, please?"

David nodded and turned in the direction of the clinic.

"David?" Natalie said, holding her umbrella high, and offering a spot underneath for his six-foot-five frame.

"Oh . . ." He looked at her as though she'd presented him with a decision that required careful consideration.

"We're going the same way," she explained lamely.

"Um, thanks," he said finally, speaking English, "but I'm already so wet I don't know what good it would do." He ducked from under the thatched roof of the pavilion and made a dash for the clinic.

"Okay," she said to the empty air. She shrugged and followed behind him, dodging the puddles that pockmarked the trail. He soon disappeared into the dense foliage ahead of her.

When she got to the clinic a minute later, David was moving the supplies off the table onto a nearby countertop.

"Here, let me help," she offered, picking up a glass canister of long-handled cotton swabs.

"It's okay. I've got it," he said without looking at her.

"Okay . . ." she said, putting the canister back and holding her palms out in surrender. He was obviously in a lovely mood this morning. She left him to himself and went into the exam room to find the supplies Dad needed. The cabinet she thought he had been talking about was full of bottled water, towels, and paper goods. She opened a few other doors, but none yielded the box she was looking for.

"Hey, David," she called into the outer room.

He appeared in the doorway. "Yeah?"

"Didn't Dad say that box was in here?"

"I thought he said right there." He pointed to the first cupboard Natalie had looked in.

She wrinkled her nose. "That's what I thought too. But I'm not finding it."

David grunted, came into the room, and

started opening and slamming shut the same cabinet doors she'd just looked behind. Trying to stay out of his way, Natalie went to the other side of the room, double-checking places she'd already searched.

When they met in the middle of a row of cupboard doors, David took a step back, tucked his hands in the pockets of his khakis, and panned the room. "Hmm, I sure *thought* he said they were in here."

"Me too." Natalie nodded.

"I'll check the other room," he volunteered.

Natalie searched the exam room again, but David's "aha!" interrupted her from the next room.

She went to the doorway. "You found them?"

He held up a cardboard box in triumph. "They were in the bottom of *this* cabinet," he said, cocking his head toward one wall. "I think your dad just misspoke." For the first time this morning, he actually looked her in the eye, and his mood seemed to lighten a bit.

Natalie crossed the room and took the box from him. "Thanks," she said. "I think Dad's kind of worked up about this morning."

David returned her smile. "He gets that

way sometimes. He'll be fine once the villagers start coming. And this weather isn't helping matters any." He lifted one end of the table with a grunt. "This is heavier than it looks."

"Here." She set the box down on the table. "This box is light. I'll just set it in the middle and carry one end." She lifted her side of the table.

He hesitated. "Well, we can try it, I guess. Is there anything breakable in there?"

Natalie peered inside the box. "It doesn't look like it. Okay. I'll swing my end around. Ready? One, two, three . . ."

They both lifted, but David's end went a full foot higher off the floor than hers, sending the box sliding. They laughed.

"You need to grow a few inches," he said.

"I'll work on that," she said wryly.

"Hang on. I've got an idea." He went to a drawer and came back with a roll of duct tape. He wrapped a length of tape around table and box, and ripped the tape from the roll with his teeth. "There. Try that."

After another false start, they managed to maneuver the table through the door. Natalie had left her umbrella lying on a counter in the clinic, and before they'd gone twenty feet down the trail, the rain had plastered her hair to her scalp.

"Yep, it's sure a good thing you brought that umbrella," David teased, avoiding her eyes.

She gave a little snort, and put out her tongue to catch a drop of rain as it rolled off her nose.

They finally deposited the table in the commons, where her father was already greeting the few villagers who had arrived. David tried to peel the wet tape from the box, but it held firm.

"Here, let me try," Natalie said, stepping close to him and taking hold of the tiny corner of tape he'd managed to loosen. "I've got longer fingernails than you." Her bare arm brushed his, and he pulled away as though she'd pinched him. She looked at him for an explanation, but he quickly averted his eyes and went to help Nate.

He barely spoke to her the rest of the morning. Natalie wondered what she'd done to offend him. Then the minute Nate gave the go-ahead, he started to head back to the mission office. "I'll come back right after lunch and move the furniture back to the clinic," he stopped and said over his shoulder.

"I can help," Natalie jumped in. "I'll be here anyway."

"That's okay," David said, shaking his head. "You don't need to."

"Oh, I don't mind. We kind of had a system going there with the duct tape." She smiled.

"No. I can get it," he said. She was sure he didn't notice her smile because he refused to look at her.

Dad looked from her to David, and Natalie just shrugged. It seemed every time she thought she and David were beginning to get along, she did something to set him off.

The rest of her morning was spent helping her father. She held down squirming, screaming toddlers while he inoculated them. With her limited vocabulary, she tried to convince half a dozen mothers to allow Dr. Nate to give their children the shot, explaining that some pain and anguish now could prevent later heartbreak. She was mostly unsuccessful at that. Natalie wished she could have found a better way to convince them, but they merely walked back to their huts with their children in tow.

The rain finally let up, and she and Dad carried the smaller supplies back to the clinic. Natalie fixed rice and beans for their lunch on Dad's *fogoriomo,* and they ate at the table outside his hut.

"Thanks for your help this morning, Nattie. I appreciate it."

"Well, I wish I could communicate better. Maybe I could have talked a few more of the women into letting their babies be vaccinated."

"Don't worry about it. We did the best we could." He stood and picked up his bowl. "Now, why don't you let me do these dishes, and you take the rest of the afternoon off. It looks like there's another storm front rolling in."

Natalie went to her *utta* and settled into the hammock with a novel she'd found on a bookshelf in Dad's hut. But her mind was replaying the morning. What was it about her that seemed to rub David Chambers the wrong way? Was he mad because she'd been speaking English? He'd made no effort to speak Timoné to her. Dad had been anxious enough getting things set up to administer the vaccine. It had been no time for a language lesson.

David was scheduled to leave tomorrow to spend a few days in San José del Guaviare. As far as Natalie was concerned, he couldn't go fast enough or stay away long enough. She was getting tired of having to tiptoe around his moods.

She wished she could recapture the laid-back way they'd had with each other that first week when Betsy was still here. She wasn't sure what had changed. Maybe Betsy had served as a buffer. Maybe David had just been on good behavior because they were company. Okay, she conceded, maybe they'd *both* been on good behavior that first week. Whatever it was, she couldn't deny that she seemed to bring out the worst in the man. For Dad's sake, she was determined to get along with him, but things were certainly more peaceful around here when David was gone.

She reread the first page of the novel, realizing that she hadn't absorbed one word her first time through. She read for a while longer, and as the clouds moved in again and the afternoon rains fell, she dozed off. She wasn't sure how long she slept, but she'd just awakened and opened up the novel again when she heard her father's voice beneath the covered stoop.

"Hey, lazybones. Are you awake up there?"

"Come on up, Dad."

Within five seconds, he was standing beside the hammock looking down at her with mock disgust.

"And don't call me lazybones," she laughed. "If you'll recall, you were the one who gave me the day off."

"Well, yeah," he said. "I thought you might want to clean your *utta* or wash your clothes or something. I didn't mean come up and lounge the day away." He reached up and gave the ropes that supported the hammock a playful shake, causing her to grab on to the sides of it to avoid falling out.

"Hey, you," she squealed.

He paced the floor for a minute, ostensibly inspecting the thatch of her ceiling and stopping to snap off a branch that had crept underneath the roof of the open porch. "You're going to have more than lizards in your house if you don't keep these branches pruned back, Nattie."

"Thanks," she told him.

When he cleared his throat and took a seat on the bench beside the hammock, Natalie realized that he'd come to see her with a purpose. "What's on your mind, Dad?"

He nodded. "I wanted to talk to you about David."

She sat up on one elbow, interested.

He looked at the floor. "I notice you two seem to have — well, let's just say that sparks fly whenever you two are together, and —"

"Dad —" She held up a hand, as though to ward him off. "I promise I'll try to get along better. It's just that he's so . . ." She let out a low growl of frustration. "I don't know. He just always has to —"

"It's not really *your* end of it I wanted to talk about, Nattie," Dad said. He rubbed his hands together thoughtfully, as if he were having trouble deciding what to say. Finally he looked up at her. "There are some things about David that you don't know — things that I think might help you understand his reactions to you."

She waited, curious.

"It's not my place to give you all the details, Nattie, but David — well, let's just say he got burned . . . by a young woman. A college girl, actually. I think maybe you remind him of that."

"What happened?" She pulled herself upright and shifted to sit on the edge of the hammock.

"I don't think it would be fair for me to say any more, Nattie. The only reason I'm telling you any of this is that I think maybe David's attitude toward you isn't just about you, but about what you represent to him. I could be a hundred miles off base,

474

but . . . well, maybe knowing this will help you to respond differently when he says something that gets your dander up . . . it might help keep things reasonably tolerable around here."

She looked askance at him. "Do you think they've been *in*tolerable?"

"That might be too strong a word, but the air has been pretty thick at times when you two are in the same room. Or the same village. Or the same continent . . ." He grinned.

She ignored his attempt at humor. "Dad, I am trying my best to get along with him, but it's not easy. It seems everything I do puts him in a . . . a mood."

"He could probably say the same thing about you. You do tend to have a mind of your own."

"And what's so wrong with that?"

"That didn't exactly come out right. What I mean is that you have a tendency to get a little bossy sometimes."

She smiled sheepishly. "Okay. You might have a point there."

He reached out and patted her knee. "I don't mean to imply that this is all your fault. Exactly the opposite, in fact. And as far as 'intolerable,' honey . . ." He swallowed hard. "You have no idea how much

I'm enjoying having you here. It's been the biggest bless—" His voice broke, which made a lump rise in Natalie's own throat.

She bounced up from the hammock and sat on the sliver of bench that was left beside him. He put an arm around her, and she leaned her head on his shoulder. "I love you, Dad."

"I love you too, Nattie." With his scarred hands he lifted her head gently off his shoulder as he stood. "Now some of us" — he cleared his throat meaningfully — "have work to do around here."

She laughed as he tousled her hair the way she'd seen him do with the Timoné toddlers that morning.

He left her alone with her thoughts, and she lay there for a long while pondering what Dad had said about David Chambers and trying to picture David with a heart broken by some college girl. Soon her thoughts of David became intertwined with thoughts of Evan. That had happened several times lately, and she wasn't sure why. Something about David Chambers made her miss what she'd had with Evan. She wondered if Evan was missing her too.

Thirty-Three

Natalie made her way down the mossy path toward the clinic. The evening breeze was cool, and the birds of the rain forest sang a cheery vesper. But Natalie couldn't seem to embrace their mood.

Ducking to avoid some palm fronds that overhung the trail, she ran headlong into a gossamer web some spider had knit across the path. The white mesh of filaments caught in her hair and stuck to the fabric of her cotton blouse. She sputtered and blew and batted, trying to disentangle herself from the gluey strands. But it was no use.

She had dreamed of Sara last night. The dream began with a joyous reunion — Sara standing in front of her, so real Natalie could almost reach out and touch her strawberry hair. But the visions quickly turned dark. Images and sounds of the party out at Hansens', of Sara's voice pleading with her, had quickly spiraled to the horror of the accident, the hospital, her jail cell. The look of unfathomable sorrow in Jon Dever's eyes.

All day the melancholy of the memories had clung to her like the spider's web, refusing to be brushed away. *How long, God? How long will this torture go on? How far away do I have to go to escape it?*

She had fallen asleep last night with a smile on her face, thinking warm thoughts about her day with the Timoné children. What had caused her to suddenly have the dream again after all this time? She'd had them often after the accident. Terrifying nightmares that began with her falling through endless darkness — and ended with the distant wail of sirens and the echoing slam of a jailhouse door.

But they'd come far less often once she'd arrived in Colombia. If she were honest, perhaps it was the thing she liked best about being here. The foreignness of the culture had erased so many of the triggers that reminded her of Sara's death. There were no sirens or hospitals or beer commercials in Timoné to torpedo the guilty memories into her consciousness. No Mom or Daddy or Maribeth or Jon. No Evan. None of the people who knew her guilt too well.

So why had the dream visited her now? *Are you trying to tell me something, Lord?*

She wiped away the worst of the sticky web and continued down the path, struggling to turn her thoughts toward pleasanter things. David had returned from San José this morning, and she had a special dinner planned. She intended it to be the first installment of a peace offering. She had planned a little surprise for her father as well. She'd had to sneak several items onto the shopping list Dad had sent to San José with David, but she had managed to pull it off.

As she started the fire and made preparations for the meal, she prayed. By the time Dad and David came to the table, her spirits had lifted a bit. As they'd taken to doing since Natalie had moved into her hut, the three Americans ate together in the clearing that served as a yard between the clinic and Nate's hut. To Natalie's relief, her father had spoken with David earlier and had pronounced that from now on English would be spoken over the evening meals.

"This is delicious, Natalie," Dad said now as he finished the last bite of fish. She had made it with a spicy cornmeal coating and fried it the way Daddy always fixed the catfish he caught on the river back in Kansas. It was pretty good, if she did say so herself.

"*You* cleaned the fish," she reminded him. "And for that I will be eternally in your debt."

"It is good, Natalie. Very good," David said, wiping his mouth on the coarse square of linen that served as a napkin, then stroking his beard as though to be sure there were no crumbs lurking there. He took a sip from his coffee mug and held it up as if to make a toast. "The thing I'm most impressed with is your coffee." Smiling, he turned to Nathan. "Sorry, Nate, old buddy, but this girl's *cazho* puts yours to shame . . . and mine, for that matter," he admitted, turning back to Natalie. "I don't know what you do different, but *this* is what a cup of coffee ought to taste like."

Natalie smiled her appreciation for the compliment. "Well, for one thing," she explained, "you guys don't grind the beans finely enough. And you need to grind them fresh every couple of days. I think the stuff in that coffee can was growing mold. It smelled like it anyway."

"When did you become such a coffee

aficionado anyway?" her father wanted to know.

"College. My roommate had an espresso machine, a fancy grinder, the whole enchilada." She grinned. "It's the one thing I learned in college that I'm really putting to use."

"What were you studying, Natalie?" David seemed genuinely interested. "Nate's probably told me, but I've forgotten."

She gave a self-deprecating roll of her eyes. "He probably *hasn't* told you since I never had a clue myself what I wanted to be when I grew up."

"Well, what kind of courses did you take?"

"Oh, Jogging 101, Women's Issues, Basket Weaving . . ."

"Well now, there's one you could actually use here," David laughed.

"Oops, that's the *one* I was kidding about," she said. "I guess I have used the jogging, too, though."

"It does come in handy fleeing from our ferocious lizards," David joked.

She laughed and, from the corner of her eye, took note of the satisfied smile on her dad's face. She had to admit it was kind of nice to have a civil conversation with the man.

Anxious to present the grand finale to the meal, Natalie casually excused herself from the table. "I'll be right back," she said, hurrying off to the clinic where she'd stowed Dad's surprise. She slid a pan of frosted cinnamon rolls from the cupboard where she'd hidden them. They weren't perfect. Even though she'd borrowed Tommi's wife's mud oven to bake them, the yeast rolls had emerged lopsided and a little too brown on the bottom. But they smelled heavenly, and the frosting alone would be a treat. She could scarcely suppress a smile as she carried the pan outside.

"Ta-da!" she sang, placing the rolls on the table in front of her father.

"What's all this?" The expression on his face when he realized what he was looking at was worth every minute she'd sweated in the airless *utta* kneading the dough and waiting for it to rise.

"It's Grandma's recipe," she told him proudly.

"Oh, Natalie . . ."

For a minute, she was afraid Dad was going to cry. But then he eagerly scooped a roll from the pan, licked a drip of frosting from his fingers, and took a generous bite.

"Mmm." He closed his eyes in exaggerated ecstasy. "Do you know how long it's been since I had one of these? Honey, they're delicious. Here, Dave, you better have one. Aren't they great?"

David took a bite and agreed while Natalie beamed. She poured another round of coffee for everyone, and the three of them visited until it was almost dark.

Finally David rose, gathered up his dishes, and took them to the stoop where the dishpan sat ready. She and Dad followed suit. David took the kettle off the fire and heated the water in the pan.

When he started to wash the dishes, Natalie protested. "Let me do that tonight, David. You're probably exhausted from your trip."

"I don't mind."

"No, seriously, I'll do them."

Reluctantly he dried his hands. "Thanks."

She took his place at the dishpan. "Ouch! How can you stand the water so hot?"

"I don't like germs," he said matter-of-factly.

"Hey," she said, "was there any e-mail?"

"Tons. It's back at the office."

"Oh, good!"

"I printed it out. Do you want it tonight? I'd be glad to bring it back over."

She shook her hands dry. "I'll just walk over with you. It'll give this water a chance to cool a little bit. Dad, do you want me to bring your e-mail back too?"

"No. I'll read it in the office in the morning. I'm going to hit the hay. Thanks again for the rolls, honey."

"You're welcome." She smiled at him, then she grabbed the lantern from the table and started off through the village with David, feeling a bit uneasy now that they were alone together. *Lord, guard my mouth,* she prayed silently. *We did so well all night. Don't let me blow it now.*

It was only a few minutes to the mission office, but the silence between them made it seem like an hour. Finally, in the interest of making conversation, Natalie asked, "So is it good to be back? Or do you like it in San José?"

They'd come to a narrow place in the path, and he was walking a few steps in front of her. He didn't turn around when he answered, "Oh, I enjoy San José, but I'm always glad to get back here."

"How is your work coming along?"

"It's going very well. Some linguistics books I ordered a couple of months ago finally came in, so I'm anxious to dig into those tomorrow."

"Oh . . . well . . . good. This might be a stupid question, but how long do you think it will be before you actually start translating anything?"

"As a matter of fact," he warmed to the subject, "I've tried out my preliminary alphabet with a couple of the worship choruses we sing. Simple ones, of course, no more than a dozen words, but Tommi could actually read them."

"Wow, really? That must be so exciting."

He nodded, and though his back was still to her, she could almost see the enthusiasm change his demeanor. "I don't know who was more excited," he said, "Tommi or me."

"Did it take a long time to teach him the alphabet?" They had reached the office, and she waited in the doorway holding the lantern high while he gathered her e-mail.

"Tommi's a fast learner," David explained. "And according to your dad, he's always been interested in books, so I'm trying not to gauge what the learning curve of the rest of the village might be based on his. I'm especially anxious to start working with Tados. His English is so good that I think he'll catch on even more quickly. He's actually been reading a little in English."

They stood on the stoop outside the office for almost an hour while David talked about his work and Natalie asked questions. Though he spoke English, she almost got lost in his references to dialects and pidgins and creoles and mother-tongue cotranslators. But a new respect for his skills and his calling to Timoné grew within her, and she found herself caught up in his excitement about what he hoped to accomplish here.

Finally David looked at his watch. "Your dad is going to think the lizards finally got you."

She laughed and put her hand out to turn his arm toward her, trying to read his wristwatch upside down. "Oh, my goodness. I'd better run."

"Let me walk you back," he said. "There's no moon tonight."

"It's okay. I've got the lantern." She held it up as though he needed proof.

"I'll go at least partway with you," he insisted.

He lit a lantern from the office, and they walked back to her *utta* in silence. "Good night, Natalie," he said softly, as he stood at the bottom of the steps that led to her covered porch. "See you tomorrow." But he made no move to leave and, instead, stood there clasping and unclasping a fist as though he had something else he wanted to say.

She cocked her head, questioning.

"That was . . ." He cleared his throat and started over. "That was really sweet — what you did for your father . . . the cinnamon rolls."

The compliment took her off guard. "Oh. Well, it was fun to surprise him."

"I'm glad I got to be in on it too." He grinned. "They were delicious."

Natalie smiled. "Thank you. If Dad doesn't polish them off for a midnight snack, there might be enough left for breakfast."

"Mmm. I'll be there."

"Well, good night, David. Thanks so much for walking me all the way back. And for the e-mail — argh!" she whined, putting a hand to her forehead. "My e-mail! I left it on your desk!"

He gave an exaggerated sigh. "You want me to go back and get it?"

"No," she sighed, appreciating the offer. "I'll get it in the morning. It's too late to read it now anyway." She affected a yawn. "And I'm sleepy. But man, I can't believe I did that."

He laughed softly and turned to go, still shaking his head.

She left the supper dishes to soak in the now tepid water, and a few minutes later, she crawled into bed. She rolled onto her back, smiling up into the darkness. Her conversation with David Chambers played over and over in her mind. It seemed that, for once, she had managed to spend more than ten minutes with the man without putting him in a bad mood — or vice versa. *Let's hear it for small victories,* she thought, growing drowsy.

As she drifted off to sleep, she thought of all the good things that had already happened in Timoné. She was getting to know her father and developing a relationship with him that she'd never thought she could have. She was contributing to the work here, slowly learning what her part was in easing the burden on her father and on David. Yet, even now, in that groggy twilight between sleeping and waking, the black tentacles of blame — the irrefutable truth of her guilt — reached out and attached themselves to her. On too many mornings, she still awakened with a strange heaviness of heart, empty of the peace and hope she longed to claim for her own.

Thirty-Four

"Okay . . . how about this word?" David Chambers said, pointing to the letters he'd printed on a scrap of paper.

"Kopaku," Tados read.

David smiled, and his pulse quickened. Tados had gone down the list David had printed, easily deciphering over a dozen simple words. The modified alphabet they were experimenting with seemed to serve the language well. Of course, Tados had an advantage, since Nate had taught him to read a bit of English, and he spoke English quite passably. The true test would come when they began to teach this alphabet to those who had never read a word of any language. David uncapped his pen and scratched out a five-word sentence across the page, using the new alphabet.

Tados looked at the paper and scratched his head, then looked up at David. *"Ques briach?"* Is this a trick?

David smiled and shook his head. "No. It's a sentence — a complete thought," he explained. David covered up all but the last word.

Immediately Tados recognized it. It was the word for "please." *"Kopaku,"* he recited, looking back to the matching entry on the list of individual words David had just given him.

David uncovered another word in the sentence. Tados sighed and stretched.

"All right, I can take a hint." Reluctantly, David began gathering up the word lists and notebooks. "Let's call it a day, Tados."

Wide lips parted to reveal a gleaming smile. "Yes, coffee break now," Tados said in English, obviously pleased with himself.

David laughed. "Right. Coffee." He tipped an invisible coffee mug to his lips and rose, dismissing the man. "And thanks for your help," David told him, reverting to Timoné. "I think the words are working well, don't you?"

Tados smiled and tapped his head. "The words are working well. Tados's mind not so well."

"Oh no, not at all, Tados. Seriously, you are catching on very quickly. I'm pleased with the way things are going."

Laughter floated up through the office

window, and David scooted back his chair and bent to peer out the window. Natalie was kneeling by the stream, playing some sort of game with a group of children.

David followed Tados outside. Natalie spoke to the native man as he walked by, then she looked up and waved at David. He waved back and remained on the stoop, watching her with the children.

They were floating little boats of some sort under the footbridge that spanned the stream. He, Nate, and Natalie had worked together all last week to rebuild the washed-out bridge, and now the children had commandeered it as a playground. Natalie and the children were dropping something into the water, then racing to the other side, screaming and cheering and splashing in the water. David watched their gleeful play, and though it only emphasized to him how young Natalie was, he couldn't help but be caught up in the delight she found in such a simple game.

"What are you racing? Boats?" he called out after watching them for a while.

"No. Sticks," Natalie called back.

"Poohsticks!" a small boy exclaimed, his shiny black hair bouncing as he ran to the other side of the bridge.

"Come again?"

Natalie turned and looked up at him, shading her eyes from the bright sun. "Don't tell me you've never heard of Poohsticks?"

"Sorry. I'm going to have to plead guilty on that one."

"David! You can't be serious. You've *never* heard of Poohsticks?"

He wrinkled his nose. "Poosticks? As in P-O-O?"

"Pooh. As in 'Winnie the.' You know . . . the game Christopher Robin and Pooh played on the bridge at the edge of the forest."

"Ohhh . . . sure, Winnie the Pooh. What's the object?"

She placed her hands on her hips and rolled her eyes in dismay. "Get down here right this minute. You have obviously lived a life of complete deprivation."

He stood, smiling at her, but unmoving.

"Come on," Natalie coaxed. She put her hand on the smallest boy's head. *"Manuel, casi alimocu por Mr. David,"* she commanded. All the children squealed and scurried to find suitable sticks for their new six-foot-five-inch playmate.

Reluctantly David came down the steps of the office *utta* and walked to the bridge. Before he knew what hit him, half a dozen twigs of various sizes were thrust into his hand.

Natalie came to his side. "Here," she said, opening his hand. She sorted through the children's offerings and picked out one pale, slender stick. "This is a good one." She took the others and placed them carefully on the ground beside the stream.

"Okay, Chago, tell Mr. David how it's played."

David smiled at Natalie over the head of a slight boy who excitedly described how they were all to drop their sticks into the water on the upstream side of the bridge. Whoever's stick came out on the other side first was the winner.

"Okay, guys. Everybody ready?" Natalie asked the children. "Go!"

A dozen sticks hit the water, and David was almost left behind in the mad rush for the opposite side of the tiny footbridge. Almost before they reached the other side, a stick floated out from under the bridge, bobbing on the current. "Hey!" he shouted, "that's mine! I won!" He cleared his throat, suddenly feeling a bit ridiculous, getting so worked up over a silly child's game.

But the Timoné children cheered for him and Natalie clapped him on the back, and he couldn't seem to help the smile that stretched his jaws until they ached.

At the children's insistence, he raced his winning stick against theirs again and again, until finally he insisted that he needed to get back to work.

"I guess I'd better go too," Natalie said. "I promised Dad I'd help him in the clinic this afternoon." She looked up at him with an inquisitive expression in her eyes. "You've really never played Poohsticks before?"

He shook his head. "I didn't grow up like you did, Natalie."

She tilted her chin toward him, brows knit in a question.

"I didn't have parents who read books to me or played games with me."

"Oh . . . I'm sorry."

"Don't be. I survived."

"Yes, but . . . it must have been diffi-cult."

"We made our peace before they died," he told her. "I think my folks did the best they knew how."

"Were they just . . . too busy?"

"I suppose that was it. My father trav-eled a lot, and my mother filled her time with her social clubs and volunteer work. What I didn't have in their time and atten-tion they made up for in material things. I never lacked for any tangible thing."

"It's not the same though, is it?"

He was drawn to the sympathy in Natalie's eyes like steel to a magnet, and yet it made him uncomfortable. "No, I don't suppose it is," he said. "Just . . . don't ever take for granted what you have with your father . . . and with your family back home."

She gazed up at him, and he felt as though she could read his deepest longings.

"Oh, David," she said, dropping her head. When she spoke again, her voice quavered. "I *have* taken it for granted. Thank you for reminding me how much I have to be grateful for."

"My pleasure," he said, tipping an imaginary hat, anxious to lighten the moment and turn the focus away from himself.

She seemed to sense his desire to change the subject. Smiling softly, she said, "You have to admit, Poohsticks is a lot of fun."

"It *was* fun," he said, meaning it. "I'm glad you made me play."

"I didn't *make* you."

"Whatever you say." He smiled so she'd know he was teasing, but suddenly it felt too much like flirting. He looked at his watch. "I really need to get back to work."

"Okay. See you later, David." She told the children goodbye, jumped the stream, and jogged down the path toward the clinic.

David watched her go while the two halves of his heart warred.

Natalie sat bolt upright on her sleeping mat, her blood racing, her mind in a state of near hysteria. She felt like she was falling, flying through the air. She heard sirens, and then she was falling into a ditch on a cold Kansas night.

"Sara! Sara!"

The sound of her own screams brought her awake, but the sensation of falling remained strong. She flailed her arms, as though to catch herself, but her hands became tangled in the mosquito netting over her head, which only caused her panic to escalate. She put a hand to her chest and felt her heart thumping against it. She forced herself to calm down and disentangled herself from the gauzy fabric.

She looked around. It was dark, but she could make out the shadowy, familiar forms of her table and chairs, the cane bench in the corner. She was in her *utta* in the village, far, far from the scene of the accident. The jungle night was still except for the white-noise *chirr* of the insects, which she scarcely heard anymore.

She lay wide awake now, trying to put

the dream from her mind. It had been so long since she'd thought of Sara. She felt guilty at the realization. She lifted the mosquito net, got up, and went to the window. The village slept all around her. She stood at the window and said a quiet prayer for each member of her family before she lay down again. But sleep eluded her.

She reached for the small flashlight that she kept beside her bed. Fumbling in the dim light it provided, she got up again and lit the lantern on the table.

Rubbing her eyes to rid them of the grit of sleep, she reached for the plastic folder where she kept her e-mails. For the few months she'd been here, she had collected a surprisingly thick sheaf of letters. Many of them were printed on the backs of David's old word lists or on the blank side of discarded documents from the library in San José. Nothing was wasted here.

She sat down at the table and began to sort through the pile of papers. Pulling out Evan's most recent post, she read it again, not sure why it suddenly seemed so important to do so.

Dear Natalie,
Hi from Kansas. Hope everything is going good for you there. I got six

e-mails from you today, so I'm going to go through them all and try to hit the high points and answer as much as I can before I fall asleep.

Am I still working? Yep. Same boring job at the gas station. At least I haven't had to work the late shift the past couple of months.

Do I ever see Jon or Nicole? I ran into Jon at a game a couple weeks ago, but Nikki was home studying. Jon said she has a pretty heavy class load this semester, but you probably already knew that. We didn't talk very long, but it seems like they're doing great. Jon's put on some weight. Nikki must be a good cook.

My folks are fine. Dad's talking about retiring, but Mom's not crazy about the idea, so I'm not looking for it to happen anytime soon. I think he just likes to get her riled.

You asked about classes. Candace Shaw (remember the redhead I told you about — from our Bible study?) is tutoring me in speech. You know how I've dreaded that class, but Candace has really helped me not to be so nervous about getting up in front of people. Anyway, things are going pretty good, but I'm ready to be out of here.

Yes, Evan, I remember Candace Shaw.
He'd only mentioned her half a dozen times in the last few e-mails. She felt a twinge of jealousy and wondered just how close Evan and Candace were getting to be. They'd made no promises to each other, she reminded herself.

Tears came to her eyes as she thought of what she and Evan had had together. He had come into her life at a time when she desperately needed a friend, a friend who understood what she had gone through with Sara's death. What they'd had was special. Yet Evan seemed no closer to sharing her interest in Timoné than he'd been when she left Kansas. Still, she was confident that she had been right to come to Timoné. Timoné offered her hope of redeeming her past — a hope that Evan could not offer.

A blanket of oppression came over her as all her guilt paraded by in a bleak procession. That day in the courtroom when she'd been declared guilty. Her days in jail. Daddy. Evan. Sara. Always, everything came back to Sara's death. She tried to brush the disturbing memories away, but the accusing images came at her like darts, and each one hit its mark, stinging as it pierced her spirit. She grabbed her head and tried to stop the flow of thoughts. *Help me, Father.*

She rose from the chair, blew out the lantern, and went again to the window. What had caused her to be so agitated tonight? *Lord, help me to put these thoughts away. Help me to dwell on things that are true and lovely,* she prayed, remembering a worship chorus they had sung in their open-air sanctuary yesterday. To her surprise, the words in her thoughts as she prayed were the Timoné words. *Quemaso dumé possu, quemaso dumé beleu.* Whatsoever things are true, whatsoever things are lovely.

She had found ready teachers in the children of the village. Tommi's young twins, especially, had taken her under their ornery wings. As they followed her through the village, they delighted in labeling everything for her — the birds, the plants, the parts of the *uttas*. The trained linguist in David might laugh at her, studying under seven-year-olds, but the vocabulary of her tutors was at a close enough level to her own that she understood them well.

And, too, it had helped that she'd begun to spend more time with the village women. She was discovering that Timoné was a very expressive language. Hand motions and facial expressions almost seemed to be part and parcel of the dialect. Their innate sign language made it easier for her to get the gist of what the women were saying. She wondered how David intended to incorporate *that* into his alphabet.

Yet only a few weeks ago she had almost despaired of ever being able to communicate, and now here she was — thinking, *praying* in the Timoné tongue. Granted, she had a long way to go, but she couldn't wait to tell David. She smiled wryly into the darkness. She almost hated to give him the satisfaction. But perhaps he had been right to force her to use the language. She was learning. Finally.

She lay back down on her sleeping mat and closed her eyes, practicing how she would tell David — in Timoné. There were a few words she would have to fill in with her own sign language, but he would allow her that. She couldn't wait to see the expression on his face when she told him.

A stab of guilt pierced her at the thought. What about Evan? The physical distance that separated them seemed to reflect a distancing in her heart from him. In truth, she suspected that Evan was experiencing some of the same feelings. Candace Shaw's name, appearing with regularity in his e-mails, wasn't the only hint she'd had.

More and more, Evan's letters were filled with talk about his future in the field of physical therapy, the clinic he would set up, the impressive salary he would earn. And though Natalie couldn't deny feeling a twinge of jealousy each time she read about something he'd done with Candace, or another mention of Evan's future that didn't include her, in a way, it was a relief that Evan was not pining away for her. For the longer Natalie was in Timoné, the more she realized that Evan would never be a part of her life here.

That's because David is here. The words came as clearly as if someone had spoken them aloud. It startled Natalie. But she knew it was true. She and David still had their moments when they snipped at each other, moments when he acted so strangely she wondered what was wrong with him. But yesterday when he had played Pooh-sticks with her and the children on the bridge, she had seen a side of him that filled her with delight — and with something else that she could not name. To her great surprise, she was finding that making David Chambers smile had become one of her greatest pleasures. She drifted back to sleep, wondering how, exactly, to deal with that fact.

Thirty-Five

Nathan Camfield's heart went out to the young boy who sat on the examination table, trying hard to be brave but grimacing in pain. Luis and some older boys had attempted to turn a lard-coated branch into a torch with the fire in the *fogoriomo,* but the hot grease had dripped down the branch and burned his hands.

They were second degree. If Nathan could keep out infection, the boy would probably heal with minor scarring. As Nate dressed the wound, he recalled the searing pain he'd experienced when he had been dreadfully burned over twenty years ago. Now he noticed the scars and striations on his own hands as though he were seeing them anew.

Nate touched the boy's arm and was trying to reassure him when David Chambers burst into the clinic. The man's face was red, his forehead adorned with huge beads of perspiration.

"Nate, we've got trouble." He was speaking English.

"What's happened?" he asked, his hand still resting on the shoulder of his patient. As David explained, Nate continued to bandage the boy's wounds.

"I was making routine radio checks. I wasn't getting a response from Conzalez. Finally Meghan came on and said that two small planes had landed on the airstrip there this morning, and there are about a dozen soldiers — Meghan called them guerrillas — milling around the village. They haven't made any demands other than forbidding them to use the airstrip and the radio, but —"

"How did Meg get through then?"

"I'm not sure, but she was obviously in a hurry to get off the air."

Nate covered the boy's dressing with a bandage and gave him brief instructions about keeping it dry, then he prayed for him. "And stay away from the fire," he scolded, as he sent the lad on his way. "Did Hank and Meghan want us to try to get to Conzalez?" he asked David when the door had closed behind Luis.

"She didn't say so. She said something about overhearing something that made her think the guerrillas were waiting for more planes and that we might somehow be involved."

Nate looked at David. "In Timoné? She didn't explain?"

David shook his head. "Like I said, it was apparent she was using the radio against their directive."

"Did you radio Bogotá?"

"Yes, the mission. It was Randall Sanderson I talked to. He thinks we ought to get out at the first chance."

"I assume that wasn't an order?" He and Dave had talked many times about their reluctance to abandon Timoné in the event of a paramilitary takeover.

"No," David said. "And I didn't speak with anyone higher up. I wanted to talk to you first."

Nate nodded, thinking. He didn't like the sound of this. It wasn't unusual for paramilitary groups to "borrow" a mission airstrip. It had happened once or twice before at Conzalez, and it happened quite frequently at San José del Guaviare — usually without incident, though two mission pilots had been shot and killed at San José a few years ago. Sometimes it was lone rangers posing as paramilitary in order to move drugs. It was hard to know whom to trust. But this had a different feel to it, and it set off an alarm for Nate. Perhaps he was just more sensitive to it all because he had Natalie to think of.

He rubbed his temples, deliberating.

Natalie. Dear Lord, if anything happens to her, I'll never forgive myself. He shut off the thoughts that tried to make inroads into his mind now. He needed a clear head. He needed wisdom from above. He turned off the generator and took out the keys that locked the storage closet. "Do you know where Natalie is?" he asked David.

"She was in the chapel with Tommi's kids when I left the office . . . something about a language lesson."

"Okay. Well, let's go hang out at the office. We can try to get through to Meghan again and see if we can find out what's going on. Maybe Bogotá will get back with something. Meghan didn't say why she thought they might be headed here?" he asked again.

Again David shook his head. "Just that she overheard them talking and that they mentioned Timoné."

"I don't know what they'd want here," Nate said, thinking aloud. "You haven't gotten any vibes from the villagers that there's something afoot here, have you?"

506

"No. Plenty of bad vibes in San José though. I told you about that. But nothing here."

The radio was squawking when they walked into the office. "Get that, would you, Dave? I'm going to get Natalie."

While David hurried to the radio and picked up the hand-held microphone, Nate flew down the office steps and jogged to the chapel.

Natalie was sitting cross-legged on the floor in front of the twins — Tommi's sons. The two little boys sat side by side on their haunches, their copper-colored knees lined up like four peas in a pod. At first he thought Natalie was teaching them English, but it soon became clear that she was the student, they the teachers.

She pointed to her eyes and asked, *"Qué vocca topi?"* How do you say that?

Paku provided the word, and Natalie repeated it back to him. Nate watched for a while, hating his reason for interrupting, amazed at Natalie's diligence in getting the pronunciations just right.

An irrational fury took hold of Nate: If this incident ended up sending Natalie home, taking her away from him again, or worse . . . it would devastate him. *Please, Lord.* It was all he could manage to pray.

God knew what he meant. He shook off the thoughts and turned his attention back to the language lesson.

Natalie pointed to her knee. *"Qué topi?"* What's this?

"Benotigua," Daric filled in.

Natalie tried to repeat the word, but instead, she used the word *benotiqué,* which meant to spit. The boys rolled on the floor, laughing hysterically.

"Qué?" Natalie whined, a quizzical smile on her face. *"Qué mi vocca?"* What did I say?

They only laughed harder, then began pantomiming a very convincing spitting contest, which was, indeed, a popular pastime for the village boys.

Almost forgetting the message he'd come to deliver, Nate laughed along with them.

Natalie glanced up from her roost on the floor. *"Hollio,* Dad," she chirped. *"Que ésta ce?"* She must have read the concern on his face because she took one look at him and reverted to English. "Something's happened. What's wrong?"

"Well, I hope it's nothing. But David just talked to Meghan Middleton, and something's going on in Conzalez . . ." Speaking English, he explained what they knew.

"Are Hank and Meg okay?" She couldn't

hide the tremor in her voice.

"As far as we know. But it sounds pretty tenuous. If things heat up over this, Natalie, I don't want you here."

"Dad, no! I'll be fine." She jumped to her feet.

He held up a warning hand. "It may come to nothing. You know we get similar reports all the time. But this one is pretty close to home." He didn't tell her that Meghan seemed to think that Timoné might be a target.

"I want to stay, Dad," Natalie pled. She spoke quietly to the twins, dismissing them in Timoné.

"Natalie, I don't even have time to discuss it right now. Dave and I are going to camp out by the radio. He's trying to get through to Meghan again."

"I'll go with you."

He let her lead the way. David was on the radio when they walked in, his voice tight.

He covered the mike with a large hand and filled them in. "I'm on with somebody in Conzalez. I'm asking for Meg or Hank, and I don't seem to be getting anywhere."

He'd no sooner said the words than Hank Middleton's voice came over the waves. "Nate? Dave? *¿Qué pasa?*" He spoke an Anglicized Spanish, which told Nate that he was being monitored.

David slid from the chair and motioned for Nate to do the talking.

He sat down and pulled the mike close. "Hank? *¿Qué pasa?* Is everything okay there?"

"Hi, Nate. We've got some guests. I guess we're going to loan out the airstrip for a bit. Nothing long term, I don't think."

Nate could tell by the strain in Hank's voice that his friend wasn't alone. He listened intently, choosing his own words with equal care. "You don't want us to come then?"

"Oh no. No need, I don't think. Had any company up your way?"

"No. No . . . not lately. Should I get the guesthouse ready?"

"Oh, it might not hurt. Some of these fellows headed your —"

"*¡Cállate!*"

Nate, David, and Natalie exchanged worried looks as a stranger's harsh bark came over the air, interrupting Hank.

"I guess I need to sign off now," the young missionary told them. "Meghan sends her love."

"Okay. God be with you, Hank."

"Thanks, buddy. You, too."

Nate signed off, and the three of them paced the room, discussing what their next action should be.

"It sounds like we could have visitors," David said.

"Yes." Nate scratched his head, deep in thought. "And I have no idea what they might want."

"Do you think they're looking for ransom?" David ventured. He glanced at Natalie, and then at Nate, as though wondering how much he should say.

Natalie apparently read his question. "Please don't keep anything from me," she said. "If there's trouble, I need to know what's going on."

"She's right, Dave," Nate said. "Please speak freely."

"Well, we sure don't have an airport or a drug stash to offer, so —"

"What about the clinic?" Natalie asked. "Could they have heard there are drugs there?"

Nate shook his head. "I doubt it. We don't have the quantity — or really even anything attractive."

"So, you think they might be planning to kidnap someone?" Natalie looked from Nate to David. Nate could see that she was trying hard to be brave.

He shook his head, still thinking aloud. "They know Gospel Vision won't pay ransom. Unless they think they can get something from a family or a government . . . You have some millionaire relatives you haven't told me about, Dave?" he said.

David laughed, but his smile didn't quite reach his eyes. "I think we need to lift Meg and Hank up in prayer."

"Of course," Nate agreed, feeling guilty that he hadn't done so already. He dipped his head in deference to his colleague. "Would you do that, Dave?"

"Sure." David stretched his long arms out, inviting them to join hands.

Nate and Natalie went to either side of David, and Nate took his daughter's other hand, closing the circle.

"*Jehovah, Jesu, ceju na, kopaku,*" David prayed, beginning in Timoné.

But then he switched to English — for Natalie's sake, Nate suspected.

"Be with Hank and Meg, Father God. Cover them with your loving protection. Give them courage, Lord, and wisdom to know what they should do. Grant them strength to endure whatever you might ask of them, and bring them safely through this day and the days to come. We ask it all in your precious name, Jesus. Amen."

Love and respect for the younger man welled up in Nate's spirit as David prayed. Beside him, Natalie squeezed his hand. It wasn't fear he felt in her grasp, but strength and support.

Whatever might happen, he was in good company.

Thirty-Six

The sun was beginning its descent into the western sky — its afternoon sojourn always fleeting here on the fringe of the rain forest canopy. They'd been in the mission office — Natalie, her father, and David Chambers — waiting by the radio for over four hours now. They'd spoken with Gospel Vision in Bogotá and with the American embassy there, but though they'd tried numerous times to reach Conzalez, they'd had no further contact with the neighboring village mission since Hank Middleton's call.

Natalie put a hand on her stomach to quiet its growling. Dad was bent over the table where the radio sat, his attention glued to the cryptic notes David made as he spoke with authorities at the mission headquarters and the embassy. She put a hand gently on her father's arm. "Dad, why don't I go fix us something to eat? I can bring it to the office."

Preoccupied, he nodded his approval.

She climbed down the steps of the hut, crossed the stream, and headed into the village. Tommi's twins, Paku and Daric, appeared out of nowhere, full of questions. They glanced at her nervously as if they sensed something was going on.

They quickly flanked Natalie and chattered away as they followed her through the village.

"Why did Dr. Nate close the clinic?" Paku wanted to know.

Daric, eyes round as snails, asked, "Is a storm coming?"

Natalie put a hand on Daric's head, reveling in the heat that radiated from his thick, shiny black hair. "No, Daric. It's not a storm," she told him, hoping she was using the right words. "It is nothing for you to worry about. Just some business with a faraway mission."

"See, I told you it wasn't a storm," Paku disputed his brother.

"Stop it, Paku," Natalie scolded. "Go play now. Both of you. I must make dinner for Dr. Nate and Mr. David."

She pushed them playfully in the direction of their *utta* and quickened her steps. Something felt different. Instinctively, she looked to the sky, half expecting to see an angry bank of clouds obscuring what was left of the sun. But the waning orb was bright and unveiled. In spite of the afternoon heat, Natalie shivered.

She debated building a fire in the *fogoriomo*, but decided it would take too long. Instead she cut some ripe mangoes, guava, and bananas and mixed them into a bowl of cold leftover rice. Then she sliced the fried flatbread left from last night's dinner into three triangles. They'd finished off a thermos of coffee at the mission office, so after she'd packed everything into a basket, she walked over to the clinic to get cold water from the refrigerator there. It wasn't much of a lunch, but it would fill their stomachs. She doubted the men would taste a bite of it anyway.

She had just come to the rise where the path narrowed before it met the stream when she heard a commotion behind her in the village. She turned and shaded her eyes, gazing into the shadows. There was frenzied movement among the trees. At first she couldn't figure out what she was seeing. It looked like giant butterflies flitting among the foliage, or a flurry of deciduous leaves, but she realized now that what she was seeing were the hands and faces of a dozen or more guerrilla soldiers. The village was teeming with men in green camouflage. As the truth registered in her mind, she took off running, barely able to breathe for the fear that lodged in her throat.

Stay calm, she told herself. *Maybe they're Colombian military.* But she knew better. Even in the short time she'd been here, she'd heard too many stories about kidnappings and guerrilla raids to believe the more palatable prospect. Meghan Middleton had tried to warn them.

Heart racing, she sprinted across the bridge and flew into the office, barely able to squeak out, "Dad, there are — soldiers in the village!"

"What? Guerrillas?" Alarm filled his voice.

"I'm not sure," she said, trying to catch her breath. "I think so."

Dad and David both leapt to their feet and met her at the door, closing it quickly behind her. They ran to the window. Not seeing anything, they turned back to Natalie and bombarded her with questions. "Are you sure? Where were they?"

She told them everything she'd seen, but before she could finish they heard the frightened cries of villagers in the distance.

"Come on," Dad commanded. He

stopped for one moment and looked hard at Natalie. She could read in his eyes that he was considering making her stay here or hiding her somewhere. But something must have changed his mind, for he opened the door, praying aloud even as he led the way to the village. "Father God, go with us. Guide us. Protect us, Lord. May your will be done in all that happens today."

He reminded Natalie of a general, leading his little army to battle. He marched them to the village commons where the soldiers were herding the villagers at gunpoint into the pavilion. As they stepped under the thatched roof of the spacious gazebo-like structure, Natalie heard Anazu, a village elder and Timoné's first convert, arguing with the guerrillas. Again and again, he insisted that the guerrillas leave their village.

The captors spoke Spanish, and though Natalie could only make out a few words, one phrase, repeated over and over, filled her heart with terror — *¿Dónde están los Americanos?* Where are the Americans?

She saw her father and David Chambers exchange anxious glances, and she imagined that her life was passing before her eyes. She saw a picture of Mom and

Daddy and her sisters weeping at her funeral back home. A strange image flashed through her mind — of three gravestones side by side. She could read the inscriptions, and they were for Dad and David and her. She shivered. Then she realized with a start that death was the more appealing scenario — there were far worse fates they could suffer at the hands of these rebels. Her own hands began to tremble.

Dad put an arm around her, and David came to her other side, moving through the crowd. The villagers were gathered in a semicircle under the pavilion, mothers holding children, young men clenching itchy fists at their sides.

Dad continued to move purposefully, ushering her and David to the front of the group in the center of the sea of bodies. Natalie expected him to exert his authority and speak with the leader of the guerrilla group, but he stopped suddenly and stood silent. He allowed Anazu to continue what seemed to be fairly civil negotiations with the intruders, though it seemed that the elder did not understand everything that was being said. The other soldiers were stationed in a circle around the commons, weapons ready, but in spite of the repeated reference to *Americanos* that peppered the leader's invective, none of them paid an iota of attention to Natalie, Nate, or David.

Finally the leader turned his back on Anazu. The Timoné elder backed slowly into the circle to stand directly in front of the American trio. He tossed a hushed command over his shoulder. Natalie understood his Timoné words clearly.

"Keep silent. Our God will hide you from wicked eyes."

The leader summoned three of his subordinates and conferred with them. While some other rebels stood guard, four soldiers began walking through the crowd looking into the faces of the villagers. Natalie's knees almost buckled as one of the rebels came to stand in front of her, looked directly at her, then from her father to David and back again to her. But it was as though he looked right through them.

For several long minutes, the guerrillas continued to walk among the hundred or more villagers who had been corralled in the commons. From time to time one of the men was prodded with the butt of a rifle and questioned: *¿Dónde están los Americanos?* But no one pointed them out.

When the leader seemed satisfied that what he wanted wasn't here, he sent a contingent to raid the *uttas* and search the clinic and the mission office.

When the guerrillas left by the river path an hour later, they carried with them a wealth of supplies, including the mission's radio, medicine, and supplies from the clinic, and David's laptop computer.

But it was vividly apparent that the spoils they took were merely incidental. They had not found what they'd come looking for — in spite of the fact that what they'd come looking for had stood close enough to smell their fetid breath and watch the pupils dilate in their eyes.

The door to the mission office stayed wide open throughout the following day, and a constant parade of villagers came and went, some stopping to help with the cleanup, some bringing food and supplies for the Americans from their own meager provisions.

As David Chambers received yet another offering from a villager, he was overwhelmed by their generosity.

"*Égracita*," he told Tommi's wife, who'd come to the clinic with the twins in tow, each of them loaded down with gifts of rice and dried fish and woven blankets. But it wasn't the gifts of the Timoné believers that touched him most deeply. Many of those who came were not converts. Some had even been openly hostile to the gospel the missionaries brought. But today they had seen the hand of God, and they seemed more open to hearing about him. Yet he was discouraged. Though he had all his important files backed up on disks and filed away on paper, still, hours had been lost in his translating work. And many more would be lost while they did inventories to determine exactly what all had been taken in the raid, and while he made trips to San José, and perhaps even to Bogotá, to replace the computer, Nate's medical supplies, and the other provisions.

Without the radio they all felt helpless. Nate had sent two natives down the river to check on the Middletons. David knew that Nate was terrified that, because of the reports they'd made to Gospel Vision's Bogotá headquarters, word would reach Natalie's family back in Kansas that there had been a raid on Conzalez and rumors of an invasion on Timoné. They desperately needed to get word to Bogotá that the missionaries in Timoné were unharmed.

David prayed they would be able to report the same of Hank and Meghan Middleton. Because of the guerrillas' insistence on finding "los Americanos," he was convinced that kidnapping had been the goal of the invaders. Perhaps they only wanted use of the airstrip in Conzalez, but whatever the case, he prayed that Hank and Meg had experienced a similar miracle and had been spared. David shook his head as he remembered again the way the guerrilla commander had looked him in the eye with a blank stare, as though he saw nothing of import — as though it weren't an obviously American face that he stared into. And while he suspected that God worked overtime on a daily basis to protect all of them in this danger-ridden jungle, he had never experienced the Lord's protection in quite such a dramatic and clearly visible way.

As comforting and encouraging as that knowledge was, another revelation nearly brought him to his knees. There was no denying it any longer.

He had feelings for Natalie Camfield that went far beyond friendly affection or respect or anything else he tried to make believe they were. He loved her. Deeply. For weeks now, his dreams, his unspoken prayers, his unbridled thoughts had all tried to reveal the truth to him, but he had denied them — until twenty-four hours ago, when he truly thought they might all die, or that *she* might die — never knowing how he felt about her. The fact that he'd wanted to take her in his arms and declare his love for her in the midst of a life-threatening guerrilla raid proved just how irrational and ridiculous his feelings were. And yet, could he simply deny them? She was so young. A mere baby by comparison. *Oh, God,* he cried out within his spirit. *Is this a thorn in my flesh that you're punishing me with? Please, Father, take away these feelings I have for her. Control my passions, Lord, because I can't seem to . . . Oh, Natalie . . .*

While her name was still in his thoughts, she walked through the open doorway, breathless, arms overflowing with yet another offering from the villagers.

"Where do you want this?" she asked.

He turned away from her and busied himself with sorting through the books that had been swept from a shelf by soldiers searching for treasure. Surely she could read his mind, see the truth in his eyes. "Why don't you just leave it over there?" He inclined his head to the far corner of the room. "I can finish up here."

Without turning to see her face, he heard the hesitation in her breath, in the almost imperceptible pause before she spoke. *She must know.*

"Okay," she said, turning to go. "I'll — I'll go see if Dad needs help in the clinic."

Outside the sun sank below the treetops, leaving the office in shadow. It was as though she had taken the light with her.

The following Sunday morning, as Natalie walked to the village commons flanked by her father and David, she couldn't help but think about their journey here two days ago. She gave silent thanks not just for her life and the lives of these two men who escorted her now, but for the miracle she had seen with her own eyes. It still sent shivers of holy joy down her spine to remember the blind stare of the uniformed soldier who looked into her face and somehow failed to see that she was American. Never mind her yellow-blond hair, never mind her pale skin, never mind the green eyes that matched her father's. Oh, how she wanted to crawl into the skin of that guerrilla soldier for just a moment and see through his eyes. What *had* he seen that day? Had God turned her, in the enemy's eyes, into a native Timoné woman for those fleeting seconds? Or had the man simply seen through her to the Timoné woman standing behind her in the crowd? She would probably never know on this side of heaven, but as long as she lived, she would never doubt that God had done a miracle that day.

She quickened her pace, forcing Dad and David to keep up. She had never been so excited to go to a worship service. Anazu was preaching this morning, as he often did. But this morning's message would be different. Natalie prayed silently that the word of what had happened would travel throughout the village; that even the Timoné who never attended their little church services would somehow hear the message.

She saw the answer to her prayers almost with her next breath. As they rounded the curve in the pathway and came into the clearing where the village commons was, the three of them halted in their steps. The pavilion was packed with people standing shoulder to shoulder, as though it were a *fésta* day. The villagers whispered excitedly among themselves, pointing and staring as the three Americans stepped under the thatched canopy that today was a church.

After several minutes, Anazu stepped to the east end of the pavilion. The crowd quieted immediately, and without preamble, the elder began to speak. Natalie didn't understand all of his words, but his expressive hands told much of the story as he recounted for the villagers what had transpired two days before.

"Many of you were witnesses," he began, "to the strangers who visited our village two suns ago. You heard with your own ears as these evil men asked us to give them our Dr. Nate and his daughter and Mr. David."

He allowed a full twenty seconds to pass, as though they needed to let this fact soak in. Then, stretching his hand out over the hushed crowd, Anazu told the part of the story the villagers did not know.

"Before the men came, I was praying to the God of Dr. Nate, now my own God" — he tapped a closed fist to his heart — "and he told me, in my spirit, that these strangers would come. He told me that I was not to be afraid. That no harm would come to our Dr. Nate and his friends — to any of us. When the soldiers came, I could not believe what my God had told me. My heart doubted. But then God spoke to my spirit again. 'I will do what I say I will do,' God said to me. And what he says is true.

"I heard his voice a third time, this time

as I saw Dr. Nate and his daughter and Mr. David walking into this place." Anazu's hands swept the arena where they stood. "This time my God said to me, 'I will make the soldiers blind.' I did not understand his words." He flashed his toothy smile and dipped his head. "I wondered, would God pluck out their eyes and drop them at my feet?"

A murmur of laughter rippled through the crowd. But they quieted immediately. Natalie turned slightly from her place at the edge of the commons, and her gaze surreptitiously swept the faces. Anazu had their rapt attention. Hundreds of eyes were on him, awaiting the rest of his story.

"When Dr. Nate walked into the village and came to stand in the very faces of the men who wanted to take him captive, then I understood what God meant. The soldiers seemed to be blind even while their eyes remained in their sockets! I told Dr. Nate that he should not speak." Anazu looked to Nate as if to say, "Isn't that right?" and Natalie's father nodded, affirming the elder's words. Again a droll smile lit Anazu's face. "God had not told me that he would make the soldiers deaf."

Natalie couldn't keep from smiling. She had never seen this side of Anazu, but she realized now that he had a rich sense of humor.

Again Anazu stretched out his arm and held his hand over the people. He spoke, and Natalie was surprised to hear her name. *Nat-ah-LEE.* Before she could wonder what he was saying about her, David leaned over and whispered a quick translation in her ear.

"You saw with your own eyes as the evil men looked into the eyes of Dr. Nate and Mr. David and walked right on by. The soldiers stood in front of our adopted Timoné daughter, Miss Natalie, and even as her banana-colored hair shone in the sun, the soldiers looked right past her."

Natalie felt her cheeks grow warm as the villagers craned their necks to look at her, but her heart was as warm as her face, hearing Anazu's reference to her as "our adopted Timoné daughter." She felt deeply honored.

Now Nate stood and stepped up beside Anazu. The elder yielded the floor to him.

"At the same time God was speaking to Anazu," her father said, "he was speaking to me as well. I came into the village ready to give those evil men a piece of my mind. I had my speech ready, and it was going to burn their ears."

Again the crowd laughed.

When they quieted, he continued, "But even while I was rehearsing my speech, God was commanding me to hold my tongue. I wanted to argue with God, but his words were unmistakable in my head." He looked directly at Natalie, and a mischievous grin spread over his face. "The real miracle is that my daughter held her tongue. I assure you that she also had a lecture ready to deliver to these men. Probably one far more scathing than the one I prepared."

Now the crowd roared, and David leaned over to again interpret what Natalie hadn't caught.

The congregation quieted, and Nate sat back down. Then Anazu delivered the coup de grâce. "You have seen this with your own eyes." He pointed a stubby finger accusingly. "You have heard Dr. Nate's testimony. You know him to be a man of truth and honor. This is not the first time you have seen the miracles of the God Dr. Nate serves, the God Anazu and his family serve. Many times over, you have seen the power of Dr. Nate's God demonstrated. Will you accept him today? Will you serve him and only him? For that is what *our* God requires."

Some of the villagers dropped their heads — whether in rejection or in prayer, Natalie couldn't be sure.

But as Dad and David recounted Anazu's sermon to her again over supper that night, filling in the words and phrases she hadn't understood, she felt certain that the Holy Spirit had moved in Timoné in a mighty way that day. She was humbled to have been a witness.

They finished their meal of donated food, and suddenly Natalie was overcome with exhaustion. Her head pounded from the stress of the last few days, and her throat felt tight with emotion, yet she couldn't bear to leave this celebration table. She poured one last round of *cazho* and sat at the table with the men as they told the story yet one more time.

Thirty-Seven

When the meal was over, Natalie started clearing off the table. Dad and David rose to help her. Dad picked up a bowl of leftover rice, yawning loudly. "I'm going to go put this in the fridge, and then if you two don't mind, I think I'm going to turn in early and leave the rest of the dishes to you."

"Sure," Natalie said. "Good night, Dad."

David suddenly seemed uneasy, fidgeting while Natalie fixed the dishwater and Nate gathered his things. After her father had gone, David stood beside Natalie, bent over the dishpan that sat on the crude table on which they'd dined.

She watched him from the corner of her eye, as he handed her dishes to dry without speaking. She knew he had a lot on his mind, but something seemed to be bothering him — something more than the hardships they'd just endured.

It had been an exhausting few days,

trying to right the havoc inflicted by the raid on the village. Thankfully, the two natives who had gone to Conzalez reported that the Middletons were safe. According to their report, the guerrillas had left Conzalez when their co-conspirators returned from Timoné. Hank and Meghan had been miraculously unharmed, but when the rebels left Conzalez, they had taken with them the Middletons' radio and other supplies — and, most devastating, their airplane. But they hoped to have another plane there from Bogotá within the week.

The day after tomorrow David would be leaving for San José to begin the overwhelming task of replacing their supplies. A small party from the two missions would fly to San José, then on to Bogotá if they deemed it necessary.

David handed Natalie the last plate to dry, took his hands out of the dishwater, and stretched to his full height. "Man," he moaned, kneading the small of his back. "I'm going to have to find something higher to put the dishpan on."

"Is your back hurting you again?" Natalie asked, tipping her head to look up at him.

"A little," he said. "Nothing a good

night's sleep won't cure." He picked up the dishpan and walked a few steps to toss the dishwater on the little plot of vegetables Natalie had planted beside the clinic.

"Oh, sure," she teased as he walked back toward her, "a good night's sleep on that soft, cushy mattress of yours. You know, you're lucky the guerrillas didn't cart that off."

He grinned. "Let me tell you, I was mighty happy to see that it was still there after those boys left."

She turned serious. "But I bet you would have gladly let them have it if they'd left your laptop behind."

Avoiding her eyes, he nodded. "You've got that right." He plopped down at the table, rested his elbows on the rough surface, and propped his chin on his hands.

She took a stool across from him. "How far behind did this put you?"

"Well, thank goodness, I had everything backed up — and they didn't take the disks. But even after we replace the computer — which could take weeks with all the travel — I'll still have to reload all the software, transfer my files . . ." He sighed heavily, puffing out his bearded cheeks and looking very vulnerable.

"I'm sorry," she said, putting a comforting hand on his arm.

"It's not your fault," he said, pulling away, ostensibly to slap at a mosquito on his other arm. "You'd better get inside," he told her, "before the bugs eat you alive."

"You know, I hardly notice them anymore."

"I wish I could say the same." He slapped at another insect and rose to go. "I'll see you in the morning."

He gave a halfhearted wave and disappeared into the encroaching darkness before she could find her voice.

"Okay," she whispered to the empty air. "Good night, David."

What was wrong with her? She should have known better than to bring up the topic of his stolen computer and lost work hours. She'd meant to give him an outlet for venting his frustrations. She'd hoped to cheer him up. But obviously she'd done exactly the opposite.

She gathered up the clean dishes and carried them into the clinic. Locking the door behind her, she walked across the yard to her *utta*. As she climbed the ladder-steep stairs, fatigue overcame her. Her muscles ached and her head throbbed. *Poor David*, she thought, as she got ready for bed. How discouraging it must be to have made so much progress, only to have those hours stolen away. Yet, as she drifted off to sleep, she couldn't help but feel a twinge of excitement. She didn't think David was aware of the progress that she was making in her own study of the Timoné dialect. Maybe she could help — really help — this time.

She had to admit that it would be a joy to work with the man. She laughed softly into the darkness, thinking how crazy that statement would have sounded in her ears a few short months ago!

David Chambers lay tossing and turning in his bed, in spite of the soft, cushy mattress Natalie had given him such a hard time about. *Natalie.* Oh, how she was complicating his life. Besides the fact that she reminded him of the whole mess with Lily, he could scarcely concentrate on his work with her around. Or even with her not around. She seemed to invade his thoughts when he was away from the village in San José or Conzalez.

As the thoughts formed in his mind, he knew he was being irrational. And unfair. Natalie had contributed much to the mission — not the least of which was a decent pot of coffee. It wasn't her fault that she drove him to distraction.

He threw off the thin blanket and sat up on the side of the bed. This could not go on. Tonight when Natalie had touched him, it was all he could do not to take her in his arms and kiss her. He had to get a grip on his emotions before he did something foolish.

"Is Natalie around?" Purposefully Nate closed the door to the office.

David looked up from the word list that had begun to blur in front of his eyes. "I think she's in the chapel."

Nate cleared his throat, and David waited expectantly.

"I want to talk to you about something, Dave."

He put his pencil down and leaned back in his chair. "Sure. Shoot."

"I want to send Natalie back with you when you go to San José tomorrow."

"She wants to leave?" His heart started pounding erratically.

"No. I — I haven't told her yet. I've been wrestling with this for days, but I've made a decision. She's probably not going to like it."

"I'm just glad I don't have to be the one to tell her." He tried to affect a wry smile, but the muscles in his face weren't cooperating.

"What happened last week was too close for comfort," Nate went on. "I could never forgive myself if anything happened to Natalie. I know you may get to Conzalez and find out that things have settled down, but I'm not willing to take that risk with Nattie. I need you to help make arrangements to get her a flight back to Bogotá — and call her mother about getting her a connecting flight back to the States."

David nodded. "Okay." He looked down at the desk, then back up at Nate. "What if we get to Conzalez and they still don't have a plane?"

"I realize that's a possibility. I want you to take enough provisions to go all the way to San José by boat if you have to. Plane or no, we've got to replace the radio and the computer and restock our supplies."

David whistled under his breath. Nathan had no idea what he was asking of him. "That's . . . a hard trip." He scuffed the toe of his boot hard on the floor. "Do you . . . think Natalie is up to it?"

Nate sighed. "I don't think Natalie is going to be up to leaving, period. But I'm not giving her a choice. I promised her mother that I'd take care of her, and that's what I'm going to do."

"You mean that's what *I'm* going to do." David's words came out harsh and accusing, born of an irrational fear that had begun to grow in his mind. How in the world was he going to spend even one day alone on a boat with Natalie Camfield?

Nate stared at him, a puzzled expression on his face. Finally he shook his head. "I'm sorry, David. I know it's asking a lot. But one of us needs to stay here, and it makes no sense for me to go. I wouldn't know the first thing about replacing the computer. If my life depended on it, I wouldn't know how to get the files you need to — download or upload, or whatever it is you do with them."

David sighed. There was going to be no getting out of this. The Timoné could do without a translator far more easily than they could do without a doctor right now.

"I'm putting a lot off on you, I know," Nate repeated now. "Someone needs to check on Hank and Meg, make sure things are still going okay there." He stopped midstride and looked hard at David, as though gauging how this plan was going over, then forged ahead. "You probably would have been looking at going on into Bogotá anyway, Dave. So it's not like that's above and beyond just because of Natalie —"

David held up a hand to silence him. "I'll do it, Nate. You know I couldn't very well say no."

"I know that. But I'm grateful nevertheless."

His smile was wry but genuine now — in spite of his growing apprehension. "You owe me big time, buddy."

"I won't forget that."

"When are you going to tell her?"

Nate headed for the door. "Right now. Pray for me."

"You'll need it."

David watched through the window as Nate walked up the incline toward the chapel. He put his elbows on his desk and dropped his head into his hands. "Oh, Father," he whispered, *I'm* the one who needs prayer."

Thirty-Eight

The waters of the Rio Guaviare overflowed its banks, and still the rains fell. Natalie Camfield huddled under a coarsely woven blanket beneath the tattered Bimini top of the pontoon boat. Damp and shivering in spite of the tropical air, she was still so angry she could scarcely think straight.

She had never liked having people make decisions for her — even when she was a little girl — but it especially rankled her now that she was a grown woman. She had felt a calling to Timoné — a calling she was sure of. She had worked hard to prove that she could be an asset to the mission. She was just beginning to make real progress with the language and felt on the brink of truly being a help to David with the translating work.

With one sentence, her father had crushed every dream, changed every plan, robbed her of her one chance to make a difference, her one opportunity to atone for what her life had been before.

She had tried to explain all that to him. She had begged and cried. But in the end, none of it made a whit of difference. And now here she was on the vessel that would take her away from her father, away from a people she had come to love. Away from the thing God had called her to do. And away from David. Possibly forever.

As though her thoughts had summoned him, David Chambers left his place beside Juan Miguel, the boat's copper-skinned pilot. David poked his head under the canopy, interrupting her thoughts. "Are you okay?"

She grunted noncommittally, suspecting that David had encouraged her father's decision to exile her from Timoné.

He started to walk away, but instead ducked and came to sit beside her under the mildewed awning, the only shelter the craft offered from the downpour.

"Are you cold?"

"A little."

"You'd think we were on a sleigh ride the way you're bundled up."

She shrugged. "I'm fine."

He started to say something, then rose to leave. But a minute later he was back, sitting across from her on the built-in bench seat. "Natalie," he started, scuffing his boot on the deck, "I know you're not happy about being here. But I know your father. He would never have sent you back if he wasn't convinced it was the right thing to do."

She made a sound between a snort and a harrumph.

"Believe me, it was a sacrifice for him to let you go."

"He didn't *let* me go," she shot back. "He *made* me go."

"Because it's too dangerous right now. And because he loves you."

"He treats me like a child!"

"You *are* a child."

She glowered at him. "Is that what you think?"

"I only know what I see."

She narrowed her eyes and drew back her shoulders. "Then look again, David Chambers. I am twenty-two years old, and —" To her dismay, her voice broke and she dissolved into tears, sobbing like the child he'd accused her of being.

He sat silent, waiting for her tears to subside.

"I'm sorry," she said finally, wiping her cheeks on a corner of the rough blanket.

"You're right. I'm acting like a baby." She sat up straighter and looked him in the eye. "Oh, David . . . I loved my life in Timoné. It was my home. And I know God called me there. I *know* he did."

He was quiet, and she tried to read his face. "You don't believe me?" she challenged.

"That's not for me to say. That has to be between you and God." He stroked his beard. "But I think maybe God interrupts our callings at times. For our own safety, or for a time of spiritual growth. Maybe that's what this is about for you, Nattie."

He rarely used her family's pet name for her, but now it warmed her heart somehow. She sat quietly thinking about what he'd said. He was looking out over the water now. The rain had let up, and the air between them was static, the only sounds the hum of the boat's motor, the soft slosh of water against the hull, and the usual cacophony of the jungle's denizens from the overgrown banks that flanked them. Finally the clouds dissipated, and Natalie peeked from under the canopy, craning her neck to see where the sun was positioned in the sky. "What time is it anyway?"

David turned his wrist over, glancing at

his watch. "We'll be at Conzalez in another hour. It's almost noon." He looked at his wrist again and shook his head in amazement. "It seems impossible that July is half gone," he commented.

"It's funny," she told him. "The calendar doesn't seem so important here. I lose track of time. I don't even know what day it is."

"It's the sixteenth."

July 16. Sara's birthday.

She must have gasped at the remembrance because David gave her a strange look. "What's wrong?"

"My — My friend's birthday is today."

"I can send an e-mail for you when I get to San José. It'll only be a couple of days late — unless we run into trouble at Conzalez."

She shook her head. "No. Sara . . . well, she died. I meant today would have been her birthday."

"Oh. I'm sorry." After a few awkward seconds, he surprised her by asking, "Is this — the friend who was killed in your accident?"

Her accident. Did he know how apt that was? She nodded, a lump coming to her throat. She'd never talked to David about Sara, though she suspected he knew her story, since Dad had left Timoné to be with her during that time.

"Anniversaries are rough, aren't they?"

She looked into his eyes. A part of her was touched, but mostly she was afraid that his sympathy would make her cry again, and then they'd both be embarrassed. "Yeah, well, everything about Sara's death is rough," she said, purposely putting a hard edge in her voice.

"I'm sorry," he said again. "Do you — Do you want to talk about it?"

"There's not much to say," she told him. "Dad probably told you about the accident."

"A little. We prayed for you a lot during that time."

"Thank you." Again her throat grew tight. "It was my fault. I was driving drunk."

He nodded. "I know."

She felt guilty that she'd gone all day without even remembering Sara's birthday. She knew Sara's parents and her brother had not forgotten. The tears came now, and she turned away.

"It's okay to cry, you know," David said.

That only made her cry harder.

"I'm sorry about what happened, Natalie. I'm sure it was a very hard thing to go through."

Her voice was a whisper when she answered, and she was speaking as much to herself as she was to David, "Sara was the sweetest girl you'd ever meet. She loved God with all her heart, and she — She made a difference in the lives of everyone she ever knew."

Natalie stared out at the murky brown waters of the Guaviare. "And it's my fault that she's dead. I was rebellious and stubborn. I'm the one who deserved to die. But instead God took Sara."

She put her head in her hands, suddenly not caring if he saw her cry. "Oh, David, I've made such a mess of my life. And just when I was doing something that might really make a difference, just when I had a chance to make it all up . . . then this happens."

He eyed her, his head tilted to one side. "Is that what your coming to Timoné meant to you?"

"What do you mean?"

"Was Timoné supposed to be your salvation? Your redemption?" He seemed astonished.

She sat looking at him, almost afraid for him to explain.

"Natalie, let me ask you a question. Have you been forgiven for what happened with Sara?"

"I — I know God forgave me," she answered.

"And Sara's family?"

"Yes. They've forgiven me. At least that's what they said."

"Then why are you still trying to make things right? Why are you still looking for forgiveness? Whose forgiveness are you really looking for?"

She contemplated his question and finally replied, "My own, I guess. Everybody else was somehow able to forgive me, but I just can't forgive myself. I don't know if I'll ever be able to." The tears were close to the surface again.

David sat forward on the bench and leaned closer. "Do you realize how arrogant that is?"

"What do you mean?"

"By your own admission, you made a terrible mistake, committed a terrible sin. And the God of the universe, in his great mercy and unfailing love, forgave you. But you're not satisfied with that. That wasn't good enough for you. You're still holding out, trying to obtain forgiveness from one last source."

He wagged his head back and forth, and the tone in his voice was close to disgust. "I'm sure glad *my* salvation doesn't depend on forgiveness from the great and mighty Natalie Camfield."

She stared at him, appalled at his audacity, yet convicted. "I — I don't mean it that way. I know my salvation is in Christ alone."

"Then why are you still struggling — what is it now . . . four years later? Why are you still trying to make things right?"

"Because I killed somebody," she shouted, throwing off the blanket and jumping to her feet.

"That's right, Natalie. You did." His eyes had turned to steel, and his gaze pierced her. "You committed one of the worst sins a person could possibly commit. And it was your best friend you killed. Someone you loved more than anyone in the world. You'll never make things right."

"Why are you doing this?" she shouted. "Haven't I suffered enough?"

"I don't know, Natalie, have you? How much do you think you need to suffer before it will all be okay? It's been four years now. Do you think another four might do the trick? Or do you think this crime might take nine years? Or ninety? How long —"

"Stop! Stop it!" She slumped back to the bench and put her head in her hands.

But he wasn't finished with her yet.

"Your problem is that you think you're the only one who's ever sinned *that* bad. Well, let me tell you something, Natalie, you're not. And as much as you want to go back in time and change what happened, you can't do that. You will live with regret for the rest of your life. Join the club."

His voice was trembling, and in spite of her fury at him, she wondered if he had just made a veiled confession.

He stood up — as far as his height would allow him under the boat's topper — and came to sit beside her on the bench. His whole demeanor changed abruptly, and when he spoke, his voice was as gentle as a spring shower. "I'm sorry, Nattie. I didn't mean to be so rough on you. But do you understand what I'm saying?"

She refused to meet his gaze.

He put his fingers under her chin and lifted it gently, forcing her to look at him. He put his hands on either side of her face, then put the back of his hand to her forehead. "Natalie? You're burning up!" What she saw in his face, heard in his voice now, was alarm.

His fingers felt cool and soothing against her skin, and she slumped against his broad chest. He kept her head cradled in his large hands, and she wanted him to hold her that way forever.

"No wonder you were shivering under a blanket. You're burning up with fever. Do you feel sick?"

"I . . . I thought it was just all the stress," she muttered.

"Are you still cold?"

She shook her head. "I'm okay."

"No, you're not okay. We've got to get you something to bring that fever down." He pushed her gently away from him and went to fetch a bottle of water from the cooler. He unscrewed the lid and handed it to her. "Here, drink as much as you can."

She took a few sips, but her throat ached, and the water tasted brackish on her lips. She handed it back to him.

"More," he insisted.

She obliged.

David left her and went to speak with the boat's pilot. He came back with a battered first-aid kit and rummaged in it until he found a packet of aspirin. After she'd swallowed the tablets, he helped her stretch out on the seat. He offered his knee for a pillow and covered her with the blanket. "We'll be to Conzalez in just a few more minutes. Meghan will know what to do."

With the shore bumping by in her line of vision, her mind flitted from one thought to another, none of them seemingly connected.

She thought of her mother in a much cruder boat, long ago on this very river as she left Timoné for the last time. It hit her like lightning: *She* had been on the Guaviare then too. For Daria Camfield had discovered that she was pregnant with Natalie shortly before she made that trip. The realization startled Natalie and made her feel closer to her mother than she ever had. And more a part of this savage land that she had grown to love.

She thought about what David had said to her moments ago. She knew his angry words had revealed a truth she desperately needed to hear. But how did one forgive oneself the unforgivable? How could she ever hope to live with the regret of what she'd done?

She wondered what Dad was doing right now. She missed him already, and suddenly she understood how hard it must have been for him to send her back.

She tried to pray, but she felt lightheaded and detached from her own body. Slowly, she closed her eyes, and soon the rhythmic sway of the boat and the cool, masculine hand pressed to her face lulled her into a deep sleep.

Thirty-Nine

David's heart sank when Conzalez came into sight. The small Quonset hangar sat gaping and empty at the end of the air-strip. He spoke quietly to Juan Miguel as the Colombian steered the eighteen-footer into the shallow inlet that served as the village's harbor. He went back to check on Natalie. She was breathing evenly, and not shivering so violently as she had been a few minutes ago, but her skin still felt as though it were on fire. He shook her gently. "Natalie, we're here."

She stirred but did not sit up. David patted her arm again. "Natalie . . . wake up, Nattie."

She squinted against the sun and gave him a frail smile. "Are we there?"

"Yes. How are you feeling?"

She pulled herself to a seated position, moaned, and put a hand to her forehead.

"Your head still hurts?" he asked.

She nodded almost imperceptibly. His pulse quickened as he noticed how pale she was. Many a missionary had been felled by malaria or dengue fever or one of a dozen other diseases that thrived in the mosquito-ridden jungle. He prayed that the raid on Conzalez had not depleted the Middletons' supply of medicine as completely as it had Timoné's. They had to find something that would lower Natalie's fever.

As Juan Miguel moored the boat, Hank and Meghan came running. "Hello!" they shouted, waving and smiling widely.

David lifted his hand, but said soberly, "Natalie is sick. She's burning up with fever."

Meghan, who was just over five feet tall, tipped her head back and looked at him with a nurse's keen observation. "Hurry, let's get her inside," she ordered her husband and David. "Has she been drinking plenty of fluids?" she asked David.

"I made her drink most of a bottle of water on the way here, but she's gotten worse. And she's complaining that her head hurts. Do you think it's malaria?"

"I don't know, David. It sounds like it could be."

Natalie offered Hank and Meg a weak

smile, and even thanked Juan Miguel for his services, but it was obvious that she was not herself.

David grabbed the cooler and another box of provisions he'd brought from Timoné and followed the Middletons as they held Natalie up on either side and helped her into their small bungalow.

He placed his burden on the floor in the galley kitchen and followed the three of them into the guest room at the back of the house. In spite of his grave concern over Natalie's health, he smiled to himself, thinking how happy she would be to sleep in a real bed.

The young missionary couple helped Natalie into the bed, while David watched anxiously. By now she was almost incoherent. Hank turned to leave the room, but David hung back, watching Natalie closely for some sign that she would be all right. *Please,* he begged heaven, *please let her be okay.*

Meghan turned from Natalie's side to look up at him. Her soft brown eyes searched his before she said quietly, "Go on now, David. I'll take good care of her."

Twenty-four hours later, the plane from Gospel Vision in Bogotá finally arrived bringing supplies and medicine. Natalie had been delirious since they had put her to bed the day before. David took turns with Meghan, sitting at her bedside, forcing sips of water and broth down her swollen throat, sponging her body with cool water, and praying as he'd never prayed before.

When Hank and Jim Logan, the Gospel Vision pilot, began to carry in the provisions, David thought he had never been so glad to see a box of pharmaceutical supplies and medication in his life.

Meghan Middleton seemed equally relieved. She took inventory, then did some quick, rudimentary blood tests before starting an IV on Natalie.

David watched as she tucked a light sheet around Natalie's shoulders. "Is she going to be all right?" he asked.

The nurse nodded. "I hope so. I wish you'd gotten here two days ago."

"She wasn't even sick two days ago, Meg. At least she never said anything." He was feeling unaccountably guilty.

Meg reached across Natalie's bed, expertly regulating the quinine solution that dripped through the IV line. "But if I'm reading the tests right, this should make a difference soon. I'm just glad the

556

plane got here when it did."

"Me too."

"I'll stay with her," Meg told him as they stepped into the hallway. "We're all praying."

"I know," he said. "Thank you, Meg."

He went out to the airstrip where Hank was filling the pilot in on the news David had brought from Timoné while they loaded the pontoon boat with a temporary radio and other basic provisions to take back to Nathan Camfield. The river had flooded its banks, so the trip back upriver would take at least twice as long.

Before Juan Miguel untied the boat, Meghan came running out to the dock. "Here! Wait," she called. She handed the Colombian an envelope and turned to David. "Could you please ask him to give this to Dr. Nate? I thought he would want to know the details about Natalie's condition," she explained.

David nodded and relayed the message in Timoné, while Meghan offered her thanks in the few broken words of Timoné she knew.

David and Hank spent the rest of the morning setting up the new radio, while Jim Logan got the plane ready to fly to San José, and then on to Bogotá, where they would check in with Gospel Vision's head-quarters and file reports on the events of the past week. There they would replace Nate's temporary radio with a more pow-erful one, and — if the organization's funds allowed — buy computers and other supplies to replace the things each mission had lost in the raids.

David went to check on Natalie one last time before he and Hank flew out. She seemed to be sleeping peacefully, but Meg sat by her bedside, obviously concerned that her fever still had not broken.

"Will you — please tell Natalie goodbye for me when she wakes?" David asked the missionary.

In spite of the fact that Meghan Middleton was a few years David's junior, she gave his hand a motherly pat. "I'll take good care of her, Dave. I promise. She'll be anxious to see you when you get back."

He dipped his head, wondering if Meg guessed how strong his feelings for Natalie were.

"Now you take good care of Hank for *me*," Meg ordered, a barely perceptible quaver in her voice.

He gave her a reassuring smile. "I'll do that. You sure you're okay to stay here alone?"

She nodded, encompassing the village with a sweep of her hand. "These are good people" — she glanced heavenward — "and I have a loving Father. I'll be fine. But thanks for asking."

Twenty minutes later, he watched Hank kiss his wife goodbye, saw the tears in Meghan's eyes and the strength they seemed to draw from each other's embrace. He sighed, a long-hidden yearning in his own heart exposed. He didn't want to die without knowing a love like this.

When the plane lifted into the air, then dipped and turned northward, David watched out the window of the small craft as Conzalez disappeared beneath the ocean of dense foliage below them. He felt the familiar tug of God's Spirit on his heart. Maybe it was time he took his own advice. Maybe it was time to forgive himself for what could never be changed. What would always be regret. *What had already been forgiven by the One who mattered most.* Wasn't that what he'd told Natalie?

Natalie opened her eyes. The room was bright with morning sun, and she squinted against its glare. It took her awhile to remember where she was, but Meghan Middleton's beautiful soprano voice drifted from somewhere in the house, reminding her quickly that she was in Conzalez. Natalie recognized the melody of an old hymn, but the words Meg sang were Spanish.

She looked across the room and out through the screened window. She wondered if David had left for San José yet.

She started to sit up on the side of the bed, but the minute she swung her legs over the edge of the mattress, she felt lightheaded and woozy. She eased back against the pillows, grateful again for the soft comfort of the cotton sheets beneath her.

She tried to call out to Meg, but her throat was parched and swollen, and her voice was weak. She stared at the wall, watching a tiny green anole lizard scale the logs and scurry across a rafter. She smiled, remembering how revolted she had been by the slithering reptiles just a few months ago. Now this little fellow, blinking at her from his perch overhead, seemed almost friendly. She thought of her beloved *utta* back in Timoné and wondered if Dad had already bartered it away for a side of venison or a mess of dried fish. She had asked him to keep it ready for her, but she had been acting like a spoiled toddler, and he hadn't been inclined to make her any promises.

More regrets. Had she ruined every chance of ever returning by her childish behavior? She knew now that Dad had only been acting out of genuine concern for her. There was no denying that Colombia was a dangerous place to be right now. But she truly wasn't afraid — not since she had witnessed God's miraculous protection and intervention during the raid on Timoné. Why didn't her father see that too?

Her thoughts drifted to the time she'd spent with David on the boat. He had said some harsh things to her, but as she played them over and over in her mind, she began to grasp the truth in what he'd said. David was right: She had been arrogant and self-absorbed in thinking that her redemption depended on her own actions, on trying to work her way out of her guilt. As David had said, the only forgiveness that counted had been granted two thousand years ago on a hill called Calvary. She owed a huge price — an unspeakable sum — for the pain she had caused through Sara's death. But that price had been paid on that lonely hill, when God's Son had hung on a cross and died. For *her* sins. No matter how shameful, no matter how devastating, no matter how permanent.

Suddenly chastened within her spirit, Natalie closed her eyes. "Oh, Father," she whispered, "forgive me. Forgive me for not acknowledging that what you did was *enough*. I know now, Lord, that there's nothing more I need to do, except live my life completely for you." She turned her palms up in her lap and lifted her hands as high as her weakened condition allowed. The action was painful, but it seemed important somehow — a physical symbol of her heart's surrender. "I accept the grace and mercy you offered me long ago. Please, Father, fill me with your perfect peace."

Even as the word *peace* left her lips, she felt the personification of it wash over her. She was flooded with unspeakable joy, and for the first time since the accident the heavy burden of guilt and shame was lifted. She drew in a deep breath and could almost feel the strength return to her body.

Outside her door, Meg had stopped singing, and now Natalie thought she heard voices in the house. She sat forward, straining to make out the words. Her heart leapt as she recognized Dad's voice. But how could her father have gotten here so soon?

She tried again to call out. "Meg? Dad?"

Within seconds, Meghan appeared in the doorway. "Natalie! You're awake." She rushed to her bedside and put a hand to Natalie's forehead, beaming her thousand-watt smile. "How are you feeling? I just talked to your dad."

"He's here?"

"No. I'm sorry . . . on the radio, I meant." Meg smoothed the sheets and, feeling Natalie's forehead again, took her temperature. Then, as though the idea had just struck her, she said, "Let me run and see if I can still catch your dad on the radio. He'll be so happy to hear you're awake. He's been worried sick about you. It was all I could do to convince him he didn't need to hop on a boat and come doctor you himself."

"Tell him *hollio* for me," Natalie croaked out. But she could tell by the sound of Meg's footsteps that she was already halfway down the hall. She lay there listening to the murmur of voices as Meg assured her father that she was doing much better.

Feeling at peace, yet desperately homesick for Timoné, for her father — and most of all, for a wise and wonderful man named David — she drifted back to sleep.

Forty

From his seat beside the pilot of the Cessna 172, David Chambers looked out over the sea of lush vegetation that swayed almost imperceptibly in the jungle breeze. He cupped a hand to his forehead and traced the edge of the Rio Guaviare with his eyes, straining to catch sight of Conzalez. He desperately needed to see for himself that everything was all right in the riverside village — that Natalie was all right.

He and Hank Middleton had spent four days in Bogotá securing supplies and filing reports with the mission headquarters and the American embassy. David had also, at Nathan Camfield's request, contacted Cole and Daria Hunter, asking them to be ready to fly to Bogotá as soon as their daughter could be moved there.

All the while he had been in the city, his thoughts had never been more than a heartbeat from Natalie. Blessedly, they had been able to get through to Meghan on the radio daily, but David needed to see Natalie with his own eyes, needed to hear her voice one last time before she flew away from him.

Natalie smelled the tangy, masculine scent of him even before she opened her eyes and saw David Chambers sitting in the chair beside her bed. The fluttering of her heart revealed her true feelings, and she was afraid she would cry at the sheer relief of finding him here.

He sat with his head down, so stock-still that for a moment she wondered if her imagination had conjured him. She freed her hand from the light blanket that covered her and reached out to touch his arm.

He started and turned toward her. The smile on his weary face was greeting enough.

"Natalie."

"David, you're back," she croaked.

He nodded. "How are you feeling?"

She gave a little shrug. Her head still hurt too much to waste words.

"Here," he said, offering a fresh glass of water with a bent straw.

She took a sip, her eyes meeting his over the rim of the glass. The water felt cool on her throat, but it was agony to swallow.

David patted her arm. "You're getting better," he told her. "Meg is pleased with your progress."

He cleared his throat in a way that made Natalie study his eyes again.

"I'm going back today," he told her. He looked at the floor. "There's no reason for me to stay —" He cleared his throat again and started over. "I need to get back, Nattie. I've lost days as it is. Your parents will be in Bogotá in a couple of days. You'll be fine here until they can fly you out."

The lump in her throat was not a result of the malaria. She stared at him, her mind reeling. The fact that he'd offered excuses before she'd even protested was not lost on her. "When . . . when will I see you again?" she whispered.

David ducked his head. "I don't know. There's no telling how long it will be before it's safe again."

"I'm afraid," she breathed.

"There's nothing to be afraid of, Natalie. You'll be safe here now. That's why we —"

"No, David. You don't understand. I'm — I'm afraid I'll never see you again."

"Stop it, Natalie." His gaze pierced her, then he turned his eyes to the floor.

"Maybe it's for the best."

"David, listen to me." The force of her words started a coughing fit. When she finally quieted, he offered her another sip of water. But she wasn't finished. "I don't think I could stand it if I thought I'd never see you again." Every syllable that she choked out brought agonizing pain, but she could not fly away from this place until she'd let him know how she felt.

"I *am* coming back," she said now, with as much emphasis as her voice could muster. "I know you might not believe that, but Timoné is my home now. I know I'm not well enough yet, but as soon as I am, I'm coming back."

She reached out and took his hand in hers. She could scarcely believe she was being so bold with him. "David, I love you. I love you in a way I've never loved anyone before. I — I can't go back without telling you that —"

He reared back in his chair and pulled his hand out of her grasp.

She shook her head and forged on, knowing she sounded desperate and not caring, "Maybe I'm a hundred miles off, David, but I . . . I think you have feelings for me too. I don't know what it is that has made you put up these walls between us. It doesn't matter to me what it is. I —"

"Natalie. Stop. You don't even know me. There are . . . too many things you don't . . . too many regrets . . ." he finished weakly.

She squeezed his arm. "Believe me, David, I know all about regret. Aren't you the one who taught me that it was arrogance to go on blaming ourselves for what can never be changed? But isn't that just what you're doing by refusing to allow yourself a chance to love again?"

Her words betrayed what her father had told her about David, but he didn't seem to notice. He gazed into her eyes, and Natalie thought she detected a spark of hope in their depths.

"Let me love you, David. Please. And give yourself a chance to love me in return."

He put a cool hand to her cheek, and there was an exquisite tenderness in his touch. He started to say something, then abruptly pulled his hand away and pushed his chair back from the bed. He stood as though it took great effort, raised a hand in an awkward wave, and turned and went from the room.

Her head hurt too much to cry, so she sent up a silent prayer instead.

The water churned brown and syrupy beneath the outboard motor. David slapped at a mosquito the size of a horsefly. Anxious as he was to get back to Timoné and the work he'd been called to do there, still his heart was heavy. The village wouldn't be the same without her. He could no longer deny that Natalie Camfield had added something to his life that he hadn't admitted was missing.

And yet the words she had spoken to him this morning had sent a chill through his bones. Surely she couldn't have known that they were the very words Lily had used. The exact words! *I love you in a way I've never loved anyone before*. It had to mean something. It had to be some kind of sign. It was what Lily had told him when he'd tried to break things off with her. She had been too young. He was her teacher! The memories came flooding back, and he hung his head with the weight of the shame they brought.

He thought — he needed to believe — that for Natalie the words had come from her heart. But for Lily, they had been mere words . . . words meant to manipulate and control. And he'd been so starved for love that he'd fallen for them like a lead anchor.

They were the words that had been his un-
doing.

The boat rounded a wide curve at full
throttle, and within a few minutes Timoné's dock came into view. Juan Miguel
shut off the motor and put a paddle into
the water, maneuvering toward the landing. David shook the thoughts from his
mind and went to help.

He was anxious to see Nathan Camfield.
He knew that Nate's spirits, too, would be
low at Natalie's absence. He took a deep
breath and willed himself to be cheerful for
his friend's sake. He could offer Nate good
news of his daughter. She was growing
stronger each day, and soon her family
would be in Bogotá where there was an airline ticket back to the States with Natalie's
name on it.

As he stepped into the tepid water to
moor the craft, he cursed that ticket under
his breath.

Nathan pushed back the bench on which
he was sitting and looked across the table
where David Chambers sat. He didn't like
the look on David's face one bit. Though
his colleague had insisted that Natalie was
gaining strength each day and that Meghan
Middleton was delighted with her prog-

ress, Dave's expression seemed to indicate otherwise. As much as he would miss Natalie here, he could scarcely wait for her to be safely back in the States, getting the best medical care and the pampering she needed to fully recover.

He had been crazy to permit her to come here in the first place. God had been gracious in allowing malaria to be the worst thing that Natalie had suffered. She could have been kidnapped or killed by the guerrillas that had raided Timoné. She could have died before David got her to Conzalez. He looked at David again and was certain that the barely concealed anguish on the man's face indicated some horrible truth about Natalie that he wasn't revealing.

"Dave, there's something you're not telling me," he finally blurted. "Give it to me straight. It's Natalie, isn't it?"

To Nate's astonishment, David Chambers put his head in his hands and groaned. Nate's heart began to pump double-time. He reached across the table and put a hand on David's shoulder. "What is it? Dave, what's wrong?"

David shook his head and stroked his beard as Nate had often seen him do when he was upset.

"Is it Natalie?"

"Oh, it's Natalie, Nate, but not in the way you're thinking. Her health is fine. She's going to be all right. It's just —"

Nate looked at his friend's anguished face, and a strange bubble of joy rose in his throat. "Would I be way off base if I guessed that you are in love with my daughter?"

David stared at him, his lips a thin line of concentration, as though he were trying to decide how to answer. Finally he sighed and the dam broke. "I do love her, Nate. I'm sorry. I didn't mean for it to happen . . . to fall in love with her. I swear to you, I tried everything in my power *not* to love her. But I do. I do . . ."

Nate smiled sadly. "David, it wouldn't surprise me to learn that she loves you in return. Have you told her how you feel?"

He wagged his head. "No. But she told me that she . . . that she loves me."

"Ah," Nate said simply.

When the silence between them grew deafening, Nate again put his hand on the younger man's shoulder. "And now she's gone, is that it?"

No response.

"David . . . Son, if I know my daughter, there will be nothing that can keep her from coming back to you." He was surprised at the comfort he found for his own soul in those words.

But David's reaction startled him. "She can't come back, Nate. I'm no good for her. She doesn't know . . . the truth about me."

Nate sighed. "Are you still wrestling with that old demon?" he asked, not unkindly. David had told him about his affair with a student when he had been a new professor. The girl had seduced him and then cried "rape" to her wealthy and influential father. It had been a hard lesson, but it had ultimately brought David to the Lord, and thus to Timoné. He'd thought David had seen that hallowed facet of the situation long ago, but judging by the pain still written on his face now, he had a ways to go to accept it. "Let it go, David. It's all past. It was forgiven long ago. I know your fine mind realizes that. Now let your heart believe it too."

"No, Nate. You don't understand. There's . . . there's more to it than I've told you."

He looked hard at David. "I see . . . Do you want to talk about it?"

"If I tell you, I'd just be trying to get it off my chest. You're right. I know it's been forgiven. But . . . it's one thing to allow myself to feel forgiven — and quite another to expect someone else . . . Natalie . . . to forgive. You know as well as I do, Nate, that sometimes — in spite of the forgiveness God offers — we suffer the consequences of our sin forever."

"Well, at least until heaven," Nate corrected. "I admit you have me curious, but it's up to you if you want to talk."

When David finally spoke, his voice was a tormented monotone, "Lily became pregnant."

"Oh." That explained a great deal. "So you have a child."

"Oh, dear God, Nate, I wish I *did* have a child!" David cried, putting his face in his hands. "No. I destroyed my child. I destroyed a precious life. Lily had an abortion. An abortion that I paid for, that I wanted . . . and encouraged."

Nate touched David's arm softly. "I'm sorry, Dave. I'm truly sorry." He was surprised by the confession and disappointed. And yet he understood only too well how a man could make such an ugly choice. Though he hadn't succumbed, he had faced a similar temptation in his own time of trial.

The years fell away and he remembered, as though it were yesterday, the day he had been with Daria when she went into premature labor with Cole Hunter's child — Natalie's sister Nicole. That baby had stood in the way of his being reunited with the wife he loved with all his heart. For one awful moment that day, Nate had considered ignoring the gift of his medical knowledge and skills. For too many incriminating minutes, he had done nothing, had considered letting nature take its course, letting Daria deliver the baby prematurely . . .

David Chambers pulled his arm from under Nate's touch, and the action shook Nate from his disturbing reverie.

Now David crossed his arms over his broad chest and hung his head in shame. "I don't deserve to ever have a child. And that's why I *can't* love Natalie . . . why I can't allow her to love me."

"What you did was not the unforgivable sin, David."

Nate wasn't sure David had heard him, for he went on, a haunted dullness in his eyes. "Natalie will be a wonderful mother. Have you seen her with the children? She just shines when she's with them. She — She deserves a chance to have children of her own."

Nate made his tone stern. "What are you

talking about, David? You've been forgiven."

"Sin . . . sin has consequences, Nate. I'm
not doubting my forgiveness. Truly, I'm
not. I accepted that long ago — gratefully.
But I know there have to be consequences." David looked at him with
pleading in his eyes.

"So you've decided that the best penalty
for your particular sin is that you'll never
be allowed to know the love of a woman
again?" David rubbed his temples and
nodded, but Nate thought he saw a spark
of hope in the tortured eyes.

"I — It only seems right."

"Oh, Dave . . . you are so wrong. What
happened to all that mercy I heard in your
voice when Natalie was going through her
ordeal? Why are you so quick to offer her a
clean slate and so determined to mete out
a harsh judgment for yourself?"

"It's what I deserve." But the words
sounded far more like a question than a
verdict.

Nate shook his head and laughed softly.
"Dave, Dave . . . You belong to the King,
man. You don't get what you deserve.
You've been bought back from all that. Re-
deemed. Remember?"

He put a hand on his friend's shoulder.

"David, if there are to be consequences, let God decide what they are. I have a feeling you're far harder on yourself than the Almighty is."

David looked across at him, and his face relaxed. "Except for Lily, I've never talked to anyone about that."

"And you're still breathing, aren't you?" Nate smiled at him. "You still have a problem, though."

David lifted an eyebrow in question.

"My daughter still loves you."

David looked Nate in the eye and asked haltingly, "So . . . if I asked your permission to love your daughter . . . even across the miles . . . knowing what you know, you'd still give your approval?"

Nate beamed. "Heartily. *Heartily*, Dave. My approval, my blessing, even a share of my bank account, such as it is . . ."

A slow smile spread across David's face. A smile that said more than could ever be put into words.

Forty-One

Natalie opened her eyes and gave a little gasp. David Chambers was sitting in the chair beside her bed, watching her. Why was he here? She sat up and looked around the room, confused. She was still in Hank and Meg's guest room. The prayer calendar on the wall was turned to July 25. The day after tomorrow she was supposed to fly to Bogotá. And then home with Mom and Daddy. Had something happened to them?

"David?" She swung her legs over the side of the bed and focused on his face, waiting for the lightheadedness to pass. "What are you doing here?"

"You look wonderful," he said quietly. "It's good to see some pink back in your cheeks."

"I thought you weren't coming back . . . before I left," she said. "Is everything all right with Dad?"

"He's fine. He misses you, though."

"Then . . . I don't understand . . ."

David stood and paced the short length of the room. Natalie sat on the edge of the bed watching him. She started to get up, but when he noticed he came and sat back down, motioning for her to stay. He took her right hand and enfolded it in both of his. Her pulse quickened as their eyes met.

"I . . . I have no idea how to say this." He gave a little laugh. "I'm a linguist, Natalie. Words are my business. But I — I can't seem to find the words I need now. In any language."

She waited impatiently, daring to hope that he was here for the reason she ached for him to be here.

"I want another chance," he said finally. "A chance to love you, a chance to deserve the love . . . the miraculous love . . . you have for me." He dipped his head, then looked her in the eye. "But there are some hard things I have to tell you first."

She waited, her eyes never leaving his face.

"Your dad has helped me see these things in a different light. And for that I will be eternally grateful. But you need to know the truth about my life — my past. All of it."

He took a deep breath, and his story

poured out of him. "Natalie, I was in love once before. Or I should say I *thought* I was in love. I know now that it was a cheap imitation . . . of what I feel for you."

She offered a wan smile, but David shook his head, as if he couldn't accept her warmth until he'd finished his story.

"The girl was my student. She was . . . a teenager . . . in her first year at the university, and she had a foolish infatuation with me. I —" David hung his head and swallowed hard before he went on. "We had an affair."

Now he looked up at her, as if to gauge her reaction. She gave a slight nod, urging him to continue.

"Lily . . . got pregnant and . . . told her father I had forced myself on her. The whole affair turned into a scandal on the campus." David let go of her hand and scrubbed his face with his hands. "I'm so sorry, Natalie. I wish I didn't have to tell you this . . . this ugly truth."

"Please, David. I want to hear it."

"Her father was furious. He was an alumnus of the college and one of their biggest contributors. He threatened to withdraw his financial support if I didn't resign. He wanted Lily to get an abortion. And . . . so did I. Without my teaching job,

580

I was in no position to support a child. My reputation had been ruined, and I was afraid I would never teach again. So I paid for her abortion. I went with her and sat in that waiting room, knowing full well what was happening to her in the back room. I resigned, and I . . . never saw Lily again."

Natalie listened, treasuring every horrible, difficult word, somehow only loving him more as she saw his honesty and his vulnerability before her, as she began to understand why he acted and reacted the way he did sometimes.

He paused and inhaled deeply. "I wish it wasn't true, Natalie. I wish to God none of it was true. I . . . I made things right with God long ago, but I'm asking your forgiveness now."

"David, you don't owe me an apology. That's all in the past."

He shook his head. "No, Natalie. My sin *was* against you. Even though I didn't know you then . . . didn't know . . . that I would come to love you, I should have waited for you. And I'll regret that for as long as I live."

"I forgive you, David," she said simply, reaching for his hand. Oh, what a blessing it was to be the one offering forgiveness instead of the one in need of it. Natalie could see that David was relieved at the mercy she extended, and yet there was one question she had to ask. "You're not in Timoné to run away from all that, are you?"

He smiled softy. "That's exactly what your dad asked me when I first came."

"So, Dad knew about this all along?"

"Not everything. Until a few days ago, I hadn't told a soul about . . . the baby." He took her hand, absently smoothing the soft skin on the inside of her wrist with one thumb. "No, Natalie. I'm not running away from anything. Maybe I was at first. Or at least maybe God's call was easier to answer because I had good reasons to want to be as far away from her — from Lily — as possible. But I promise you, I am here now because God has work for me here. I believe I have a clear call."

She nodded, feeling everything he said resonate within her. Hadn't that been her story as well? But she couldn't escape from herself. David had helped her see that.

"Oh, Natalie," he said, "if I could go back and change things, I'd never make the same decision again. I hope you believe that."

"David," she whispered. "Oh, David, do you know how much I understand that? I've spent four years of my life wanting to go back and make a different decision than the one I made the night Sara died."

"But we don't get that chance, do we?"

"No. We only have today."

"And, God willing, tomorrow," he said, reaching up to caress her face. "But the wonderful thing is, I truly believe that this has all been part of God's plan for my healing."

Her heart soared with the truth of it, and she reached up to place her hand over his. David cradled her head with his other hand, drawing her close, gently kissing her forehead and each eyelid. Then he leaned away to gaze into her eyes.

"Thank you, Natalie . . . for understanding."

She nodded and smiled softly, and he drew her into his arms again and held her as though he would never let go.

Natalie awakened the following morning with a lightness of heart she hadn't felt since childhood. She dressed and went out to the Middletons' kitchen. David was sitting at the table, an empty mug and his open Bible in front of him.

"Good morning, sleepyhead," he said when he saw her. He closed his Bible and rose to give her an awkward embrace. But his boyish smile told her that his spirit felt as carefree as her own.

"What time is it?" she asked, yawning.

"Almost ten. Are you hungry?"

She nodded, feeling suddenly rather shy with him. "Where are Hank and Meg?"

David pulled out a chair for her and she sat down. "Meghan's back in the clinic. Hank's working in the hangar. Meg left some coffeecake for you. Does that sound good?"

"Mmm. Wonderful. I can get it, David. You don't have to wait on me."

"I know," he said. "I don't have to . . . but I want to."

He served her breakfast and waited while she finished eating.

"Do you feel well enough to go for a walk?" he asked as he put her dishes in the sink.

"I'm not sure how far I can go, but I'd love some fresh air. Let me go get my shoes on."

Natalie went back to her room, brushed her teeth, and tied her hair up in a ponytail. She slipped on her shoes, and when she reappeared in the kitchen, David was waiting by the back door.

"I'm ready. You're sure I'm not keeping you from something?"

He put an arm around her shoulder in reply and guided her through the door. The air was already warm and the humidity thick, but it was a beautiful morning.

"Hang on," David said, leading her to the back of the building and into the clinic. Meg was at her desk, deep in concentration over the laptop.

David rapped softly on the doorpost. "Just wanted to let you know I have your patient," he told Meg. "We're going to walk a bit."

Meghan looked up from her work. "Oh, hi. Hey, Natalie! You're looking great. You feeling okay?"

"Much better . . . better every day now, really."

"Good." The nurse nodded her approval. "Well, have a nice walk. Just don't overdo."

"I won't."

"She won't," David echoed.

He closed the clinic door behind them and turned Natalie toward the west edge of the village. With the sun at her back, her physical strength returning noticeably, and her spirit finally at peace, Natalie didn't think things had ever felt so right with her world. David's arm draped lightly around her shoulder made it just about perfect.

"Oh, David," she sighed, looking up at him, "why do we make things so hard for ourselves?"

"I don't know," he said, putting a hand up to run his fingers absently through the strands of her ponytail. "But look at how much we've learned along the way."

She nodded her agreement. "All this time I thought I was coming here to make a difference, to somehow make up for the horrible thing I did. But instead, God brought me here to teach me something about himself. To make a difference in *me*."

"And yet, you *have* made a difference, Natalie. In Timoné. In me."

She acknowledged his words with a smile. They talked and walked, and by the time they reached the middle of the village Natalie was growing weary. She knew it would be wise to turn back, but she couldn't bear for their time together to end, so she said nothing. They walked on through the settlement, greeting villagers here and there, making precious discoveries about one another as they talked. They came to a pier that jutted out over a small inlet, and together they walked out to the end of it. Taking off their shoes, they sat and swung their legs over the side. The water felt cool and refreshing on Natalie's toes.

"This reminds me of the pond on our farm," she told David. "When I was a little girl I used to walk through the pasture to the pond and pretend I was on some great adventure." She sighed. "I could never have imagined where the real-life journey would take me."

David gave her shoulders a squeeze. "I'm just glad your journey brought you here." He gazed across the water, silent for a long minute before he spoke again. "I think the quest I was always on — when I was little — was to know what it felt like to be loved. To be part of a family."

"Oh, and I had all that and never really appreciated it. I'm so sorry for you, David . . . I wish . . ." She let her words fade away, not knowing what else to say.

He gave her a squeeze, as if to reassure her. "I was closer to my parents in their last years. We made things right between us. And God has done some serious healing in my life. But I know there are things about myself — not good things — that are there because of the way I grew up. You need to know that about me, Natalie. I'm not always this easy to get along with."

She smiled up at him. But she heard the longing in his voice, and though she knew she could never undo what he'd suffered, she wanted a lifetime to love him, to make up for all the love he'd been deprived of. She sighed again. "Oh, David. I don't want to go back — to the States. I want to go back to Timoné with you. I'm so much better now." But even as she said the words, a deep cough racked her body, and she was powerless to suppress it.

He patted her on the back and waited for her to catch her breath. "You need to recover completely, Natalie. Go back and spend some time with your family, heal, give things a little time to simmer down politically here, and then you *can* come back."

She sighed. "But how long could that be, David? Oh, I'm too impatient. And I do miss Mom and Daddy. It will be good to see them again. But tomorrow? We . . . we've just found each other. I'm not ready to let you go so soon."

David smiled. "It'll be all right, Natalie. I promise you. It will all work out."

He stood and stretched, rubbing the small of his back in that way that was now so familiar to her. "I'd better get you back before Meghan comes looking for you."

He helped her to her feet and they started back, following the riverbank. Above them, a low droning sound filled the sky. As though their movements were synchronized, David and Natalie both turned and lifted their heads, shading their eyes from the glare of the tropical sun. The buzz grew louder overhead, and Natalie pointed to a dark spot in the sky. A plane circled lower and lower.

"Were you expecting supplies today?"

"Maybe." There was an expression on David's face that she couldn't read. "We'll go by the airstrip on our way back. Are you sure you're feeling okay?"

"I'm tired, but I'll make it."

They walked on, watching the plane fly lower and lower and finally disappear into the trees. They heard the change in the whine of the engine and knew it had landed on the airstrip that was part of the mission compound.

Natalie watched David. He seemed to be deep in thought, and she felt her heartbeat quicken with fear. What if this was another guerrilla raid on the village? They'd lost so much already. If the invaders took the radio again, how would they let her parents know what had happened — or get word to Dad back in Timoné? Natalie's breathing grew labored as they quickened their steps toward the airstrip. Fear mushroomed within her.

The Quonset hangar came into view, and they watched the plane taxi slowly toward it and come to a stop. Natalie and David stood at a distance and watched as the Colombian pilot emerged. Natalie breathed a sigh of relief when she saw that the pilot was not wearing the uniform of the paramilitary. The pilot turned to hold the door for a passenger who was dressed in light khakis and a white shirt. The man stepped from the plane, head bent. His build and carriage seemed familiar. Natalie's breath caught. It couldn't possibly be, but it looked like —

He cleared the plane's wing, straightened, and glanced in her direction. "Nattie!"

"Daddy!" Incredulous, she turned to David, who stood smiling beside her. "David? It's my daddy!"

She started running, and though her lungs burned in her chest and her head felt as though it would float away from her body, she didn't stop until Cole Hunter's arms were wrapped tightly around her, holding her up. She felt another pair of arms go around her, and she looked up into Mom's blue eyes. Her gaze moved from Mom to Daddy and back again. Tears were streaming down both their faces, and Natalie's eyes brimmed too. For five minutes, they cried and hugged and laughed, then cried some more.

"Did you know they were coming?" she asked David, suddenly remembering that he was standing there, looking on.

He nodded, grinning.

"You must be David," Cole Hunter said, reaching out to shake his hand.

"Oh, I'm sorry!" Natalie cried, putting a hand to her mouth. "I'm not thinking straight." She left her mother's side and stepped forward to put a possessive hand on David's arm. "This is David Chambers. David, these are my parents, Cole and Daria Hunter."

David shook each of their hands in turn. "Very pleased to meet you. Natalie has told me a lot about you."

Hank Middleton walked over from the hangar and joined them now, and Natalie made introductions again.

"I've heard a lot about you," Hank said.

Cole looked at her with mischief in his eyes. "I'm afraid to ask what she's been saying about us."

They shared the nervous laughter of

newly acquainted friends, while Natalie looked on in awe, still unable to believe they were actually here.

"Meghan will be anxious to meet you," Hank said. "Why don't we go on up to the house."

With Hank and David leading the way, and Natalie tucked tightly — happily — between her parents, they started for the mission compound.

Natalie napped for several hours that afternoon, but that night they all stayed up past midnight, visiting and laughing and catching up on each other's news.

Finally Hank and Meghan showed the Hunters to their room and called it a night. David and Natalie were left in the living room, where David was to sleep on the sofa.

"Oh, David," she sighed. "I'm so happy. You knew they were coming all along?"

He nodded. "It was Nate's idea, but I was happy to make the arrangements because it bought me several more days with you," he confessed sheepishly.

Tears filled her eyes. "Thank you, David."

He crossed the room and took her in his arms. "Oh, Natalie . . ."

He bent to kiss the top of her head, tightening his embrace. She raised her face to his, and their lips found each other. Tenderly, he kissed her once and then again. Then he held her away from him. "I'd better let you get to bed," he said, his voice a breathless whisper.

She stood on tiptoe and kissed him once more.

The next three days were a gift, unlike anything Natalie had ever known. There were moments when she didn't think she could possibly contain the joy that filled her. Besides the precious time with her parents in Conzalez, she experienced a new freedom in her communion with her heavenly Father. In letting go of her self-imposed guilt, a hindrance to her prayers had seemed to fall away with it. Now she praised God with unfettered joy and sought his counsel with a newly surrendered will. She hungered for God's Word as though she were famished and spent hours reading her Bible and praying.

One afternoon as she sat reading in the cool shade on the Middletons' patio, she came to a verse in the second chapter of Ephesians that seemed to give voice to everything she had learned over the past few days. It was a scripture she must have read a dozen times before, but suddenly the words had life. They spoke to her as though they had been penned for her alone.

For it is by grace you have been saved, through faith —, she read, *and this not from yourselves, it is the gift of God — not by works, so that no one can boast. For we are God's workmanship, created in Christ Jesus to do good works, which God prepared in advance for us to do.* To think that all along, when she had been trying to work hard enough to earn the right to be forgiven, he had already paid the price. Not only that, but, according to the Scriptures, even the very work she was doing in Timoné had been prepared in advance by the God of the universe — for her! Work that not only would benefit the people of the village, but that would change Natalie's very being. It was a staggering, humbling thought.

Then there was David. As much as she'd loved him before, she saw him with new eyes now. Each day, as they sat together on the patio or walked the short distance that Natalie could manage about the village, the attraction they'd always felt for each other deepened. Natalie prayed for strength to keep her heart reined in. *Don't let me run ahead of you, Lord,* she prayed. But before she whispered the words, she knew in her spirit that David was the man God had made for her — the man who shared her calling, who understood her frailties and loved her in spite of them. The man who completed her.

Each hour they spent together, the friendship that had grown between them matured. And the love they'd dared to declare for each other hardened and set, like strong cement, impervious to the rains that would surely fall in time.

Forty-Two

Natalie carried Meghan's laptop into the guest room and plopped cross-legged on the bed, placing the computer on a pillow in front of her. She opened the e-mail program and typed Evan Greenway's address into the appropriate field.

Dear Evan, she typed. The words she'd pecked out dozens of times since she came to Timoné, blurred through her tears as she wrote them now, possibly for the last time. It wasn't that she was having second thoughts about David, or that she had any regrets. But still, it was hard to say goodbye to someone who had been such an important part of her life for such a long time. She blinked away the tears and put her fingers on the keyboard again.

You might have heard that I've been ill. I'm in Conzalez right now, recovering from malaria. I've never been so sick in my life. It was scary for a while, but I'm much better now. The Lord has used this time to teach me some very important lessons. Mom and Daddy are here with me, and they'll be bringing me home to recuperate for a while. But I'm coming back to Timoné, Evan, as soon as I can. I know this is where God wants me.

I understand now that Timoné has never held any attraction for you, and I apologize for trying to put my calling off on you. I wanted to have the best of both worlds, I guess. I wanted to be with you, but I felt drawn to Timoné. I still believe it was God who drew me here. I was a little mixed up about his reasons, but I'm beginning to figure some things out now, and I'm happier than I've ever been in my life.

Because I don't know for sure how you feel about me after all this time, it's hard to know what to write. I'm just going to tell you the truth and pray that you aren't hurt by it. I have fallen in love with David Chambers. David shares my love for Timoné, shares my calling to Colombia, and I believe in my heart that he is the man God intended for me.

You were a wonderful friend to me, Evan, and I'll always be grateful for the time we had together. I know we didn't make any promises to each other before I left, but I feel that I owe you an explanation. If this hurts you, if I've ever led you on, I'm sorry.

I trust that God is working in your life as he is working in mine.

She scrolled back over what she'd written. Satisfied, she signed her letter and filed it in the outbox for Hank to send the next time he flew into San José. She trusted that, because Evan belonged to God, the events of his life were being divinely charted just as the events of her own life were. She smiled to herself, thinking that now she might even be happy to find out that Candace Shaw had become more than just a tutor to Evan Greenway.

After breakfast Monday morning, Daria went with Natalie out to the cool shade of the porch to sit. Meghan was already at work in the clinic, and the men were loading the plane for their trip to Bogotá as well as getting David's provisions ready to go back on the boat to Timoné. David was leaving this afternoon, and tomorrow morning Daria and Cole and Natalie would fly home.

It had all gone too quickly. But it had been wonderful to spend this time with her daughter here in Colombia, to see how much Natalie had come to love this country Daria had once called home. Natalie had grown up so much in the few months she'd been here. Last night Daria and Cole had lain awake in the guest room next to Nattie's and marveled together at the changes they'd seen in her. And while they had begun to suspect from Natalie's letters that there was something between David and Natalie, seeing them together had left no doubt.

"I wasn't ready to like him one bit, Dar," Cole had told her. "But I do. I like him a lot. I wish he wasn't quite so old, but it's obvious that he loves Nattie. And he's good to her."

Daria had laughed softly.

"What's funny?" Cole said.

"It's just interesting that you think David Chambers is old. Oh, to be as 'old' as he is again! You're no spring chicken, my darling."

"Well, you know what I mean. I don't like to think of Nattie widowed young or nursing an old man someday down the road. She's in love. I'm sure she hasn't thought that far ahead."

"I'm sure God has," Daria chided.

"You're right, as always," he'd whispered, pulling her close.

They'd fallen asleep in each other's arms.

Now, seated across from Natalie on the porch, Daria fanned herself and took a sip of the chilled sweet tea Meghan had brewed for them. "Natalie, I'm crazy about David," she said, "but I'll have you know I'm not so crazy about his calling. I suppose there's no question that you'll be going back to Timoné?"

Natalie nodded. "As soon as I can, Mom. It's *my* calling too."

"Oh, Nattie, I know. But as a mother, I don't like it one bit." She sighed. "What about Evan? What happened with him?"

Natalie shook her head. "There's nothing between us anymore, Mom. From the sound of his letters, I think maybe he's found someone else. A certain 'Candace' has come up in his e-mails a lot lately."

Daria rubbed the corner of the table-cloth between her thumb and forefinger. "This love for David isn't . . ." She began.

"On the rebound?" Natalie shook her head vigorously. "No, Mom. Not at all. I think things were really over with Evan be-fore I ever left Kansas."

"Well, I had to ask."

"I know. And I did write to Evan to let him know what's happened. I owed him that much."

Daria put a hand on her arm. "I'm so happy for you, Natalie."

"Thanks, Mom. I'm so glad you and Daddy could come and meet David. I wish you could come to Timoné sometime."

Timoné. Daria winced, struggling to stay clear of the whirlpool of memories that threatened to pull her in. She didn't know whether she could handle seeing the place where she had left Nathan, could handle seeing him there still caring for the people she'd left so long ago. "Maybe someday, honey . . . maybe someday."

"Don't worry about me, Mom. I know this is where I'm supposed to be. Somehow, I just know it . . . right here." Natalie put a hand gently over her heart. "And . . . well, Dad's there. And he needs me."

"Oh, Nattie, more than anything, I'm so happy that you've had this time to get to know your father. You can't imagine how much that means to me."

She covered her daughter's hand with

her own, and they exchanged teary smiles.

Natalie's eyes held a knowing beyond their years, and she said, "I think maybe I do know, Mom."

Natalie lay down midafternoon for yet another Nurse Meg–prescribed nap. David had promised that he would wake her before he left for Timoné. But she had lain awake for the past half-hour thinking and praying. Her thoughts were not troubled, though she didn't know how long it might be before she saw David again. Instead of feeling panic at his going, she felt perfect peace. Instead of feeling gloomy about the weeks — perhaps months — they would be apart, she felt anticipation for the things God would teach her while she was away — and for the reunion she and David would have when finally she was able to return to her beloved Timoné.

She was just thinking of getting up when she heard a soft knock at her door. David stepped into her room, and the rich aroma of coffee and buttered toast wafted from the tray he held in his hands. "Hey, sleepyhead," he said, putting the tray on her nightstand and placing a warm hand on her cheek. He helped her sit up in the bed.

She yawned and smiled. "I think surely

I've slept as much in these last two weeks as I have in my whole life."

"You just keep it up. It's the best thing you could do to get well now."

"It does make the time go more quickly," she told him. "I'll be grateful for that while I'm back in the States." She had almost said "while I'm back home," but what she had told David that day on the river was true — *Timoné* was her home now. And even more so since she'd come to love David.

He went to the window and rolled up the bamboo shades, letting the light stream across her bed. She watched him as he stood, illumined by the tropical sun. She loved the way that sun had burnished golden highlights in his dark hair and beard, and coppered his skin as deeply as the natives'.

He seemed to have a new serenity, and she thought it amazing that they each had so recently found the peace for which they'd longed. To the end of her life, she would carry deep regret for the sorrow her foolish, rebellious actions had caused. But she understood now that God was a God of deliverance and redemption. There was no sin so great that he could not forgive, no tragedy so profound that he could not bring something good out of it.

She fell back against the down pillows, savoring their softness. "Oh, how I wish I could take this bed with me when I go back to Timoné."

David turned and looked at her, an odd expression on his face.

"What's wrong?" she asked.

He sat down on the edge of the chair beside her and enveloped her right hand in both of his. "Natalie, if I have my way you won't need a bed."

She pushed herself up again, supporting her weight on her elbows. "What are you talking about?" Surely, after all they'd been through together, he hadn't changed his mind about her going back to Timoné.

A slow smile painted his face as he brushed a strand of hair from her forehead. "I have a perfectly lovely bed in my *utta*."

"But . . . what about your back? I couldn't ask you to —"

"I wasn't offering to give up my bed. I was — I *am* offering to share it with you, Natalie."

Before the meaning of his words congealed in her mind, he slid from the chair to sit beside her. Turning to her and taking her face in his hands, he placed an exquisitely tender kiss on her parched lips.

"Natalie Camfield, I love you and I want you to be my wife. There's nothing I long for more than to have you lying in my arms every night before I fall asleep."

She gave a little sigh and leaned over to lay her head upon his strong shoulder. "Oh, David . . ."

"Is that a yes?"

She heard the smile in his voice, and she nodded into the soft fabric of his denim shirt, unable to speak.

"You go home, get well," he told her. "I'll be counting every minute until you're in my arms again." He stood now, kissed his fingertips and, bending down, transferred the kiss to her lips with a featherlight touch. "*Mi carru.* My love."

Then, without another word, he turned and ducked through the doorway.

Acknowledgments

I would like to thank the following people for their roles in bringing *After the Rains* into being:

Miss Linda Buller, who will soon celebrate her ninety-first birthday, and whose many years as a missionary in Colombia have been an inspiration to me.

Police Chief Jim Dailey, Judge Ted Ice, Gerry Loomis of the Harvey County Sheriff's Department, County Attorney Matt Treaster, Joyce Roach, Vern Schmidt and others in local law enforcement agencies who patiently answered my many questions.

Dr. Mel and Cheryl Hodde, the wonderful writing team who make up Hannah Alexander, for providing information on the medical aspects of this story.

Tom and Diane Tehan, doing the Lord's work in Thailand, for sharing invaluable information and literature on the work of translator linguists.

Author Gayle G. Roper, who unknowingly provided my theme in one of the chapters of her wonderful book on contentment, *Riding the Waves* (Broadman and Holman, 2001).

Others who helped with research on various topics: Melody Carlson, Jason Efken, Larry Greene, Cyndi Kempke, Erin Pennington; and my children, Ryan and Tobi Layton, Tarl Raney, Trey Raney, and Tavia Raney, who brought my memories of life as a preteen and teenager into the twenty-first century.

Those who read my manuscript in its early stages and offered suggestions and encouragement: Lorie Battershill, Meredith Efken, Kim Hlad, Cyndi Kempke, Terry Stucky, and my parents, Max and Winifred Teeter.

Dan and Jeanne Billings, whose charming Victorian bed-and-breakfast, the Emma Creek Inn, near Hesston, Kansas, provided a lovely writing retreat away from the cry of the telephone, doorbell, and dirty laundry — and came complete with a nice fat tomcat to warm my feet. Thank you, Alex.

My incredible editors at WaterBrook Press, Erin Healy, Traci DePree, and Laura Barker.

And as always, my biggest supporter, encourager, and the love of my life — my husband Ken.

———————————

A note to my readers: As in *Beneath a Southern Sky*, the villages, native people, and dialects of Timoné and Conzalez — while based on actual people groups of South America — are fictionalized as portrayed in *After the Rains*, and are the products of my imagination.

For more information, or to write me, please visit my Web site at www.deborah raney.com. I love hearing from my readers!